PRAISE FOR ANDREW MAYNE

"In Mayne's exciting second Jessica Blackwood novel, the cunning FBI special agent applies her magician training to investigating a bizarre explosion . . . A fast-moving thriller in which illusions are weapons for both good and evil."

—*Publishers Weekly* on *Name of the Devil*

"Science supersedes the supernatural in this action-packed follow-up . . . With snappy prose and a smart protagonist, this is an adrenaline-fueled procedural with an unusual twist. Great reading."

—*Booklist* (starred review) on *Name of the Devil*

"Mayne, the star of the A&E show *Don't Trust Andrew Mayne*, combines magic and mayhem in this delightful beginning to a new series . . . Readers will look forward to Jessica's future adventures."

—*Publishers Weekly* on *Angel Killer*

"Professional illusionist Mayne introduces a fresh angle to serial-killer hunting . . . Mayne forgoes gimmicks, instead dissecting illusions with human behavior, math, and science without losing sight of the story's big picture."

—*Booklist* on *Angel Killer*

THE NATURALIST

OTHER TITLES BY ANDREW MAYNE

JESSICA BLACKWOOD SERIES

Black Fall
Name of the Devil
Angel Killer

THE CHRONOLOGICAL MAN SERIES

The Monster in the Mist
The Martian Emperor
Station Breaker
Public Enemy Zero
Hollywood Pharaohs
Knight School
The Grendel's Shadow

NONFICTION

The Cure for Writers Block
How to Write a Novella in 24 Hours

THE NATURALIST

ANDREW MAYNE

This is a work of fiction. Names, characters, organizations, places, events, and incidents are either products of the author's imagination or are used fictitiously. Any resemblance to actual persons, living or dead, or actual events is purely coincidental.

Published by Thomas & Mercer, Seattle

www.apub.com

ISBN-13: 9781477824245
ISBN-10: 1477824243

Cover design by M.S. Corley

Printed in the United States of America

To my friend Gerry Ohrstrom, for his contagious support and enthusiasm for science.

CHAPTER ONE

1989

The woods were wrong. That was the only way Kelsie could describe it. There was just something not right. She stared off in the direction Trevor had gone, unsure if she should try to track him down or stay put next to the tiny red tent and wait for him to return from his bathroom break.

He'd laugh at her if she said she was scared, so Kelsie dug through her backpack, searching for the roll of toilet paper she'd borrowed from the Conoco station restroom thirty miles back. She found it wrapped up in the cords of her Walkman, resting on the mixtapes Trevor had made for her back at Boston College.

Trevor was a lanky journalism major with a mop of black hair that usually covered his eyes. They'd met at an off-campus party and bonded over a mutual love of prog rock and board games. The first evening they spent in his dorm they listened to *Tubular Bells*, played Stratego, and drank cheap wine. She was pretty sure she was in love right there but waited two months to tell him.

Her parents hated him. Her father, a bank executive, couldn't get over the phrase *journalism major* and her mother still hadn't gotten over her own first marriage, made in college. Trevor was just another fling to them. No more significant than Kelsie's date to junior prom.

Trevor's parents were divorced and lived abroad. He barely spoke to them, and Kelsie soon followed suit with her own. When he proposed a cross-country hiking trip during summer break, she said yes without hesitation. To further her independence from her parents, she only told them she wouldn't be returning home for the break. She ignored the phone messages left at her dorm. To hell with them.

That was two weeks and a thousand miles ago. As Kelsie looked out into dark-blue forest, she wished very much she'd gone home and tried to talk them into accepting Trevor. The trip had been fun, mostly. But she saw Trevor's temper occasionally and was terrified of doing anything that might make him roll his eyes and remind her of how ignorant she was of the most basic hiking and camping skills.

"Trev?" Kelsie called out as she started along the path she'd seen him go down.

There was no reply.

"You bring any TP, babe? I got you a roll . . ."

She walked ten yards, looked back to make sure she could still see the tent, then went a few more.

The woods were transitioning from day to night. Crickets chirped, and some enormous, shadowy bird—an owl?—flew overhead, returning home or heading out somewhere.

Kelsie still got chills thinking about their hike in the Appalachians, when she saw a huge flock of black birds and pointed them out to Trevor as they flew across the dusky sky. There were so many of them. She'd stared up in awe as they swarmed past.

"Those are bats, babe," he'd explained.

"Bats?"

"Yep. There's probably a huge cave nearby."

"Cool," she'd replied, trying very hard to pretend she meant it. She didn't sleep at all that night. Every flicker of shadow on the wall of the tent sent a shiver down her spine.

That was nothing compared with now.

She reached the spot where Trevor should have been. It was a V formation of logs and formed a natural barrier where even she'd feel somewhat comfortable.

But he wasn't there.

Maybe he took another way back?

Her body was half-turned when she noticed the pale leather of his hiking boot. She knelt down and picked it up.

It had been wedged under a root, as if he'd tripped and slid out of the shoe. Only he wasn't lying in front of it. He wasn't anywhere.

"Trev?" she called out timidly. She was too afraid to raise her voice.

The trees were growing darker and the twilight fading. Kelsie decided to go back to the tent and tried to visualize Trevor waiting for her, smiling. She took the boot and headed back to the campsite.

For a moment she panicked when the tent wasn't visible, but as she got closer she could make out the red fabric in the dim light. There was still no sign of her boyfriend.

"Babe?" she called out.

He'd pranked her once, and she'd denied him sex that night in retaliation. She was pretty sure he'd gotten the message but hoped that this was just a relapse.

Kelsie set the boot by the front of the tent and tried to decide if she should go inside and wait or try to make a fire.

Make a fire, she decided.

It was when she knelt down to the small circle of rocks to ignite the dry leaves that she noticed a tree stump that hadn't been there before. Half the height of a man and as black as night, it was standing between two evergreens in a spot she would have sworn was empty a moment ago.

Her breath frozen in her lungs, she quickly looked to her left and then her right to make certain that she wasn't mistaken. When her gaze returned to the stump, it was gone.

The woods were moving.

There was an explosion of motion, as if a shadow leaped out at her.

The next thing she knew, she was on her back and the frozen breath was trapped under the incredible weight of something standing on her chest.

Her fingers felt thick, coarse hair, like on her mother's paintbrushes. The smell was coppery and rancid.

She saw the flash of claws but didn't understand what happened until seconds later when she felt her warm blood drip down the cold flesh of her stomach.

Trevor had told her that there were bears and mountain lions in these woods. Kelsie had no idea what attacked her. All she knew as she lay paralyzed, bleeding out, was that she'd never heard of an animal that wounded you, then just sat there, watching you die.

CHAPTER TWO
ICE MACHINE

> A scientific man ought to have no wishes, no affections, a mere heart of stone.
>
> —*Charles Darwin*

Red and blue police lights splash off the chipped chrome letters spelling **ICE MACHINE**. I'm standing in front of the motel vending machines with my plastic pail in my hand, lost in thought. Where does the water for the machine come from? Is it from some local stream? Do they filter it? Is the water sealed inside an internal reservoir before it's frozen into cubes?

I just read a paper that described a new bacterium found deep inside ice caves. It evolved from photosynthesis to chemosynthesis—literally eating the rocks to survive. It could also chew through the charcoal used in most filters like soft ice cream.

So far it hasn't been shown to be harmful to humans . . . which makes me wonder if it would be useful for dissolving the mineral buildup of kidney stones. So many questions . . .

So many questions . . . I barely notice the squeal of tires as a vehicle comes to a stop behind me. I turn and see that it's an armored van and that the parking lot has filled with a half dozen police cruisers, each with a pair of county deputies ducked behind, guns drawn and shotguns pressed to their shoulders. Every eye and weapon is trained on the rooms across the lot from me.

"Get down," someone whispers harshly.

A man in black slacks and a tie covered by a bulletproof jacket is hiding behind the driver-side door of a Ford Bronco parked beside me. I can see a badge on a pendant, but his gun isn't drawn.

He waves me away. "Go back to your room."

Everything is happening in slow motion, but I can't move. All I can do is crouch and watch from behind his rear bumper.

Four men in black tactical gear with metal face masks leap out of the back of the van and run toward the row of rooms across from us. One of them is carrying a thick metal cylinder. He rams it against a lock, and the door bursts open. Guns pointed inside, two men rush into the room while the others keep them covered.

There's a tense silence.

From inside someone shouts, "Clear!"

One of the armored men steps outside and makes some kind of hand signal while shaking his head.

The other armored men exit after him, letting three deputies enter, followed by a tall woman wearing a jacket and a cowboy hat. She's got tan skin, like leather, with laugh lines and crow's-feet I can see across the parking lot.

After peering into the motel room, she steps back into the parking lot and scans the cars in the lot. She points to one, and a deputy calls out its plate number on his radio. Everyone is quiet as his voice carries across the parking lot.

The man who told me to get back relaxes and stands up from behind his door. He catches my reflection in his driver-side mirror and wheels around to face me. "Didn't I ask you to go to your room?"

"I . . . can't." I look to the deputies surrounding the door. "I don't think they'll let me."

It takes a moment for this to register with him. I'm still processing what just happened.

"Holy shit." He narrows his eyes. "Are you Dr. Cray?"

"Yes . . . Theo Cray. What's going on?"

His hand touches his hip where a gun sits. He doesn't draw but keeps his palm on the handle.

The man's voice is low and measured. "Dr. Cray, for your safety, may I ask you to slowly set down the ice bucket and place your hands in the air where I can see them?"

I don't think. I just follow his directions.

"Now would you get on your knees?"

I'm wearing shorts, so gravel digs into my knees, but I'm too numb to feel any pain.

He steps over to me, his hand never leaving his pistol at his side. "I'm going to stand behind you to make sure you don't have a weapon." I watch him out of the corner of my eye. His free hand goes to his other hip. "May I put handcuffs on you for my safety?"

"Okay." He has a gun. I'm not sure I can say no. I'm too afraid to ask why he feels the need to cuff me.

After the cold metal restraints are quickly, but not forcefully, clicked around my wrists, he asks, "Is it okay if I lift your shirt?"

"Sure," I say weakly.

I feel cold Montana air on my sweaty back.

"I'm going to pat your pockets now."

"Okay."

He puts a hand on my shoulder, pinning me down as he feels both my pockets. "What's inside there?"

I panic as my mind blanks. "Um . . . my room key. Wallet. Um . . . phone."

"Anything else?"

I think for a moment, afraid of getting the answer wrong. "Uh . . . a Leatherman."

I smell the scent of latex as he pulls on a pair of gloves. "May I remove them from your pockets?"

"Yeah. Yeah . . . of course."

In movies there's a lot of yelling when this happens. This man talks to me like he's a doctor. He never raises his voice. He never threatens me.

He removes everything from my pockets and sets them several feet away from me. Close, but out of my reach.

"I need you to wait here for a moment while we clear this up."

"Clear what up?"

He doesn't answer. Instead, he puts his fingers to his lips and makes a loud whistle. The woman in the cowboy hat looks to see who made the noise.

Her eyes narrow on me. "Cray?" she shouts.

The man nods. Dumbly, I nod, too.

Everything up until now has unfolded with the disorienting calm of a medical exam. Now things go into overdrive as all the energy and attention aimed at my motel room pivot toward me, like the barrel of a cannon.

I feel scores of eyes staring at me.

Some of them angry.

I'm being scrutinized. Judged.

I have no fucking idea why.

"What's going on?" I ask again.

The woman in the cowboy hat walks over in quick strides. She's imposing as she stares down at me like I'm a sample in my lab. I catch a glimpse of a blade on her belt.

"Did he try to run?" she asks with a slight drawl, never breaking eye contact with me.

"He's been very cooperative."

"Good. Dr. Cray, if you can continue to cooperate, this will all be over in a little while."

There is absolutely nothing reassuring about the way she says that.

CHAPTER THREE
SAMPLE

I'm a scientist. I observe. I analyze. I make guesses. I test them. I may be intelligent, but I'm never truly in the moment.

As a kid reading comics, I wanted to be Batman, the Dark Knight detective, but the character I had the most in common with was the Watcher, the bald, toga-wearing being who showed up in Marvel comics and just . . . watched.

Right now I'm watching my life like the rise-and-fall flow of a sequence of numbers on my computer screen as I search for a correlation.

Detective Glenn, the man who found me at the motel, is sitting across from me. We're having a perfectly ordinary conversation. We avoid the obvious questions, like why I have plastic bags over my hands.

I don't think I was technically arrested. As far as I can tell, I agreed to all of this. Not all at once, but incrementally. I think this is what they mean when they say someone was held for questioning. The cuffs came off the moment Glenn sat me down at the conference-room table, but the bags remain taped to my wrists. I'm clearly a specimen.

Glenn is so calm and disarming, I forget from time to time how I got here. The handcuffed trip in the back of a police cruiser. The guns pointed in my direction. The angry, disgusted looks for which I have no explanation.

I study Glenn as he observes me between polite exchanges about Montana weather and Texas winters. He's got receding blond hair and watchful gray eyes sitting in a worn face like an aging baseball pitcher trying to guess how the batter will respond to his next toss. Although his last name is Scottish, his features are very Dutch.

I try asking again what this is all about. His only answer is, "We'll get to that. We have to clear some things up."

I offer to clear up whatever I can right now, but he demurs, acting disinterested in what I might have to say. Given the two dozen law enforcement agents who swarmed my motel and the present situation of my hands and feet, I suspect they're very interested in me.

A dark-haired woman in a lab coat knocks on the conference-room door. Glenn waves her in.

She sets a toolbox on the counter, then dons a mask over her mouth and nose. "Is that running?" she asks, pointing to a video camera I hadn't noticed in the corner of the room.

"Yes," replies Glenn.

"Good." She turns to me and slides the bags off my hands.

The bags were obviously there to preserve evidence from when they . . . detained me to now. Evidence of what?

"Mr. Cray, I'm going to take some samples." Her voice is loud. I assume so the microphone can hear her. She examines my fingernails and points them out to Glenn.

He leans over and stares at my cuticles. "You have them cut very short. Why is that?"

"Chytridiomycosis," I explain.

"Chy—?" He gives up on pronouncing it. "What is that? A disease?"

"Yes. A fungal disease."

The technician lets my hand drop. "Is it contagious?"

"Yes," I reply, surprised by her reaction. "If you're an amphibian. I don't have it. At least, I don't think I carry it. But I spend a lot of time studying frogs in different environments. I have to be cautious that I don't spread it."

Glenn makes a note on his pad. "That explains why you bought your boots three days ago?"

I don't ask how he knows that. "Yes. What I can't sterilize, I destroy and replace. I might be a bit overcautious, but some people think the decline in amphibian populations might be due to researchers unintentionally spreading it."

"So you travel around a lot?" asks Glenn.

"Constantly." Is that saying too much?

"Studying frogs?"

"Sometimes . . ." I'm not sure how much to offer. He hasn't acted all that interested to this point, but that could have just been a ploy to get me anxious to talk.

Glenn pulls a folder out from his portfolio and flips through some printouts. I try not to notice, but I can see through the paper. They're Internet searches about me—faculty pages, research articles, interviews.

The technician uses a small pick and a swab to go underneath my fingernails. She's very gentle. I'm surprised that she didn't know what chytridiomycosis is, but I guess I shouldn't be. Although she's dressed like a scientist, she's a technician who specializes in gathering forensic samples, not examining them.

After shifting through a few pages, Glenn glances up at me with a puzzled expression. "Bioinformatics? You're a biologist?"

"Not exactly. It's a cross between computational science and biology."

Although he's trying to make his questions seem broad and ignorant, I can tell Glenn is intelligent and listening to what I say and what I don't. Since I have no idea where he's going with this, I keep answering in earnest.

"We use the tools of computational science and apply them to biology. Mostly in genetics. For example, DNA. It's so complex, you need computers to try to understand it."

He nods. "So you're a kind of geneticist?"

"No. I study DNA from time to time, but that's not my area. My current area is phenotypic plasticity."

He looks over at the technician, who is shaking her head, then gives me a raised eyebrow. "I'm going to go out on a limb and say that has nothing to do with plastic."

"Not quite." I search for one of my cocktail-party explanations and remember how much I hate to explain my work to nonscientists. "Did you play sports in high school?"

"Football."

"Did you bulk up for that?"

"Twenty pounds of muscle I wish I still had." He gives a self-conscious grin to the tech.

I suspect that when they're not grilling suspects and looking for damning evidence under their fingernails, they're just like any other coworkers with their own in-jokes.

"Gaining muscle like that is something mammals can do and reptiles can't," I go on. "We can dramatically change our muscle mass. A silverback gorilla gets more food, increases his testosterone, and literally gets bigger muscles and a silver back . . ." I pause. "I don't mean to bore you."

Glenn shakes his head. "No, Professor. Please continue. I find this kind of thing fascinating."

"Well, phenotypic basically means the code in our DNA that makes us. Plasticity applies to how it can have variability. For example, Chinese children are growing much taller than their parents. Their DNA didn't change. It already had built-in code to adapt to increased amounts of protein, larger womb size, et cetera. Obesity is another example. We evolved for an environment where calories were scarce, so we can triple our body mass if we're not careful. That's a downside to phenotypic plasticity."

"So you're up here looking at animals that can change their body type?"

"Basically. In particular, were-phibians." I smirk at my quip I've said a hundred times in front of slightly amused students.

Glenn and the technician don't share in my joke.

"Were-phibians?" asks Glenn.

"Were-frogs, or tadpoles, to be more precise." I awkwardly continue. "Wood frog tadpoles are quite interesting. If you get too many of them in a pond, one or more go through a change. Their jaws and tails get bigger and they go from herbivore to cannibal. They resemble mini-piranhas and start eating other tadpoles. When the numbers go back down, their jaws and tails return to normal, and they're just like any other happy little tadpole waiting to grow up into a frog."

Glenn takes a moment to let this sink in. "Interesting. Were-frogs. I get it. And you're looking for them?"

"Not exactly. I'm studying the environment that creates them. I don't think it's a behavior exclusive to tadpoles. It can be on a smaller microorganism scale, or human size."

Glenn arches an eyebrow. "Humans?"

"Yes. You can see this in the womb, where one fetus takes nutrients from another, causing varying birth weights. In vanishing twin syndrome, probably one in ten pregnancies results in a twin, but one is absorbed by the other. Did the mother cause this? Did the evil twin? If so, the evil twin always wins.

"Within a contained environment, like a pond, one organism spontaneously regulates the population, then returns to normal. Apex predators—a dominant animal at the top of the food chain—is going to be emergent when the population gets to a certain size. You see this with cannibal rats, spiders, and even with computer programs."

"A sheep turning into a wolf?" asks Glenn.

I think for a moment. "Perhaps. It's a bit harder to find these behaviors in domesticated populations. They're extremely homogenized and intentionally culled. But in livestock going feral, like pigs, you see them reverting to different forms. It happens in dog packs, too."

"Huh. Well, this is very interesting, Dr. Cray." He turns to the technician. "Caroline, do you have everything you need?"

"One second." She swabs around my thumb and places the Q-tip into a plastic bag marked **Right Thumb**. "That'll do it." She puts all her samples into a bag, seals it with tamper-evident tape, and displays them to the camera before leaving.

I observe the camera observing me, wondering who is on the other side playing the Watcher.

Glenn stands up. "Dr. Cray, if you have a moment, I'd like to get your professional opinion on something. And we'll see if we can find you some shoes."

While I'm relieved my hands aren't in handcuffs or plastic bags anymore, I'm concerned at how Detective Glenn's ears had perked up when I mentioned a specific word.

Predators.

CHAPTER FOUR
SELF-INCRIMINATION

Detective Glenn is still cordial and treating me like an invited guest as he leads me down a hallway. "I appreciate your cooperation, Dr. Cray."

As we walk past open offices and people glance up from their desks, I notice I'm being scrutinized, and not casually.

Clearly, I'm a suspect, or a person of interest, as the news says. But they won't tell me what for.

At this point I should be more tense, but strangely, the fact that I'm being kept in the dark makes it easier to deal with. It's not like waiting for the results of a screening for an aggressive form of cancer. Not knowing the stakes is somewhat dreamlike and unreal.

Glenn unlocks a room lined with filing cabinets with a large table in the middle. "Have a seat, Dr. Cray."

"Call me Theo," I say as I sit down. I normally correct people earlier, but I've been a little preoccupied. "I like to reserve 'doctor' for the medical kind." I save him my diatribe about people with bullshit EdDs and PsyDs that I've run into in academia who couldn't pass a fifth-grade science exam all insisting that they be addressed with the same reverence as the head of oncology at a research hospital.

"Just Theo?" Detective Glenn riffles through some filing cabinets behind me, pulling out folders. "Aren't you a genius or something?"

"You mean the award? That's MacArthur. I won a Brilliance award. It's a bit different. The name is atrocious. I don't put it in my bio."

Glenn sets the folders on the table and takes a seat across from me. "Come on. Obviously you're a genius of some kind. Admit it, you're a real smart guy."

He's playing to my ego, trying to work me. But toward what? "Not smart enough to know why I'm here."

He waves his hands in the air. "It's just procedural nonsense. We'll be done soon."

Which could mean me back in handcuffs.

"As a biologist—excuse me, a bioinformatic . . . What do you call yourself?"

"It changes at every conference. I just say computational biologist."

"Okay. As a clever guy, I want to show you some photos. Different cases. I'm curious to know what impressions you get."

"Impressions? I'm not a psychic."

"Poor choice of words. I'm just curious to see things through your eyes. Humor me."

I want to point out that I've been humoring him for the last two hours. But I don't. I'm not very confrontational.

He pushes a folder toward me. The edges are worn and the label faded. I open it and find myself staring at a man's split-open head. One eye stares at the camera while the rest of his face is missing. Splattered blood covers the tile beneath his head. I close the folder and push it away. "Ever hear of a trigger warning?"

"What?" Glenn takes the folder back and glances at the contents. "Jesus. Sorry about that one. I meant to give you this." He pushes a different folder across the table. "What do you make of this?"

It's an image of a cow with bloody marks around its neck and a slit-open abdomen. "In my professional opinion?"

"Yes."

"This is a dead cow."

"Yes. But how?"

"Is this a test?"

"No. It's been a mystery around here. More of a joke. The rancher says it was a chupacabra. Others say aliens. It definitely looks like coyotes gnawed at its stomach. But the marks on the neck are a mystery."

"Seriously?" I examine the wounds again.

"Absolutely."

I examine the trauma and try to remember everything I know about cows, which isn't much, but enough to have a notion of what happened. I toss the photo back on the table, unsure if I'm being tested. It seems rather obvious now. "Do you want my answer or the path to the answer?"

"The path?"

"Yes. How I arrived at my guess."

He smirks. "Okay, Professor, give me the path."

"As I said before, I study systems. A system can be DNA. A cell. A body. A pond. A planet. We all function in different systems. What system do we see here?" I push the photo toward him.

"Well, by the coyote bites, we see where the cow sits on the food chain."

"Sure. But what other system?" I point to the bloody markings on the neck. "What could cause this? Have you found it on other animals?"

"Yes—"

I interrupt. "I'm going to guess on sheep. But not pigs or horses. Correct?"

Glenn nods. "That is correct."

"Well, the answer should be obvious."

"Obviously . . . and that is?"

"Coyotes."

"Okay, but what about the marks on the neck?"

"All of those animals I named share a system. What is that?"

"A farm," Glenn replies.

"Let's be more precise."

"A ranch?"

"Yes. And what makes a ranch a ranch?"

His gives me a nod as he begins to get it. "Usually a fence."

"A barbed-wire fence. That's how we contain the system. It works great for cows and sheep. But it's too short for horses, and pigs can burrow under it. The only things getting killed here are the animals that are stopped by a barbed-wire fence. Sheep and cows."

"So they're getting stuck on the fence and the coyotes find them, then drag them away?"

"Perhaps. I imagine the coyotes have learned to chase them into the fence. The cow gets cut up, but not stuck. It keeps running until it bleeds out. Maybe miles away from where it hit the fence."

"Impressive. Well, you're a genius in my book." There's something about his praise that feels exaggerated. He rests his hands on the remaining folders. "These are a bit graphic. Random cases. I'd like you to look at them and see if you get any sciency thoughts."

He slides the stack over to me, but I don't touch them. "Is this why I'm here?"

"Just humor me again, Professor. Trust me, no one else here is as charming to deal with as me."

I decide I don't want to find out what he means by that. As far as I can tell, I have nothing to be implicated for, so making some observations shouldn't be a problem. Anything to get out of here sooner.

There are two dozen photographs of bodies, bloody handprints, and random items. The photos are of at least three different people: an elderly woman who looks like she was beaten to death, a man with cuts and stab wounds, and a bloodied young woman whose face isn't visible in any of the images.

There are also photographs of bloodstained clothes, cell phones, money, and tree trunks, along with some other, pristine items.

I'm lost in my thoughts as I pore through the photos. Detective Glenn is a million miles away to me. So is the camera in the corner of the room that's still watching. And presumably the Watcher.

I gather the photos into four piles and sort through them one by one. I see insect bites, poison ivy rashes, a hand resting on a closed pinecone. I don't know where to go with any of this. The cow was easy—it was just one photo.

After a few minutes, I look to Glenn for some guidance and notice the polite smile is gone from his face.

He's staring at a pile in the middle. His eyes flick to the camera for a brief second; then he looks at me, regaining his composure. "Dr. . . . Theo, why did you put those photos there?"

My stomach clenches. Something has happened. Something that makes me look bad.

I spread out the photos from that pile, hastily trying to explain myself. "These look like different angles of the same victim."

He pulls out the photo of the bloody pinecone and another of a purse on a log. "There's no person in these photos, yet you put them into that pile." He drops the photos back onto the fanned pile. "Why?"

"Oh." I gather up the photos and thumb through them again. "I wasn't really paying attention. Random, I guess."

"There are two dozen photos here. You separated the six that were all from the same case. What are the odds on that?"

"High. So I guess it wasn't that random . . ." I try to understand my own reasoning.

"No. It would appear not."

I point to the numbers on the bottom of the photos. "These are case numbers, I'm guessing. They all match up. Mostly. It looks like a coding for a date."

Glenn takes the photos and studies the numbers. "These shouldn't be here." He shoots an annoyed glance at the camera. His shoulders slump. "So you just looked at the numbers? That's why you put those in one pile." He shrugs and lifts his palms in the air, frustrated. "I guess that makes sense."

I should keep my mouth shut. I can't. My desire for logical explanations is a compulsion—a dangerous one at that. "No. That's not how I knew."

The cords in Glenn's forearms tighten. His whole posture goes stiff. His voice is calm and controlled as he asks me, "Then how did you know they're all from the same crime scene?"

CHAPTER FIVE

INDEX

I can tell Detective Glenn has spent a lot of hours working on being calm and composed in extreme situations. I suspect nothing has been an accident so far. The "accidental" photo of the split head was because he wanted to see how I reacted.

His composure slipped when he saw me pile the photographs together. It caught him by surprise. I think that up until then he'd been only casually entertaining his suspicions. His lack of aggression was an asset. If I'd picked up on that, then I probably would have realized sooner what was going on.

There's a reason I haven't seen the sheriff—the woman in the parking lot—for hours. She wears everything on the surface. Glenn glides along the bottom of a deep ocean. I suspect she's the one who ordered the SWAT team to knock down my door, while Glenn is the one with the nuanced approach who got me to willingly hop into the back seat of his car like a frightened stray.

"Why did you group those photos together?" he asks again.

I face them toward me. "It was a subconscious thing."

His voice becomes cordial again. "Is there something you want to tell me, Theo?"

"Yeah. I suck at botany. I could never remember all the names." I point to a small, barbed weed. "It's not milk thistle. Related, though." I point to the weeds in the other photos. "It's only in the ones I piled here. Which means these were taken at the same time of year."

He picks up a photograph and stares at it. "Weeds?"

"Yes, weeds." I wave my hand at the other photos. "I organized the others for different reasons." I point to the old woman photos and ones I thought were related to them. "There's distortion in the lens. You can see that in the lower corner where the straight lines are." I touch another stack. "These are clearly film prints transferred to digital using a scanner. Probably from the 1990s."

"Probably," Glenn echoes as he softly shakes his head.

There's a knock on the door, and someone calls for Glenn to join him in the hall.

"Excuse me," he says before stepping out.

I can hear them talking but not the words. I'm curious but try not to look too interested, because the camera is still watching me.

Detective Glenn walks back in and falls into his seat, somewhat relaxed. "Can I give you some advice, Dr. Cray?"

"I'm sure I could use it."

"If you ever find yourself in a situation like this again, god forbid, don't say anything until you talk to a lawyer." He taps the stack of photos. "That's some spooky stuff. You might even say incriminating."

"I was just being honest."

"I noticed. Almost to your own detriment. Speaking of which, I was curious why you lingered on the head trauma photo."

"So, that was planned?"

"Oh, yeah." He nods. "I wanted to see if you had a normal revulsion response or wanted to start touching yourself."

"And I lingered . . ."

"Yep. Cops and doctors do, too."

"I was a paramedic."

This gets a raised eyebrow. "Really?"

"Yes. But that's not why I lingered. I was looking at how the blood dripped across the white grout between the tiles. It had me thinking of bone."

Glenn squints one eye. "Bone? You're an odd one. I don't know if you realize how odd." He passes his hands over the photos. "Want to know what was most interesting to me?"

"Please tell."

"Never once did you mention the bodies. You noticed everything except them."

Even I have to admit that's a little peculiar. "I guess people are not my area of expertise . . ."

He lets out a small laugh. "I'm realizing that."

"So . . . am I free to go?"

"You were free at any time. Technically, we never arrested you."

I eye the door suspiciously. "When you say I'm free," I say, "am I *free* free? Or is this the kind of thing where you're going to keep after me for . . . god knows what this is about?"

"You're free. You're not our guy."

"Your guy? Can you tell me what this is about now?"

"Yes, Professor. For a hot moment you were our number-one suspect in a murder investigation. The district attorney was already trying to decide what tie to wear to your lethal injection." He eyes the camera again, then lowers his voice. "Out here they're a little jumpy when it comes to this kind of thing. They were eager to get to you to preserve any evidence of your guilt."

I feel a bit numb. "Me? Why me?" The photos should have made it obvious, but sometimes I'm so detached I don't draw straight lines.

"Are you kidding? You're a wet dream of a suspect. Aloof genius scientist. You come in here talking about apex predators. It was too good."

I feel a kind of burning on my skin as this washes over me. Glenn is relaxed, yet I'm afraid it's still an act.

He notices my discomfort. "Seriously"—motioning to the door—"you can walk out right now."

I turn my head toward the door, half expecting to see armed guards waiting to haul me away. "If this is a game, I don't know what I'm supposed to do. I don't know what you want me to say."

"I'm sorry, Dr. Cray. I know this is all a bit of a head trip."

I step outside myself for a moment and see how I must appear. As an EMT, I saw shocked people all the time. That's what I'm feeling right now.

My eyes fall to the topmost photo. A woman's hand, soft, almost elegant in its pose, dangles in the frame, splatters of red dripping from the fingertips. Her palms are caked in dirt and her own blood.

I spread the other photos out on the table and look at each one again.

Detective Glenn had mentioned I noticed everything except the people in them.

I'm noticing now.

There's no picture of her face.

It all makes sense now. I know the reason why I'm here.

A different kind of weight sinks onto my shoulders. After a long pause, my eyes drift up to Glenn. He's watching me intently.

I find the strength to say what I don't want to. "I know her . . ."

CHAPTER SIX

FIELDWORK

Detective Glenn watches me for a reaction as he says the name. "Juniper Parsons."

I don't have one, which, I suspect, is a reaction in and of itself. My first fear was that he was going to say the name of someone close to me—of which there aren't that many. The hand in the photo could have belonged to a half dozen women I've worked with or the daughter of an acquaintance.

The only woman I've been involved with recently—and that's stretching it—is Allison. I think I'd recognize her hand immediately. I'd spent long nights caressing her wrists and intertwining our fingers as we talked about everything from old Bob Hope road comedies to the smell of the desert air in the Gobi.

If it had been her in the photos, my body would have reacted first with some kind of primitive physiological response—dilated blood vessels, skin hackling, a knot in my stomach.

Right now I feel a fleeting sense of relief that I don't recognize the name. Fleeting, because a higher emotion—the kind our social brains tell us to feel based upon internal, not external, experiences—tells me I should feel guilty. Guilty like a chastised dog sitting in the corner, not because he knows taking food from the table is bad, but because he's done something inappropriate he doesn't understand.

My nonreaction is observed by Detective Glenn. While it may support my innocence, it probably reinforces his perception that I'm more detached from the people around me than usual. I'm a caricature of the aloof scientist.

I'm bad with names. I roll Juniper's through my head over and over. Did he mean June?

June isn't a vivid memory. She was a student of mine when I started teaching full-time six years ago. I was close enough in age to most of my class that it made it difficult to manage the need to be professional with the desire to be accepted by what would appear to be my peer group.

She was a zoology major, considering a jump to ethology, the study of animals in their environments. I'd been teaching my holistic approach to understanding systems. Forget the names and conventions we're accustomed to: invent your own. Not every animal with an identical name behaves the same when it's in a different ecosystem. An Inuit who survives by hunting whales weighing more than the mass of everyone he's ever met lives a vastly different lifestyle than a San Francisco vegan who never eats anything that doesn't spend its life cycle buried in dirt.

We had a handful of conversations after class. I think I went out for pizza a few times with her and some other students after a lecture. She never worked in my lab, and as far as I know, we never exchanged texts or talked on the phone.

I glance back to Glenn, after what has been a very long moment. "What happened to her?"

"Do you remember her?"

"I believe so. She called herself June. Maybe she felt Juniper was a bit much."

"Three days ago, we got a call from her mother. Juniper was out here doing some research and hadn't checked in. We sent someone to her motel room. She hadn't been there in at least as long. Everything was intact. The only thing missing was her car. Which we found at a repair shop getting a new transmission.

"This morning two hikers found her body. It went from a missing-persons case to a potential murder investigation. The first thing we do in a situation like this is identify anyone who might know the victim.

"Your name came up." Glenn doesn't elaborate, keeping his cop secrets to himself as he waits for me to say something.

Is this where I protest or stay quiet?

After waiting a beat, he continues, "Two scientists who knew each other in the same area doing research . . ."

I guess it's my turn to respond. "I had no idea she was here. Juniper and I haven't spoken in years."

Glenn gives me a noncommittal shrug. "She had your book on her iPad. Some of your research, too. That led us back to you again. A little too much *Law & Order*, first act, I know. But real life sometimes plays out like that."

"But now you know I didn't do it?" I try to make it a statement, but it comes across as a question, a desperate one at that.

"I think we can reasonably rule you out. If it makes you feel better, we also pulled in the mechanic at the car shop and had local police question her ex-boyfriend. You weren't our only suspect . . . just the most interesting one."

"What's changed in the last hour?" I'm afraid to ask too many questions. Just as quickly as the accusing finger points away, it can point back.

"Our medical examiner was able to make a more thorough examination. I would say we can conclusively rule you out as a suspect."

My eyes dart to the photo of her elegant hand dangling in despair. "Okay, but who did this to her?"

"Not who, Dr. Cray. What."

CHAPTER SEVEN

ISLANDS

"As you've no doubt gathered, the injuries were quite severe," Detective Glenn begins. "At first it appeared to be a knife attack of some kind. One arm was almost detached and the head nearly severed. We found bloody footprints and handprints stretching for almost a hundred yards. She was attacked and chased down. Possibly repeatedly. She was then dragged under a log. It took place less than a half mile from the interstate. Not exactly deep woods. But these kinds of things can happen anywhere. As you're now aware, our policy is to get as much evidence as possible before it goes cold."

"These kinds of things?" I try not to focus on the graphic images.

"A bear attack. We weren't sure at first." His voice trails off for a moment. "We get several encounters a year and on average one fatality." He points to me. "Scientists account for almost half of them. A close second are self-professed grizzly experts. Juniper appears to have been at the wrong place at the wrong time.

"We found a partial paw print and what appears to be bear fur in some of the wounds. An expert from Fish and Wildlife confirmed the wounds are consistent with a bear mauling."

"A bear." I let it sink in. Doing research in Montana and Wyoming, you're constantly on the watch for them. I keep a can of bear spray in my pack whenever I set foot in their territory. I've seen hundreds of them. Even grizzlies. I give them a wide berth, and they've always reciprocated.

I'd never done any field research with Juniper, so I have no idea how well trained she was. But she never struck me as a stupid girl.

Even still, bear attacks are so exceedingly rare. Which is surprising when you realize how closely we come in contact with them when we're out in the woods.

Put a wildlife camera in your campsite overnight and you'll be surprised and possibly frightened by the amount of nature that comes strolling and slithering through.

You can find a hungry bear within earshot of a highway where electric Teslas whiz by under automated control and kids sit in back of RVs obliviously watching *Star Wars* on a big-screen TV as microwave popcorn pops.

Nature is there, even if you don't recognize it.

"Two days ago a hiker called in to report that he'd heard the sound of a woman screaming not too far from where we eventually found Juniper. He said he and his friends went to investigate but couldn't see anything."

Glenn lets out a small sigh. "Easy to understand out there. I once stood on the bumper of a Cadillac that had been covered by mud and brush, looking for that self-same car. I got hell for that one."

I'm not one to talk. I tell myself it's because of my intense focus. "Do you have any idea why she was out here? Not doing bear research, I hope."

He flips through his notepad. "Insular biogeographical analogs?"

"Islands," I reply. "She was looking for islands."

"Islands? Up here?"

"That's what I call them. Generally speaking, they're ecosystems that are isolated from the outside. In the case of islands, it's the ocean that separates them. In a desert you might find an oasis. Or even in a dense jungle, you might find caves with isolated life.

"Remember how I mentioned animals filling different parts of an ecosystem? Even tadpoles becoming apex predators? It sounds like Juniper was looking for pocket ecosystems that are more self-contained than they appear from the outside.

"You can find them in unusual places. Caves, like I said, or on the side of cliffs. You can even find them in man-made environments like a cruise ship or the top of a building. Their degree of isolation varies. But the more remote they are, the more likely a few species are to adapt to fit all the roles you see in a larger system." I realize I'm droning on again.

"Keep going."

"Well, from a bioinformatics point of view, it gets really interesting when you don't limit yourself to traditional taxonomies. Sociologists see emergent structures in everything from prisons to computers playing poker."

I see a connection between Juniper's research and what I taught and feel a twinge of guilt. "I used to tell my students that computer models are informative, but they can only tell us so much about external systems. We have to compare and contrast. You have to go outside. You have to explore the unexplored . . ."

Detective Glenn notices my hands. I tend to flex them and squeeze them when I'm stressed. Right now my fingers are going white from the lack of blood.

"Are you okay, Dr. Cray?"

I shake my head. "No. I just remembered a conversation I had with June . . . Juniper. She asked me for advice." It becomes more vivid. We were at the pizza place near campus with a group of other students. She'd slid into the bench next to me. She had bright brown eyes.

She flicked her hair back and gave me a small grin. "So, Professor Theo, what advice would you give an aspiring scientist?" She'd propped her elbow on the top of the bench. I'd slid back to give her a little more room. This got me another smirk from her.

I recall being very afraid of coming across as one of the lecherous professors who corner young coeds like desperate wolves, then act surprised when they're told that their field has a long way to go toward being more hospitable to women.

Her body language was lost on me. It might have been flirty in the way that some girls learn is likely to get them a response from males who might otherwise dismiss them. I don't know. All I saw was the question.

I gave her a heartfelt response. She pulled back from my space only to prop her head on her hand, elbow on the table, and listen intently.

I thought she was humoring me as I went on. I know now that she wasn't. She took every word very seriously.

Those words, my words, got her killed.

CHAPTER EIGHT

FRONTIERS

From Pliny the Elder, who died rushing ashore to Pompeii after Mount Vesuvius erupted, to modern times, being a scientist can be dangerous. Expert pathogen seekers have lost their lives trying to combat diseases. We've lost astronauts in reentry and ocean explorers to the depths of the sea.

Even the laboratory can be a dangerous frontier. Madame Curie was killed by the elements she was helping us understand. Virus hunters in level-five containment facilities, where every molecule of air is scrubbed, have lost their lives when a tiny pinprick ruptured the tip of a glove.

Sometimes carelessness is the cause. Other times it can just be the fact that we don't understand the nature of the thing we're trying to study. Or it can just be bad luck, being in the wrong place at the wrong time.

In telling my students to go out into the world, turn over rocks, and poke their noses into overlooked places, I perhaps take for granted that they'll exercise caution. Or maybe I'm guilty of understating the dangers you just can't account for.

Although I spent a good part of my youth in the woods, now, with my spectacles and absentmindedly combed hair, I'm sure to my students

I look not much different than agoraphobic English professors and two-legged lab rats who only see the light of day on their way to the student center's vending machines.

I'm by no stretch a survivalist. My limit for the outdoors extends to how much fresh water and granola bars I have in my backpack. My understanding of the forest is more abstract and theoretical than practical in many situations.

Yet I learned something about the outdoors from my stepfather and had some common sense knocked into me by my ROTC drill instructors, who rightly regarded my intellectual curiosity as a battlefield handicap in most situations.

And in dismissing what little I do know, I think I may have set Juniper up for what happened.

Detective Glenn takes a call, and I sit here looking at the outstretched hand of the poor girl.

Her fingers permanently curled in agony when her body stopped producing the coenzymes that prevent the stiffening of muscles we call rigor mortis.

You only have so many hours in a semester to impart upon your students what's important. I'd create endless different lesson plans trying to distill what I thought was absolutely critical. Somehow I managed to find the time to let them play video games on the lecture hall video screen—showing how hip I could be while teaching them how even a digital ecosystem can follow emergent rules.

Now I regret spending so much time on that nonsense, or on movie days when we'd watch a film like *Avatar* and try to rationalize an alien life cycle.

I should have been teaching them about survival.

The video games and the movies are a selfish indulgence. I have never been the popular professor, good at making jokes or just talking to my students. I'm often disconnected and isolated. These so-called fun teaching tools are my attempts to show them that there is a connection between the cool things in their lives and the world I live in.

Looking at the photographs of poor Juniper, I feel as foolish as a history professor strutting into class in a Captain America costume.

I should have been teaching her and her classmates to be safe, not trying so hard to get them to like me.

Juniper should not have been out there alone. Someone should have known where she was. She should have been packing a gun. She should have done all the things I don't do . . .

Impulsive, curious, and oblivious, she may have learned more from me than she should have.

"Dr. Cray? You okay?" Glenn asks.

I realize I've gathered the six photographs of Juniper into a pile and clutched them close to me. Embarrassed, I set them back on the table.

"I'm sorry." I push my chair back. "I should probably be going. If it's okay?"

"Yes. Of course." Glenn stands up and goes over to the door to open it for me. He stops before turning the knob. "I was just on the phone with Fish and Wildlife. They've got their best tracker here. We're going to catch this animal. If that's any consolation."

I give him a weak smile. "We both know that it isn't. The bear was just being a bear." I take a gulp of air into lungs that don't want to move. "She should have known better."

"Don't blame her," Glenn replies.

I glance up. My words are terse and filled with self-loathing. "It's not her that I blame."

CHAPTER NINE

MIDNIGHT

A deputy drops me off at the motel parking lot in the late afternoon with a cardboard box containing my shoes, laptop, and other stuff they took from my room and my Explorer.

The door to the motel room still has a splintered frame where the tactical unit knocked it in. I should probably ask the front desk to put me in another one, but I just don't care.

I shut the door behind me and use the chain latch to keep it closed. The bed is still unmade, but it looks like my pillows have been moved. If I had to guess, someone went over them with a sticky roller, gathering up hair. I suspect they weren't just looking for Juniper's blood. They were also searching for any other signs of her.

While Detective Glenn and I spoke, a technician was doing a cursory examination of what they found.

If a long brown hair had been discovered in my bedsheets or in the shower drain, I can bet that Glenn would have innocently asked if I was here alone or had any company. It would be the first step toward establishing if I was a liar and a potential killer.

Up until I left the sheriff's office, I could tell Glenn was taking a careful measure of me. He's met hundreds, perhaps thousands, of guilty persons. I'm sure he has his own patterns to look for. Everyone is unique, yet we all overlap in the way we react.

It would be easy to call me unemotional. And perhaps I am, if you use a literal definition of the word.

When my father died, I went from an outgoing if not extroverted boy to very withdrawn. My mother sent me to several psychologists. She was worried that I wasn't dealing with my grief appropriately.

Sitting in their offices, I could really only articulate my feelings in yes-or-no fashion. When given a written quiz by one therapist, Dr. Blakely, that asked me specific questions about how I felt, what was going on in my head became apparent—at least to Blakely and myself.

Blakely sat my mother in a chair beside me and told her bluntly that I was managing this as well as could be expected. I wasn't a sociopath or unfeeling. I just didn't express how I felt or even recognize it the same way other people did, or in the same time frame.

The trouble is we expect the *emote* part of emotion. Humans are social primates, and our experiences have to be externalized to be acknowledged by others.

Mother never saw me cry. I used to think that's what bothered her and why she sent me to the different therapists. When I was a little older and had the benefit of perspective—plus some insight from her second husband, Davis—I finally realized why she kept trying to get a second opinion.

She never cried.

Mother couldn't admit her own guilt at not expressing the emotions people are supposed to when a loved one dies.

I have no doubt she felt the loss of my dad deeply. I know she loved him dearly. Everyone did. He was a selfless human who died trying to help other people.

I never judged my mother's sense of loss by how she acted. It was as plain as an equation. When Dad died, the echoes of boisterous laughter and the light he seemed to radiate throughout our home were gone. A stranger to our house could sense that something was missing.

In retrospect, it reminds me of the stories my stepfather told about taking the train from West to East Germany when he was stationed in Berlin. Davis said it was like going from a color to a black-and-white movie.

When Dad was alive, the world was filled with color. Afterward, color only existed as a number on a list of hues. Everything felt muted.

My reaction to Juniper's death was a slow burn. Glenn may now believe I didn't kill her, but as I lie in my bed staring at the ceiling, I wonder if he thinks I'm the type of man who could.

What was I supposed to say when he mentioned her name? How was my face supposed to move? I don't know. I'm sure the right response wasn't to do nothing and stare blankly like a Greek statue.

At the end of the interview, Glenn gave me a second chance to react like a normal, feeling human being when he said they'd catch the bear. My response was that of a scientist, not a red-blooded man who should be driven to revenge for this injustice.

To be clear: I hate that fucking bear.

It may have been doing what comes naturally, but so does Ebola or cholera. I'd wipe them from the face of the planet if I could.

Bears are fascinating animals that share more similarities with us than we realize. They've adapted to almost as many environments as we have. They're an extremely successful and intelligent mammal.

They deserve our protection.

But not this one. Too stupid to know that harmless young woman was no threat, it has to die.

Right now I wish I were out with the hunters trying to track it down.

That's what I was supposed to tell Glenn. The right response was anger and the desire to do something.

He probably thinks I'm something worse than unemotional.

A coward.

The real men, men who never met Juniper or were in positions of authority over her, are out there in the woods seeking her killer.

I'm in a climate-controlled room, behind a mostly locked door, sulking over my inability to let people know how angry I am.

No judgment Glenn could pass on me would be harsh enough.

I'm pathetic.

Unable to express my frustration, I'm even worse than pathetic: I'm impotent.

I lie motionless until my phone rings.

It's Detective Glenn.

"We got him," he says enthusiastically.

"Where? I want to see it."

CHAPTER TEN

THE BEAST

I pull my Explorer into the Highway Department lot at the edge of the forest where they keep road-clearing equipment in a shed. A crowd of men surrounds something under the solitary streetlight.

At least twenty people are standing in a circle. Trucks with gun racks partially block my view of them and what they're gathered around. Most of the vehicles are local and state government.

I park and get out. The distance from me to the thing under the light seems like a football field. I'm conscious of every step yet feel like I'm not getting any closer.

The camera flashes from the circle's center light up the tall pines like silent lightning. The scent of hot coffee fills the cold air along with the sound of laughter.

Take away the trucks, the iPhones, the box of doughnuts, and the rifles, and this could be a scene from the Lascaux Caves, where twenty thousand years ago men would gather to celebrate their victories on the hunt.

I'm the interloper, while they're the heroes that go after the monsters that kill the fair maidens. I'm the bystander here to see the face of the monster but have no right to participate in the backslapping and congratulating.

"Dr. Cray!" Detective Glenn shouts to me. He breaks away from a man in a Forest Service uniform to step over to me.

I half expect him to ask me what I'm doing here, even though he invited me.

He shakes my hand. There's a grin on his face. He only knew Juniper as a corpse. For him, her story began when she was found dead in the woods and has ended happily with the vanquishing of the monster.

The same for the other men.

The main character in their drama is the bear. Each man a protagonist, the animal the antagonist. Poor Juniper is merely an inciting incident. She's nothing but a name and a cause to them.

I'm not angry with them for this. At least they did something while I gazed at my navel.

Glenn introduces me to a man with a peppered beard and a Fish and Wildlife jacket. He's wearing shorts with a pistol strapped to his waist. "This is Kevin Richards. He tracked the animal and killed him."

I shake his hand.

"I'm sorry about your loss." Richards gives me a solemn look. I sense he's the kind of hunter that doesn't relish in the death of any creature.

I can't think of anything to say. I just nod, too embarrassed to admit the biggest loss I'm feeling is my sense of pride.

I catch a glimpse of brown fur between a break in the crowd.

Richards clasps my shoulder. "Let me show you."

His gesture is supposed to be comforting. It's emasculating. I have to resist the urge to shake it off.

He's the triumphant knight showing the scared villager the dead dragon. As if to say, "Don't be afraid. I have it covered, little man."

The crowd notices Richards and Glenn approaching and splits apart so we can see the thing.

A large blue tarp is splayed across the gravel. In the middle sits a mountain of fur, splattered with leaves and twigs.

I can see the dark red of blood on the body, but they don't appear to be the bullet wounds.

In fact, there's only one visible wound on the animal: an entry mark on its right temple, just behind the eye. It was a master shot and a quick death.

The bear's eyes are still open. Its jaws wide in a snarl with sharp fangs visible. The creature's claws jut out from its paws like steak knives.

This is the monster that killed Juniper.

This is the nightmare that took her life.

It's big, even for a grizzly.

I should feel hatred looking at it.

Some instinct should make me want to grab a hatchet and start hacking the beast into pieces, demonstrating my rage. I can't even muster the anger to spit or shake my head.

I look at it and all I see is a bear.

Just a bear.

The snarl on its face was probably just a spasm after getting shot. When Richards pulled the trigger, the animal more than likely had its head down as it tried to smell if there was something to eat under a log.

It was killed in a moment of peace, not in the middle of an epic battle. It died quietly and unaware, as it should have.

As Juniper should have, in old age.

I pity the bear. His path and Juniper's never should have crossed. Had she been ten meters downwind, the bear would be nestled into his sleeping place right now and Juniper would be grabbing a slice of pizza and glass of wine at the parlor in the next town. Both would be happy and content.

Instead, we have a dead girl in the morgue and a dead bear spread out on the ground, the target of derision and hate.

I glance over at Richards and offer my weak praise. "Good job."

He gives me a knowing nod, not really knowing what I'm thinking, and walks away with Glenn.

I stand over the bear and stare at the creature without really looking at it.

"Excuse me," someone says from behind.

I turn around and see a young woman in a deputy uniform. She's holding a thick envelope. "Are you the biologist?"

"Yes."

"I was told to bring these here." She hands me the envelope. "My husband has to leave for work, so I have to head back." She looks down at the bear. "Holy shit. What a monster," she says, then rushes back to her car.

It takes me a moment to realize I'm holding the envelope. The eyes of the bear appear to be looking up at me.

I slip my hand inside and touch several glass vials. At first I think they're some samples they took from my field kit. I pull one out and read the label.

PARSONS, JUNIPER 8.04.17-H.C.M.E.

The dark material inside is unmistakable. It's blood. Dark and clotted. This was taken from a wound. I examine several other vials. All have the same markings.

I'm holding her blood.

Inside this is her DNA. The recipe for making a Juniper Parsons is in my fingers.

Of course, if I could coax the genetic material into an egg and get it to split, even forgetting the information lost from not knowing the original DNA surface methylation, it wouldn't be Juniper.

From the act of fertilization to the moment she slid closer to me in the restaurant years ago, the world around her affected her, molded her into the Juniper I remember. That girl is gone, and I never really knew her. Her DNA is no more Juniper than her photograph.

I read the label on the envelope.

TO: DR. LIAM GOODSON. FISH AND WILDLIFE

That explains why I was just given several vials of blood. I flag down Richards. He's in a conference with Glenn and several other men.

"Excuse me. A deputy just gave this to me." I hand the envelope to Richards.

He glances inside, then nods. He gives it to an older man with a goatee and thick brown glasses. "Goodson, I think this is for you."

Dr. Goodson takes the envelope and checks its contents, then smiles blandly at me. "Dr. Cray? We'll use this to confirm that this is the right bear," he explains to me as a matter of professional courtesy.

I assume they're going to look for her blood on its fur and in its stomach.

I nod and begin to walk away, then stop and turn around to ask Dr. Goodson a question. "What made you think this was the bear?"

"We found blood on its claws and fur," he replies, then points to a toolbox, not too different from one I use, sitting on the tailgate of a truck. "Tested it. Are you familiar with hemoglobin field kits?"

"Ah, of course." He's referring to small testing vials that contain agents that change color if they're in the presence of human blood. It's a quick way to tell if a blood sample is human or some other animal. He's probably got several in his kit for other types of blood. It's one of the ways they catch poachers.

I head back to my SUV and sit there for a few minutes staring at the crowd still standing over the body of the bear.

I'm trying to process everything that's happened.

When I woke up this morning and walked to the ice machine, the last thing I expected was to be part of a drama involving a dead girl and the hunt for a killer bear.

It's all over, and I'm still reeling and confused.

Reeling from what happened and confused by my own actions.

I let the fingers of my right hand loosen from their tight grip and stare at what I'm holding. Looking at it doesn't give me any answers. Only questions.

Foremost among them: Why did I feel the need to steal a sample of Juniper's blood?

CHAPTER ELEVEN

THE PHILANTHROPIST

When I wake up, the vial of blood is on my nightstand next to three empty cans of beer. I know I should give it back. Even though there weren't any serial numbers, or a list itemizing the contents of the envelope, someone might notice it's missing.

I'm pretty sure this counts as tampering with evidence, even if there's no longer a murder investigation.

Why did I take it?

I'd like to think it's because collecting samples is second nature to me. I teach a whole class on how to improvise field kits from Scotch tape, pen casings, and anything else you can find lying around.

My lab is a magpie collection of random things. Some are immediately important; others don't strike me until later on.

Curious holes in a caterpillar cocoon I came across helped explain why a flower grew in one environment but didn't catch on just a few hundred meters away over a hill. An entomologist colleague recognized the holes as termite bores. Not exactly natural enemies, but in this instance, whenever a caterpillar tried to cocoon on a tree branch, this species of termite tore open their tiny home, allowing in harmful parasites. The caterpillar died, never making it to the next stage where it could flap around, spreading pollen.

Absentmindedness is the most innocent explanation of my actions. Bio-kleptomania is at least understandable. The rest are a bit ghoulish.

A mistake we make too often in science is thinking that having a name for something is the same as understanding it. A skeleton in a museum or a drop of blood can only give you part of the picture. Juniper's blood is just that—one pixel of the image.

You could probably tell more from her discarded dental floss. At least I would know what she had for dinner, her dental health, and possibly the DNA of the last person she kissed.

I put my motivations aside and get up to use the toilet. At midstream, my phone rings.

I wash my hands with only symbolic thoroughness and check the caller ID.

It's Julian Stein. He's the philanthropist behind the foundation that gave me my grant. Despite the rather sketchy nature of my application, he's the one that pushed it through, like he's done for me in the past.

Julian is fucking brilliant. He was a child whiz who sold his first software company when he was seventeen. He went on to become a venture capitalist and rich as hell.

For a guy that has it made—house overlooking the Golden Gate Bridge, New York penthouses, and red-carpet walks from the indie films he's helped produce—I can't tell you the number of times he's told me how much he envies me.

It's a funny thing. When I'm worried about whether the university is going to pick up my contract and how I'm going to pay my rent, it seems ridiculous that a guy who's flown presidents on his private plane would look at me with envy.

But when I'm out in the field, or even on my computer, and discover something exciting because I had the free time to do it, I understand.

I came to his attention when *WIRED* magazine did a story on an oddball discovery of mine. I discovered a way to use a local phone book or mailing list to anticipate which cities were going to see flu outbreaks first. I made a list of predictions based on a couple of factors. The biggest one was the number of people in a city who shared a last name.

People who share last names tend to be related and get together more often for meals and are less guarded about eating off one another's plates and exchanging germs. This creates pockets of infection over weekends that soon extend to schools and work. The presence of convention centers added to the calculation.

It wasn't a hard rule, but it had some useful explanatory power. It remains to be seen if it's just a theory that fits the available data.

Julian called me after reading the article and encouraged me to do more research along those lines.

I'd hesitate to call us friends. He lives his life in five-minute chunks, and you're keenly aware that as soon as this conversation ends, he's going to go to the next name on a very long list of people he talks to.

I answer the phone with a slightly froggy voice. "Hey, Julian."

His voice is somber. "Theo. I heard. How are you holding up?"

I hesitate to ask what he heard. About my arrest—well, it wasn't an actual arrest—or about Juniper. With Julian, there's no point in wondering how he found out so quickly.

I decide to say the thing a slightly less self-interested person would say. "Poor girl."

"Did you know her well?"

"Not really. I hadn't talked to her in years. I didn't even know she was working near here." Did I just try to state my innocence a little too forcefully?

"I gave her a grant a while back."

"You did?" To be honest, other than an occasional conference I go to that Julian throws, I have no idea who he's funding.

"Not much. But when I heard she'd been one of your students, it was an automatic yes. She's actually cited you a few times."

Damn, she would have been better off never knowing me. "I had no idea. I only knew her as an undergrad."

"I'm looking through her Facebook page right now. A lot of outpouring for her. She must have been something special."

I wish I knew. I put Julian on speakerphone so I can try to find her on my laptop. The first link is her Twitter profile. I click on it, and a photo pops up.

It's her. She's smiling.

I haven't seen that face or that smile in years. It comes back vividly.

She was a pretty girl. Not in any conventional way. I think I remember now—her father was Irish and her mother was from Haiti. She could pass as Brazilian or any other beautiful mélange. She was one of a kind.

I steal a guilty glance at the vial of her blood next to me. At least we still have her DNA . . .

It's a perverse thought. Even for a biologist.

"I've heard they caught the bear."

"Yeah. I saw it last night."

"I guess that's good."

"You guess?"

"They took me in for questioning," I say, half confessing.

"That doesn't surprise me."

"Maybe not. But for a little while they thought I'd killed her."

"That's fucking scary."

"No kidding."

"Thank god they got to the bottom of that one quickly enough."

"Yeah . . . ," I reply slowly.

"Yeah? You're not instilling confidence in me."

"What? I didn't kill her."

"I never doubted you," he says sharply.

"It's just . . . you know the thing about first impressions? Often they're an element that's spot on."

"Theo, you're losing me here. What are you saying?"

"I don't know. It's just, well, the one detective I spent time with. He was smart. Street smart. I don't think he's the type to go off on wild tangents."

"But they realized it was a bear and found it."

"Yeah. Yeah." I pick up the vial and rotate it around in the beam of sunlight streaming through the gap in the door. Something reflects back.

"You talk to the parents yet?" asks Julian.

I squint and see a fleck of hair. It's a short, straight bristle, not anything you'd see on a human—at least a healthy one.

"Theo?"

"Hey, Julian, do you know any bear experts?"

"We funded an ursine diversity project. Want to talk to them?"

I don't know what I'd ask. "No. Um . . . I got a sample of her blood and maybe a hair from the bear."

"You collected this?"

"No. Not exactly. Never mind." I set the vial back on the stand.

"Want to have someone look at it?"

"Nah, Fish and Wildlife is on it. I'm just being morbid, I guess."

"You're being a scientist. We can wait and see what they say if you want . . . although I'm not sure they'll do much beyond confirming the bear. I'd be curious to know if he had anything wrong with him or if there was something about Juniper that caused the attack. That whole PMS thing attracting bears is a myth, right?"

"To be honest, I don't know if there's enough data points. Anyway, getting into this probably crosses a line."

"Maybe," Julian says. "But let me ask you a question. If it was Juniper that had a vial of your blood and some bear hair, would you want her to have someone look at it?"

"Yeah. But I don't know her well enough to know if she'd want that . . ."

"Trust me, I'm sure she would. Send it."

"All right." Anything to get rid of it.

"You talk to her mom yet?" he asks again.

There's something about the way he says *yet*. As if this is a duty I'm supposed to perform.

Shit. Of course I should call. I'm such an asshole. The normal human thing is to call them and tell them you're sorry.

I hesitate. "No. I was trying to get her number."

"The police didn't give it to you?"

I didn't even think to ask. "I . . . I was getting around to it."

"I'll text it to you. I'm going to call later. It'd be good if you did it sooner than later. Being her favorite professor and all."

Favorite?

"Yeah. I'll do that now."

"All right. I'll send a courier over for the sample. I've got a rapid turnaround lab I'll tell you about later."

Thorough as hell, Julian.

We say goodbye, and I stare at the number for Juniper's mom.

How do you even put into words how you feel about this? How do you begin to explain why it's your fault?

I know sitting here in the dark won't get me any closer to an answer. I just dial the number and hope for once in my life I'll know the right thing to say at the right time.

CHAPTER TWELVE

BUTTERFLIES

"Hello?" Juniper's mother's voice sounds a bit stressed, yet still strong. For her, the nightmare began when Juniper went missing a few days prior. She's had some time to adjust, I guess.

"Hi, this is Theo Cray. I had your daughter in my class a few years ago? I wanted to call to give you my condolences." *Condolences*—what a meaningless way to say I have no idea what to say.

"Professor Theo?" Her voice lifts. "Thank you for calling. It means a lot to me."

"I don't know if they told you, but I'm in the same area." *We'll leave out the part where they thought for a moment I'd brutally murdered your daughter.*

"Yes. I know. Juniper had mentioned it."

"She had?"

"Oh, yes. She kept track of your research. I don't have to tell you how much you inspired her."

Me? "She was a delightful student."

"Did she ever tell you that you're the one that stopped her from dropping out of college?"

"Um . . . no." She never really told me anything, because I never bothered to treat her as anything other than a name on a roll-call sheet.

"She was having a rough time. Boy problems, and her father had died a year before. It was a stressful period. She says you gave her hope. She wanted to be like you."

Be like me? A socially ignorant bystander to the world?

"Thank you for that. I don't hear that very often." *Never* would be more accurate.

"I'm sure you're being modest. It means a lot that you called."

She should be yelling at me. "I just wish . . . I'm sorry." My voice breaks. "I wish I could have been a better teacher. I wish I could have told her to be more careful. I'm sorry, Mrs. Parsons, I shouldn't be saying this to you."

"It's okay. I'm still trying to deal with it." I can hear the sound of her holding back tears. "She was my little girl. Now she's gone."

"I'm so sorry." I take a breath and wipe my nose.

"Dr. Theo, why was she alone out there?" Her voice goes from cordial and in control to distant.

"I don't know. I don't even know what she was doing out here. I wish I could have spent some more time telling her how to be careful." I feel guilty for blaming her and immediately try to backtrack. "I mean . . . I just . . ."

"She was always careful. She spent summers in Yellowstone working with the forestry service. She'd encountered lots of bears and always knew to stay clear. But . . . I guess the one time you're not looking."

This is the first I've heard she'd done forestry-service work. She had more training than I thought.

Now I feel even more guilty for attributing her death to her carelessness. It's comforting to blame the misfortune of others on their own actions. It's also wrong.

She probably had more outdoors skills than I do. Which makes the way she died all the more senseless.

It's the wrong time to ask, but I have to know. "What was Juniper doing up here?"

"Something to do with fish genes, I think."

The map where they found her body wasn't anywhere near a pond or stream. But she could have just been hiking for fun.

Still, as a fellow scientist, not to mention a former teacher of hers, I should at least find out a little more about what she was researching. It's shameful that it took her death for me to even be aware that one of my students had gone off to do her own interesting things.

"Did you see it?" she asks.

I have to take a moment to figure out what she means. The bear. The monster that killed her baby.

"Yes, I saw it last night. We caught it yesterday."

What an utter lie for me to say *we*.

"Thank you for helping catch it. It makes me feel better that it's not going to hurt anyone else. Of course Juniper wouldn't have wanted the thing to suffer. She was that way."

Of course she was. "It was a quick death. The hunter got it in one shot."

"Good. Juniper would be upset with me, but I'm glad you all got the fucker." She pauses. "I'm sorry."

"There's nothing to be sorry about."

"Are you sure you got him?"

For a moment I think she's challenging my version of the story where it's *we* that got the bear. I'm about to confess; then I realize she's asking if we got the right bear.

"They seem to think so. They do tests for that kind of thing."

The vial of Juniper's blood and the hair from the bear is sitting on my nightstand. I feel better about taking Julian up on his offer to have it analyzed. "I'm going to double-check," I say, feigning authority. "I have some friends who can do some of their own testing."

"Thank you. Thank you, Dr. Theo. That means so much to me. I'm glad you're there."

I feel some relief that her mother has justified my transgression.

"Of course," I say magnanimously, and completely full of shit. "Please, just call me Theo. And if there's anything I can do for you, let me know."

"She had her car at a repair shop. I hate to be a bother. The police can send me her things, but . . ."

"I'll take care of it. Just give me the name of the shop and where she was staying. I'll handle the rest."

We say our goodbyes. I make a mental note to follow up with her on the phone in a few days. I can't just treat this like sending an obligatory Mother's Day card.

This woman lost everything that was important to her. As far as she's concerned, I was important to her daughter. The very least I can do is respect that and look in on her from time to time. I'm sure it would be what Juniper wanted.

Juniper, the more I hear about you, the more interesting you become.

What were you doing out here?

CHAPTER THIRTEEN

WALKING DISTANCE

Bryson's Auto Repair sits on a patch of gravel along the highway, seated between long stretches of pasture near where the tall trees of the forest begin. Its presumed namesake, Bryson, in his fifties and wearing grease-stained overalls, looks up at me from under the hood of a Subaru Outback as I pull in.

I spot what must be Juniper's Jeep sitting in the noon sun on the edge of the lot next to a pickup truck and a Toyota Camry that's missing a hood and fender.

Bryson walks out to my SUV to greet me. "So you're the other one?" he says as I climb out.

"The other one?"

"The other fella they took in."

Ah, I get it. Of course. Glenn had mentioned that they had another potential suspect before they realized a bear killed her.

He's a few inches shorter than me but has a thick build. I only see one car lift and a small winch. He probably keeps fit lugging heavy parts around all day.

"Yeah," I say. "Looks like the one they were after walks on four legs."

"I suppose," he replies.

I point to Juniper's car. "Her mother asked that I make arrangements. She lives in North Carolina. Any idea how to get it there?"

"The tow company that brought it only does in-state. But I know a car service that will cost you about eight hundred. If you got a few weeks, you can take out a Craigslist ad and see if anybody working up here for the season wants to drive it back."

"You think that'll work?"

Bryson shrugs. "I dunno. But if you got the time."

"Actually, I have to be back in Austin in about a week. Fall classes are starting. Maybe I'll try the ad for a few days."

I'd hate to ask Juniper's mother to pay for this. Worst-case scenario, I'll put it on my credit card and figure out later how I'm going to manage the expense.

Bryson looks over my shoulder at my Explorer. "You planning on getting new tires soon?"

I'm about to dismiss him as a huckster when I actually look at the tires and realize I have almost no tread on the front ones.

He's noticed my hesitation. "I'm not trying to hustle you. I can replace the front ones with a couple of discounts. The rear ones will last you another little bit. It'll only cost you a hundred and fifty."

"Each?"

He lets out a small laugh. "Pardner, if I was going to rob you, I'd never let you see me coming. Hundred fifty for the both and I'll throw in an oil change."

"That would probably be a good idea."

"I got a lounge with Wi-Fi if you want to wait. Of course, there's not much else to do." He nods to the forest. "Even if they caught the thing, I don't think I'd go walking around up there."

"Probably right."

He points to the field of grass next to the metal building. "It was like a Hollywood movie. They landed the search helicopter right there."

"Here?" I turn back to the forest. "Wait, is this where Juniper was found?"

"Three miles up the road. Between here and the Mountain Cloud Inn."

The Mountain Cloud Inn was Juniper's motel.

I hand Bryson my keys. "I might go for that walk after all."

I take my day pack out of the back seat and strap it around my waist. I don't plan on going into the woods. I just want to follow the road a bit.

At least that's what I think. To be honest, I don't have much of a plan.

❦

The highway cuts through the forest like a skinny canyon. I stay on the gravel easement in case a distracted driver comes hurtling down the road.

It's a strange change from the grazing land to the evergreens. In between there are patches of tall wild grass—an ecotone. The trees and the prairie are in a battle for turf. The wild grass straddles the middle, where the rocky flatland gives way to the softer forest ground.

On the edge of the highway, where the asphalt is cracked, daisies and weeds pop through like tiny little islands. Miniature ecotones. If I were looking for a bacterium that could eat oil, I'd be collecting samples of dirt from the middle of busy freeways. I don't know if I'd find one, but I'm sure I'd discover something interesting.

I lift my gaze from the road to the surrounding forest and try to look for what Juniper was searching for out here.

The smart thing would be to pull up her latest research applications or, at the very least, read her blog. But I am still taken aback by events and can't bring myself even to spend much time on her Facebook page. Her face keeps appearing, haunting me.

The first mile I walk is a gradual incline as the road begins its wayward journey into the mountains. The second begins to get a little steeper.

I keep my eyes on the trees for any sign of where Juniper was found. Undoubtedly, the sheriff's department used some kind of marker.

I see a few faded-orange forestry markers but nothing else. To my knowledge, they haven't released anything other than a general area description to the public.

The connection between this forest and the map I spotted in Glenn's office isn't obvious to me—and I spend all day looking at maps of real and artificial landscapes.

A tractor-trailer truck blows past me and heaves a great gust of wind over my body.

I should have asked when Juniper brought her car into the garage. Did she have to do a lot of walking?

I make up my mind to give it another ten minutes and then turn back. I have no idea what I'm looking for, much less what Juniper would have been doing out here, other than walking from her motel to the car shop or back.

The hills on either side of the highway are too steep to form a pond or any body of water bigger than a tree trunk. The only fish would be the ones that fell out of a bird's mouth.

When I'm contemplating turning back, I spot a blue ribbon tied to a tree. It looks brand-new. A dozen yards into the trees, before it gets too thick to see past, there's a thicker yellow ribbon—the kind of tape you see at a crime scene in a movie.

This is the spot. Or rather, the spot on the road that takes you to the trail that leads you to where it happened.

I really should go back to the garage now. I have no business out here.

Yet . . . I walk into the forest to find the place where she was killed.

CHAPTER FOURTEEN

Yellow Line

The ancient Greeks believed that the world began with chaos, a void without form. From this shapeless heap the Titans and the gods emerged, bringing forth man. In his most evolved form—which the philosophers saw as themselves—he tried to put order to this chaos, seeking symmetries and rules to the universe.

It was this rule seeking that created the idea of philosophy and, much later, science.

A scientist is someone trying to see order in chaos. Sometimes it simply can't be done, as science tells us via quantum mechanics and chaos theory. A thing can be one way or the other without any means to predict why it is so.

I'm hiking up the hill because I want to make sense of chaos. We have an event: Juniper's death. We have a cause: the bear. I don't have a why, and the police haven't divulged what led to this encounter.

The first yellow ribbon was just a marker, as I suspected. Ten yards beyond it is another.

I find five yellow ribbons that lead to a small area of level ground.

This is where I see the first red ribbon.

It's tied around a tree trunk. Below it is a dark blotch on the bark.

Blood.

To be precise, a partial, bloody palm print.

Juniper touched this tree as she was dying.

I spot four more red ribbons in this small clearing and three red flags on the ground.

Some of the ribbons mark where parts of the tree were carefully removed to take back to the medical examiner. Some of the spots on the ground are simply holes where the dirt and blood was shoveled free.

The holes are small. Not quite what you'd expect to find where an adult bled to death.

I kneel down to inspect one of the stains. The ground feels waxy, like clay. Beads of moisture collect on the surface as the minerals behave hydrophobically.

Some dirt repels moisture. Other kinds, like parched desert soil, soak it up greedily.

You'd have to dig down to know how much blood was shed. From an initial examination, it doesn't look like much. She may have already bled out by the time she came to rest here.

I wipe my hands on my shorts and see the second row of yellow ribbons. They lead higher up the hill.

The pattern is becoming clearer. I'm still surrounded by chaos, but it's pointing in a direction.

I climb the hill and find my footing a little unsteady as small rocks slide free underneath me. I can only imagine what it was like for Juniper to stumble her way through the brush.

Two red flags mark where drops of her blood splattered plants.

The yellow trail ends at another tree where Juniper rested her hand. Oddly, it's on the side of the tree facing the road and not the one oriented deeper into the woods, where I assume she first encountered the bear.

There's a much longer path of yellow ribbons leading even higher. I climb the trail, careful not to step on any red flags hiding behind logs or shrubs.

As I place my right foot down, I freeze. It's not a sound that makes me stop—at least not one I'm conscious of.

It's the older part of the brain that's connected to atrophied or extinct sense organs.

I've had this before.

The first time was when I was fourteen and my stepfather took me on a hike in West Texas. I stopped from time to time, unsure of something. Davis remained quiet.

When we got back to camp, he asked me if the hike felt odd. I told him it did but couldn't explain why.

He gave me a knowing nod, then retrieved his rifle from the truck. "Follow me."

We backtracked a mile and came to a stop at the very point I first got that strange feeling. I watched as he squinted and surveyed the surrounding area. His attention fell on a large boulder.

I followed him around to the other side. Davis squatted down and motioned for me to do the same. He pointed to a small patch of mud.

A paw, larger than my fist, had rested there. I recognized it from a hunting guidebook. It belonged to a mountain lion.

That's what we both had felt.

"How did we know?" I asked.

"Maybe we smelled another carnivore. Maybe we heard it. Just keep in mind, it was aware of us long before we were aware of it."

That was a sobering reminder that would be illustrated to me over and over again.

Right now I get the feeling there's something out here with me. Running would only establish that I'm frightened prey. Acting too brazen might present me as a territorial challenger.

The best course of action is caution. I slip my hand into my day pack and grab my can of pepper spray.

There's one more trail of yellow ribbons to follow. Following it could mean bringing me to where Juniper was first attacked by the bear.

While I saw a dead bear, that doesn't mean it was the bear that killed her. Bears and lightning do as they please and can strike in the same spot as much as they choose, despite what experts tell us.

I should carefully walk my way back to the road.

But I still have chaos.

I want order.

Mace in hand, I keep climbing the hill.

Every noise, every prolonged stillness makes me stop and take measure of my surroundings.

I don't see any predators lurking behind trees. But that doesn't mean they're not there.

I reach the last yellow flag and see one red one planted in the ground.

Although the forest floor is covered in pine needles, I can tell the soil is different here.

It's full of blood.

CHAPTER FIFTEEN
RESTING PLACE

A morbid image comes to my mind as I look at the dark stain on the ground. In the Rorschach way our brains leap to connections, I think of a snow angel.

Juniper struggled here on the ground. Her arms windmilled as her blood spread out around her.

Was she fighting the bear? Trying to climb out from underneath it?

The fact that she had the strength to find her way to her feet and make it down the hill astounds me.

How would I have reacted? Would I have panicked and gone into shock?

Juniper was a fighter. She was a brave girl who didn't give up until her body physically couldn't go any farther.

As a paramedic I'd hear about people dying of the simplest wounds. Others would survive accidents that would be fatal to others. Vital organs and arteries matter, but so does the will to live.

Something stirs in the trees. I stand up and make a slow turn as I gaze into the forest.

The part of my vision primed for patterns doesn't spot any.

There could be a dozen animals, from bear size to mouse, within twenty yards of me and I wouldn't see them.

Mindful, yet transfixed by the circle of blood, I kneel back down and try to make sense of things.

What brought Juniper and the bear to this spot?

Was it stalking her?

Did she surprise it?

Was she foolishly stalking the bear? Stupid as it sounds, more than one idiot has been killed doing this.

I stand back up and look down the hill. I've seen plenty of yellow and red flags, but no other colors.

What about her backpack or shoes? Do the police have some special ribbon for where they find a person's belongings?

I can't imagine Juniper came this far into the forest without even a water bottle—even if she was just hiking between the garage and the motel.

And I still can't understand what would bring her all the way up here. There aren't any ponds or lakes. The largest pool of liquid is her bloodstain.

There aren't even any rotting logs where a bear would find something worth eating.

Juniper's and the bear's presence here are just so random.

Bears can have very wide territories. I guess it's possible it was on a long hike of its own.

To be honest, I don't really know much about them. I'm standing in the woods speculating about the behavior of two creatures that are quite alien to me.

My ear twitches at the sound of a twig snapping. I wheel around to empty forest.

I hold my breath and freeze, waiting for it to move again.

I know I'm facing in the right direction. I just can't see what made the noise.

All my attention is focused on a small area where two trees stand a few feet apart.

Something is there.

I decide the best course of action is a careful retreat. Pepper spray ready at my waist, I take a step backward, never looking away. I take another.

Something stabs into my ankle. I jerk reflexively and fall.

My back slams into the ground, and the wind is knocked from my lungs. My head slaps into a rock, and the corner of my vision begins to fade like an old television.

I fight passing out.

Twigs break as something rushes through the forest.

Rushing toward me . . .

I try to raise the pepper spray, but my hand comes up empty.

The exertion uses too much blood, and the dark fingers of unconsciousness grab me.

One of my last sensations is the smell of blood.

There's the warm trickle from the back of my head, but the blood I'm feeling isn't my own.

I've fallen into Juniper's snow angel.

A shadow falls over me as I pass out.

CHAPTER SIXTEEN

Sniper

When I come to, I'm leaning against a tree trunk. The back of my shorts and hoodie are soaked in blood. At first I think it's my own; then I realize I fell into the pool of Juniper's.

The last image of the shadow falling over me comes back. I jerk in fright and try to get to my feet, but my knees are too weak.

Something rushes through the brush. I bring my hands up like a scared child.

"Take it easy," says a man's voice to my left.

Detective Glenn steps up and leans over me. He's got one hand on his phone. The other is holding a bloody cloth. He touches it to the back of my head. I try not to twitch.

"The good news is most of this isn't your blood. The bad news is that you've desecrated a murder scene."

"I'm sorry." I look at the stains on my fingers. Juniper's blood is all over me.

"It rained last night and made the pool bigger." He holds up a finger in front of my eyes. "Blurry?"

"No."

"Well, there's more good news. We're not going to have to chopper you out of here."

"I'm okay. Give me second."

The back of my head stings. But that should go away. There's no funny smell, and I don't feel dizzy, which means I probably don't have a concussion. Probably.

"You hit the rock over there perfectly. Right on the sweet spot."

"I was . . . startled."

"No kidding." Glenn checks for a dry spot, then sits down. "What the hell are you doing up here?"

"I thought it would be a great place to fall on my ass." I glance over at the pool of Juniper's blood, then shake my head. "Jesus Christ."

"Yeah. Not a graceful moment. You still haven't answered my question. Why are you up here?"

"Mrs. Parsons, Juniper's mom, she asked me to take care of her car."

Glenn cocks his head. "Up here? I don't think there's much parking. You sure you're okay?"

"Back at the garage. What's his name? Bryson. He's changing my tires. I thought I'd go for a walk."

"And ended up here?" Glenn asks skeptically.

"I saw the ribbons. I was curious. What are you doing here?"

"I don't have to have a reason. But if you have to know, tying up loose ends."

I think back to the sense I had of not being alone. "You were watching me."

"Yep. Ever since you got here."

"And you didn't say anything?"

Glenn looks to the side as he tries to remember something. "What do they call it? The observer paradox?" He shrugs. "I figured it would be more interesting if I saw what you did if you thought you were alone."

"But I knew I wasn't alone."

"Maybe. But I bet you thought it was a bear or cougar stalking you."

He's right. "It might as well have been. You were quiet. Military, right? What did you do in the service?"

"Spotter."

A spotter is a soldier who accompanies a sniper and helps them identify targets. "Of course. I guess if you'd been a sniper, I'd be dead already."

"I think you did a pretty good job of taking yourself off the battlefield."

I reach back and feel the tree trunk. Slowly, I stand up, using it to brace me.

"You okay?"

"Yeah. I think so." I wipe away the leaves stuck to my clothes. "How did Juniper end up all the way down the hill after losing so much blood up here?"

Glenn stands up and raises an eyebrow. "What makes you think we found her down there?"

"It's closer to the road. I'd assume she met the bear deep in the woods and tried running toward the road."

He shakes his head. "No. She died right here. Exactly where you fell."

"She ran up here?"

"Ever been attacked by a bear?"

"Five minutes ago I thought the answer was yes."

"Well, I haven't. But I would imagine my only instinct would be to run any way I could."

"Yeah. You're right. I guess it's easy to overanalyze things when you're not about to die. Still. It seems counterintuitive."

Glenn folds his arms and looks around. "All right. As a scientist, can you tell me what she may have been looking for up here?"

"Not a clue. Her mother mentioned something about fish. Obviously there aren't any around here."

"Nearest lake is through Brookman's Pass. That got filled in with a mudslide a month back. The only way there from here is a two-day hike. Half of that through pasture." He points toward the road. "On the other side of there are a few ponds. But you can't get there from here, as they say."

"Interesting. I'll do a little more digging to find out about her research."

"Let me know. It's also possible she was looking for a shortcut."

"I think she was brighter than that."

Glenn acts as if he's trying to hold something in. He shakes his head. "If her teacher is any example . . ."

"Don't judge her," I reply coldly. "I may be a klutz, but from the looks of things, she went down with a hell of a braver fight than I did."

"No. You're right. That was out of line." He replies with a grave tone. "Tough girl."

"I wish I'd known her better."

Glenn lowers his voice. "Come on, now that you're out of the hot seat, you can level with me. You knew her pretty well, didn't you? Maybe had a little rendezvous in town?"

I'd punch him if he didn't have a gun and I wasn't a coward.

All I can fight back with is a hurt look. Hurt that he'd think that of me. Hurt that he'd think that of Juniper.

"Don't be an asshole."

He holds up his hands in surrender. "Sorry. It's the detective side of me. I'm always poking. I wanted to see how you'd react."

"What difference does it make now? She's dead and you got the bear."

"True. I guess it's like research. If I ever meet someone else like you, I want to know what's going on inside his head."

I'm not sure I like the idea of him still probing my motives. "Have you ever met anyone like me before?"

"Actually, when I first met you, I thought I had."

"Was he a bumbling goof like me?"

Glenn studies me for a moment. "No. He was a killer. As cold a man as you could imagine."

"A killer?" My stomach churns.

"Fourteen confirmed kills, to be accurate."

My skin goes cold at the comparison. "A serial killer?"

"I wouldn't call him that."

Glenn's observation isn't amusing. "Then what? A mass murderer?"

"No. A sniper. I was his spotter."

I don't know what to make of that comparison and just manage to mutter, "I'm only dangerous to myself."

"Maybe. But I still get the feeling I wouldn't want to see you angry."

CHAPTER SEVENTEEN

GenBank

When I get back to my motel room, I notice a voice mail from Julian. "Call me . . ."

"What's up?" I ask a minute later.

"I'm about to send you a fat file. We got DNA back."

"That quickly?" I check my watch. His courier picked it up less than twelve hours ago.

"I have a rapid DNA testing start-up, Xellular—with an *X*."

"Of course. You named it, I bet. I don't think I've heard of them." This was the lab he was alluding to. Of course it's his own.

"Yep. And you probably wouldn't have heard of them. They're not in academia. Our main client is the CIA. They use us to identify terrorists and figure out after the fact who they hit with a drone strike. Money is no object, so they were willing to foot the bill on rapid testing. The upside is that we'll be able to make it commercially available soon."

"Sounds good. Although I don't know what to expect out of Juniper's DNA. If there was some kind of hormonal or pheromonal thing, it would have been in the blood plasma."

"No," he corrects me. "Theo, this is the bear's DNA."

"The bear's? I didn't realize there was a follicle in the sample. It just looked like a short hair shaft."

"There wasn't. We got it from the shaft."

"I didn't think that was possible." Accepted wisdom is that hair only contains mitochondrial DNA, or mtDNA, passed from mothers to their children with little change. Men don't pass it on. Changes in mtDNA are so slow, mainly due to random mutations, that you can use hair as a kind of genetic clock to see when populations split. As far as identifying individuals, it's pretty useless. The mtDNA of you and all of your maternal cousins is effectively the same.

Nuclear DNA, or nuDNA, is the DNA that contains the combination of your mother's and your father's DNA that describes you. This is how you tell one individual from another. This is how you'd try to clone someone or identify their involvement in a crime.

Whereas blood and skin cells contain nuDNA along with mtDNA, hair, the part that grows above the shaft, is made of dead cells not thought to contain any nuclear DNA.

"Hey, something Theo Cray doesn't know," Julian says in a mocking tone. "They thought you couldn't find any nuDNA because of the keratinization process. As the hair cells died and hardened, it was believed to be destroyed. Since we're finding genetic material in fossils long after the DNA half-life should have destroyed it all, it's not unreasonable to have suspected that there might be some viable DNA in hair.

"The real challenge was scrubbing the rest of the stuff away. Some Chinese researchers figured out a couple of years ago how to use laundry powder to do that. As it turns out, we've been designing custom enzymes for cleaning microchip wafers. We found an even more efficient formula for finding DNA."

"That's great. So how's your dinosaur park coming?"

"Insurance is going to be a bitch. Anyhow, I figured it might be interesting to compare the bear that got Juniper with others involved in attacks. Who knows, maybe they're susceptible to some kind of mad-bear disease."

Julian wants a rational explanation, like me. "I don't know if we'll be any better at predicting criminal behavior in bears than we are in people."

He makes an awkward cough. "Sometime when I know I'm not being recorded, we'll have an off-the-record, politically incorrect conversation about that. Francis Galton was on to something."

"Galton was a racist," I reply.

"I don't mean that part. Anyway, I'll send you over the DNA file. I haven't had a chance to upload it to GenBank and find out what subspecies it is. I'm sure Fish and Wildlife already knows all that, including what it had for breakfast. What I know about bears I learned from watching the Muppets."

Julian knows this is perfect busywork for me. It's a way for me to deal with the situation on my own terms. I thank him, then hang up.

The e-mail with the zipped file follows shortly after. DNA in software form is just a text file with a list of location numbers, followed by sequences like acaagatgcc attgtccccc ggcctcctgc tgctgctgct ctccggggcc acggccaccg.

Remarkably, you can take this information—which describes the order of the bonds of guanine, adenine, thymine, and cytosine to a sugar and phosphate group—and plug it in to a machine that will recreate the DNA by dripping nucleobases one by one into a solution.

Researchers have e-mailed text files across the Internet, uploaded them to DNA replicators, and then dropped the DNA copy into "blank" cells, which have then started up and become identical versions of the original organism.

It still blows my mind that you can e-mail life like you can cat pictures. Any day now we'll read about some researchers actually e-mailing the cat across the Internet.

The text file is pretty useless by itself unless you're familiar with specific sequences and their locations. To make sense of it, you load it into a program called a viewer, where you can more easily understand what you're looking for.

The search for the genetic origins of disease involves looking at specific regions and trying to identify differences. We thought we'd have cancer and other illnesses licked once we could sequence the whole genome. The trouble was that even assuming the condition was related to just a handful of genes, looking at a sequence couldn't tell you if it was turned on or off in the body. But we're making strides.

GenBank is the largest public repository of genetic information. It's filled with DNA samples from just about every animal on the planet that's managed to find its way near a DNA collection kit.

The original database fit into a few hardback books. They didn't contain whole genes, just known base pairs. The most recent version has 165 billion base pairs that would fill seven million books.

Fortunately, it's available in an online database.

I upload the file Julian sent me. A moment later it spits back the results: *Ursus arctos*.

A brown bear. In North America we call them grizzlies. Just like the one I saw back at the snowplow shed.

Beyond telling me it belongs to a population in the Wyoming and Yellowstone area, GenBank doesn't have any additional information.

I guess I shouldn't be too surprised. So I do a search for any groups that have more specific DNA information on local bear populations and find a research group working out of Montana State called Ursa Major.

On a lark, I dial the number on the website.

A woman answers. "This is Dr. Kendall."

Okay, words . . . "Hello. Um, this is Dr. Theo Cray."

"What can I do for you Dr. Cray?" She's polite but to the point.

I'm sure her group is all over Juniper's bear attack. I'm too embarrassed to tell her exactly why I'm calling. To be honest, I'm not sure even I know why.

"Dr. Kendall, I've been doing some research in the area on different fauna and I was wondering if you have a database of bears you've tagged or tracked?" I'm not sure how to flat-out ask her for access.

"Yeah. Send me your e-mail and I'll give you a log-in. What university are you with?"

"Texas. But right now I'm working on a Brilliant grant."

"Ooh, a brilliant man," she teases.

"I've begged them to change the name."

"Just e-mail me through the website I'm guessing you found me on and I'll send it to you. And if I ask for a Brilliant grant, maybe you could put in a word for me?"

"Absolutely."

Science can be like that. Just give off the right signals and you're accepted.

Five minutes later I'm in her database poring through hundreds of entries describing different brown and black bears they've counted.

Each one has a code, like UA20.22.06. Some also have nicknames from field researchers studying their behavior: Honeypot, Paddington, Paddington 2, Winnie, Booboo, Tricky Dick.

The associated entries explain how they came by their names. Some are random—Tricky Dick was a black bear that managed to get three different sows pregnant at the same time.

It takes me a little while, but I manage to find the DNA database. I upload the file Julian sent me and quickly get a match for the bear hair from Juniper's wounds.

I pull up the animal's file, and his name gives me a chill.

Ripper.

CHAPTER EIGHTEEN

Apex

Ripper's file contains information collected from hair traps—strands of barbed wire used to snare follicles (the part with nuDNA)—scat, paw prints, and tracking points from when they had him GPS collared for a year.

It's like an NSA database on the animal. It literally tells me what he had for breakfast on some occasions. Moose. Lots of moose.

Ripper got his name because of how he'd slice open the stomachs of his prey. He preferred long gouges.

Maybe to savor the moose juices? I can only imagine why.

There's also a lineage showing his relatives and offspring. He's known to have one surviving cub, just called UA.354.222. I assume that means nobody has even made a connection between an observed bear and his offspring's DNA.

The GPS tracking dots overlay onto a map showing his range. Apparently his stalking grounds are ten miles from here. Although it's not unusual for a bear to go outside his territory.

Unfortunately, the GPS information ended last year, so there's no telling how far he traveled before ending up in this neck of the woods.

A list of hair traps shows a slightly wider range. It appears that many of these data points came before he was collared.

It's odd—probably because I don't know any better—that he never ventured over the ridge until now.

Maybe he killed Juniper because he was in unfamiliar territory? Detective Glenn mentioned something about a pass getting shut down from a mudslide. Ripper might have been going on a trek and found himself stuck here.

It's all speculation on my part.

People tend to think that scientists are experts in all things, when in fact we can be so specialized we know less than a layperson about many scientific topics—like bear behavior.

In the file I also find a photo of Ripper when he was tranquilized for the GPS collar. He looks a lot like how I saw him when he was lying dead on the blue tarp. Ferocious and peaceful at the same time. Here he's missing a claw on his left front paw.

Claws are basically sharp toenails and grow back after time. I think he had a full set when I saw him. Do they grow back annually?

Still, I'd like to compare. Even though they haven't done a press conference yet, there has to be a photo online.

Sure enough, a few searches later, I find that the *Bozeman Chronicle* has an article. It's a menacing shot of Ripper, his snout facing the camera with his canines bared.

Suspected Killer Grizzly Caught by Fish and Wildlife

BOZEMAN, Mont. Off-the-record sources have confirmed that a tracker with Fish and Wildlife has positively identified and killed the grizzly bear believed to be responsible for the death of a scientist who was doing research near Filmount County. A contact at Wildlife Genetics International said the grizzly has been DNA matched to a bear known as UA.223.334.

The press is going to go nuts over the bear's nickname when that gets out.

I check Ripper's file again to see if anyone at Ursa Major has updated his file since the capture.

The most recent entry was last year. I guess the grad student in charge of it is a bit overburdened.

As I close the browser window and the case on Ripper, something catches my eye.

I reload the page to see what it was.

This is odd.

UA.221.999 / "Ripper"

This index number is different from the one in the article.

Do bears have multiple entries?

I type UA.223.334 into the database to see if they're cross-referenced.

A new file appears on the screen.

UA.223.334 / "Bart"

It's a description of a totally different bear.

This one has hair-trap samples much closer to here. I pull up a photo. It's a long-distance shot of him walking across a meadow.

Bart looks an awful lot like Ripper, but even to my untrained eye, they appear to be different bears.

Though I know a bear can put on several hundred pounds before winter and I'm not sure how you tell them apart, to be honest.

I download Bart's DNA file and load it into a viewer.

This is curious. He and Ripper are related, but there are lots of different gene sequences. About what you'd expect from distant cousins. But not what you'd get from the same animal.

I check the article and the database again just to be certain.

Yep, these are two different DNA samples.

Somebody made a mistake somewhere.

I'm on the Wildlife Genetics International website as fast as I can type. There's a number. I dial it, at even more of a loss as to what I'm going to say than when I called Ursa Major.

"WGI, to whom may I direct your call?" a woman answers.

"Hello, can you connect me with the laboratory supervisor for sequencing?"

"That would be Dr. Whitcomb. One second."

"This is Travis," says a man with a youthful voice.

"Dr. Whitcomb, sorry to bother you. I'm in the field and can't reach anyone back at the medical examiner's lab. Um, could you resend me the file for the bear they killed yesterday?"

"Resend?" He sounds annoyed. "I haven't even sent it out yet."

Damn. I think of a cover. "Sorry. Someone misinformed me."

"No problem. I got it right here. Where should I send it?"

In my haste, I give him my university e-mail. I'll think of a reason later for plausible deniability if someone asks.

I thank him. "Quick question, how did they know it was UA.223.334 without the DNA?"

"How'd they know it was that bear? Beats me. They all look alike to me. I'd ask your tracker."

I hang up and take a deep breath. I'm a horrible liar and can't handle the stress.

Worse, I've crossed an ethical line here. I'm not sure if I broke a law, but this could bite me in the ass.

Travis's file comes through my e-mail. I load it into the DNA viewer software.

The sample they say came from the bear I saw on the tarp is Bart's DNA.

The most likely explanation is that Julian's lab made a mistake. I frantically dial his number.

"What's up?" he asks.

"Your lab. Did they mix up the hair sample by chance?"

"I doubt it."

"Are you positive?"

"I can promise you two things: first, that lab probably never even touched bear DNA before this, and second, if we made those kinds of mistakes, wars could get started. What's the problem?"

"Nothing. Nothing. I'm sure you're correct." Somebody fucked up, big time. "I got to run." I hastily hang up.

The article mentioned a press conference was going to be held in a couple of hours.

They're about to say they caught Juniper's killer.

They didn't.

The DNA in the hair in Juniper's wound came from a different bear than the one they killed.

That means her killer is still out there.

CHAPTER NINETEEN

All Clear

I introduce myself as Dr. Theo Cray at the front desk of the sheriff's office and get directed to a conference room. I pretend I'm supposed to be there and a deputy obligingly escorts me to where Detective Glenn, Sheriff Tyson—the wide-shouldered woman I first saw in the motel parking lot—and several others are gathered.

Richards, the Fish and Wildlife tracker, and Glenn stop their conversation and look up as I enter.

"Dr. Cray?" says Glenn. "I'm sorry, did someone ask you to come down here?"

In a situation like this it's better to just jump in instead of trying to explain yourself, so I direct my blunt question to Richards. "How did you know that Bart was the bear that killed Juniper?"

He searches Glenn and Tyson for an explanation to my intrusion. They shrug, so he obliges me. "We found the victim's blood on its fur, and DNA matched the bear we were looking for."

"Yes. But how did you know to shoot Bart? How did you know he was the right bear before you killed him?"

Glenn interrupts. "I'm sorry, Dr. Cray, why are you here?"

"I'm here because the hair in Juniper's wounds doesn't match Bart's DNA."

There's a silent pause in the room. After a tense moment, Sheriff Tyson speaks up. Her voice is low and measured. "How did you get Juniper Parsons's blood?"

I give her the matter-of-fact answer. "One of your deputies gave it to me by accident. I decided to have it analyzed."

"You decided to have it analyzed?" she asks. "That's called stealing evidence."

I don't like the menace in her tone. "Let's deal with that later. What's important right now is that the bear that killed Juniper isn't the same bear that you killed." I turn to Richards. "No offense."

Red-faced from the accusation, he slams his hand onto the table. "We found her blood on the bear!"

I don't mean to insult the man, but facts are facts. "Yet DNA found within Juniper's blood sample connects to a different bear. Maybe Bart stumbled across her body?" I face Glenn. "Hell, I stumbled into her blood. I got it all over me. You saw."

This gets him a sideways glance from Tyson.

Glenn sighs and explains to the room. "The curious Dr. Cray decided to visit the murder scene."

"And who told him where it was?" Tyson asks, her voice rising.

"I found it on my own," I interject. "The little flags on the highway aren't exactly inconspicuous if you're looking for them."

"And why were you looking for them?"

I give her all my reasons at once. "Because one of my students was killed. Probably because I'm a horrible teacher. I felt like shit about it. I wanted to give her mother answers. I don't know. I just went there."

A redheaded woman on the other side of the table speaks up. "How did you get bear DNA from Juniper's blood?" She's maybe in her early thirties. Pretty face, not much makeup.

"The sample I was given came from a wound on Juniper. There was a hair sample in it."

"With a follicle?" She turns toward a man to her left. I recognize him as the coroner.

He shakes his head. "There weren't any follicles in the samples. We checked. Just shafts."

The woman swivels back at me with a condescending look on her face. "It seems like your lab was looking at mitochondrial DNA. Maybe they should go back to school."

My face goes hot at the insult, but I respond coolly. "I know you don't get all the news out here, but you can pull nuclear DNA from hair shafts, if you know what you're doing." Pretty cocky for a guy who didn't know that this morning.

"Is this true?" the medical examiner asks her.

She shrugs. "I don't know. I'll have to ask around."

I try to calm myself. "I have access to resources," I say, regretting the pompous tone.

"I hope they involve a good attorney," says Sheriff Tyson darkly.

"Hold up a second," Glenn interjects. "Before we slap the bracelets on him, let's hear him out. Dr. Cray knew the victim and is understandably agitated by what happened."

Tyson makes a show of checking her watch. "Make it quick."

No one offers me a seat, so I go over to the whiteboard and grab a marker. I draw a quick map of the area and put an *X* where Juniper was found.

"This is where the sample I was given came from." I put another *X* where they killed Bart. "This is where Richards found Bart. Close enough to make sense." I draw a wide circle. "In fact, this is Bart's range from the Ursa Major database. As you are aware, he was a known grizzly. The likely suspect.

"But the sample from Juniper's scene had hair that belonged to a bear from much farther away. It may have been trekking into Bart's territory. She could have been caught between them. Did you find any DNA at her death scene from Bart?"

The medical examiner replies, "We found hair that was consistent."

"Hair from a grizzly, yes? But no DNA?"

He shakes his head.

I draw a wide circle around Juniper's *X*. "So we have no proof Bart was even there. We do have proof of the other bear."

"So you say," replies the woman. "But you're the only one who has the magical ability to pull DNA from hair shafts. I'd love to have that power."

I suddenly figure out who she is. "You're Dr. Kendall?"

"Yes."

"I'll help you independently verify it." I'm sure Julian would give them access to his lab. "The important part right now is that having a press conference and saying you caught the bear would be irresponsible and inaccurate. There's still a killer grizzly out there. Worse, we don't even know why he killed Juniper."

Sheriff Tyson directs her intense focus on Richards. "Is this possible?"

He takes a deep breath. "We found her blood on the bear."

"Yes," she says, "but bears are known to sniff around others' kills."

"True. It's common." Richards tilts his head in defeat. "It's possible. Very possible. Damn. I hoped we caught the bastard. This is bad. And worse, I may have killed an innocent bear."

"Cancel the press conference?" asks Glenn.

Tyson shakes her head. "No. We've established how she was killed. We can announce that part of the investigation is closed. We'll tell people to use caution." She glares at me. "You better be right about this."

Her intensity makes me step backward, bumping into the whiteboard. "I've been very thorough."

"Looks like he was all over my database," replies Kendall as she looks at something on her phone, probably data logs. "Did you find a match?"

"Yes . . . it's UA.221.999." I wait a beat before telling them his nickname. "Also known as Ripper."

"Christ," Glenn mutters. "That's all we need. A grizzly named Ripper on the loose."

"Are you sure that's what you matched?" Kendall asks.

"Completely," I say confidently. "I checked several times."

She shakes her head. "Then it appears you've made a mistake."

"A mistake?"

Kendall lets out a sigh of relief. "Dr. Cray, UA.221.999, also known as Ripper, died last year."

"Died?" I try to process the word.

"Yes. I inspected his corpse myself when we retrieved the GPS collar. Ripper is very dead." She points to the whiteboard. "What we have there is probably contamination. Maybe Juniper brushed up against old hair that was on a log. Maybe Bart still had some of Ripper's in his fur. I don't know. What I do know is that she wasn't killed by a ghost bear."

I can feel the eyes of everyone else in the room on me as they come to realize they've been entertaining a fool.

Kendall gives her head a small shake.

"Thank god," Richards mutters.

My limbs grow cold. The marker falls from my fingers and rolls across the floor.

"Dr. Cray, would you step outside?" commands Sheriff Tyson. "I'm going to talk to Detective Glenn after the conference and decide if you should be arrested or sent to a psychiatrist."

Her words don't faze me as the new reality sets in.

Kendall's revelation isn't what she thinks.

"Don't you see it?" I ask quietly.

They ignore me and return to their discussion about the conference.

My stomach begins to churn.

They don't get it.

It's so obvious.

It's why they arrested me in the first place.

It's why Juniper ran the wrong way.

The pattern is clear.

"Don't you see it!" I shout.

All eyes turn back to me.

"Deputy," Tyson shouts to the open door. "Would you escort this man out of here?"

I ignore her and slam my hand against the spot on the map where Juniper was found. "Are you that dense? She wasn't killed by a bear! She was murdered by someone who wanted to make it look like that!"

The room is silent.

I get how I sound. But I know if I bring a sample back to my lab and find out it's contaminated and I'm certain it didn't happen in the lab, that means it had to have happened in the field. The only way hair from a dead bear ended up on Juniper's body was because someone put it there.

I can't even fathom how or why, but this is where reason has led me. Unfortunately, no one else is seeing it as clearly as I am.

Two thick-necked deputies rush inside, reacting to my outburst. I'm slammed against the wall, handcuffed, and dragged away before I can explain.

CHAPTER TWENTY

FRAMED

I'm shoved inside a small room with a metal door and a narrow reinforced-glass window. There's a bench along the back wall. It's a holding cell of some kind but without a toilet. It's not meant for a long stay, I hope.

The ceiling is solid and the walls concrete.

Holy shit, I realize. I've been locked up.

Jesus Christ.

I collapse on the bench. Part of me wants to pound on the door and insist there's been some kind of mistake. But I know they'll just see this as more crazy-man behavior.

The looks on their faces as Sheriff Tyson's goons hauled me away . . .

They thought I was raving mad.

I was mad. I still am. Mad at them for ignoring what's in front of them.

They pulled me in with a SWAT team welcoming party because something about Juniper's murder looked like a man could have done it.

I never saw the autopsy photos, but it seems clear to me that a bear attack and human attack should look pretty different.

For some reason, this one didn't, at first.

They were looking for a man and found me. When they found bear hair in Juniper's wounds and had a chance to examine her more closely, they let me go.

Her blood on Bart cinched the case.

Open, shut.

They chose not to see the rest. Maybe because it's too fantastical. But it fits the evidence.

Juniper was attacked near the road, yet ran away from it. Why?

The simplest explanation is that she may have been brought to the clearing blindfolded and had no idea where she was. She simply ran.

Ripper's hair showed up in her wounds. The hair was well preserved enough that we could get nuDNA out of it—a near impossibility under ideal conditions. Unthinkable for hair that has been out in the open for a year.

The odds of Ripper's hair showing up in the wound are astronomical if you're assuming a purely natural explanation. Charles Manson's hair would be a more likely find.

Nothing from Bart was found at the murder scene. If he wallowed in her blood like I did, then there should have been some trace.

Yet, miraculously, Juniper's blood showed up on the bear miles away.

If the bears were people, you'd call it a frame-up.

A frame implies a framer.

Someone had access to Juniper's body and Ripper's hair. Later on they lured Bart to her blood.

This leads me to a paranoid revelation: everyone in the conference could be a suspect.

Richards is the most suspicious, but he hadn't behaved as I'd expect a guilty man to behave. His responses were natural: he wanted to get the bear that killed Juniper. He was frustrated that he might have killed the wrong animal.

If he was Juniper's killer, the smart thing would have been to go with the vibe of the room and point a finger at me. But he didn't.

As for the others: Sheriff Tyson is as cold as ice and Detective Glenn is a mystery to me, but I'd think the both of them would find better ways to cover up a murder.

It doesn't make any sense. And I'm no judge of character.

It's probably not any of them. That'd be too Agatha Christie.

Hell, maybe I'm deluded and it's exactly as they say.

Yet my gut says no. There's a pattern here.

Hopefully they're in the conference room right now weighing what I said.

Kendall seemed bright. She has to be bothered by the fact that her dead bear's DNA showed up a year later and miles away. It's just not rational.

Rational or not, I'm the one locked up.

I rap my knuckles against the metal bench, wishing this was a dream. Unfortunately, it's very real.

I'm such an idiot.

I'm in here and the killer is outside somewhere, long gone.

He has everyone fooled. Down the hall is a room full of cops and wildlife experts that don't even believe he exists.

Jesus. It's a scary thought.

It's one thing to kill someone and not leave evidence or hide the body so it's never found, but to be able to murder someone and have everyone think it was an accident of nature?

That's some kind of genius.

A shiver rolls down my spine when I think of the implication. This was either planned for a long time or done by someone who is very good at killing. Maybe both.

The presence of Ripper's hair implies they planned on it looking like a bear attack. They just didn't expect that someone would be able to get viable DNA and discover that their generic grizzly wasn't so generic.

I remember Glenn mentioning some hikers hearing screams and investigating. Was the killer caught off guard? Had he been planning to take her body somewhere else but had to flee?

It'd be so easy to bury it out there where nobody could find it. That's what I would do . . .

Maybe that was the plan but he got interrupted?

He left behind Ripper's hair and took some of her blood with him to leave for Bart.

Getting it on Bart wouldn't have been too difficult. Bears are curious. All it would take is a bucket of fresh meat to draw him in.

Maybe. I don't know.

I shake my head. All this conjecture is giving me a migraine.

I look up at the sound of a key in the lock. Detective Glenn steps inside.

"Please, hear me out," I insist.

He jabs the edge of a file folder toward me. "No, Dr. Cray, you're going to sit down and shut up." He nods to Sheriff Tyson standing in the hallway, watching. "If you can't do that, I'm going to take her advice and have you sent for a psychiatric evaluation. Got it?"

I nod my head and slink down.

He leans against the door frame and flips open the folder. "I did a little more digging." I think he's going to talk about the case, but my hopes are dashed when he looks up from the folder. "I've looked into your background. It seems like you have a reputation for causing problems."

Fuck. Here it comes.

Time to shoot the messenger.

CHAPTER TWENTY-ONE

TROUBLEMAKER

As Detective Glenn reads selections from the folder, Sheriff Tyson watches me closely. Her face is inscrutable. She's intimidating as all hell.

"You have a sealed juvenile file in Texas," Glenn says. "But I find a mention of you being arrested for building bombs as a teenager and a child getting hurt. Care to explain?"

I stare at the floor. "No. Not really."

When I was thirteen and still dealing with the loss of my father, I took up chemistry. I learned how to make bombs from household chemicals, and I'd go into the woods and blow things up.

That would have been fine if a friend—more of an acquaintance—hadn't taken my bomb-making parts and tried to explode a car sitting in a shopping center parking lot.

The car was barely damaged. But his younger brother got acid burns on his arm. His parents went apeshit.

The first thing he did was tell the police I put him up to it.

Protesting my innocence was hard when they found my lab under my bed.

Thanks to a very understanding judge, I only got community service for it.

My mother was obviously thrilled.

This was shortly before she married Davis.

I never would have pulled that kind of thing with him in the house. For one, he would have insisted I never let my friends near my lab equipment and that I keep it safely locked up.

Detective Glenn notes out loud that I was fired from my first faculty position.

Again, my stubbornness.

From his point of view, without the details, I probably look like a know-it-all prick.

I could try to explain to him the details, but he's not in a mood to listen. He's reading me the riot act in front of Sheriff Tyson.

Maybe this is for show.

I don't know.

The best course of action is to shut up. Tyson is primed to punish me. I'd probably be able to get away with swiping the blood sample. But getting away would still mean a trial, a lawyer, and I can bet for damn sure she's going to make certain I spend a few nights in a cell before I see a judge about bail.

"We had the press conference," says Glenn. "We explained the possibility of another bear."

I refrain from pointing out that makes no sense if Ripper is pushing up daisies.

He continues. "We'll have another look in the lab for possible contamination. Other than that, we're considering the matter closed." He snaps the file shut and tosses it on the bench beside me. "Understand your situation?"

I nod sullenly. Glenn steps aside.

Sheriff Tyson stands in my way. "You have two hours to clear out of my county. If you start running your mouth, you're going to be back in a cell for tampering with evidence. Furthermore, if you insist that this is a murder investigation, take one guess at who gets arrested first."

Glenn escorts me out of the building and to my car. Neither of us says anything.

There's nothing to be said.

Clearly, he doesn't believe me. The only reason I'm not back in the cell is because he took pity on me and told Tyson I was going through some kind of grieving process.

Hell, maybe I am looking at things all wrong.

I pack my bags at the motel, hop on the interstate, and decide I can deal with Juniper's car later.

Eight miles later I pass a sign that says I've left the county.

A quarter mile ahead I spot a motel.

The stubborn part of me, the part that got me fired, makes me click on my turn signal and pull into the parking lot.

CHAPTER TWENTY-TWO

THE GRAPH

This is insane. I toss my motel room key on the dresser and fall down on the bed. I should be working on my research. I have enough field samples. The smart thing is to drive back to Austin and finish what I can before the semester starts.

That's the rational, logical thing. Or is it?

When Juniper's body was found, the hunters went out to find her killer—the brave men of the tribe ventured out to defend their own. They may have never met her, but she was still part of the human race.

No other animal draws boundaries as far out as we do when it comes to protecting other members of our group.

My instinct tells me Juniper was killed by a man—or a woman, not to be presumptive.

It's what fits the facts.

Then why do the people who are experts on this kind of thing not see it?

What do I know that they don't?

Their medical examiner is competent enough, it would seem. Richards and Kendall know more about bears than I ever will. And

Detective Glenn is no fool. After the animal was tracked down, he was still on the case.

If this was the first act of a movie, I'd be pointing the finger at him. I'm not very good at reading people, but in all my interactions with him, his suspicions were always directed at me.

I can't rule anything out. Except one thing: I'm not the kind of person that could talk to someone for an hour and have any idea one way or another if they're guilty.

All of those people collectively know more than me. Yet, here I am, staring at the ceiling, convinced Juniper's killer walked on two feet.

Why?

What do I know that they don't?

It's not any one thing. My expertise isn't deep in any field. My papers, my research, my life have been about drawing connections from very different fields. My domain is how things are related.

I trace life cycles. I look at gene flows. I build computer models and search for real-world analogues.

I seek out systems and circuits. Whether it's the nitrogen in our bodies that came from fertilizer plants or it's our genes for coding specific proteins that evolved a billion years ago.

Systems can go laterally through space. Others move linearly through time.

I get up from the bed, pull some maps out of my backpack, and tack them to the wall with glue dots.

I'm not a detective. I'm not a forensic specialist.

I'm a biologist and a computer programmer. These are my areas of expertise.

I stick a red circle where Juniper was found. Next to it I place a green one to represent that she'd physically been there. I place another on the car repair shop and another on her motel.

These are places where we know Juniper had been alive. It's part of her graph. I place another on where she was working on her postgrad at

Florida State and another where she lived in North Carolina. The final dot I place on Austin, where she was in my class.

These are points in her life graph. In a computer I can create a version that shows this over time. But right now it's simple enough to see.

This is Juniper's story.

Her life started in a delivery room in Raleigh. It ended in a forest in Montana.

What brought her to that point?

Life is decided by thousands of external and internal forces.

Her death could have been a random event, initiated by someone catching a glimpse of her as they passed her walking on the highway.

It could be someone she's known for years, all the way back to North Carolina.

Maybe some FBI profiler could look at her wounds and tell you if it was personal or not. I wouldn't know. And since the experts think it was a bear, I don't know what credibility I'd give them right now.

I place a black circle next to the two by her body. This is her killer. We know at one point he was in the same place as her.

I place another where Bart was killed. Our killer was in that area at some point as well.

To be precise, I don't know that the killer was there. It could have been an accomplice. Graphs don't always measure actual locations of organisms. Sometimes they just map their influence. For now, I'll just use black circles for the killer's graph of influence.

The killer's graph . . .

I sit back and take it in. I only have two data points, but that's a start.

In my field, a graph can be just as illuminating as an actual animal or its DNA. Sometimes more so, because it can tell you how it lived and not just the color of its pelt or the arrangement of its genes. Sometimes less so, because a graph can be misleading. Too many unrelated data points leave you looking at chaos.

Sorting through chaos is why I developed MAAT. She's the software I use to sort through thousands of points of information and find patterns.

MAAT is based on how I think, but much more advanced.

I built it using source code from a research project designed to find genes that contribute to longevity. It's AI that builds better algorithms with each iteration. Each time becoming more and more complex.

I couldn't tell you how the current version of MAAT works, just that she does. Sometimes.

When the researchers who developed the core AI behind MAAT asked it to figure out what gave a strain of fruit flies its longevity, it pointed to the genes that regulated resveratrol—the same chemical in red wine that has been tied to human longevity. When they tried to figure out why the software singled that out, the answer was a string of data that no human could understand.

What MAAT could tell you right now from the data points on my map is what is already obvious.

She's really useful when you give her thousands or millions of points.

Points I don't have. The killer is just two black dots in time and space. But . . . in the absence of firm data, the other trick is to give her assumptions.

If we were looking at mating cycles, and Juniper and her killer were two mountain lions, I could tell MAAT the frequency that a female is in estrus and an estimate of the male's range. That information would give me an estimate about when they would encounter each other again. If a male mountain lion had multiple females it bred with and they had specific ranges, I might be able to predict where else he would show up.

And if there were general rules about the kinds of places they reproduced, I might be able to narrow down candidate spots based on available geographic information.

From all of this, MAAT could give me a dozen or so places where I could plant wildlife cameras and reasonably expect to catch the two large cats doing it, even over an area of dozens of miles—all of that based on three data points and general information not specific to an animal.

The problem is I don't have any more data to put into MAAT.

I know nothing about the killer.

He was born at some point. He met Juniper. At some point after that, years or minutes, he killed her. His last appearance was getting her blood on Bart. Then he vanished from his graph.

I need more data than what's on my map.

From where?

If I don't have data, then I have to use the next best thing . . . which is also the worst best thing.

Assumptions.

I need to make guesses.

On a real graph these wouldn't be black circles. They'd be half black, half white. They're maybes.

Sometimes they lead you somewhere interesting. Other times they derail you for months . . . or years.

Our war on cancer has been filled with countless maybes. Billions of dollars and millions of human hours have been spent chasing after a pattern we can't even begin to guess at.

Even still, we've made some progress. Many of those maybes have panned out. People live longer than before because not all that effort was wasted. And for every maybe that turns out to be a no, we still move forward.

I need some maybes and assumptions about the killer.

I can't be worried if they're wrong. I just need a starting point.

Let's make some . . .

Juniper's killer was clever because he got away with it. That's a hard thing to do. He was either very lucky or experienced.

Okay . . . let's go with experienced.

Oh, shit. Sometimes one assumption makes something else automatically true.

An experienced killer implies that he's done this before . . .

I open up my laptop and do a search for bear attacks in the United States and Canada.

I'm not sure what I was expecting, but there's only been a handful in the last ten years.

The Fish and Wildlife Service has detailed reports. Most of them are in deep woods. I look for any within a few miles of a highway.

There are two. In the first, three years ago, a self-proclaimed grizzly expert was killed. I'd personally rule that a suicide.

The other was six years ago. A woman was found bleeding to death on a road. She died on the way to the hospital.

Experts decided that she'd also been killed by a grizzly. The report shows diagrams of wounds and a photo of a tissue sample. There's even a hair. But no DNA analysis was done.

The bear they caught was identified by the victim's blood on its pelt.

That sounds familiar—just like Juniper.

The hair on the back of my neck raises. It's my own animal sense telling me I'm looking at something dangerous.

I put a red and a black circle where the other victim was found and a black one where the accused bear was trapped.

It's fifty miles away in a different county, making Detective Glenn and the others seem less suspicious to me.

This has happened before, somewhere else.

But two red dots don't make a pattern. Not yet.

I need more data.

CHAPTER TWENTY-THREE

The Human Circuit

A wider search of bear attacks is a dead end for me. They're supported by finding human remains in the animal's scat. This doesn't mean the killer couldn't have left the victim to be scavenged by bears. Apparently bears are not very picky eaters. It just means that these look exactly like bear attacks. There's nothing suspicious to them, unlike Juniper Parsons or the other woman, Rhea Simmons.

I pull up an article on Rhea. She was twenty-two and apparently hitchhiking her way across the country. Born in Alabama, her family had no idea she was in Montana.

Scanning through a few more articles, it seems like they'd been estranged for a few years. The first they heard about her whereabouts was when the police called.

What a horrible phone call to receive.

Rhea was a loner. A photo of her shows a hippie chick. The kind I'd seen around campus, struggling to figure out their place in the world. For Rhea, it was trekking out on her own.

Her case is promising, but there just isn't a pattern yet, other than both she and Juniper were independent young women. Our killer may have a type, but there doesn't appear to be enough alleged bear attacks to support a pattern.

Alleged . . . *alleged* implies someone to make the allegation . . .

If a bear kills you in the forest and nobody finds the body, is it a bear attack?

No.

It's a disappearance.

Hikers said they heard Juniper's cries. Rhea made it to the road.

What if nobody had heard Juniper? Would the killer have left her in the open?

Or would he have buried her?

The same for Rhea. If she'd never made it to the road, would we be looking at a missing-persons case?

I get a chill. If Rhea's killer had managed to hide her body, she'd never have been a missing-persons case. At least not for months or years. Probably not in Montana.

Her parents didn't even know where she was—or seem that concerned.

We're used to the high-profile cases on cable news shows. The kind where a wife or husband vanishes under suspicious circumstances. Or when a daughter is last seen leaving somewhere and never checks in.

All of them have one thing in common: tight family structures.

What about the loners? What about people living on the fringe?

If the toothless woman who panhandled outside the 7-Eleven went missing one day, who would report it?

People drop out all the time. Drugs, psychiatric problems . . . there are a multitude of reasons.

More than once I've received concerned phone calls from parents worried because their child hasn't called home in weeks.

It's usually just a phase. Sometimes it's not. People—especially young people—can begin to disconnect bit by bit, then fall away entirely, if only for a time.

I remember the story of a twenty-three-year-old California girl found dead in her car in a Walmart parking lot. Not only had nobody reported her missing, but she had been dead for three months. She killed herself, then rotted away in a heavily tinted car as people walked back and forth just a few feet away.

I Google missing-persons information and come across the webpage for the FBI's National Crime Information Center. They have a listing for missing persons—a list of people who have vanished under suspicious circumstances. According to this, there are eighty-four thousand missing people right now in the United States.

Holy shit, that's a lot of people.

To be sure, many of these are people with drug problems or other issues that made them easy to drop out.

But eighty-four thousand people? That's like the city of Boulder, Colorado, disappearing.

And these are just the people where someone picked up a phone and told the police they were worried. Who knows how many more are unattached to a family group?

How many go missing and nobody knows?

You could have scores of serial killers out there and nobody would notice. My skin goes cold. We probably do.

What about Juniper's killer? Is he responsible for more than her and Rhea?

How could I possibly know?

I look up some more data points and make a creepy discovery.

Montana and Wyoming have more missing persons per hundred thousand people than any other states except Alaska, Oregon, and Arizona. What the hell?

This could have to do with how the data are collected. One extra check box on a form can skew things out of proportion.

But still . . .

I click on the link to the Montana Missing Persons Clearinghouse.

The first things that appear are the photos of two smiling young girls. Below them is a Native American couple and their child.

There are a lot of young women on the list. The same for Wyoming.

I count at least a dozen women who fit Juniper and Rhea's age range. Most, if not all, are probably runaways, many no doubt fleeing bad situations. Or, worse, leaving with men with ill intentions.

But I also have no reason to assume the killer limits himself to women.

There's usually a strange thrill when I encounter a new data set. I can't quite describe it. This time I feel guilty when I look at the faces of the missing.

I pull a box of colored thumbtacks from my luggage and push an orange one into my map for every missing woman over the age of eighteen in the surrounding states.

I do a new search to narrow it down by city. It's depressing how little attention these missing-persons reports get. The data are scant.

The even more depressing thought is that the current state of their investigation is probably limited to having their name on a list and a report collecting dust in a filing cabinet.

Unless the police have clear evidence of foul play and a suspect, many of these women may never be found.

After a few minutes of pinning data points, my map begins to fill with orange thumbtacks. I find myself reluctant to shove them in; they feel like nails in a coffin.

I notice something odd but don't want to jump to conclusions.

This is getting too complex for my map. Fortunately I have a portable video projector. I connect my laptop and use my bio-geo mapping software to create a virtual map I can project on the wall.

I still like to stand next to things when I look at them.

All my orange dots pop up. I use a shader control to color counties by population. This helps me see whether the orange dots are correlated to population density.

There's no way for me to know what's good data and what's bad, let alone what's missing. But to paraphrase the Supreme Court's statement about obscenity, when it comes to patterns, I know them when I see them.

I plug all the variables into MAAT, comparing missing-persons reports with population data. I also find some statistics on the percentage of reports proven to be runaways who are safely returned. This filters things a bit.

MAAT draws a wispy, dark-purple loop around my map. It goes off the frame and then returns to curve around.

It's a graph showing a connection between missing persons that lie outside what you'd expect from a given population size. It also follows certain interstate highways, but not others.

In biology you become accustomed to different ways data can represent itself. Salmon returning upstream and herd animals have very linear patterns. Birds follow loops.

I'm looking at another pattern.

One that's very familiar to me.

It's a predator's circuit.

I furiously type away, searching for the pattern imprinted on my memory.

I find it. It's not the same shape, but it has similar symmetry. I could write a formula for a fractal that would generate patterns just like these.

But it's not just a pattern, it's a behavior.

The behavior generating the pattern on my wall, the one where Juniper's killer is hiding, matches this other behavior quite clearly.

The creator of this other pattern is an efficient killer that has remained unchanged for millions of years. It's developed a sophisticated system for hunting predicated upon always staying on the move, allowing it to return to the same points again and again without its prey being any wiser.

I flip back and forth between the patterns. I have to sit down.

It's the same pattern as a great white shark's.

CHAPTER TWENTY-FOUR

The Pitch Experiment

Analogies and maps can be dangerous things when you take them too literally. A map is just a representation of something. Even a photographic map can't tell you if the terrain is now covered by snow, or if a morning rain has made a path too muddy to traverse.

Juniper's killer's circuit is like the hunting pattern of a great white shark, but only because the two of them have acquired similar behaviors.

Great whites don't try to hide their kills, mainly because tuna don't form police forces and seek revenge. But they're careful to avoid overpredation in certain areas, lest the fish remember this is a bad spot. Killing too much sends a signal to the system to change its patterns—kind of like leaving bodies around would tell the cops that something is up.

Besides being careful not to overkill and create a disruption, sharks use camouflage, like our killer. The great white has countershading that helps it blend into the sea floor when looked at from above and appear invisible when looked at from below.

The killer—I don't know what else to call him—almost certainly also has his own camouflage. He probably doesn't attract too much attention to himself. By hiding the bodies or making the ones he can't hide look like animal attacks, he cloaks his presence from prey who, just like a pod of seals, may not realize they have a killer in their midst until it's too late.

Sharks also have a specialized organ called the ampulla of Lorenzini that enables them to sense the electrical activity of hiding prey and see through the blood in the water during a feeding frenzy.

Likewise, the killer probably has his own set of skills for spotting victims. He's not just looking for a physical type—he's seeking out a particular kind of vulnerability.

The Montana and Wyoming missing-persons reports only tell me about locals and people who were known to come through the area and vanished. Every year, hundreds of thousands of people visit during the summer to vacation and work at seasonal jobs.

Some of my students make money during semester breaks serving tables and staffing summer resorts like the ones here.

How many young people drift through this area on their own, without their parents knowing or caring where they are?

Based on this, the killer could have many, many more victims.

But right now it's just conjecture.

The only way to see if a model has value is to use it to make a prediction you can test.

All I can guess with MAAT at this point is the approximate number of people who will go missing and the probability that within six years we'll get another bear attack resembling Juniper's and Rhea's.

Six years is a long time. Some scientists wait their entire lives for the eruption of a volcano, the return of a comet, or some other infrequent event.

The most insane I've heard of is the pitch-drop experiment started at the University of Queensland in 1927. It's a funnel of pitch designed to measure the material's viscosity. Since the experiment started, only nine drops have fallen from the funnel, making the viscosity of pitch 230 billion times that of water. The two times a drop fell while a webcam was aimed at the experiment, technical problems prevented researchers from observing the rare event.

The longest-running experiment ever is a metal ball hanging on a thread between two metal bells. Each time it touches a bell, a battery gives it a charge and knocks it into the other bell, where it discharges the current.

I saw this myself while visiting Oxford for a conference. The ball vibrates almost imperceptibly between the bells, but you can see it with the naked eye.

It's been doing that since 1840. Even the battery, a dry cell, is the same one installed almost two hundred years ago.

Science can require patience. But I can't wait six years for Juniper's killer to fake another bear attack.

I can't even wait six days. The semester is starting, and I'm already going to be late for faculty meetings.

I could go to Parvel, the town near where Rhea was found, but the trail is probably cold. I don't even know what a warm trail would look like.

And all I can imagine finding out is that her death looked a lot like Juniper's.

What I need is some way to confirm at least part of my suspicions.

The suspicions—or rather, my assumptions—are that Juniper's killer has done this multiple times and his attacks resemble an animal's. I make a note to figure out what that means, precisely. All I know is that Detective Glenn initially thought a man might have been the suspect.

Knives?

I also believe that in most cases the body is never found.

So . . . all I need is an unreported animal attack and a body that was never found.

Yeah, easy . . .

I turn back to the missing-person dots projected on the wall. A couple of them are in the thick purple band of the killer's circuit.

That doesn't mean he's responsible for any of them, but if you knew of two different seal-mating areas and there was a spot in between where seals were known to go missing, it wouldn't be unreasonable to suspect there's a shark that travels through there.

The most recent one was seventeen months ago in the town of Hudson Creek. A woman named Chelsea Buchorn was reported missing. A friend of hers, Amber Harrison, reported to the police that she thought her friend was abducted.

Harrison said they were walking through the woods and she lost track of Chelsea.

It's a rather odd account. I can only find two news stories about what happened. The first one describes Amber as being agitated and telling conflicting stories. Police had no evidence of foul play and released her.

If I was going to try to read between the lines, it sounds like they went off into the woods to get really high. Amber wouldn't be the most credible of witnesses if she was on something.

However, she and Chelsea would also make ideal victims.

Hudson Creek is a four-hour drive. I throw all my stuff into my Explorer and leave the room key with the clerk.

God knows why she imagines I needed a room for just four hours.

CHAPTER TWENTY-FIVE

HUDSON CREEK

Hudson Creek is a decaying strip of buildings on either side of the highway, clinging to the road like barnacles on a rotting pier. If this were an ecosystem, I'd say it was on the verge of collapse.

FOR SALE signs litter stretches of property with dilapidated buildings that look like they haven't had two-legged occupants in years.

Occasionally I spot signs of life. Aluminum-sided trailers covered in faded paint with clothes dangling nearby on lines. Someone lives there, if this is what you can call living.

I've seen plenty of poverty in my travels. Not all of it radiates despair. I've been to slums where the electricity falters at night, but the live music keeps going. I've visited shantytowns where a new pair of shoes is as rare as a Tesla, yet people wear homespun clothes as vibrant as any I've seen.

Hudson Creek has none of that. There's no new construction. No signs that the town is fighting for life.

The only things not falling apart are the shiny new cars I occasionally spot in weed-infested driveways.

These people have mixed-up priorities.

Or do they?

Would you invest in landscaping if you knew your property values were going to keep declining? Maybe it's better to spend your money on an escape pod with leather seats and a Bluetooth system.

How people get the money for the fancy four-by-fours and Corvettes is beyond me.

I guess there's always some kind of commerce. Once upon a time, Hudson Creek may have been a mining town or played some crucial role for the railroad.

Now? It's a place between here and there.

Yet according to the purple trail MAAT had displayed, there's a high probability the killer has been through here. Several times. He's driven down this same highway and stared out his window at the run-down houses I'm looking at.

Did he see it as a decaying carcass to be preyed upon?

The town where Juniper was staying was a smaller-scale Hudson Creek. Her motel had a burned-out neon sign and bare plywood on one side. Bryson's Auto Repair was a junkyard that only functioned as a business because one person knew how to change tires and oil.

A tractor-trailer truck barrels around my car, frustrated at my gawking. I step on the accelerator and head toward what the GPS says is the city center of Hudson Creek.

Along the way I pass the only new construction I've seen for miles. It's a huge service station catering to truckers. Next to it is a diner with a parking lot full of cars.

City hall may be a mile down the road, but this is clearly the center of what's alive in this town.

When I seek answers as a biologist, it's not too hard to know where to start. I can either call the local Fish and Wildlife office or the Farm Bureau.

In another country, I start with the biology department at the biggest university and then work my way through a network of connections until I can find someone who knows something about an arboreal rat or a species of flowering plants.

If I were a cop, I'd probably just roll into the nearest police station and ask to speak to the investigator in charge.

Having just been kicked out of the last police station I visited, I'm not too eager to do that.

However, there's another resource I've used when I'm in a strange country and the locals are distrustful of strangers.

It's never failed me. I don't need my GPS to find it; I just have to watch for it. Even in as sad of a place as Hudson Creek, I'm sure I can find it.

Sure enough, I see a cross next to a small church. There's an old Ford Focus in the parking lot.

In every country and every town I've been in, no matter how far away from civilization, I've always been able to find a priest, a nun, or an imam willing to help me out.

I decide to start my questions here and pull into the parking lot.

The church consists of three buildings attached by a covered walkway. When I knock on what looks like the office, there's no answer. The other doors are locked.

I hear the sound of a lawn mower from the other side of the building. When I round the corner, I spot a man in a T-shirt on a John Deere, mowing the field that runs from the back of the church to a forest line.

I wave to him, and he cuts the engine. Thinning gray hair; he looks to be about sixty. We walk toward each other.

"What can I do for you?" he asks when we're close enough not to have to shout.

"I was looking for the"—I do a quick glance back at the sign on the road to figure out what denomination of church this is; it's Baptist—"minister."

"You found him." He wipes a grimy hand on his jeans and offers it to shake. "Call me Frank."

"I'm Theo Cray. I'm a professor visiting from Texas."

"Professor? Theology?"

"No. Bioinformatics." I make feeble small talk because I don't know how to get to the point.

"Is that like robotics?"

"No, sir. I'm a biologist who stares at a computer screen and sometimes goes out into the real world."

"So what brings you here?"

"It's a little complicated."

He takes a look at his watch. "The good news is I'm due a break and a glass of tea right now. I can handle a little complicated and spare a glass. Follow me." He steps past me and leads me toward the office. He asks over his shoulder, "What are the basics?"

"I want to ask about a girl that used to live here."

"Who is that?"

"Chelsea Buchorn?"

He stops walking and faces me. The smile is gone from his face. "What exactly about Chelsea do you want to know?"

This stops me in my tracks. In biological terms, I'd describe his posture as suddenly defensive, if not hostile.

CHAPTER TWENTY-SIX

The Lawn Mower Man

I don't know what to do. All I have is the truth. "I lost someone under similar circumstances."

"You lost someone?" Some of the edge has left his voice.

"Yes. A student. I was looking for a connection."

"A connection with Chelsea? Did they know each other?"

It's a question I never even thought of. It seems unlikely, but it's worth looking into. "I don't know."

"So why are you asking me?"

"I don't know anyone here. I saw your church and thought you might know the people around here."

His body relaxes. "Ah. I understand. Let's go get the iced tea and I'll tell you what I know. It's not a lot. Chelsea wasn't a member of our church."

He leads me into his office. I take a seat opposite his desk while he pours two glasses of tea from a pitcher kept in a small refrigerator.

The room is small, lined with bookcases. A window overlooks the highway. Pictures of what look to be his children at different ages line the walls, along with various awards. His desk is cluttered with notepads and a laptop.

Frank moves a book out of the way and places a glass in front of me, then takes his seat behind the desk.

He takes a long sip, then cools his brow with the glass. "We used to have someone who did this. The lawn, that is. We used to have people do a lot of things around here."

"I'd think someone would volunteer."

He lets out a small laugh. "Not so much, these days." He shrugs it off. "Who did you lose?"

"Her name was Juniper Parsons."

"The girl that got killed by the bear?"

"Yes, her." I'm about to blurt out my suspicions but decide to phrase things carefully. "That's what they think. But I've heard there's still some suspicious circumstances."

"Suspicious? How?"

"They interviewed two people as potential suspects before they settled on the bear." I don't point out that one of those suspects is in the room. "I've heard they don't all agree about the DNA evidence." That's true, if I'm included in that *all.*

"Interesting. So how is this connected to Chelsea?"

"I'm not sure. But she disappeared under similar circumstances."

Frank shakes his head. "Chelsea didn't disappear. She left town. Her friend—what's her name, Amber—isn't exactly what I'd call reliable. The pair of them had run away several times on their own before. They get caught up with the wrong boys. Or rather, they're drawn to them. Either way, nobody here takes it seriously. Chelsea just moved on. It happens."

"It's serious enough for her to be on a missing-persons list."

"They put her on there because of Amber's mixed-up stories. Even Chelsea's mother doesn't believe it."

"So you don't think anything happened to her?"

"No. Not here, at least. She was a lot of trouble herself. Loved to make up stories. She probably loves the fact that some people think she's a victim."

"But you don't?"

"I don't know for sure. But she'd cleaned her stuff out of her apartment before she allegedly went missing. That sounds rather odd."

"I hadn't heard that." Of course, if Chelsea was killed, the killer could've broken into her place and taken her things. I wouldn't put that past someone forward thinking enough to bring grizzly hair to a crime scene.

Frank seems elusive about something, but he appears to genuinely believe that Chelsea skipped town.

For a man of God, he doesn't seem to hold her or Amber in very high regard. Maybe in his eyes, they're just another couple of lost causes in a town that makes a minister mow his own church lawn.

"Do you know of anyone around her age that's left?"

"A few. But it's normal. There's not much out here for young people. My kids live in Colorado and Vermont, but I wouldn't call them missing. Even if they don't call all that often."

"How does your wife feel about that? Empty-nest syndrome?"

Frank's face tightens. "She's helping my oldest daughter in Colorado with her kids."

I've been around enough broken families to catch the code words for a separated couple. Even in this day and age, that's got to be embarrassing for a Baptist minister. A big part of what they do is relationship counseling. His own split might discredit him some in the eyes of his congregation. Even if not everyone is meant to stay together.

"You married? Or was Juniper close?" he asks me.

The question comes out of left field. "Me and Juniper? No. She was my student. Never married, either."

"Sorry. I hear stories about professors. Don't mind me."

So do I. "Well, I haven't seen her in years. Technically, she has her doctorate now and probably teaches—or taught—undergrads. So, it wouldn't have been inappropriate, I guess. Not now . . ."

It's a strange thought. In my mind I keep seeing the twenty-year-old girl awkwardly sitting next to me in the pizza parlor. She certainly looked a little older in her photos, but I wouldn't call it aging. She was twenty-five. A little on the young side for me, but nothing that would have batted an eye on campus if she had a graduate degree and wasn't one of my students anymore.

I shake the thought out of my head. I'm here because I feel paternal toward her, not because of some unspoken romantic feeling I had for her.

"Do you know how I could get in touch with Amber?"

"Amber? Why?"

"I just want to hear her side of the story."

Frank releases a small groan. "She's a piece of work. Trouble. She's been arrested several times. Not exactly what I'd call reliable. Dishonest, to be more like it."

He's pretty judgmental for a man whose job is to help people find forgiveness. "Just the same, it'd give me some piece of mind."

"Suit yourself." He taps into his computer and writes a number down on a slip of paper. "I used to coach the girls' high school soccer team. Here you go."

"Thank you." As I get up, I think of a way to reciprocate. "I noticed some bags of fertilizer in the mower shed."

"Yeah, I use it to keep the lawn nice and green."

"It's surprisingly so. Most of the fields around here are brown. Just so you know, though, that's an industrial-grade fertilizer. I'd cut it down to a third or so. You'll have to mow less often, but the grass will look as good."

Frank smiles as he holds open the door. "That explains a lot. Someone donated it to me without any instructions."

He heads back out to his mower, and I return to my Explorer.

In my car I dial Amber's number and get her voice mail.

"Hi, um, this is Theo Cray. I'd like to talk to you about something . . ." I leave my number and hang up, not knowing what to say.

Leaving even an innocuous voice-mail message is awkward for me, much less when I want to talk about an alleged murder.

Two minutes later I get a text message from a different number.

this is ambyr. meet me @ king's diner in 2 hrs. 1004BJ3004ATW

The numbers and letters don't appear to be an address or anything else that makes sense, but King's Diner is the one I passed by the massive truck stop.

Hopefully, she can tell me what the code meant, as well as what really happened to Chelsea.

CHAPTER TWENTY-SEVEN

Troubled Young Things

Amber—or "ambyr," as she called herself in her text message—is half an hour late. The waitress pours me another cup of coffee as I pick at a cherry in my pie.

"Want something else?" she asks, noticing I haven't touched it.

"No. I'm fine. Thank you."

She gives me a polite smile, then moves on to another table. She looks just shy of thirty. Dirty-blonde hair to her shoulders, athletic, small-town pretty.

I like the way she makes small talk with the other patrons and their kids as she bounces around the busy place. There should be at least two more servers here, but she manages to keep things moving, dropping off food, running the register, and taking care of food prep.

The diner is immaculate. The wall by the register is filled with framed photos of men in uniform. There are service patches pinned up as well.

I'd imagine that for some in a town like Hudson Creek, the best prospect was going into the military.

The part of Hudson Creek that's not the new 88 Service Station or the King's Diner is oil stained and run-down. Across the street is a motel that looks like zombies would feel at home in it. Next to it is a convenience store plastered with ads for high-alcohol-content beers. In front of it, two men in their midtwenties lean against the hood of a truck, eating microwave hot dogs and burritos. Their truck suggests redneck, but one of them wears a hipster knit cap and the other a Halo T-shirt.

I'm debating whether or not to text Amber back when my phone rings.

"Where are you?" asks a young woman.

"King's Diner."

"You're not in the diner, dumb ass? Are you?"

"Yes. You said—"

"That's not what I meant. They watch the diner. I'm out back by the old car wash."

"Oh, I'll . . ." She's already hung up.

I hurriedly drop money on the table and head outside.

What did she mean by "they"?

Her paranoia is infectious. I walk out to the sidewalk and glance around. Between here and the 88 are half a dozen parked trucks. Behind the diner is a small, open lot with rusting cargo containers.

The car wash, actually a large truck wash, is a crumbling block of concrete covered in vines. It resembles an ancient temple.

Tall weeds stick through the cracked asphalt. In a few decades you'd never even know there was something man-made here.

I walk around the back of the truck wash and see a girl smoking a cigarette as she texts on her phone.

She's wearing a hoodie and sweatpants. Her hair is tied back in a ponytail. Underneath the heavy eyeliner is an attractive young woman who looks like she's getting over a cold.

"I won't bite you," she says when she spots me.

I glance around, looking for the "they" she warned me about.

She notices my anxiety. "They never come back here. We're fine."

"Are you Amber?" I ask, stepping closer. Nearer to her I can see she's got a lot of makeup caked on. Probably to cover acne.

"I hope so." She gives me a smile. "How much did you bring?"

"Bring?"

"Money."

Is she in hiding and needs help? I pull my wallet from my pocket and start counting bills. "How much do you need?"

She looks down at the cash and steps close to me. "Now we're talking." Her breath is overpoweringly minty. Like she just used mouthwash.

Out of nowhere, she grabs my crotch.

I stare at her hand, confused. "Um . . . I just wanted to talk."

She leans in and whispers into my ear, "That's what they all say."

After a confusing moment, I manage to overcome my shock and pull her hand away.

She looks over my shoulder.

There's the sound of squealing tires as the truck from the convenience store comes skidding around the side of the building. The two men inside the cab are looking at me with murder in their eyes.

"Oh, shit!" says Amber before she runs away.

The driver pulls the vehicle to a stop and flies out of the cab with his friend behind him. "What the fuck are you doing with my sister!"

"I just wanted to ask her a question!" I plead, holding my hands up. He has a metal baseball bat in his hands.

He bolts straight for me and slams the bat into my stomach. I crumple to my knees.

His companion kicks me in the ribs, and I fall onto my side.

"There's been—" My words are cut off as I try to fend off a flurry of blows with my hands.

The brother, the one in the knit cap, slams a fist into my jaw and my face falls into a patch of leafy spurge. I lose consciousness, perversely wondering if the weed broke the asphalt or if the hot-and-cold cycle of the weather allowed it to spring through.

CHAPTER TWENTY-EIGHT

Cherry Pie

I come to some unknowable time later and manage to move from the ground to lean on the building. My side hurts like hell. I spit out a mouthful of blood. The red saliva lands on my shoe.

My battered ribs shriek as I bend over to retrieve my empty wallet. I shove it back into my pocket and, using the hand that isn't swollen, give myself a spot check for broken bones. There's lots of sore muscle, but no sharp pain from fractures or suspicious clicks. Only an X-ray can tell for sure, but I think I've at least dodged that bullet.

My stomach roars in pain, though. I lift my shirt and see a bruise the size of a football. I remember the brother swinging his bat into it.

I hobble toward my Explorer in the King's Diner parking lot but collapse twenty feet from the bumper. Footsteps come running up behind me. I lie flat on the ground and stare at the blue sky.

My waitress from earlier leans over me and says, "Dumb ass" under her breath. Amber's word for me. Apparently a regional favorite. The waitress still looks pretty, even when chewing me out.

"Did you just call me a dumb ass?" I ask over the pain.

"Do you want me to call the cops?"

"No," I reply as I sit up, fighting back white waves of agony.

"Then, yes. You're a dumb ass. Do you want an ambulance?"

"No. I don't think so." I look back at the diner. "Can I just go sit down?"

She gives me a cross look. "I should kick you off my property."

"Lady, give me a minute or two and I'll leave this fucking place, gladly." The second time today I've been asked to get out of town.

She watches me get to my feet, not offering a hand but making sure I don't fall down again and split my head in her parking lot.

"Don't worry," I say through gritted teeth, "I won't sue if I fall."

"Don't worry, I don't have any money," she snaps back.

Using handrails and seat backs for support, I make my way back to my original seat. Which was dumb and pointless, because it's the farthest booth from the door.

She ignores me while I use paper napkins to soak up the blood in my mouth and make an impromptu cleansing scrub using a glass of water and table salt.

I have a first-aid kit in my Explorer, but it might as well be in the next state.

I take stock of my wounds. I'm bruised up, but it's nowhere near as bad as it could have been. With some Tylenol and sleep, maybe a medicinal beer or two, I'll be fine in a couple of days. I'll look like shit, but I'll survive this.

Whatever *this* is.

The waitress stops at my table. "You able to walk out of here now?"

"Yeah. Sorry." I wad up my bloody napkins. "Just one thing"—for the first time, I notice her name badge—"Jillian. What happened back there?"

"Are you that dumb?"

"Apparently."

She rolls her eyes. "You got played. They rolled you. Let me guess, your wallet is empty?"

"Yeah. But you act like this happens all the time. Why don't the cops do something?"

"You said yourself, you didn't want to call them. They never do."

"'They'? I don't understand. Who are 'they'?"

"The other johns."

"Johns?" Amber's words to me before I got my ass kicked come back to me. "Wait . . . did she think I was trying to hire her as a hooker?"

"Real good naive act." Jillian shakes her head, then starts to walk away.

"Please," I plead. "Just a second."

She turns around. "What?" she says, agitated.

"I had no idea. I only wanted to talk to her about Chelsea Buchorn."

Jillian comes back to the booth. "What about her?"

"How she disappeared. That's why I'm here. I just wanted to ask her what she saw."

"Why do you care?"

"I just lost a friend. Her name was Juniper. They say a bear got her. I don't know." I stare down at the table and hold my head in my hands. I feel myself breaking down. "I just want to know what happened." Red blood falls onto the white Formica. I wipe it away with my sleeve.

Jillian takes a seat across from me. "You really weren't trying to hook up out there?"

"God, no! I thought she knew something. The way she talked about 'them' watching . . ."

"She meant the police."

"Oh. Great." I pull my phone from my pocket. The screen is cracked, but it still works. Using trembling fingers, I pull up her text message. "What does '1004BJ3004ATW' mean?"

She stares at it, taking only seconds to decipher it. "Do you really want me to say it?"

"Yeah. I don't get it."

"Imagine the first three numbers are a price. Four means 'for,' as in for something."

I stare at my phone. "BJ . . . oh, crap." You'd think as much as I work with numbers, the code would have been obvious before. "And ATW means 'all the way'?" I look across the table at her, my cheeks hot with shame. "I'm such an idiot."

"Not everyone can be a rocket scientist."

"CalTech's program actually accepted me. But I turned it down to study biology at MIT."

Her lips curl into a bemused grin. "Are you a scientist?"

"When I'm not getting my ass kicked by the brothers of prostitutes."

Jillian pats my nonswollen hand. "You really are a babe in the woods. That was her boyfriend-slash-pimp. The whole thing was a setup. If you'd been a local, she would have you meet her in a motel or in your car. Didn't the whole thing seem suspicious to you?"

Holy crap, I'm an even bigger idiot than I realized. She had me for a mark the moment I left my confused voice mail message.

"If it's common knowledge, why don't the police do something?"

"Because you're not a local. Hudson Creek has bigger problems. Did you get a look at her face?"

"Yes. Of course."

"I mean did you notice the makeup?"

"Huh? Yes. I thought it was because of lingering teenage acne."

"We call that meth face."

Then the mouthwash was because of her breath. As a hooker, she had to make herself presentable.

Crap, now I get it. I've read about this. Seen it on TV. The run-down houses and the new cars—it's like Southeast Central LA in the 1980s, when crack was an epidemic. Out here it's meth.

"How bad is it?"

"Two police officers were arrested last month by state police for trafficking. But it's worse than that."

I nod to the wall with the photos of all the soldiers. "I'd think you'd get better police out here."

Jillian looks at the faces of the men for a moment. "Those are the ones that didn't make it back. Hudson has another distinction besides meth. Per capita, we've provided more Special Forces than any other town. We've also lost more men than anyone else."

So this town is what happens when you kill off the best and the bravest. You're left with a cancerous epidemic that turns the young into violent sociopaths.

And you create the perfect environment for a killer to come and go as he pleases.

"Do you know anything about Chelsea?"

"No," Jillian replies. "I was at Fort Bragg when she went missing."

"Military?"

"Reserve. My husband was, too."

"And now?"

"I'm out." She sighs. "And he never made it home. This was his parents' place."

I can't think of anything to say. My pain seems rather insignificant at the moment.

Jillian slides out of the booth. "I've got to check in on the other tables. And don't worry, I'm no longer kicking you off my property."

"Thank you. Do you know anyone who could tell me about Chelsea?"

She shakes her head. "The only person I know of that knew her well just had your ass kicked so she could buy meth."

"Delightful."

CHAPTER TWENTY-NINE

Open Wounds

Between her rounds, Jillian fills me in with more town gossip, then gives me the name of a motel with the lowest number of sheriff department raids.

The Creekside Inn is from a bygone era when color TV was an attraction like Wi-Fi is today. The manager, an older man with a goatee, is leafing through a stack of fly-fishing magazines when I walk in.

He gives my face one look and decides he doesn't want to know the story behind the bruising.

I get the key and limp to my room. It takes me three trips to get my luggage inside. A futile act, given that I don't expect to be here more than a day or so, just long enough to feel up to the drive back to Austin.

I make a nest for myself on the bed, using pillows to make it easier for me to sit up. In a moment of absentmindedness, I set my laptop on my stomach and feel a flash of pain.

There's a nice yellow color surrounding the bruise. It's a beauty. I'm pretty sure I can make out the brand of boot Amber's friend was wearing.

Hudson Creek has become one painful dead end for me. The one person I wanted to talk to nearly put me in the hospital.

Determined to not be a complete quitter, I do an Internet search to see if Chelsea might have any less violent friends I can speak to.

An old Instagram photo shows her partying with three "best buds." One I recognize as Amber with a shorter and lighter haircut. The other two girls are tagged Gennifer and Lisa.

The photo was taken in a kitchen. They're mugging at the camera dressed in pajamas, holding cans of beer. Just four girls having a fun Friday night.

And now one is missing, probably dead. Another is a hooker frequently involved in felony robbery.

I find Gennifer's last name: Norris. She pops up in a database of Montana mug shots looking older than she should. She was booked for intent to traffic.

Lisa Cotlin managed to get out of town. I find some wedding photos in Tampa that Chelsea liked. The groom is wearing a marine uniform.

At least one person had a happily ever after.

I can't find anybody else besides these three who was in regular contact with Chelsea. Gennifer disappears from her social media stream not too long after the party photo.

Chelsea's updates are mostly photos of landscapes and various cats and dogs from around Hudson Creek.

If I could describe it in one word: *lonely*.

These are the kind of photos you take when you're walking back and forth between two forgettable places, texting on your phone, looking for some kind of escape, when a random dog pokes his nose up above a fence and gives you an unconditional smile.

I don't know anything about Chelsea, but these photos are how she looked at the world, or at the very least, the parts of it she thought worth remembering or sharing.

Her last photo before she went missing is an antique metal headboard.

Always wanted one.

Underneath is a comment from Amber.

Bitch, you know I'm going to tie you up to that!

It's the kind of playful innuendo I overhear all the time in the classroom. I don't read anything more into it.

Although it's a little odd that she'd buy a new piece of furniture before deciding to leave town. Not as unlikely as signing a new lease, but still, an indication that if she did move on, it was a last-minute decision.

I'm startled by a knock at the door. I wince getting up but take some satisfaction that I only audibly groan once.

Cautious, I glance through the peephole and see the motel manager standing there holding a bag.

I open the door. "Did I forget something?"

He raises the bag. "Jillian brought us some dinner." He motions toward a picnic table at the front of the property. "If you can make your way there, we can enjoy one of the last nice evenings before it starts getting cold."

I put on my shoes and meet him. A beer is waiting for me when I sit down.

"Gus Wheeler," he says, holding out his hand for me to shake.

I return the gesture. "Still, Theo Cray."

He pulls out two foam containers along with some napkins and condiments. "Hope you're not a vegetarian."

I open my container and get a whiff of the bacon cheeseburger inside. "I've given it up several times. This would make me do that again."

Gus doesn't make much conversation at first. I'm too focused on chewing my food without opening up the cut in my mouth.

It's a beautiful evening. He stops eating to look at the colors of the sky as the sun sets behind the mountains.

"Every night, it's like a brand-new painting. It's always different, but nothing changes." He nods toward town. "Some things do."

"How long have you lived here?" I ask between french fries.

"I was born in Helena. I moved out here to teach at the middle school in Quiet Lake. Eventually I started teaching at Hudson Creek High and became principal."

"You're an educator?"

"I started off that way. Then, when things got worse, I felt more like a warden."

I had gotten some of the story from Jillian, but I want to hear his version. "Worse? In what way?"

"Where do you want to start?"

"How far back does it go?"

"How much time do you have?"

"All night."

CHAPTER THIRTY
Lost Girls

Gus opens up a second beer and continues. "People try to figure out the cause of things. They want simple explanations. Hudson was wounded long before it became infected. Used to be a trading post. It was called Swanson's Creek back then. Trappers and Indians would come through here and more than likely get themselves swindled.

"That went on for a while before someone burned the trading post down. A while later silver was found in the hills." He jerks a thumb toward a distant range. "There used to be a mine there a hundred years ago. Hudson was where you'd go to get drunk and go to the whorehouse. Loggers would come in from the camps. The two biggest businesses were silver and vice.

"As the town grew, men started having families. The vice never really went away, but the rest of the town grew big enough to hide it.

"When things get bad, the trouble comes to the surface. Now"—he shakes his head—"trouble is all we have."

"Jillian mentioned the police officers who were arrested."

Gus leans in closer. "Notice how many shiny cars there were in front of shitty houses? Hudson has two industries: pumping gas into the long-haul trucks and methamphetamine. The two aren't unrelated. I don't blame the young people with any sense for leaving."

"Why didn't you leave after you retired?"

"I didn't retire as much as have my school close under me. We fell below the required attendance and the state shut us down. As far as why I'm here? Lots of people homeschool their kids now. Lots of people not qualified to do that. I tutor and try to help out." He locks eyes with me. "You know what it's like to be a teacher. You can't give up on them."

I wish I had his determination. I feel guilty for taking a compliment that doesn't apply to me.

"Do you remember Chelsea Buchorn?"

"Oh, yeah." He gives me a sideways look. "I heard you had a run-in with some of her former friends."

"Yeah. That was . . . a mistake."

"I'm going to tell you this, and you have every right to not believe me, but they're not bad kids. They do bad things, but if circumstances were different, I don't think they'd be pulling that kind of thing. Probably dumb stuff, but not to that degree."

The kicks to my stomach felt pretty bad. "Why doesn't anyone stop them?"

"Was there another young man there? Kind of a nerdy-looking one?"

I remember Amber's boyfriend's crony jumping out of the truck. "Yeah."

"That's Devon's friend Charlie York. His father is the chief of police."

"I see."

"Actually, it's a bit more complicated. Chief York is in Colorado getting cancer treatment. Or that's the story. Rumor has it that he's trying to dodge a federal indictment. The two they arrested were just the tip of the iceberg.

"Half the city council has cars in their driveways they can't afford."

This seems like a nightmare. "How does that work?"

"It's not like they're being given bags of money. Well, some are. The more honest ones—rather, the ones that try to see themselves as that—they're getting paid rent on property they bought for next to nothing or profits from businesses they were practically given."

"By who?"

"Whoever wants to keep doing business here and not get hassled. When this was a mining town, it was the owners of the cathouses and the saloons. Later it was the moonshiners.

"When meth came to town, it got worse. We'd lost a processing plant. Honest people were taking dishonest money."

"Everyone?"

He leans back and squints down the highway. "You see that bass boat dealership?"

"Yeah."

"Connor is the owner. He and his wife are good friends of mine. Nice folks. He sells two or three boats a week. Great business for around here.

"Do you think he asks everyone who steps on his lot where the money came from? He just built a new house on what he's made selling boats. That's how most people here make their money. They do it honestly, selling to dishonest people.

"The problem is that when you know where your money is coming from, whether you're making it legally or not, you're resistant to things changing. You stop caring about getting rid of meth in Hudson Creek and start talking about getting rid of the violence. Like Las Vegas.

"You resign yourself to the fact that you're always going to have crooked politicians and police, but just as long as you're safe."

I got mugged because I was an out-of-towner they thought was here to do something illegal. If I went to the police, I probably would have found myself in jail.

Gus continues, "The reality people are facing is that all you can really do is push it below the surface. You ignore the problem and then find out your daughter is working as a prostitute or your son is beating up people trying to cook meth on the side.

"The price for all those shiny new cars is Hudson Creek's children." He takes a deep breath. "It's like the old stories where a town would drown a child in a lake to prevent flooding. You do it enough times and your lake runs dry, your children are gone, and all you have left is an empty lake filled with skeletons."

I don't know what to say. So I turn back to the reason I'm here. "What do you think happened to Chelsea Buchorn?"

"I want to believe she decided to leave. What do I think really happened?" He stands up and faces the mountain where the mine was located. "Let me show you."

I get to my feet with some strain and stand beside him.

"See the notch just below the ridge?"

Orange and purple clouds are visible just beyond. "Yes?"

"About twenty years ago, some surveyors found a skeleton there. And another and another. They were dead at least fifty years by then.

"That notch is about a mile off the path that led from the mining camp to Hudson Creek. The nearest building was a cathouse.

"They found at least twelve bodies before they gave up. All of them young women. All of them probably prostitutes that worked either in the whorehouse or the mining camp.

"We still have the town newspapers from back then. Not one, not a single one, ever mentions a missing girl.

"Old-timers just assumed they moved on. At least twelve girls didn't. That's just the ones they found. Who knows how many others were never seen again by anyone. Those hills could be filled with lost girls.

"Back then, just like now, whenever people look the other way when evil is around them, the wicked will find it. Chelsea wasn't the first. She won't be the last."

Gus and I quietly eat the pie Jillian prepared for us.

My gaze keeps returning to the notch where the forgotten girls were buried. How many other places are there? How many more children were lost?

We say good night and I head back to my room to chase down some ibuprofen with a medically inadvisable amount of beer.

When I wake up the next day, as sore as should be expected, I make a decision not to head back to Austin just yet.

I still want to talk to Amber.

CHAPTER THIRTY-ONE

STALKER

When I wake up and feel coherent enough to think, I send a text message to Amber.

> We need to talk.

Half an hour goes by and there's no answer. I decide to be more direct.

> I don't care about what happened. I want to talk about Chelsea. I think I know what happened to her.

Another half hour and no answer. I decide to just call her.

A robotic voice tells me that her phone isn't accepting calls.

She's blocking me.

Of course. I'm sure I'm not the first person to call her after falling for their stunt.

I drive to the 88 Service Station for coffee. Walking through the brightly lit aisles, I see a shelf full of prepaid cell phones and purchase one for fifty bucks.

I open it in my front seat and play around with it. I'm surprised to find out that it's more fully featured than I would expect for the price. By no means is it as good as my iPhone, but it has a web browser and runs Android apps.

An interesting realization hits me: if I'd paid cash, this phone would be totally untraceable to me.

I go back into the store and buy another one with money from an ATM. In theory, the phone could be connected via the ATM withdrawal if someone knew the time of purchase and checked the ATM's history log. But it seems secure enough. I have no idea why that's even important to me.

I guess, given what happened yesterday, a little more caution might be a good idea.

I put away the phone I bought with the credit card and text Amber on the one purchased with cash.

I'm not angry about yesterday. It was a mix-up. I wanted to talk to you about Chelsea.

To be honest, I'm mad as hell. But I just want to find out what she knows and get the hell out of this town.

I sit in the parking lot and drink my coffee while I wait for her to respond.

An hour goes by. Frustrated, I call her and get her voice mail.

I try to make myself sound as casual as possible. "Hey, Amber. This is Theo from yesterday. I'm not mad. I don't care about the money. I just want to talk about Chelsea and what happened to her. Um, I'm not a cop or a weirdo. I lost someone, too. I just want to compare notes."

I hang up, thinking that's about as sincere as I can possibly get.

There's no immediate text back from Amber like yesterday.

I get the feeling she's not going to have anything to do with me. For all she knows, this could be a setup.

I try to look at it from her point of view. I'd be paranoid as hell. She probably thinks I'm out to kill her.

Mentioning Chelsea might only make her more frightened.

I need to figure out another way to reach out to her.

On my burner phone I do a Google search for a website that locates people. It takes me fifty dollars to get her most recent address.

It's eight miles away.

Google Street View shows Devon's pickup truck in the driveway. The sight of it makes me ache.

Crap. This isn't going to be easy.

I don't want to confront him again.

I go back into the 88 and buy two cans of Mace. The clerk is the same one that sold me the burner cell phones. He doesn't bat an eye.

With my face bruised up, this has to look sketchy as hell. I'd call the police on me.

But apparently in Hudson Creek, this isn't all that unusual.

When I drive by the address, Devon's pickup is still in the driveway, just like the aerial image on Google. Seeing it close up makes me start breathing heavily.

I keep my window up and don't stop. It takes me two miles to calm down.

The house had two stories and a large yard. It wasn't terribly rundown, but it was cluttered. Three other cars were parked nearby.

They looked beat-up and not the kind of vehicle I'd expect the son of a police chief to drive.

The report on Amber said she owned a Honda Civic. I think I remember seeing one in the yard as I drove by, trying not to be seen.

My plan is to pass by the house every hour until the truck is gone and Amber is there alone. No way am I going there when Devon is around.

The truck sits there for four hours. At one point Amber's car is gone, but it's back when I drive by again.

When I turn the corner and see the truck has finally left, I feel a strange, perverse rush of excitement.

I park my Explorer in front of the house. I'm too scared to pull into the driveway and get trapped.

My face looks like crap, so I pull a baseball cap over my head and put on a pair of big aviators. When I step onto the road, my leg is trembling. My knee doesn't want to support my weight.

I guess this is what they call spaghetti legs.

I should just get back into my Explorer and head home.

Yesterday was a warning. I'm getting too deep into this.

But there are answers here. Or at least the potential for answers.

My legs finally find their courage, and I walk up to the front door. I also have two cans of Mace in my pockets.

Three aluminum chairs sit on the porch along with dirty ashtrays and crushed cans. In one of the ashtrays there's a glass meth pipe.

Through the window I can hear a television and see someone lying on a couch.

A dog starts barking when I knock. I step back from the door. Somewhere inside a young man says, "Hold up."

I hear scuffling feet and the sound of the dog being pushed into another room.

The young man who answers the door has messed-up hair, bad teeth, and a bug-eyed expression. "Yeah?" he says drowsily.

"I'm here to talk to Amber. Is she here?" I have to use every ounce of control to avoid stammering.

I keep glancing over his shoulder, afraid Devon or Charlie is going to come running at me with the baseball bat. The only thing that stirs is an interior door when the barking dog throws his body against it.

The house is a pigsty. Dirty plates and takeout containers litter the floor. There are piles of clothes everywhere. Filled ashtrays sit on the arms of the couch and on the floor. Glass pipes are strewn about without care.

The place has a funky smell whose source I don't even want to guess at.

My greeter shouts upstairs, "Amber, one of your gentlemen callers is here."

"Who is it?" she shouts down.

"Ask him the fuck yourself. I'm not your butler." He gives me a "What can you do?" look and rolls his eyes, then returns to the couch.

Footsteps sound from the top of the stairs, and I feel my heart skip a beat.

Afraid that she'll see me and run, or worse, I turn away from the door and stare out at the street.

She reaches the bottom of the steps. "Yeah?"

I turn around, staring at the ground. "I just wanted to ask you about Chelsea."

"What about her?" She's studying me, trying to remember me. Suddenly it hits her. "What the fuck!"

She rushes to slam the door. I stick my foot in the way.

"I'm going to call the police if you don't get the fuck away! And I'm going to tell them you tried to rape me," she says, trying to close the door.

The guy on the couch watches with amusement.

"Call the police," I bluff, then decide to double down. "I'll call the state police. Let's see what they say."

She stops pushing on the door. "Fuck off."

"Amber, I don't care about yesterday. It was a case of mistaken identity. I met with you because I thought you might be able to tell me what happened to Chelsea. I wasn't trying to hire you as a hooker."

"I'm not a hooker, you fucker!" she screams at me through the gap in the door.

I try to keep my voice calm. "I don't care. I just want to know what happened to your friend." I pull my foot away and step back from the door, making a point to hold my hands up. "Please."

She watches me through the narrow space. I step all the way to the brown grass.

"This isn't some kind of payback?" she asks in a calmer voice.

"It's not. Juniper Parsons, the girl they say got attacked by a bear, she was a student of mine. I was her professor."

She opens the door a little wider. "For real?"

"For real."

"Keep back." She steps outside the house and takes a seat on the top of the steps leading from the porch, then pulls out a pack of cigarettes and a lighter from her sweatpants.

I lower my hands as she lights her cigarette. She keeps looking at me suspiciously, then scans the street. After a few calming puffs, she finally says, "Nobody believes me. Even Devon thinks I'm a joke."

CHAPTER THIRTY-TWO
Besties

Remembering something from a psychology class on body language, I take a seat below her on the dying grass. Amber puffs away. I give her a moment to calm down. She also looks a little glassy eyed and may still be high.

Finally, when both our pulses have dropped, I say, "Tell me about Chelsea."

She frowns, then blows smoke out of the corner of her mouth. "I don't know. We were best friends since forever. Always getting into trouble together." She gives me a quick glance. "Not that kind of trouble, at first. Just usual kid stuff. Staying out late. Boys. Stealing beer." She shrugs, takes another drag. Sends another plume of smoke into the air. "But yeah. When things got so boring around here, we got into other stuff.

"Her mom kicked her out of the house. I'd been in and out of mine. We knew some girls were making money doing stuff. And, well, we liked to party. There's fuck-all nothing else to do up here. We weren't like lot lizards or nothing like that."

I make a mental note to look up "lot lizard" later.

"What about the night she went missing? What was going on then?"

"We were just going to get high. I had a strip of acid. We'd take it in the woods. Most people would be scared shitless. We loved it. You'd be out there on the ground listening to nature, staring at the stars. It was peaceful."

"Is that what happened that night?"

She stabs out her cigarette and lights another. "That was the fucked-up part. We never even took it. We was walking along out there and we heard a noise. You get wild boar and such. We laughed, pretended it was a monster or something. I took off running. She ran after me, then fell back.

"I went to look for her. I thought she was playing hide-and-seek or something. But she wasn't. I saw her standing there, like she was listening for something. I was starting to call to her, and then I saw it, past her. I screamed before she did. I thought it was a bear. There was this shadow." Amber holds up her hands in an arch over her head. "I thought it was a bear on his hind paws. Only he starts moving like a man; then he runs toward Chelsea. She hears me scream; then she screams. Then there was nothing. I couldn't see her in the shadows. Everything got real quiet.

"Something told me to run like hell. So I did.

"It was following me. I could hear it. Then I heard Chelsea hollering. I think it turned back to finish her. I just kept running." She swallowed, licked her lips. "I know I shouldn't have left her behind. She was my best friend.

"I'd parked on the roadside. I got in and just drove as fast as I could, straight to the police station.

"But I didn't go in right away. I started panicking. Thinking maybe I was high. Maybe I imagined the whole thing. I know that sounds crazy.

"It was stupid of me, but I decided to try to sleep it off. When I woke up, the sun was shining. I was still in my car.

"I went inside the police station and told Charlie's dad everything I remembered."

"But they didn't believe you?"

She shakes her head. "No. They said I was making things up. They said Chelsea's room was cleaned out. Her car was gone. That doesn't make any sense." Her voice gets defiant. "I know she was there that night. I picked her up. We took my car, left hers behind."

"Is it possible she played a prank on you?"

"I wanted to believe that. But for this long? Ha-ha, Chelsea. Where the fuck are you? Nobody does this for that long."

"Is there anyone in town that would want to kill her?"

"Chelsea was the nicest person you'd ever meet. But she slept around a lot. Older men, especially. I think a few of them were glad she went away.

"Did anyone kill her? Hell, this is Hudson. Anything is possible. You hear about that Indian family that went missing?"

I remember them from the missing-persons database. "Yeah."

"What the newspapers don't say is that they were running their own little meth lab. Without permission. That's why they disappeared." She grins knowingly and lowers her voice. "Know who the last two people to see them were? Bower and Jackson."

"Bower and Jackson?"

"The police officers who got arrested for trafficking crystal. That's how fucked-up things are around here."

"Has anyone else ever mentioned something like what you saw the night Chelsea went missing?"

"I talked to some Chippewa guy. He grew up on a res. He said they have lots of stories like that. I don't believe any of that. What I saw was a man that wanted me to think he was an animal. But I saw him walking, plain as day." She narrows her eyes. "I thought they caught the bear that killed your girl."

"They caught a bear. But there's nothing that ties it to her."

Amber watches a flock of birds fly overhead. "At least you know she's gone. You have something to bury. Everyone around here is pretending Chelsea is out there somewhere having a gay old time. But they know. They know Chelsea's dead. They just don't care."

I can feel the sense of loss she's experiencing. It's a quiet desperation, like clinging to a rope in a fog.

"Do you remember the spot where she disappeared? Where you saw the man?"

"Round about. I took the police there."

"Did they find anything?"

"Are you kidding? They spent about ten minutes, then left. They didn't give a fuck."

"So it was never made a crime scene?"

"They didn't make it a *crime*." She stabs the air with her finger. "They didn't care!"

The words come out of my mouth without thinking. "Can you tell me where it happened?"

Before she can answer, I hear the familiar sound of squealing truck tires.

"Shit," Amber mutters. "My boyfriend is here."

Here we go again.

CHAPTER THIRTY-THREE

Bad Prince

I feel my spine stiffen as Devon's boots stomp across the grass. He comes to a stop over my shoulder, his shadow falling over me.

My right hand grips the can of Mace in my pocket, but my fingers are trembling. I don't know if I'll be able to pull it free quickly enough, let alone muster the nerve to squeeze the trigger.

I'm terrified that trying to defend myself will only aggravate him further. Last time he took my money but left me well enough to walk away. Fighting back might put me in the hospital, or worse.

Amber looks over my head at Devon and gives him a little nod. "What's up."

"Who's he?" Devon asks.

My body slackens a little when I realize he hasn't recognized me under my hat and sunglasses. I keep my head down and avoid looking up at him, lest he see the bruise on my face and recognize his handiwork.

"He's nobody," Amber replies. "Just an old friend of Chelsea."

"Friend or customer?" Devon replies with a mocking tone. He walks past me without turning to look. "Make sure he knows your pussy is no longer on Craigslist."

"Fuck you." Amber flips him the bird as he steps inside, closing the door behind him.

Amber shuts her eyes and shakes her head. "You probably think I'm a horrible person."

I keep my voice low, afraid he'll hear me inside. "Aside from what happened yesterday, I think you're swell."

"Yeah, whatever. We only started doing that after a trucker roughed up some girl from Quiet Lake. They fucked his shit up when they got to him.

"Devon was getting pissed when he saw the guys calling me. It was one thing if they were a local, someone we knew who was okay."

I'm trying to understand the relationship dynamic. "Is Devon your . . ."

"Pimp? Fuck, no. I'm not a fucking whore," she says sharply.

"I was going to say 'boyfriend.'"

"Oh. We have an open relationship. Not that it's any of your business."

I'm embarrassed by the whole discussion. "I didn't mean to imply anything."

"You have a judgmental face."

"I'm a scientist. I look at everything this way."

She tilts her head toward the house. "Devon wanted to be a scientist."

"Really?" I say a little too loudly.

"He loves all that shit. He's got a Neil deGrasse Tyson T-shirt and everything. We used to get high and watch *Bill Nye the Science Guy.*"

Out of nowhere, this makes me laugh. My stomach protests in pain, and I try to stop moving.

"Yeah, fucked-up, I know. You ever watch *Sesame Street* wasted? It's like it's made for two-year-olds and stoners."

"No. I've never gotten high all that much. As an undergrad I was on a trip to the Amazon and a local medicine man gave some of us something that I still can't identify. We sat around in a circle drinking it, thinking it was a bonding ceremony.

"Turns out they were just messing with the out-of-towners. I sat in a tree for hours convinced I was a spider monkey. When I got back down and explained what I experienced, the medicine man asked me how I was so certain I wasn't a spider monkey that got high and thinks it's a scientist."

Amber taps the side of her nose. "That guy knew what he was talking about. How are you so sure?"

"Sometimes I wonder."

She leans back and stares at the passing clouds. "Chelsea and I used to have those conversations all the time. We'd wonder if this world was the real one. When we were little girls, we'd always be looking through closets and random doors, hoping we'd find one that led to another place. Like Narnia. Something different."

She leaves out "someplace better," but I know what she's trying to say.

She tugs at a weed. "When we got older and realized that we weren't going to find that door, we started thinking that world was around us, but we couldn't see it. I don't mean like a Doors song or nothing. Just that we get used to calling things by names and thinking about them in a certain way.

"We started making up our own names for stuff. Like the phone was the far talk box. We'd call the TV a magic window. We'd come up with names for people, too. Chief York was the Evil Baron. Charlie was the Bad Prince. We had names for everyone. Reverend Goat, the Red Witch, the Bad Wizard—he was a meth cook." Her voice drifts. "Anyway. Stupid stuff."

I feel a connection to this lost girl. "It's not stupid at all. I teach a whole class on nomenclature. I explain how using different names, but ones that still fit, can give you a different understanding of things."

"Like how?"

I think for a moment. "Take Hudson Creek. It's not much of a creek, but the whole town and everything around is in its valley. Actually, it's kind of a bowl between the mountains. On the other side are a couple of different towns. One is more in the mountains—lots of summer rentals, right? The other seems like a nice enough place. What makes this town different? What name would you give it?"

She doesn't hesitate. "Hell Mouth. This isn't hell, but the entrance can't be far. We're all circling the edge, waiting to fall in."

"I don't know about all that, but I'm sure you get more than your share of wicked passing through." I think of the dark-purple bands MAAT showed me. I wonder what I'd see if I used data from last century. Was Hudson Creek still on the devil's highway? From what Gus told me, it would seem so.

"Amber, if I give you a map, can you show me where you last saw Chelsea?"

She thinks it over, then shakes her head. "I'm not sure."

"Could you at least tell me some markers to look for?"

"They're hard to find."

I'm frustrated that she's suddenly become a dead end. Maybe the subject is still too painful.

"How about I show you myself?" she offers.

"You mean, go back there?"

"I'm not scared," she says defiantly. "If the devil wanted me, he would have come for me when he got Chelsea."

Amber is a tortured soul, but I admire her bravery.

Going there sounds like a horrible idea, but I agree anyway.

CHAPTER THIRTY-FOUR
FIELD TRIP

When I return to Amber's house later that afternoon, Devon's truck is still parked in front. So I text her to let her know that I'm here. She texts back, b right there.

I'm not sure what I'm looking for out there. But if the police never did a thorough investigation, who knows what still might be up there? A piece of fabric, a shoe, anything that backs up Amber's story would help me know if I'm looking in the right direction.

But for what?

I only have a few more days before I should head back to Austin. As things are, it's going to be tight getting everything ready for class. I'm already going to have to beg off a couple of faculty meetings. These are usually pointless anyway, but not being there has political consequences. My contract is up for renewal. It's best to play nicely.

There's a knock on my window. I look up from my phone and nearly piss myself. Devon is standing there. He motions for me to roll down my window.

I reach my hand toward the shifter to put the Explorer in drive, but I hesitate when he steps away from the door and holds his hands up.

"I just want to talk to you," he says.

I fumble for my Mace and hold on to it tightly before cracking the window.

"Amber says you're going to where she says Chelsea went missing."

"Yes," I reply hesitantly. "That's what I wanted to talk about yesterday."

"Yeah, yeah. A mix-up." He rests his hand on the door frame. "I can't let you take her up there alone. For all I know, you could be a whack job."

I take off my sunglasses and point to my bruised cheek. "Do I strike you as the violent type?"

"You might be pissed and all. But that was a mistake. That was Charlie's fault. He thought you were someone else."

"Who is that?"

"I don't know. Some guy that likes hitting girls. Fucking you up was wrong, but we never hit any women. Anyhow, I'm coming with you." He grabs the handle to the back door.

"The fuck you are," I shoot back, making sure the doors are locked.

Devon walks back to my window. "Listen, I'm sorry about what happened. Here." He shoves his hand into his pocket and pulls out a wad of bills. "Take it back. Charlie's got the rest." He feeds the bills through the crack in the window like a vending machine.

I watch the money fall into my lap. When I look up, Amber is walking out of the house in a jacket.

"Is he okay with it?" she asks.

Devon looks at me through the window. "Well?"

This keeps getting worse. "Fine. But you're sitting up front so I can watch you." I know that's something you're supposed to do, but the idea doesn't make me feel any safer.

"Sure. Cool." He goes around the car and gets into the passenger side. Amber climbs into the back behind him.

It's an awkward drive for the next few minutes. I keep a watch on Devon. Each time he moves, I twitch.

In the rearview mirror, I check to make sure Amber isn't getting ready to strangle me with piano wire.

Finally Amber speaks. "I had to tell Devon where I was going. He pointed out you could be the guy that got Chelsea. Going off with you alone would be kind of stupid."

These people are afraid of me?

"Amber is a bit too trusting," Devon says.

"That would explain you in my life," she replies.

"Woman, I'm the best thing that happened to you."

"Oh, lord. If this is the best, I don't want to go on." Amber shakes her head and stares out the window.

Devon reaches for the radio, and I shove my hand in my pocket. He notices. "You carrying?"

Carrying? He means a gun. It might be better if they think I'm armed. "I'm always careful." I add, "I told some friends where I was going to be."

"We did, too," Devon replies. "Never know."

"No, you don't." I give him an anxious glance, but he's staring at the houses as they pass by.

After a few minutes he speaks up. "Amber says you're a scientist? What kind?"

"I studied biology. But I'm in computer science, too."

"Cool. Cool. I wanted to be an astrophysicist."

What a loss to the scientific community.

"I had straight As until my senior year," Devon explains. "That's when my mom got sick. I graduated, but barely. I guess I should do some online stuff. I watch the Discovery Channel all the time."

"High," Amber says from the back seat.

"Carl Sagan got high a lot."

"He was also Carl Sagan," I reply, regretting it, but Devon laughs.

"True. True. So, Dawkins or Stephen Jay Gould?"

"You've read them?"

"Yeah. *The Blind Watchmaker* is one of my favorite books ever."

The debate between Richard Dawkins and Stephen Jay Gould was whether the genes or the whole animal was the principal driving force of evolution. It was actually one of the reasons I got into bioinformatics.

To an amateur scientist, asking where you stood on Dawkins versus Gould was the equivalent of asking who your favorite sports team was.

The debate died down when people began to appreciate the notion that evolution is a very complex process and saying the animal or the gene is the deciding factor is too simple.

"I side with Dawkins," I reply, so Devon won't murder me in the woods. "But it's complicated. One of the things I study is how we define genes. As you know, there's a biological definition for it as the smallest unit of inheritability. But things are more complex. I tend to think about things in terms of systems or processes. Some systems can be reduced to a few bits of DNA. Others involve entire ecosystems."

"Where do you draw the line at the organism?"

Apparently, Devon is more intelligent than I realized. Granted, our first meeting wasn't under the best circumstances.

"I've heard it argued that we're just space suits for mitochondrial DNA," I reply. "Another thought is that we're just moving cities of gut bacteria. We carry more bacterial DNA than our own. Not by length, but unit. An alien might not recognize us as what we think we are."

"I'm not sure I recognize us as us," says Amber.

"We're constantly changing." I point to the darkening sky. "As the seasons change, some of our genes switch on or off. Genetically, we become slightly different organisms. Other things can do that, too." I don't think I want to bring up my were-frog research right now. "Nature controls us more than we want to admit."

I catch Devon staring at his reflection in the passenger mirror. His eyes are sunken and his skin ragged from his addiction. "That's for sure. That's sure as hell for sure."

This bit of introspection doesn't comfort me as I drive into the woods and away from civilization and safety.

CHAPTER THIRTY-FIVE

Dark Paths

We park my Explorer on a side road just past a small plot where a sad pizza parlor sits next to a tiny convenience store. Two miles up the highway is an RV park.

I imagine either Amber or Chelsea had business in one of those places.

We begin walking up a small trail. Amber leads the way, while Devon is a dozen yards behind me, which does nothing to make me feel better about my choice to come out here with them.

I was foolish to agree to meet Amber under such shady circumstances yesterday. But coming here with them after what happened? Sheer stupidity.

One hand is in my pocket on the Mace. The other tightly grips the heavy flashlight I keep in my SUV. I have lighter, more modern ones, but they wouldn't make as good of a club.

"What'd you and Chelsea do up here? Lez out?" taunts Devon.

"Get away from assholes like you." Amber stops by a large tree stump at the top of a hill. "This is where we'd meet up. You could probably make a fortune on all our empties out here." She kicks at a faded piece of metal.

"Not to mention the dildos," Devon says, still in jerk mode.

"At least they can stay hard."

Devon mutters something about fucking a subway tunnel, then goes over to a tree to take a piss.

"Is this where it happened?" I ask.

She points down the hill to a flat area. "Over there. We were walking from the other direction. I saw the shadow up by here before it broke into a run."

"On how many legs?" Devon asks after zipping up.

"Two, dumb ass."

He shoots me a look. "That's not what she said at first."

"I always said he was a man," she explains to me. "He may have crawled some. I don't know, it was dark."

"You were high," Devon adds.

"Not that high. Not yet."

I walk down the hill to where she said Chelsea was last seen. There are a few rocks and rotting logs on the ground. I grab a stick and use it to turn over the dirt.

If this had been sand or something else porous and dry, you might be able to still see blood. It just looks like soil to me.

"What should we be looking for?" asks Amber.

I give her a shrug as I stand up. "I don't know. A shirt. Her purse. Something that says she was here."

Amber and I spread out and start kicking through brush and rocks. Devon sits on a log and watches us.

Not sure myself what we should be looking for, I ask, "You remember what she was wearing that night?"

Amber sets down an empty beer can. "She had a blue coat that came down to her knees. Knit cap. Jeans."

Other than beer cans and silver Mylar candy wrappers, there's no sign of Chelsea.

I'm not sure what I was expecting. A bloody shoe that matched the foot of a long-gone Cinderella? A confession from the killer?

We spend the next half hour searching while Devon types away on his phone.

"Thank you for your help," Amber says to him sarcastically as she passes him.

"I'm just here to make sure you don't get raped and murdered." He nods to me, then grins.

Amber glances back in my direction. "Maybe you're afraid we'd just fuck while we were up here alone."

Devon's smile fades. "He don't look rich. But go ahead. See if I care. Fuck who you want."

Their squabble is making me uncomfortable, so I give them some distance.

I keep hoping one of us will have that magic eureka moment where we find the clue that solves everything. It's not happening.

While I think Amber is sincere in her own way, I don't think she's all that reliable. If I'd known she and Chelsea came out here to drop acid, I'm not sure I would have made the effort to come to this town. Especially if I knew I'd get an ass kicking.

"How much longer do you two want to keep doing this?" asks Devon.

"Until you leave us alone so I can blow him."

"Christ, already. I'm going back down to the car." He turns to me. "Can I have your keys so I can wait inside?"

I don't trust the situation. I'm afraid that'll be the last I see of him or my Explorer. Devon had been friendly, but I wouldn't put anything past him.

"No," I say as forcefully as I can. "You're the last person I'd trust with my keys."

He raises the hem of his sweater and shows me the butt of a pistol. "If I wanted to take them from you, I'd have done that." He drops his shirt, concealing the gun.

My leg begins to shake. I try not to show it.

Amber sprints over to face him. "Jesus, Devon! He already thinks we're psychos. Why did you have to do that?"

Devon raises his hands. "I was only making a point." Over her shoulder he says to me, "That wasn't a threat, man. Sorry."

My leg's shaking subsides a little. "Why don't you help us?"

"Look for something that didn't happen?"

Amber makes a cross face. "You said you believed me."

"I'll say anything to get laid."

"Asshole." She stomps away. "That's the problem around here, everyone is full of shit."

It's getting darker, and I'm beginning to think I should call it before things get too tense. Part of me is still afraid that this is all for show and I'm being set up for something. After my beating, the world looks a little different to me.

"Can't you do some science shit?" Amber asks.

"It's not like a magic power," Devon sneers. "Maybe he's got one of those *CSI* methane probes in his truck. Do you?"

"Not quite. I'm not a forensic technician . . ." My voice trails off as I think about what he just said.

I was looking for signs of Chelsea—clothing, a possession. Maybe hair on a branch or something from the killer.

The thought of looking for Chelsea herself never struck me.

I keep thinking it would be like Juniper's murder scene, where she was found lying on the ground. What if Chelsea's killer had a little more time to prepare or to clean things up?

If he didn't take her with him and he didn't leave her for dead, that would mean she's buried somewhere around here.

There's acres and acres of potential ground to cover and no way to search it in my lifetime.

But what if I do use some of my science powers?

"Are you okay?" Amber asks.

"He's thinking," Devon says. "Or getting ready to flip out and kill you."

"Shut up."

It hits me. "I know where to look."

CHAPTER THIRTY-SIX

Biodiversity

"You've never been here before," says Devon. "Or have you?" His hand goes toward his gun.

I get the sense he's a very scared and jumpy kid trying to cover it up with this false bravado. "Relax. No. I just thought up some science shit. See that?" I point my flashlight at a leafy green plant with small white flowers. "That's mallow-leaf ninebark. And that's western meadow rue. Those are the droopy ones."

"Do they grow over graves or something?" asks Amber.

"They grow over a lot of things."

Devon is now interested and starts looking around with his light. "Here's some ninebark." He points to a patch of the plant. "Over here, too."

"I found some, too," says Amber.

I walk over to inspect what they've found. "Good. Good."

"What do you want us to do?" asks Devon.

"Keep looking."

After a few minutes he points out, "It's everywhere."

"The meadow rue, too," adds Amber.

"I know. We're doing a survey. You can tell the difference? Right?"

They both agree.

"Okay. We're going to add another one." I point to a white grass with tiny white flowers. "This is bear grass. Any time you see one of these, call out the name. Got it?"

"Is there going to be a prize?" Devon jokes.

"We'll see. It's only a guess."

We spend the next half hour calling out the different plants as we spot them.

"Ninebark, bear grass," Amber shouts.

I walk over to where she's standing. It's by the thick roots of a tree. "Keep going."

I move us down the hill toward the small valley between the ridge on the side farthest from the road.

We keep within sight of one another. The calls are a little less frequent. I decide to give it a little longer.

"Ninebark, bear grass, and meadow rue. I hit the trifecta," Devon exclaims. "Neat trick. Was this to keep our eyes on the ground?"

I rush over to him. "No. This was to see if we could find the three of them together."

Sure enough, all the wild plants are represented here. He's standing in a small flat area at the base of a steep incline. The hill is bare, with loose rocks poking through the soil.

It's a great spot. Lots of erosion from uphill. Something buried here would only get deeper and deeper underground every time it rained.

Amber walks over to us. "Is one of these something that grows over dead people?" She doesn't hide the dread in her voice.

"I couldn't tell you what a dead body would cause to grow. Except maybe more of something if it was decaying quickly and fertilizing the plants near the surface.

"If it's down deep, then I doubt it. This really is outside my area."

Devon kicks at the plants with his foot. "So what are you looking for?"

"A sign that someone was here. That someone was digging in the dirt."

"These plants are everywhere." Devon pulls at some bear grass.

"Yes. But in how many other spots were all three here?"

"None."

"Why?" I scan the ground for anything unusual. "Or rather, why aren't they growing together elsewhere?"

"Because they don't like each other," Amber answers.

"Exactly. The plants create their own herbicides that kill off rival species. But it takes a while for one to win out.

"When you dig up the soil, you're basically tilling it and creating a free-for-all for anything that wants to take seed there."

Devon gets to the point. "So what is here?"

"Probably nothing. It was just a theory."

"Let's test it. You have a shovel?"

I never planned for this. "I don't know if we should be digging here." The thought that Chelsea could be under my feet is making me anxious.

Amber chimes in, "So, what? We're going to go into the police station and tell them we found some pretty flowers? We might as well go home."

"Give me your keys," says Devon. "I'll go get the shovel."

I hand them over without much thought.

As he reaches the top of the hill, he shouts back, "See you later, sucker!"

I spin around. He shakes his head and laughs. "Whatever you two are gonna do, hurry it up."

"He's such an asshole," Amber groans as she stares at the ground.

I think I can tell what she's wondering—is my friend really down here?

Devon's jackass behavior is because he's nervous. For Amber, this could be vindication.

A sad vindication. For as long as people said she was full of shit, there was the possibility in her mind that they were right.

Chelsea could be out there having a great life.

If Amber is right . . . if I'm right . . . she's rotting away beneath our feet.

I feel her shoulder touch mine. I awkwardly put a hand on it. I don't know what to say.

"I'm sorry you lost your friend," she whispers, probably thinking of her own loss, too.

"Me, too. I wish I'd known her better."

"You guys are too slow. Or too quick," Devon chides as he comes skidding down the hill with the shovel.

He sees the tears in Amber's eyes and shuts up.

"Here?" he asks, pointing to the ground.

We step back. "Yeah," I say. "It's as good as any. It could be several feet down. We'll probably need to dig a few different holes."

He scoops up a pile of dirt, uprooting the plants. I examine the soil, trying to figure out how to tell if it's been disturbed.

Devon tosses aside another pile. I grab a handful and start poking through it with my finger, looking for some clue. This could take forever.

He stops digging. "Want me to take over?" I ask.

I look up when Devon doesn't answer. He's staring at something. Amber steps up behind him, then suddenly puts her arms around his waist.

It only took three camping shovels of dirt in the very first place we decided to look.

Dirty, but as plain as could be, a bright blue coat is lying there.

Amber buries her head in Devon's shoulder. I look up at him in disbelief. He covers his mouth and shakes his head.

"Holy shit. Holy fucking shit."

I'm not sure which one of us said it. But I know we are all thinking it.

CHAPTER THIRTY-SEVEN
Remnants

I remind myself that it's just a blue piece of fabric we're looking at. We don't know that it's a coat, let alone Chelsea's.

"Is it her?" asks Amber, as if Devon and I have the answer.

Devon lowers the shovel and looks at me.

This was all theoretical until now. It's a strange blend of the thrill of discovery and horror as the reality sinks in.

I came to Hudson Creek on little more than a lark, because of an educated guess based on the slimmest of data. My gut and MAAT thought that there was something here that fit the pattern of Juniper's death.

Now I'm staring at what may be proof. The analytical part of my brain is exhilarated; the neurons that get pleasure when I solve a Sudoku are euphoric.

But is it what I think it is?

Is it Chelsea?

Devon nudges the coat with the tip of the shovel. "Should we dig it up?"

My first impulse is that we should go straight to the police. But with what? A photo of the coat on a phone?

Assuming we could convince them to come out here, something they weren't too enthusiastic about before, what if it is just a piece of blue fabric?

I'll look foolish.

There's only one solution. "We have to see what's under there."

Devon begins to reach down to grab the coat. I clutch his wrist to stop him. "Hold up." I'd done that more than once in the field or the lab when a careless student let their excitement get the better of them.

I take out a pair of latex gloves from my day pack and slip them on. I keep them around for dealing with specimens that could do me harm, or that I could kill through my touch.

I squat down and carefully grab the coat. If I had the proper tools, it would be better if we removed more dirt before pulling it free, in case it falls apart.

I slowly lift the fabric, and it begins to slide out of the dirt. It resists for a moment, and I get a nauseated feeling at the realization Chelsea could still be wearing it.

Gently, I pull back the coat a little more. A pungent odor wafts through the air.

Devon makes a choking noise as he turns away. Amber covers her mouth and steps back but doesn't take her eyes off the hole.

I've encountered lots of dead things in the field, but this is probably the worst smell I've ever encountered.

I pull my shirt over my mouth and nose and lift the coat entirely free of the earth. It's in tatters.

At first I think it's just decomposing; then I notice five long gouges in the fabric.

Setting it aside, there's something marble white underneath.

Using two fingers like a trowel, I scoop away the dirt and reveal a forearm, wrist, and fingers.

"Fuck," Devon whispers.

I stare at the arm in silence, not sure what I'm supposed to do now. Keep digging? Confirm that it's Chelsea? Make sure it's not some elaborate prank?

No. This is proof enough. It has to be her.

My doubts seem silly to myself on one level, because what else could it be? But on another, a voice is telling me this can't be real. It refuses to believe.

The excitement of being right is obliterated by the fact that things are so much darker than I could imagine.

"Hand me the shovel," I say to Devon.

"Are you going to dig her out?" he asks.

"No. We're going to cover her back up." I take a garbage bag from my pack and lay it over the body, then start heaping dirt on it.

"Why are you burying her?" Amber asks through tears.

"Because we have to let the police do it. This is a crime scene."

"Yes, but why are you burying her?"

"So the animals don't get her," Devon explains.

"We'll put her coat in a bag and take it with us. But we have to protect this for now."

Amber wipes her nose on the sleeve of her jacket. "Should we call 911?"

"We should drive Amber's coat there," says Devon. "Get Charlie to meet us at the station. It'll be easier than explaining on the phone."

I put the dirt back in place and drag a log over the grave. "This is to make it easier to mark and make it harder for any scavengers to find the body."

Chelsea's made it this long without being dug up, but now that we've disturbed the body and the scent of decaying flesh is spreading throughout the forest like blood in the water, animals from all around know there's something here.

The light has begun to fade, and we're less than an hour away from full darkness.

"I think I'm going to be sick," says Amber.

I feel the same way. "You guys go back to the car. I'll be there in a second, after I bag the coat."

Devon gives me a nod, then escorts her up the hill.

After they're out of sight, I bag the jacket, then grab the log they saw me put over the grave and drag it ten yards down the gully.

Considering the inauspicious circumstances under which we met, I don't trust them. I have no reason to think they'd do something to the body, especially since police should be here within the hour, but the scientist in me is telling me to take extra precautions.

When I return to the Explorer, Amber is in Devon's arms.

"Can we drop her off at home?" he asks. "I'll get my pickup and meet you at the police station."

It's a legitimate request, but I feel better for having moved the log. "Of course."

The drive back to their house is quiet. Amber cries softly in the back seat, dealing with the realization that her friend is truly dead.

Devon shakes his head and mumbles under his breath, "Holy shit. Holy shit."

CHAPTER THIRTY-EIGHT
Informant

The Hudson Creek police station parking lot is almost empty at this time of night. There are a half dozen parked police vehicles and two civilian cars. The lobby is brightly lit behind glass doors.

I grab the garbage bag containing what I presume is Chelsea's coat and walk toward the building.

So much has happened in the last few days. From being suspected of Juniper's murder, to the ridicule I received in the conference room at the Filmount County Sheriff's Department, it's been a strange trip.

Thankfully, with the evidence they'll hopefully find at Chelsea's burial site, they'll be able to build a case and find justice for Juniper.

I get a guilty pleasure at the thought of Sheriff Tyson realizing her mistake and Detective Glenn having to admit that he judged me wrong.

I have to remind myself this isn't some professional dispute in a journal over the results of a research paper. Two girls were murdered, and maybe many, many more.

My goal is simply truth. I have to take my ego out of this.

I step inside the police station, and the desk sergeant looks up at me. She's in her midthirties, thick farm-gal build, and could probably easily take me in a fight. There are two other uniformed cops sitting behind her, engaged in conversation. One of them has his feet up on a desk.

"How may I help you?" she asks in a no-nonsense tone.

I can only imagine the crazies she deals with at night.

I read her name badge. "Sergeant Palmer, I'd like to report a lead in Chelsea Buchorn's disappearance."

She scrutinizes me for a moment. Probably noticing the bruise on my face. "Buchorn? Didn't she move away?" As she says this, she picks up a clipboard and flips through it. "Ah, here we go. I didn't realize this was categorized as a missing person." She sets it down. "And you say you have evidence about an abduction?"

I set the garbage bag on the counter. "I think she was murdered."

Palmer eyes the bag and places her hand near her sidearm at her waist. "I'm going to have to ask you to step back from the counter."

I move back. "Sorry. I know this looks weird."

"Just have a seat on the bench over there." She points to a wall across from the long desk, then calls to the two policemen talking leisurely in the corner. "McKenna, Gunther, you guys want to step over here?"

They see Palmer's posture and hop out of their seats to see what's going on. The one with McKenna on his name badge is tall with a thick black mustache. Gunther is shorter and stockier with red hair.

"What's up?" asks McKenna, shooting a suspicious glance toward me.

"This fella says he knows something about the Chelsea Buchorn disappearance."

"I thought she just moved away," replies Gunther.

"That's what I said." She holds up the clipboard for them to look at.

McKenna takes it from her and reads it over. "I guess state police put her on there." He shakes his head. "They need to update this."

"What do you think you know?" Gunther asks me.

"I found her body."

McKenna lowers the clipboard. "Come again?"

"Her body. I believe I found it." I nod to the garbage bag. "I think that's her coat."

Gunther moves over to the bag. "When you say you found her body, do you mean you found something you think belonged to her and think her body is nearby?"

As he says this, he begins to open the bag and releases the putrid stench of decaying flesh.

"Oh, shit!" Gunther says.

McKenna pulls a pair of blue gloves from a pocket. He grabs the coat and pulls it free of the bag.

In the stark white light of the police station, I notice what I thought was dirt is the dark reddish-brown stain of blood.

Gunther eyes the slashes in the coat. "Holy shit."

McKenna puts the coat back in the bag. "Where'd you find this?"

"Off Highway 90. I have a GPS position."

McKenna ties the top of the bag in a knot. "Carole, call Steve Whitmyer. Get him up here."

She picks up the phone.

"Gunny, get a map and have Mister . . . what's your name?"

"Theo Cray. Professor Theo Cray." I added my title in an effort to not sound like a crackpot but end up looking like an ass.

"Well, Professor, could you write down on the map where you found the body?"

Gunther motions me over to a desk. He digs around through a drawer, then pulls out a map. "So how did you find this body?" he asks as he finds me a pen. His face seems to have lost its color.

"I was looking for it."

"Looking for it? How long've you been searching?"

"Maybe an hour?" I'm searching the map.

"An hour? That's pretty good luck . . ."

"I'll say. But I had a good idea where to look." I tap the spot on the map. "I also had Amber Harrison and her boyfriend Devon helping me."

Gunther doesn't say anything for a moment. "Huh. Well, mark it on the map." He slides a notepad next to the map. "Use this to make any notes."

I circle the area and start writing down the specifics about the log and how to find the body.

Gunther walks away to talk to McKenna and Palmer. I use Google Maps to check the location against the map they gave me.

Over my shoulder I notice the three of them are having a small conference, their voices too low for me to hear.

Amber and Devon should be here by now. They also said they were going to have their friend Charlie, the police chief's son, meet us.

I send Amber a text.

Where are you guys?

I go back to my notes about the body. When I finish, McKenna is standing over me. "Is that it?"

"Yes. I'd be happy to go there and show you."

"If we can't find it, we'll bring you out there. In the meantime, I'd like you to tell Officer Gunther everything you know. We have a conference room over here."

Gunther walks me down the hall, and I have a strange déjà vu about the first time I was pulled into a room to talk to a police officer.

He thought I was a murderer.

The way Gunther keeps a careful distance and watchful eye on me, I don't feel like I'm being treated merely as a concerned citizen.

There's still no response from Amber and Devon.

CHAPTER THIRTY-NINE

ACCESSORIES

The so-called conference room looks strangely like an interrogation room.

There's a video camera in the corner, just like the last one I was in. Gunther unlocks a cabinet and flips a few switches. The red light blinks to life.

"I'm bad at taking notes," he explains, nodding to the camera. "This is just so we can understand, in your words, how you found the body."

He's trying to be friendly but comes across as patronizing. There's also something distant about him. He doesn't possess Detective Glenn's smooth ability to glide you through a conversation.

"First off," he asks, "how'd you get that shiner?" He points a pen toward my face.

"It's a long story." I'm not sure now is the time to try to explain a case of mistaken identity that started off with two meth heads thinking I was looking to hire a hooker.

Two meth heads who still haven't texted me back . . .

I get a sinking feeling at the thought that Devon and Amber are back in their house getting wasted. Christ, that's all I need.

"We've got some time. McKenna is waiting on Detective Whitmyer before they head out."

"I fell," I reply. It's not the entire truth, but I definitely remember falling when I was getting my ass kicked.

"You fell?" He makes a note on a piece of paper. "That's the kind of thing wives tell me when their drunk husbands abuse them."

I'm trying to find a way to change the topic, but Gunther thankfully drops the matter and moves on.

"What makes you sure you've found a body?"

"Oh . . . I forgot." I pull my phone out of my pocket and pull up the photo I took. "Here . . ."

Gunther takes it from me and stares at the image of the pale white hand. "You took this?"

"Less than an hour ago. Right where I said."

"Hold on." He gets up and leaves the room with my phone.

I'm normally nervous enough when it's out of my sight. Having it in the hands of some suspicious cops in a corrupt police department while I've found myself pulled into not one but two murder investigations makes me extremely anxious.

What happens if Amber and Devon text back while they have my phone? Can the police look through anything they want, since I basically just handed it to them?

Even if they can't legally, that doesn't mean they won't.

Although Detective Glenn and company seized my phone and laptop, they never asked me for a password.

There's nothing incriminating on there. Maybe some personally embarrassing e-mails and a web-browsing history you'd expect from a lonely guy on the road. Nothing weird. Nothing worth passing around.

I'm tempted to get up and go find my phone. I relax when I feel something in my pocket. My personal phone.

I'd taken the photo with the burner I bought at the 88. There's not much on there . . .

That's not quite true. The only thing on there is my conversations with Amber. But I've already told them about her and Devon.

Maybe the burner is suspicious, but it can't be any more incriminating than anything I'm ready to say.

Gunther walks back in the room and hands me my phone back. It's still on the photo of the corpse.

Not that it would be difficult to look through everything else, then go back to that image.

He slides a business card to me. "E-mail the photo and anything else you have to this address."

He waits until I finish sending the image. "That certainly looks like a body."

"You get many people making that kind of thing up?"

"You'd be surprised," he says flatly. There's something about the way he's watching me, almost defensively. "So how did you find the body?"

"Like I said, I was looking for Chelsea."

He makes a note. "Did you know Chelsea?"

"No. Never met her."

"Did you just read something online? Do you work for some kind of missing-persons agency?"

"No. I teach bioinformatics. I use computers in biology."

"I didn't realize that was special. I thought everyone uses computers."

I can't tell if he's just being an ass or not. "Well, we use special simulations and processes to understand certain things. This is how I found Chelsea, or rather the body I believe to be hers."

"A computer told you?"

I'm not prepared to go into how MAAT works. "Sort of."

"A computer told you where she was buried?" He can't hide his skepticism.

"No. No. Not quite." I'm starting to get agitated. "The computer, I mean the program, told me that Hudson Creek would be a highly probable place for the murder of a young woman."

Gunther says nothing. He just waits for me to fill in the rest.

"I entered into my computer all of the missing-persons reports and looked for ones that may have been potential murders. This one, Chelsea's, was the closest."

"Closest to where you live?"

"No. I'm from Austin. I was in Filmount."

"Filmount? Where the girl got killed by a bear?"

"Yes. She was a student of mine. And I don't think it was a bear. That's why I came here."

"Because you think a man killed these girls? One of them you know personally?"

"Yes. Exactly."

"Give me a second. Let me see if Whitmyer is here." He leaves the room again.

I check my phone for anything from Amber and Devon. Still no response. I text them again.

It's going to look bad if my two witnesses are high as a kite when they show up.

I start to get more anxious. What if they're avoiding me?

My biggest fear at the moment is that Chelsea's body won't be there. It's nerve-racking to leave your most important piece of evidence out in the open like that.

I can't imagine why Devon or Amber would want to hide her corpse. Although I did hide the location because I didn't trust them.

Gunther comes back in with two cups of coffee. "Whitmyer—he's the acting chief—he just left to go look for your body." He notices the phone in my hand. "Any word from Devon and Amber?"

"I'm trying."

"Those two aren't the most reliable. We'll send someone by their house."

I pray they're not wasted.

"So a computer program told you where to find the body? Man, is that an app or something? I'd love to have that."

He thinks I'm batshit crazy.

I don't blame him. I stop and think about what I've been saying. I'm surprised I'm not in handcuffs already.

I have to clarify some things before that happens. "Amber showed me where she last saw Chelsea. We did a search around the area for signs of a burial."

"Like a marker?"

"No, though that would have been helpful. What we looked for was different plants growing together. It's a sign that the soil has been recently disturbed. Plants create their own herbicides to fight for resources. Eventually one takes over a small plot of land."

"I don't think they taught me that in academy."

"Well, if one of your instructors was a botany professor who was a Nobel Prize winner teaching postdocs at MIT, then it might have come up." And I think I just won the contest between us of who can be the smuggest dick.

"Nope. They just taught us how to pepper spray suspects and choke them with our nightsticks without leaving any bruises."

There's no humor in his voice, just ice.

I remind myself that two of his fellow officers are in jail, his chief is a suspect in a meth ring, and people around here think they might be "disappearing" people.

I force a laugh, desperate to diffuse the tension. "Then let me stay on your good side. I'm just here because I'm trying to do the right thing."

Gunther doesn't flinch. He just stares at me.

Shit.

There's a knock at the door that makes me jump.

Palmer pokes her head inside. "Lawson just went by Amber and Devon's place. Neither of them are there."

"What about Charlie?" I ask. "Anybody call him?"

"McKenna did. Charlie says he hasn't heard from them all day." She studies me for a moment, then leaves.

Damn. Amber and Devon are the only two who can corroborate how we found the body. Now they've taken off.

Undoubtedly, they're nervous about all the attention this is going to bring to them.

"Tell me how you got your black eye." Gunther doesn't ask, he demands.

CHAPTER FORTY

PROBABILITY

Turns out Officer Gunther is a bully. I've met his type before. My policy has always been to avoid conflict and give them what they want.

Telling him how I got the black eye could make things bad for Devon and Amber. I'm bitter about what happened and still feel the pain, but I pity them.

There's also the complicating factor of explaining why I went to meet a known prostitute in the shadiest situation you can imagine. If I heard the story secondhand, I wouldn't believe my story. Sure, the single professor just wanted to meet the young girl in the abandoned building to talk . . .

I have to draw the line with Gunther. My knee is shaking at a frantic tempo. It takes all my effort to keep it from spreading.

"How did you get the bruise?" he asks again.

"I'm not here to talk about that," I say feebly.

"You're here to talk about whatever I ask you."

I look up at the camera facing down on me. "I think I want to speak to an attorney now."

"You haven't been accused of anything."

I think about the fact that someone else will see this video. "I'm happy to talk to someone else. Just not you."

His face flashes with anger. To anyone watching this, I've professionally embarrassed him. He was hoping to get me to say something that would implicate me in some way. I was talkative. Now I'm not, because he's an asshole.

Gunther pushes himself away from the table, knocking it hard enough to bump into me.

If he's a cop they didn't arrest, I'd hate to meet the ones they did.

He stands up and leans on the surface. "You think you're so fucking smart?" His hand goes into his pocket and pulls out a key ring.

It's the key he used to start the video camera recording.

Shit. He's walking back to the cabinet with the VCR. "Everyone saw you come in here all bruised up."

Fuck. Fuck. Fuck.

There's a knock. Gunther jerks his head toward the door, pissed about the interruption. "What?"

Palmer speaks through the doorway. "Whitmyer wants you on the scene."

"What the fuck? I'm talking to the witness."

She motions for him to step into the hall. He goes, reluctantly, glaring at me every step of the way.

The door is open a crack. I hear her whisper.

". . . he says they found a body."

"Then I should be getting him to talk," Gunther growls.

"Whitmyer said specifically for you to leave him be."

"Fuck," he barks, followed by the sound of a fist hitting a wall.

I hear him stomp away.

Palmer steps inside. "Are you okay? Can I get you anything?" She's polite and sweet. The contrast is jarring.

I don't know the politics of this place, so I'm afraid to say anything, but I can't help it. "Do I have to talk to him again?"

She steals a glance down the hall, then turns back. "We've all been under a lot of pressure lately."

"I've heard."

She lowers her voice. "Chelsea was his cousin."

Holy shit. Those four little words change the context of everything that just happened. Gunther is still an asshole and a bully, but I understand him a little more. I think.

Palmer motions for me to follow her. "Let's go back up front. I have to watch the station. Everyone is out at the scene."

I take a seat next to a desk filled with mug books.

"Whitmyer says he's bringing in state forensics in the morning. Right now they're trying to lock down the scene."

"Is it her? Chelsea?"

"I don't know. I doubt they've even attempted to disturb the grave any more than necessary. They'll want a forensics team to come do a thorough excavation."

That makes sense. I'm used to the Hollywood notion that every police station has a whole forensic department ready at all hours of the day.

"So you're some kind of bear expert?" she asks.

"No. I'm a biologist, but bears aren't my specialty." Not even close.

"Oh. I'm sure you explained it to Gunny, but how did you know where to look?"

"Amber's account and looking for some unusual vegetation."

"Oh." She blinks at me, then drops the topic and goes back to her work. I don't have the nerve to ask what happens next, so I just sit there.

About an hour later a clean-cut man in his early forties wearing a thick coat comes walking into the station.

He nods to Palmer, then addresses me. "I'm Whitmyer, the acting police chief. Are you the gentleman who found the body?"

I stand up. "Yes, sir."

"Good work. Gunny told me that you're a biologist and you looked for some special plants that grow over bodies."

Christ already. I should just write a book on the subject. "Basically," I say, too tired to explain.

He walks over and shakes my hand. "Well, thank you. We haven't confirmed it's Chelsea yet. But I'm guessing it is." He nods to the garbage bag on the counter containing her coat. "This hers?"

"Yes."

He throws a glance at Palmer. "Did anyone think to put this in evidence?"

"Sorry. McKenna just left it."

Whitmyer takes a pair of gloves from his pocket and slides a mask over his face. He was probably using them at the burial scene.

He carefully unties McKenna's knot and peers inside, then quickly seals it back up. "Carole, can you see to it that this gets locked up?"

Palmer takes the bag down the hall.

"Looks like Amber and Devon skipped out," he says.

"Why would they do that?"

Whitmyer points to my bruised face. "Devon?"

"It was a miscommunication. I wanted to talk to Amber about what happened to Chelsea. They thought it was something else."

He gives me a knowing nod. "Do you want to press charges?"

"No. I'm just here to find out what happened to Chelsea and the connection to Juniper Parsons."

"The girl that was killed in Filmount? Bear, right?"

"I don't think so. That's why I came here."

"Well, we'll let the state police do the forensics on that. Where are you staying?"

"The Creekside Inn."

"Gus's place? He's a good guy. Are you going to be here tomorrow?"

"Yes. I have to get back to Austin at some point. But I can stick around a few more days."

"All right. We'll get a formal statement tomorrow. In the meantime, go get some rest."

Whitmyer's calm and professional demeanor is a relief. A sane voice in all this insanity.

He walks me to the front door. "Thank you again. I've got to get on the horn to Sheriff Tyson and find out what she knows." He pauses. "Did you speak to her back in Filmount?"

Cold water runs through my veins at the thought. "Yeah . . . they weren't too interested in what I had to say."

"I'm sure this will pique their interest."

I get the feeling that could be a bad thing.

CHAPTER FORTY-ONE

STASIS

There's a knock on my motel room door at 11 a.m. I didn't sleep much, even as exhausted as I am. I spent part of the night gathering all of my notes and putting everything together on a thumb drive for the investigators.

I treated it like a report for a science journal. I want them to have a clear understanding of my thought process and the sequence of events that led to discovering Chelsea's body—this could be vital to my freedom.

I also put in some data generated by MAAT and instructions on how to use the online version on my web server. I'm sure the FBI and other agencies have better, more specific tools, but local ones like Hudson Creek may not have access to them.

Along with how I found Chelsea, I put together all of the information on the pattern of the killer.

In the hands of someone who knows more about criminal investigation and forensics than myself, it should be a good start.

I'm just one man, and I found another victim in a day. With the involvement of real law enforcement agencies, they could catch this guy before I make it back to Austin.

There are two e-mail messages asking why I missed faculty meetings. I type brief replies, stating that I've been helping with a law enforcement investigation.

It feels good to type those words. Chasing frogs and strange attractors is one thing, but fighting crime, making a difference, that's something else.

I made a list of all the things they should look for in Chelsea's body. Despite conventional wisdom, stainless steel can be a hotbed of bacteria. Forensic technicians should try growing bacteria taken from Chelsea's and Juniper's wounds as well as baseline samples from the surrounding soil.

If they find a culture common to the wounds but not to the soil or the unpunctured parts of their bodies, it's an indicator that the killer used the same weapon. Once they find the suspect, testing any sharp objects for the same bacteria would put him in both places.

I put together a section detailing the laboratory procedures I'd use to get a statistically significant result. I also explain how they could use DNA markers from the bacterial culture to identify it beyond just a species.

Maybe with some of their data I could use MAAT to make more specific predictions for other clients?

That could be an interesting project. The next time I speak with Julian I'll put the bug in his ear. He'd probably love that kind of thing.

I get out of bed and answer the door. There's a police officer standing there. A young man with a badge that says Wojtczak.

"Professor Cray?"

I nod and wipe the sleep out of my eyes.

"I've been asked to follow you over to the police station. They want to get your formal statement."

"Okay. Let me get a couple things."

He waits patiently while I get dressed and gather up my notes.

"So you're the guy that found the body? I heard you discovered some kind of plant that only grows on dead people."

Ugh, the grapevine. "It's not quite that simple." I sling my backpack over my shoulder. "Any word if they've tracked down Devon and Amber?"

"Not yet."

"Have they exhumed the body yet?"

"Not that I know of. State police forensics were all over it this morning. They got there early. I think the head medical examiner was doing an on-site examination."

I'm glad they're proceeding carefully. Chelsea's burial site could yield lots of interesting data points.

We arrive at the station, and I'm led to a conference room significantly larger than the one Gunther interrogated me in last night.

I freeze in the doorway when I see Sheriff Tyson sitting at the far end of the table next to Detective Glenn.

The scene sets off a painful flashback. Of course they should be here, but the stress from our last interaction still haunts me.

Glenn looks up at me. "What happened to your eye, Professor?" His tone is cordial.

"Long story."

I'm given a spot to sit at the other end of the table.

Whitmyer enters the room wearing a polo with the Hudson Creek Police logo. His boots are muddy. He's probably been out there since this morning.

"Professor Cray." He shakes my hand.

"Is it her?" I ask.

He gives Tyson a glance. She nods back. I guess they have some kind of arrangement for how the case is going to be handled. I'm glad to see them working well together.

"It is, Professor. It's Chelsea Buchorn. Now, since everyone is here, I'd like you to take us through the series of events that led you here." He gestures to my black eye. "I wouldn't leave anything out. This is about Chelsea and Juniper."

I explain to them everything I said to Gunther. I give them an overview of MAAT and how it led me to Hudson Creek. I explain precisely how we found the body and give them some references in case they want to check up on them.

It's exhausting. They interrupt me a few times for details, but there's no finger-pointing. There's no accusations.

When I finish, I set the thumb drive on the table. "It's all here. How to find the next one, I think."

All through this, Sheriff Tyson watched me carefully. She let Glenn ask the questions. Occasionally she pointed to something on a list, but she never spoke.

When she finally does, it startles me.

"Professor Cray, I want to apologize for how we treated you. It was obvious you were under a lot of stress dealing with the death of a friend. We should have listened to what you had to say."

I'm beside myself. My tongue fumbles for words. "Thank you."

Detective Glenn stands up. "I respect your perseverance." He begins to applaud.

The entire room starts clapping. It's a surreal moment. I feel myself welling up. "I just wish Juniper didn't have to die. Or Chelsea."

Whitmyer picks up the thumb drive and plants a firm hand on my shoulder. "I'm going to make sure Fish and Wildlife gets a copy of this."

"Great. Great," I reply before it sinks in. "Wait? Fish and Wildlife? What about the law enforcement agencies?" I look around the room, confused.

"I know this is stressful for you," Whitmyer says. "I spoke with Sheriff Tyson and Detective Glenn about the prior incident. Grieving is hard to deal with.

"We're happy to find you some help. We have a few counselors out here. Good ones."

I search their faces for an explanation. "What about the murder investigation? What about getting the killer?"

Whitmyer exchanges glances with Tyson and Glenn. "Theo, I know you don't want to accept this. But it was a bear. Just like Juniper. Dr. Wilson, the chief medical examiner for the state, is returning with the body right now. He says all of the wounds are consistent with a bear attack."

"But she was buried . . ." My voice begins to rise.

"Bears do that," says Glenn. "And she was out there a long time. You pointed out yourself how erosion would help conceal the body."

I'm having another flashback to the last time I was in this situation. Getting excited only put me in a jail cell.

From the way Tyson is watching me, I can tell she's counting down the seconds until I lash out.

I want to flip the fucking table over and scream. I don't.

I stay calm.

"What about Amber Harrison's statement?"

"I took her initial one," says Whitmyer. "She was as high as a kite. And she mentioned the possibility of a bear."

"She's convinced that it's a man now," I reply, trying to keep the edge off my words.

"Maybe so. But a statement made now, if we could find her, wouldn't carry much weight. How reliable are memories the farther out you get?"

Not very. I just nod my head. "But they're going to do a full forensics examination?"

"Absolutely." He gives me a smile.

"And the data I collected?"

"I'll look it over myself. But just listen to me. Fish and Wildlife might get a lot out of this. So don't throw that out."

"Okay," I say softly. "May I leave?"

Whitmyer escorts me to the lobby. "I want to shake your hand. Thank you."

"You're welcome."

"Long ride back. Are you leaving today?"

"If you don't need anything else," I answer quietly.

"I'm sure we'll be talking a lot on the phone."

I say goodbye and step outside. I can feel his eyes on me as he watches the sad Professor Don Quixote walk away.

There's nothing left for me to do.

I tried.

I really tried.

Time to go home.

A van pulls into the parking lot. It's marked **Montana State Medical Examiner.**

Inside is Chelsea's body.

I shouldn't care. But I do. I should be leaving. But I don't.

CHAPTER FORTY-TWO

RESURRECTIONIST

Science is filled with people who had to step outside what was considered socially acceptable. Roman physician Galen and Renaissance genius Leonardo da Vinci were forced to exhume bodies to better understand how they functioned. Because of this transgression, both men saved countless lives with their discoveries.

I tell myself I'm trying to save lives and this isn't just a matter of proving that I'm right. There's a killer out there, and the room full of people I just left can't see the obvious.

I have to psych myself up for this. If I think about it too much, nothing will happen.

Stepping behind an SUV, I observe two men in medical examiner jumpsuits exit the van and enter the police station's rear entrance.

If it had been any other kind of van, I never would have considered this. If her body was locked away in a morgue somewhere, it would be as far away from me psychologically as the surface of Mars.

But the van I'm staring at is a Dodge Sprinter. The same type used as an ambulance. When I worked as an EMT, the Sprinter was as familiar to me as my office.

It's the familiarity that makes me feel like this isn't a trespass. There's also the fact that I could have taken samples from Chelsea's body when we found her.

I didn't, because I thought investigators would do a more thorough job of tracking down her murderer. I was wrong.

I wouldn't know how to pick a lock if you put a gun to my head. Luckily, all of the Sprinter ambulances I worked with had a secret switch for unlocking them in the event you lose your keys while responding to a call.

A lockout could cost lives.

It doesn't start the vehicle. It just opens the doors. All of them.

On mine, the switch was in front of the driver's side front wheel.

I make sure nobody is around, then step over to the vehicle and reach down and feel for the button.

Nothing.

I try the same spot on the passenger side. My fingers touch something rubbery. I press it.

Click.

My skin tingles. Adrenaline floods my body. It's the sensation of solving a complicated puzzle.

I move to the back of the van and try the door. The handle lifts and opens.

An indescribable feeling of anxiety crashes over me. I tell myself not to hesitate and just do what I need to do.

I slip inside and carefully close the door behind me.

Gripping my penlight in my teeth, I slip on a pair of rubber gloves.

The body bag takes up half the van. From the shape under the black rubber, it's obvious rictus set in with her limbs in an awkward position.

Now is not the time for me to analyze the agony she went through.

I've done dozens of dissections in school. This should be no different—except for the degree of decay.

My day pack has sample vials, but I forgot to pack a mask. Ugh. This is going to be unpleasant.

No time to dwell on that oversight. I slide back the zipper.

The smell is overpowering. I try to avoid breathing.

Where it's not covered by blood and dirt, Chelsea's corpse is as white as chalk.

Finding a wound isn't difficult. There are so many of them.

Her body is riddled with slashes, like stripes on a tiger.

I understand why they think this is an animal attack. It's so vicious. Her head is nearly torn off.

In the face of this, I'm beginning to have my own doubts.

There's no time for that. I have to remind myself that science led me here. No matter what I think I see, there are more precise tools to understand what happened.

I fill a few small vials with thickened blood and tissue from three different wounds: one on the neck, another on her arm, and one from a gouge just below her left breast that ripped open her shirt.

Looking at the tracks in some of the wounds, I can see where the medical examiner also made collections.

If I want to do my bacterial experiment, I'll need a sample from Chelsea's skin in a location where she wasn't wounded.

Underneath her jeans, where one of the elastic bands for her underwear is still tight, I'm able to make a dirt-free swab.

This should be enough. At some point I'll need to get some samples from the burial site. It's probably swarming with police right now.

That can wait a few days.

A few days . . .

I have to be back in Austin.

Maybe if I drive out here after class and return Sunday night?

This isn't the time or place to go over my academic calendar.

I shove the containers into my pocket, then carefully zip up the bag.

Just like that, she's back inside her pouch. I doubt that even if the ME knew someone else had taken samples, he could tell you where.

My gloves are covered in dirt and dried blood, so I peel them off inside out and pocket them.

When I put my ear to the door to listen for anyone, it's silent.

I have a moment of panic when I can't find the latch to open the door. What if this van can't open from the inside?

My fingers grasp a handle, and I feel a wave of relief. The thought of being stuck back here with this stench all the way to Helena is frightful.

Slowly, I lift the handle and ease the door open just wide enough for my body to slip through.

I set one foot on the pavement and sense something is wrong.

Over the odor of Chelsea's rotting flesh, I smell smoke.

When I turn around, I see Officer Gunther toss aside a cigarette and glare at me. "What. The. Fuck." His hand goes to his gun. "On the ground, now!" he screams.

Fuck. Fuck. Fuck.

CHAPTER FORTY-THREE

FALL GUY

Human psychology is a concept I can grasp in the abstract, usually after a given moment has passed, but there's something about the anger in Gunther's eyes and the primal way his nostrils are flaring that tells me that he's furious with me—and not just because he caught me trespassing. There's some kind of connection between him and Chelsea beyond being cousins. I violated that.

I also realize that in a few moments I'm going to be on the ground, handcuffed and facing felony charges for tampering with evidence, as well as whatever this state's laws are concerning stealing material from a corpse.

My little inquiry, finding out what happened to Juniper, my life—all of that is going to take a detour if I don't find a way out of this situation.

I remain standing and try my first option. "I just wanted to take a look at the wounds."

"On the fucking ground." His words come out like white-hot metal spittle.

He draws his pistol and aims it right at my face. I'm one centimeter away from a trigger being pulled and a bullet shooting through my forehead, puncturing my skull and leaving a two-inch exit circle in the back of my head, spraying my brains behind me.

"I can find out who did this . . ."

I notice that my hands are already up. Psychologically, this means that I've already committed to his authority. He caught me doing something wrong, and I physically admitted to it by taking on a subservient posture.

If I could have taken this back a few seconds, I would have smiled and not acted surprised when I saw him—instead of gaping at him in surprise, a startled, scared man giving off all the body language of guilt.

In a moment, if I don't fully submit, he's going to take a step forward and place the gun against my head as he uses his handcuffs to arrest me. He's trained not to shoot someone standing still—but someone resisting an arrest in any way that threatens his safety is fair game.

Usually when cops kill unarmed people, it's because they perceive some threat as they make physical contact, or they get scared and squeeze the trigger, not realizing how much pressure they're already placing on it.

Some cops carry guns with heavy triggers, like five or six pounds, in order to make it more difficult to accidentally fire. Gunther strikes me as a two-pound trigger. He's more than confident he'll know how to handle himself in a critical situation. The next few seconds may determine that.

I remain still as he walks around me, but I keep talking. "There's something unusual about the wounds. I think there's more here . . ."

He reaches up and grabs my right wrist and pulls it behind me. I don't resist, knowing I'll get the muzzle of his gun pushed into my kidney.

I try a different tactic, using his name and a shared goal.

"Gunther, we can solve this thing."

The handcuff squeezes tight around my wrist.

Damn it. He's not going to be talked into letting me go free out here. Gunther is fully committed. His fury is being channeled into what he was trained to do.

He grabs my left wrist and pulls it behind me. As he does this, he holsters his weapon, confident that he can draw it before I could theoretically take the upper hand physically.

Now is my time to act. What happens in the next few seconds is going to determine my fate.

The cuffs are tightened again until they dig into the flesh of my wrists. He places one hand on my shoulder and another on the chain and presses me flat against the back wall.

I have to go out on a limb here. I noticed something about Chelsea when I examined her and something about Gunther. They both have the same wide forehead and hair color. Faint, but present. The kind of trait you might see a lot at a family picnic.

Gunther's reaction is more than a genetic protection reaction.

It was an overreaction. It was shame.

My only way out is by going down.

"I know what you did."

He pauses for a half second as he pats me down.

"I won't tell anyone."

He stands up and hovers near the back of my head. I can feel his breath on my neck.

"What the fuck do you think you know?"

I don't have any reason to think he had anything to do with killing Chelsea—although I have a strong suspicion he knows he had something to do with why she became so vulnerable.

This is what I have to attack.

"I know she's your cousin."

He slaps a palm into my back, slamming me into the wall. "Keep your mouth shut."

This isn't a denial. His reaction is an admission that he's ashamed of his connection. If saying that caused this reaction, what I'm about to say is going to really get a response.

I brace myself, then say it . . .

"I know you fucked her."

Bam! He kicks the toe of his boot into the back of my knee, and I stumble. A fraction of a second later, he grabs my neck and trips me over his leg.

I hit the concrete on the side, and it hurts like hell. But this isn't enough. It's not nearly enough.

"You fucked your cousin and turned her into a whore."

"Shut the fuck up!" Bam! He lands a kick into the middle of my back.

I writhe in pain and see his bright-red face. There's a bulging vein on his forehead—the same forehead he shares with Chelsea.

I do some quick math.

"How old was your cousin when you fucked her? Fourteen? Fifteen?"

"You think you're funny?" He reaches down and slaps me in the face. The impact is so hard I can feel it in my jaw.

But it's still not enough.

I fake a smile and grin up at him, giving him a target for his fury.

"I mean, was it mainly the charge of fucking a family member, or do you just like fucking little girls?"

The first punch to my head makes me see purple and red.

The second makes my neck give way, and I crack my skull on the pavement.

My last beating was from amateurs. This one is from a trained sadist.

The next blow is so hard I don't even feel it when I pass out.

CHAPTER FORTY-FOUR

Inpatient

I know I'm in a hospital. When, where, and why are a mystery to me. A female doctor with chestnut-colored hair, pink glasses, and faint wrinkles on a tan face is shining a light in my eyes.

She's got a pretty face, but she elicits a feeling of vulnerability from me that's stronger than any sense of attraction. I want her to mother me, which I suspect she's been doing.

"Theo? Are you awake?"

She says something else to me, but my face erupts into an explosion of pain as I try to speak.

"Don't say anything. We have your jaw wired shut."

I glance down at my wrists to see if either of them is chained to the bed.

They're not.

This doesn't mean that I'm not under arrest, but their presence would have been absolute confirmation that I was.

I look around the room, trying to see where I am.

"This is Blue Lake Hospital," the doctor says. "You've been here two days. You're lucky Officer Gunther found you. He'll be coming by later to get a statement about the men who attacked you."

So that's the story, and Gunther will be coming by to make sure that I stick to it.

I have no memory of what happened after that last punch, but I can imagine.

Gunther probably uncuffed me and put me in his squad car and drove me to this hospital. I'd be willing to bet it's not the closest one to the police station.

This is the situation I was trying to create. Had he arrested me, I would have been seriously screwed and facing jail time. However, I wasn't expecting the beating to be so savage.

The one I got at the hands of Devon and company was just meant to scare an out-of-towner. Officer Gunther's beatdown on me was pure fury. It was primal.

For a brief second I got a glimpse of what Juniper and Chelsea saw in their last moments—except I suspect theirs was far more terrifying. Mine was just brutal.

"Just nod if you feel alert enough for me to tell you what's going on."

I give her a nod. She moves a chair close to the bed and has a seat. Her name tag says Dr. Talbot.

"You had a dislocated jaw. It popped back in pretty easily. Nothing is fractured. But I want to keep it stabilized for another day. It'll be swollen for a few more, and I don't recommend you eat any monster-size hoagies for a month. Understand?"

I nod again.

"You've got a costal cartilage fracture. That will hurt for a while but should take care of itself. Your face is pretty banged up, but your looks should come back. If you had any to begin with. If not, now is a good time to think about that nose job." She gives me a smile. "So, the prognosis is nothing permanent. But you're going to be sore for a while. I'll give you some pain meds for the short term. We'll see how you do in a few days. I recommend ibuprofen or beer after that."

I hold my hand in front of my face and tap the palm.

"You want a mirror? Think you can handle it?"

I nod. She pulls a small hand mirror from the drawer in my bedside table and holds it up to my face.

My cheeks are fleshy lumps of purple and yellow. There's a long blue line along my jaw surrounded by burst blood vessels.

As a paramedic I saw the results of a lot of beatings. You could almost deduce the incident by the kind of trauma inflicted. Bar fights had lots of eye injuries around the orbits and cracked ribs when the assailant had their victim on the ground and just took shots kicking at them—basically what happened to me when Amber's friends let loose.

In domestic violence calls, I'd often notice a lot of burst vessels around the face, as the attacker would slap their victim over and over. Slapping was some kind of punitive response, not defensive. It's meant to inflict pain, whereas a punch is intended to incapacitate.

After Gunther punched me, he started slapping me. I struck a deep personal chord within him. This wasn't just because I humiliated him over his sexual involvement with Chelsea; I touched on something else—impotent rage. He couldn't be there to protect her, a girl he helped make vulnerable. So instead, he diverted all that energy toward me. As I lay on the ground unconscious, and Gunther opened his fist to slap me, I don't think he saw my face. It could have been his own, or more perversely, Chelsea's.

Talbot pats me on the knee. "I'm going to let you get some more rest. If the swelling comes down, I might take the bandage off your head later on today. You're a pretty fast healer. Try to keep that up."

After she leaves, I stare at the curtains. Daylight trickles through swaying branches, creating a hypnotic pattern as the wind rocks them. Through a tiny slit I can see the snowcapped peak of a mountain in the distance.

I'm in a serene mental place because of all the painkillers. If I don't move my mouth, I can almost forget the trauma my body went through. Better enjoy it while I can. In the next few days, it's going to be excruciating.

And after that, then what?

CHAPTER FORTY-FIVE

DEPARTURES

I'm making notes on a yellow pad Talbot was kind enough to provide for me after she noticed I hadn't touched the remote for the television.

I've been thinking of a kind of equation, a simplistic version of MAAT. I found Chelsea's body fairly quickly once I understood how to narrow down the search area to find soil that had been recently disturbed. While I don't know how well the local flora would cooperate in other areas, this worked pretty well for this part of Montana.

The equation is more of a program, a kind of if/then decision tree. It starts with calculating the likelihood of there being a missing person who fits the vulnerable profile and comparing it to geographical information and population density. In theory, I could change some of the variables and apply it elsewhere. Instead of looking for vegetation variations, I might use topological data to calculate where a killer might decide is the most remote yet accessible location to hide a body. Forensics specialists will use methane probes to look for decomposing bodies. Another means might be to use sonar to look for soil density and thermal imaging at certain times of day. A body buried underground would lose heat differently than surrounding earth.

Another thought is to use lidar—lasers that map the 3-D landscape. Had I the opportunity, I would love to see if there was some kind of subtle indentation or outdent roughly the same size as a body. This could be statistically significant and provide another way to scan a large amount of area in a short time.

There's a knock on the door, and Dr. Talbot pokes her head in. "Good, you're up. Let's check on that mug of yours."

She sits on the edge of my bed and gently probes the contours of my face. I'm fascinated by her eyes. She's clearly making a clinical assessment, but there's obvious compassion there—not necessarily for me as a person, but for my body, for me as a patient.

"Let's see here. Blink if it hurts."

She traces her fingers down my jawline. There's a subtle pain, but nothing like yesterday. I don't blink.

"Good. I'm going to take these off."

She unwraps the bandage that has been holding my jaw clenched and sets it aside.

"Okay, slowly, open your mouth. Stop when you feel pain."

I get my teeth apart a fair distance before I feel something sharp in the back of my mouth. I stop there.

She measures the distance between my teeth with a small ruler. "Not the most scientific tool, but my dad was a vet and it worked for him. The good news is you can move from straw food to anything that fits on a spoon. I'll send you up some soup. Sound good?"

"Yes, ma'am," I reply in a scratchy voice.

"Let's get some liquids in you. In the meantime, we have a special visitor."

I look toward the door, hoping to see Jillian walk through. Instead Office Gunther enters.

My whole body trembles for a moment. I don't know if it's a high-level response or something from muscle memory. Either way, I feel my stomach knot up, and I grow cold.

"Look who it is, Theo. The man who rescued you." Talbot gives me a warm smile and a squeeze on my shoulder. "I bet you're glad to see him."

I glance up at Gunther and nod. "You have no idea."

"I'll leave you two to get to the bottom of this." She stands up and walks over to Gunther. "It's nice of you to check in on him."

"Yes, ma'am," he replies uneasily.

To be honest, I'm relieved to see that he didn't slip the lie on like a new pair of shoes. That would make me suspect that he's a sociopath. Instead, he just awkwardly accepts the praise, trying not to look at my bruised face.

He shuts the door behind her and takes a seat in the corner. Eyes toward the floor, slack posture. He doesn't want to stare at me and see the damage he's done to my face.

"You shouldn't have been in that van," he says after an uncomfortable silence.

Right now he's wrestling with what he did, trying to decide if he made the wrong choice in not arresting me.

"They're not going to find Chelsea's killer," I reply.

"How do you know?"

"I saw what happened with my friend Juniper. They'll do the same thing all over again."

Relieved that this conversation isn't going to be about what he did to me, he finally makes eye contact. "You don't know anything about me and Chelsea."

"I think you cared about her a great deal." I leave out that he's also very ashamed of what she became.

"I was like a brother to her. Her parents weren't around much, and I had to look out for her." He pauses. "When she got older . . ."

It's a small town. The number of available women is very limited. It's why first-cousin marriage is the norm in so many parts of the world—that, and it makes it easier to retain property in zero-sum societies.

"When I saw you coming out of the back of that van. What the fuck, man? And then when you opened your mouth and just wouldn't shut up. What the hell were you doing back there?"

"Looking for bacteria and hair samples."

"They do all that science shit in the state lab."

"Not like I can. They're twenty years behind the tools I have access to."

"Oh, yeah? How good are those tools of yours in court?"

"I don't give a damn about court right now. I want to find a killer."

"You're serious?"

"Serious enough to run my mouth so you'd kick my ass instead of me getting kicked out of the state and not being able to finish what I started."

He shakes his head. "I knew you were trying to piss me off."

"And I'm here instead of in jail."

"You still could be."

I point to my damaged face. "You could have said I was resisting arrest and maybe got away with it. But not now. You were my get-out-of-jail-free card."

"Maybe. Maybe not." He stands up. "I brought some of your things by. Your backpack is in the closet."

"Is this where you tell me to get out of town?"

"I don't give a fuck what you do. Just stay clear of me. There's something off about you."

No shit.

After he leaves, I muster the energy to get out of bed. While my strength is there, the pain medicine has my balance a little off. I think I'll skip the next round of pills and see how I manage.

I take my pack out of the closet to get my laptop. When I unzip the top, there's a plastic evidence bag sitting on top of my clothes.

Inside are the samples I took from Chelsea's body.

He left them for me.

CHAPTER FORTY-SIX

ACADEMIC

I close my eyes and ease my mouth open wide enough for the forkful of cherry pie. The back of my jaw feels like a metal grinder is attacking my nerve endings, but I endure long enough to get it into my mouth, then quickly retract the fork.

The crumb crust hits my tongue first, followed by the tart cherries, and then an avalanche of sweet whipped cream topples over everything as I swirl it around. The pain fades to a dull background roar as I focus on the taste.

When I open my eyes, Jillian has slid into the booth next to Gus. They're both giving me the same odd look.

"Would you like me to put that in a blender for you?" she asks.

"Maybe you'd prefer to be alone with that pie?" says Gus.

"Sorry. First solid food in days." I scoop up another piece. "It's delicious, Jillian."

"But it hurts to eat it."

"Only when I open my mouth. It's well worth it."

She reaches out and pats the back of my hand. "Then keep shoveling it in."

I notice her fingertips linger on my knuckles for a moment, then slide away, caressing the spaces between my fingers. I don't know if it was intentional, but it was certainly sensual while it lasted.

She takes a long look at my face. "I can't believe they haven't caught the animals that did that to you."

I'm extremely uncomfortable lying to her and Gus, but I don't want to start anything that's already over. "I'm sure it was a case of mistaken identity."

"Too bad you didn't get a good look at them."

"Yeah. Too bad."

I catch Gus taking a quick glance at Jillian, then turning back to me. "So, Dr. Cray, will we be seeing more of you at this table in the future?"

"I'm supposed to be back at school on Monday. Classes are starting."

"I bet you can't wait to get back," says Jillian.

"Yeah . . ." I use my fork to trace the cherry filling across my plate. It resembles the gashes I saw in Chelsea's body, and I no longer have my appetite. "But I've been thinking I shouldn't jump right back in just yet." I point to my swollen face. "I'm not sure if my students need to see this on their first day."

"Can you take time off like that?"

"Sure. It's just a freshman course. There are plenty of adjuncts that can handle that kind of thing."

This is far from the truth. I might be able to get my department head to sign off on an absence of a day or two if I get someone to cover it, but more than a week at the start of the semester is asking for a dismissal.

I'd been trying to figure out what I was going to do and my mouth just told me, more or less. Maybe it was the way Jillian asked. Maybe it's the image of Chelsea's corpse and the thought that Juniper's killer is still out there.

I'm going to have to notify the school I won't be there at the start of the semester. I catch a glimpse of my face in the reflection off the napkin holder and realize that Officer Gunther may have done me another favor.

Dr. Bacall, my boss at the college, is a big-city elitist who thinks the rest of the world is filled with backwoods, knuckle-dragging cavemen. All I have to do is drop her an e-mail explaining that I was attacked by some hillbilly out here and send her one of the photos I took in the hospital bed.

"So, Gus, do you think I might be able to rent that room out from you for another week or so?"

"We can work something out. I might have a discounted rate if you help me with a few things."

I catch a faint smile on Jillian's face. "Well. I've got some tables to check on. Glad to see you might stick around a little."

Gus watches her leave, then turns to me. "What are your plans for that situation?"

"Situation?"

"Do you need a microscope for everything? The girl likes you."

"Oh. She's great. But I'm not going to be around for that long."

He stares up at the ceiling and shakes his head. "You're the dumbest smart person I've ever met. That's part of why she likes you. You're a fling. Not a long-term romance. A happy convergence that lasts just long enough."

I look nervously over my shoulder to make sure she's not within earshot. "That's not why I'm here."

"Suit yourself. So why are you here?"

"To find out who killed Juniper and Chelsea."

"Is that all? A thousand law enforcement officers in this state and you're the one that's going to find the killer?"

"A thousand law enforcement officers in this state and not one of them even believes there's a killer. I'm starting to think maybe the murderer is not that hard to find once you know where to look."

"Then what?"

"What do you mean?"

"You find this killer. Then what happens? Do you arrest him? Do you go to the newspapers? Do you kill him?"

"Jesus. I'm not Batman. I . . . I don't know. I tell the police."

"The same police that think you're crazy and there's a killer-bear epidemic?"

"I don't know."

Gus stares at me, making me feel like a child. "This isn't a research paper. This doesn't end with a summary conclusion and a graph. You're talking about finding a killer and telling the world who that is. Along the way, you're going to be turning over some rocks that don't want to be moved. Look at your face."

"I'm not sure what you're talking—"

"Whatever. One of Chelsea's boyfriends come for you? Somebody get antsy when you told them you found the body?"

"What are you saying?"

"I told you that this place is a festering wound. You've had your ass kicked twice just for asking questions. What happens when you get closer?"

"I don't know."

"That's the problem, Theo. You only see what you're paying attention to. You're likely to trail bear tracks all the way back to the bear. Then what?"

"I'll just have to be careful."

"You've been piss-poor at that. You want my advice? You go flirt with Jillian. Take her to dinner tomorrow and a movie. You give her a deep kiss if she can bear to look at your swollen mug, remind her that she's an attractive woman, then you head back to school and go be a professor on Monday morning. Maybe one day you write up how you found Chelsea's body. End of story."

"I can't let it go," I shoot back. "First Juniper. Now Chelsea. Who else is out there? What kind of man would I be if I just left?"

"A living man."

"I've been passive for too long."

"If you stay, the professor has to go."

"What does that even mean?"

Gus points his finger directly at my face. "You're a fucking victim. A slow-motion accident waiting to happen. To be honest, I don't doubt that you are capable of finding this killer. That's what scares me. I'm afraid you're going to go off hunting down some clue and that's the last we ever hear of you. If you're right about what or who did this, then there won't be a body. There won't be a crime scene. You'll just be a statistic." He nods toward Jillian's direction. "And every night she and I will be sitting here looking out this window thinking about what happened to you, knowing that you're dead in some shallow grave in the middle of nowhere."

"You said if I stay, the professor has to go. What does that mean?"

"This is no place for an academic. If you decide to stick around, you need to think like a hunter. You're no longer an observer."

"And how do I do this?"

"I'll give you my shotgun, for starters. You also need to start carrying a pistol. We'll do some target practice to make sure you don't kill yourself. And I'll wake you up tomorrow morning and spar with you a bit. I'm rusty, but I think I can teach a broken mess like you how to do a better job of blocking a punch than you've been doing."

"I appreciate that."

Gus shakes his head. "It won't be enough, though. The only way to stop being a victim is to think like a killer. And I don't think you have that in you."

CHAPTER FORTY-SEVEN
Bayesian Casualties

Five days later the sun is dipping into the valley to the west, carving long shadows out of the fading orange light as I stick my shovel into the ground and start on my fifth hole, telling myself that I'll call it a day after this.

Two years ago a missing-persons report was filed for a nineteen-year-old girl named Summer Osbourne. She lived in the town of Silver Rock, three miles down the road from Hudson Creek. My program singled this area out as a high probability for the killer.

While Summer didn't appear to have fallen as far down the social ladder as Chelsea, her disappearance is all the more suspicious because of that.

I went out of my way to see if Chelsea was just a fluke or if MAAT is really on to something. Deep down, I know it's not a fluke, but the scientist in me tells me to check my own hypothesis.

When MAAT put a big red flag here, I decided to check up and see if there were any missing-persons reports that fit the profile. There were six in the last ten years. Summer was the most recent.

My other reason is that Chelsea's case isn't going anywhere. There's a complete lack of urgency. They've issued a preliminary report of a possible mountain lion or bear attack and sent her body to Bozeman for more analysis.

I'm done being the crazy guy showing up in police stations with a wild story about a killer who makes his crimes look like animal attacks.

My goal is just to gather as much evidence as I can. Right now, that means finding another body.

I take a break from the shoveling and look at the woods around me. I'm only two hundred feet from the highway, but it feels like I'm a thousand miles away.

Gus's shotgun is sitting in my duffel bag within reach, and I have his pistol tucked into my waistband. It didn't take much convincing to get me to carry them.

For my own sake, I used up a box of ammo making certain I still knew how to handle a gun. While I'm sure I'll be able to point the pistol away from me, I'm not too sure if I'll be quick enough or psychologically prepared to use it if I have to. But some protection is better than nothing. My usual can of bear spray probably won't be enough if I meet the killer out here.

Of course, the odds of me randomly running into him in the woods are astronomical. Randomly . . .

I scrape away another layer of dirt and reveal a dirty piece of purple fabric.

Everything drains from my body. There's no thrill of being right. It's just an overwhelming sense of dread.

I drop the shovel and slip on a pair of latex gloves to dig with my hand.

As I carefully remove the dirt from the surrounding area, the outline of a head begins to emerge. The fabric is a T-shirt. When I pull it back, a ghastly white face is looking up at me with milky, azure eyes that match the morning sky. Strands of blonde hair lie across her face—almost as if they are waiting for her to brush them away.

I uncover the torso, revealing a naked chest with dark, dirt-clogged gashes across her small breasts.

Summer's abdomen is split open, with her stomach, a fetid, stinking mass of swollen intestines, sticking out.

I need to get samples, but I have to take a break. The eyes are too much for me. They should be more decomposed, but the T-shirt and surrounding soil chemistry somehow preserved them. It's as if she's still seeing the last thing she ever saw.

I step back and lean against a tree, catching my breath, trying to hold it in.

Be a scientist, Theo. She doesn't need someone to mourn her right now. She needs someone to find out who did this.

I turn back and kneel down to continue excavating around her.

As I brush the dirt from her arms, I think about when Summer was a child and her mother bathed her and scrubbed her. If her mother had any idea what fate the world had in store for her little girl, would she have ever let her go?

The arms are predictably stiff. I raise the right one high enough to take a photo of the gashes and get a tissue sample. For a moment, it obscures her powerful eyes. But when I set it back down she's still staring up—almost as if she's looking to God for an answer.

Nobody is home, darling. And if he is, he doesn't care.

My ear twitches, and I get the feeling that I'm being watched. In the moment I try to analyze the sensation—it's like a tickle across my back.

First I just move my eyes slowly across the surrounding trees. When all I observe is forest, I turn my head slightly.

Forty feet away, up on the hill, are three sets of glowing eyes catching the setting sun.

Wolves.

Large ones.

They probably smelled her corpse long before I reached the shirt. Attracted by the scent, they gathered to watch and wait.

I can't leave her here. I buried Chelsea because nothing was around that would dig her up.

The moment I leave Summer, no matter how deep or what I cover her with, the wolves will come for her. They know she's here.

I have to take her with me.

The sun has set by the time I fully unbury her. I placed my flashlight on the edge of the hole, facing the wolves, but they vanished when I wasn't looking.

As I gently lift her body and move her to the plastic tarp I've laid down, I spot silvery eyes watching me from much closer.

They've walked around my cone of light and are just a few yards away.

Wolves are supposed to be people-shy, and attacks are exceptionally rare. I'm not sure what the data set looks like for humans all alone in the forest next to a decomposing corpse.

I lay Summer in the middle of my blue tarp. Her knees are slightly bent, with white flesh showing through tears in her black leggings. As I try to bundle her up, drops of my sweat hit her face and slide down her dirty cheek like tears.

The snarling sound of one of my watchers snaps me back to the present.

Summer's muscles have degraded long past the effect of rigor mortis, making her body flexible enough to bend over my shoulder in a fireman's carry.

I place my duffel bag over my other shoulder and use the flashlight to guide my way back down to my car.

My gray shadows follow me in the dark, making futile growls, hoping I'll drop the body.

But I don't. Nor do I ever reach for my gun or the shotgun—even to fire a warning shot.

These creatures are opportunistic cowards, afraid to take on something larger than them. Perhaps not unlike the man who killed Summer.

I hope.

I pray.

CHAPTER FORTY-EIGHT

INERTIA

Police Chief Shaw is standing near the tailgate of my Explorer with his flashlight aimed at Summer's face. Dressed in a T-shirt, parka jacket, and track pants struggling to contain his expanding stomach, the light is the only thing about him that resembles law enforcement.

"Who is this girl, again?" he asks.

"Summer Osbourne," says the lean deputy with receding auburn hair. He was the only one at the station when I arrived. It took him all of two seconds to call his boss down to the station after I showed him photos of the body in the back of my Explorer.

"Osbourne?" replies Shaw. "I don't recall anybody by that name."

"I think you might have known her daddy. He goes by MacDonald," the deputy explains.

"They live out by Finley stables? That big house? Daddy owns an irrigation pipe company?"

"That's them."

"What were there, six of them MacDonald kids?"

"Five including Summer. She was a stepdaughter."

"Summer MacDonald?" Shaw shakes his head. "She ran off with that fella from Wyoming." He turns to me. "You say her name was Summer Osbourne?"

"That's the name on the missing-persons report."

"Well, there's your problem. They never get around to updating them. Some kid runs away for a few days, and their parents come down here and make us go through the hassle of making a report, then don't bother to tell us when they come home."

I get frustrated at the backwoods-genealogy quiz. "Chief, this girl ain't goddamn ever a-comin' home."

He spins the light around and shines it in my face. "You watch your mouth, son. You show up here in the middle of the night with a half-naked dead girl in your trunk. That is suspicious." He turns to his deputy. "Didn't some fella show up with a body in Hudson Creek?"

"The second bear attack," replies the deputy.

"Jesus Christ," I groan. "First, it wasn't a bear attack. Second, I was the guy that found that body."

Chief Shaw's squinty eyes stare at me for a moment; then he comes to life, using the flashlight to gesture at Summer. "You're telling me you found another girl just like this one?"

"More or less, yes."

He turns to his deputy, "Is he for real?"

"That's why I called you down, Chief."

"That's one hell of a coincidence, you finding two bodies. Don't you think?"

I realize the closest this guy has ever been to a murder case more complicated than a domestic dispute is what he's seen on television.

"I'm a scientist. I'm working on a new detection procedure. I was looking into Summer Osbourne's case because it was similar to Chelsea Buchorn's and Juniper Parsons's."

"A detection procedure?"

"Just ask the people at Hudson Creek. They know all about it." Right . . .

"And you just brought the body here? Don't you know that's tampering with evidence?"

"When I uncovered it, wolves showed up."

"Wolves never bother anybody. They're cowards."

"I wasn't worried about me. I was worried about her. They're scavengers. They knew where I dug her up."

"If you were worried about wolves eating her, then why did you dig her up?"

Is this a serious question? I take a deep breath. "I wasn't sure if she was buried there until I started digging."

"If you had a notion where her body was, why didn't you just come tell us?"

Seriously? "I didn't want to waste your time in case I was wrong."

"Well, now I got tampered-with evidence. What am I supposed to do about that?"

"An hour ago you didn't even think this girl was missing. You have a heck of a lot more to go on now."

"Carl, go take a statement from him. I'm going to get the doc over here to take the body. Call Warren over at Fish and Wildlife." He pauses for a moment. "And call in Jefferson with the fingerprint and forensic kit. I want to make sure this girl didn't die in the back of this SUV."

Carl stares at Summer's body, then turns back to the chief. "From the looks of that girl, I don't even think this had rolled off the assembly line by the time she was killed."

"Just do it, Carl."

"Yes, sir."

I spend the next two hours making a statement and answering questions about my whereabouts. Chief Shaw then has me fingerprinted and photographed and runs them through their computer to make sure I'm not a mass murderer.

I then take a trip with Chief Shaw, Warren the Fish and Game guy, and another deputy to show them where I found the body.

The wolves are long gone, of course, but the shallow grave where I found her is just as I left it.

It's midnight before they finally release me. As I leave, I overhear Warren explaining how bears will sometimes bury their victims to come back to later.

Great, guys. Believe whatever you want.

I just hope nobody forgets to contact Summer's mother and tell her that her baby is never coming home.

Too exhausted to drive back to Gus's motel, I get a room in the next town over.

I fall asleep making *X*s on a map MAAT generated for me. They go clear across the state, following the purple band of the killer's hunting pattern.

Each one is another potential Summer or Chelsea.

I prepare myself for more awkward encounters with local law enforcement as I keep digging up bodies.

At some point their default answer can't be "A bear did it."

I hope.

CHAPTER FORTY-NINE

Body Count

Lily Ames was from a town near Seattle. Her parents last saw her nearly two years ago when she decided to hike across the country. There was some mention of seeing Yellowstone and Montana.

Two days after Summer, I find her under three feet of dirt two hundred miles from the nearest park entrance.

Her throat has been slashed to the point that her spine is visible at the back of her neck. Lily's eyes are filled with terror. There's a yellow bruise on the side of her face, implying she suffered some kind of injury long enough before her heart stopped beating.

Using my trowel, then my hands, I unearth the rest of the area around her legs and inspect the soles of her feet. They're a bloody mess.

She ran before he killed her.

He was toying with her.

I place a plastic sheet over her body, then fill in the hole.

I put an orange flag as a temporary burial marker so the police will know where to find her when I call in my anonymous tip.

Michelle Truyols was from Alberta and worked her way down to Montana by waitressing at first, then turning to prostitution at some point before reaching the border. According to a newspaper account, a friend said she met some guy who was a long-distance trucker with a drug problem. Michelle may have picked up that problem.

Her body is sixty feet from the road, behind a small ridge in the same kind of shallow depression like the others. There are bruises all over her right arm, as if she was literally grabbed off the street and dragged here.

Long gouges run from her back to her stomach, as if she was struck down from above, then pinned to the ground.

I take my samples and photographs, then seal her back up in the ground with another orange flag for the police.

Stephanie Grant's final resting place is under a clump of mixed vegetation just like the others. I can spot them pretty easily now by matching the growth pattern to the time the women went missing. It's become extremely precise. Our killer has a preferred victim and a preferred type of location for burying them. I found her by standing on a hill and just looking. Her body almost called to me.

I've become numb. Five bodies so far. Each one lost and nearly forgotten.

Being the first person to lay eyes on them—to even know they exist—is unsettling.

Every one of the red dots in the purple band in MAAT's map has proven a hit. This tells me something very frightening.

Statistically speaking, when your probability estimates keep knocking it out of the park, something is wrong. It's not that MAAT is so accurate—it's because there are many, many more bodies out there than red dots.

MAAT is just showing me the ones with 90 percent probability or more. When I adjust the range to include 50 percent or more, something terrifying happens.

My two dozen dots turn to hundreds.

I know how to find one kind of burial. Who knows if the killer has other methods of disposing of bodies? I could just be finding the impromptu killings he doesn't have the time to do a better job of hiding. That said, he seems to be doing a good enough job.

Montana has a million residents and even more tourists visiting every year. There's also the traffic of people driving through the state, crossing the country and going to and from Canada.

A watchful eye would be very good at spotting vulnerable prey—the kind most likely to vanish without much fuss.

Just like I've become accustomed to spotting the depression and the clumps of vegetation that signal a body is buried below, the killer might be able to gauge in a glance a victim's vulnerability.

It could be the outward signs of drug addiction. Or it could be from watching them and realizing they have no immediate family or friends in the area.

It scares me to think this is a skill that the killer could get better and better at until he is utterly fearless.

As I tamp down the dirt around Stephanie's grave and place her flag, I have a realization.

While it's important that I keep locating the bodies, unless I find their DNA and get a match, I'm not going to catch the killer from some careless clue he left behind.

I have to understand how the killer thinks. I have to know why he does what he does.

I'm not going to find that buried in the ground out here. I have to go to the places he's been and see what he's seen.

I have to pretend I'm the killer.

CHAPTER FIFTY

ANTHROPOLOGIST

It's been ten days since I left the hospital, and I've been ignoring e-mails from my supervisor, too afraid to read what they say. I'm getting closer, but I need more information.

Dr. Seaver, a middle-aged anthropologist currently teaching at Montana State University, leads me down the steps into the basement where his specimens are held.

"You want to see the good stuff?" he asks, giving me a somewhat fiendish glance over his shoulder.

I found his name doing a search for any information on ritualistic killing in the area. Seaver, originally from Cornell, is currently part of an interdisciplinary study examining violence and human culture. He caught my eye because he wrote a paper comparing contemporary homicides with historical precedents.

We reach the end of the stairs and come to a narrow passage between rows of cabinets. The sparse lightbulbs do little to fight back the darkness.

The air is musty with the scent of decaying things. It's an anachronism compared with modern, climate-controlled labs and vacuum storage.

"The real lab is over at the Museum of the Rockies, but that's paleontology, primarily. Pre-Holocene. Our study certainly goes back that far, but most samples are quite contemporary by comparison."

He leads me into a small room with a workbench. Five skulls sit in separate clear plastic boxes. The color of the bone ranges from dark brown to almost bleached white.

"Here, put on a pair of gloves and take a look." He removes the first skull and hands it to me. "What can you tell me about this?"

The skull is mostly complete, minus the jawbone. The brow appears slightly thick and the cheekbones wider than an average European, but it appears contemporary. "Asiatic?"

"Correct. How about this one?"

He places another skull in my hands. This one has similar features with a slightly higher brow. "Native American?"

"Correct again."

The third one gives me some trouble, but I estimate it as being sub-Saharan. The fourth as Central European and the last from Southeast Asia.

"Perfect score on identifying the general ethnicity, Dr. Cray."

"I took a lot of anthropology classes."

"But you failed to see the forest for the trees," he replies.

I glance back at the skulls, trying to grasp what I missed. Seaver picks up the middle one and drops it back into my hands. The face still tells the same story. This one is European, by all indications. I look for any other features, examining the teeth for dental variations. I can't spot any.

I rotate the skull to look at the occipital bone. There's a correlation between thickness and shape among races. In whites you can often see sex dimorphism—tell the males from the females—by features on this bone.

It's just above the bone that I see what Seaver is trying to get me to see: a massive fracture. I examine the other skulls and find similar trauma.

"They were all murdered."

"Exactly. And in the same way: blunt-force trauma to the back of the skull. Not the kind of thing you do in battle. It's the way you kill someone in a kneeling or prone position. In my research, approximately 25 percent of the deaths in prehistoric burial sites come from violence. Statistically speaking, outside of infant disease, the number-one cause of death was another human doing the killing.

"This is the norm up until the development of agriculture. Even then, violence didn't steeply curve until the age of reason. And this violence wasn't committed by a statistical few. It was regular folks. Once upon a time I might have been the one holding this person down while you clubbed them in the back of the skull."

I'm unsettled by the casual way he suggests this. I get the impression he's imagined this scenario quite a lot.

He lines the skulls up in a row. Their haunted eye sockets stare out at us.

Seaver points to them, calling out their backstories one by one. "This one was murdered six thousand years ago in what's now Hungary. This one died three thousand years ago in China. This one died one thousand years ago in Wyoming. This one was sent to me by the Genocide Project; the victim was from a mass burial in Darfur five years ago. The last one was found in the woods in Colorado twenty years ago. We still don't know who they were or why they were killed."

"Savage," I reply.

"No, Dr. Cray." Seaver shakes his head. "That's the point. These are far from the most savage deaths I've come across. These are the humane ones. They were killed dispassionately. I have other skulls and bones with hack marks and stab wounds inflicted long after the victim was deceased. I have collarbones with tooth indentations, not from cannibalism, but from someone trying to bite the victim to death, after they were incapacitated. I can show you murder sites that would make the most hardened Nazi concentration camp commander want to vomit." He waves at the skulls. "This is killing. Murder is what you're interested in."

"What's the difference?"

"Killing is a solution to a problem. Murder is something you do because you want to. You divorce your wife because you don't love her. You murder her because you hate her."

The man who killed Juniper certainly took great pleasure in the act. He could have strangled her or slit her throat. But he didn't. The act of killing was his purpose. Which leads me back to the method.

"Have you ever heard of someone making a murder look like an animal attack?"

"Disguising it after the fact?"

"No. Killing someone in the same way an animal would."

"Virtually all acts of premeditated killing in warfare involve some kind of animal symbolism. Animal mascots for military units. Wearing animal claws and teeth. Prehistoric man would wear the skins of other predators to assume their powers."

"What about the act of killing itself? Are there cases where someone has consciously used killing methods like an animal's?"

"Ah, that's more challenging. Up until when we went out into the savanna, we were opportunistic omnivores that only ate things much smaller than ourselves. We had to invent the spear and throwing projectiles because our teeth and fingernails weren't adapted to hunting.

"Mimicry would be a very inefficient way for someone to try to kill, with a few exceptions."

"Exceptions? Such as?"

"Certain weapons that would resemble the way an animal would strike."

"Like what?"

"Follow me."

CHAPTER FIFTY-ONE

SHARK TEETH

Seaver guides me to a different part of the basement and takes a dusty cardboard box down from a towering shelf. He lifts the lid and reveals a flat club with triangular white teeth sticking out around the sides, like a chain saw blade.

"In Hawaii they call this a *leiomano*. They use tiger shark teeth for the blades. It's somewhat similar to the obsidian *macuahuitl* clubs they used in Mesoamerica. This one was found in a mound in Illinois. The teeth were from a great white shark. The Mound Builders obviously traded far and wide to have access to those."

He hands me the club. The tips of the teeth are still sharp. I'd hate to have this slice into me.

"The amusing thing about this is that some anthropologists regard this as a more humane weapon than a sword, proof in their minds that their wielders were more kindhearted than we give them credit for. The reality is that this is the kind of weapon you make if you don't have iron or bronze. When you get cut by this, you die of infection from a hundred different wounds you can't sew up as easily as one gash."

I hand it back. "I don't think anyone would mistake the victim of this for a shark attack."

"No. For the Hawaiians it was more symbolic. You're talking something practical?" He returns the weapon to its box and the box to its shelf, then walks away. "Let's go down a few rows."

Seaver removes a long, curved knife from a drawer. "This is a *karambit.* It's designed to resemble a claw. Fairly practical. You can find modern versions in most knife shops."

He digs through another drawer and pulls out a metal handle with sharp nails. "This is the head of a *zhua*, a clawed staff used to pull men from horses and rip away shields."

I examine the hooks at the end. This is close but wouldn't leave the deep gouges I found in the victims.

We go over to another cabinet, and he sorts through some boxes until he finds the one he's looking for. "Ever heard of a *bagh naka*? This one is from India, but there have been variations in other cultures. In the nineteenth century, the raja would have men fight each other with these until their skin peeled off." He unfolds a piece of cloth and holds up a set of metal knuckles with four long blades sticking out.

I'm stunned. While I could imagine what kind of weapon the killer would use, I didn't imagine that it was something that had ever been used widely.

"Here," he says, extending it toward me. "Hold it. In the Great Calcutta Killings, Hindu girls were given these to protect themselves."

I grip the weapon in my hand. The claws stick out an inch or so over my knuckles. I can easily imagine how a version of this with blades like the karambit could resemble an animal claw. If you cast the blades from an actual bear claw, the similarity would be even more pronounced.

As I hold the bagh naka up to the light, I get an image of the gashes across Chelsea's body. I slide the weapon off my hand and set it down. I tell Seaver I want to get some photographs, but really I don't want to touch it anymore.

"Have you ever heard of anyone using something like this to kill someone? Here? In the United States?" I ask.

"It wouldn't surprise me if some martial arts nut went after a roommate with one, but no. To kill someone with this, you'd have to be strong."

I think of the deep gouges in the girl's bodies. "How strong?"

"I don't know. But strong enough to hit an artery."

I pick the weapon back up and use my phone to capture it from every angle.

"Thank you, Dr. Seaver. Just one more question. Have you ever heard of anyone mistaking a human attack for an animal attack?"

"There were reports of wolf attacks in France several hundred years ago that might have been the work of a man. That gave rise to werewolf legends in that region."

"What about around here?"

"Like the wendigo?"

"I've heard the name. But I don't know much about that."

"It's an Algonquin legend. A half-man creature that eats people. Indigenous people took them very seriously. But that's more associated with cannibalism. Is that what you mean?"

"Not quite. But that's worth looking into. I was just wondering if you had heard of any recent cases of people mistaking a person for an animal."

"No. Not recent."

"Well, thank you for your time."

"Unless you consider the 1980s recent."

"Pardon me?"

"The Cougar Creek Monster? It's a kind of local story, but it made it into a few of those silly cable television documentaries."

"Wait, what's that?"

"I moved here after, but that was this area's Mothman or Bigfoot for a while. Hikers near Red Hook said they spotted something lurking around their campsites at night. I think maybe even shots were fired. I don't remember much else. Everyone was talking about it; then it just went away."

"What did they say they saw?"

"A man walking on four legs. Like a big cat. Or the other way around. I'm sure you can look it up."

"Did it ever attack anyone?"

Seaver shrugs. "Maybe? I think there was some account of a camper getting clawed across his chest." He gestures with his hand, tracing a path across his body I'd seen too many times in the past few days.

"Thank you, Dr. Seaver."

I leave him in his basement with his skulls and weapons of murder.

CHAPTER FIFTY-TWO

UNSOLVED

In June of 1983, a group of seventeen campers, most of them recently graduated from Chilton High School, took a trip to Beaverhead National Forest. The first and only night of the camping trip, something happened. The details vary among the accounts I've been able to find in the public library in nearby Red Hook, but the general story is fairly consistent.

The hikers spent several hours trekking through the woods to a remote spring. Along the way several of them thought they were being tracked by a large animal, possibly a bear or a mountain lion.

There had been other reports in the area of people spotting something in the woods watching them. This creature would stand on two legs to observe them and then slink off into the brush when noticed.

The Chilton High campers reported seeing something that was tall and lithe, too skinny to be a bear. Although they never saw it clearly, they reported the skin as being more light brown or tan in color than the black or brown of a bear.

After they made camp, three of them went into the woods in search of firewood. They came running back after a hiker said he spotted a large cat sitting on a log watching them.

One of them claimed that it gave chase to him, but when he looked back, he saw glowing yellow eyes at the same height off the ground as his own.

The other campers dismissed this as a prank or a confused sighting of a mountain lion and decided they would be safe in numbers.

At some point after 2 a.m., when the last of them had left the campfire to go to sleep, several of the campers said they were awoken by the sound of something prowling outside their tents.

One member of the party, who'd brought along a rifle, went out to investigate but didn't see anything.

Sometime after 3 a.m., the camp woke to the sound of screaming.

This is where the versions begin to differ.

True Tales of Mountain Creatures says a large, catlike creature walking on two legs tried to drag one of the girls out of a tent, only to be stopped by a group of campers, one of whom was clawed to death and carried off.

Big Sky Mysteries says the students saw a ghostlike apparition of a Native American on the outer edge of the campsite commanding a large cougar to attack the campers, only to vanish as quickly as he appeared.

Angel Encounters claims that the boys in the group stumbled upon the girls in some kind of consensual sexual congress with half-cat male spirits and took issue with it.

Perhaps the most accurate account—at least the one that best aligns with the experiences of the campers—is an article in the *Montana Tracker* detailing the encounter and claiming that one of the students received an injury when something climbed into his tent. The article is accompanied by a black-and-white photograph of four students sitting on a couch animatedly explaining their experience.

There's an oddness in their expressions that could either be the face a trickster makes when trying not to let on that it's a gag, or the confusion and awkwardness of dealing with this much attention. From the tone of the article, it's quite clear that the reporter didn't take them all that seriously.

It would seem that nobody else did, other than the sensationalist authors of the books I found in the library.

It's an easy story to discount. You have a group of high school kids off in the woods, already primed for hijinks. Add to that whatever they were drinking and smoking, and you have the perfect opportunity for an actual animal encounter to get blown out of proportion.

But when I look at the photo from the article, the expression of a dark-haired girl on the edge of the couch strikes a chord. She resembles outwardly how I felt when I was first interrogated by Detective Glenn—confused and frightened.

The caption lists her only as Elizabeth L. I don't know what the other students saw that night, or if they were just trying to push themselves into the story, but she has the eyes of someone who witnessed something she'd rather put behind her.

Unfortunately, a first name and only the first letter of the last isn't much to go on. Unless . . .

I get up from the table and ask the librarian if they keep high school yearbooks.

Ten minutes later, I'm back at the table with three editions of the Chilton Champions Annual, scanning through the pages for Elizabeth L.

It's not hard to find her. Each graduating class is only about fifty students.

Her face leaps out immediately. She's smiling and looking forward to a happy future—a far cry from the frightened girl in the other photo.

The yearbook lists her last name as Lee. Her best friend is Brandy Thompson and her favorite quote is "'Cause tramps like us, baby, we were born to run."

An Internet search finds an Elizabeth Lee Collins living in the town of Lodge Pine. Property records list an address. When I type the address into a search engine, I get the phone number for Lodge Pine Aquaculture Supply—which I assume sells equipment to fish farms.

I have her number now, but do I call her? Chasing down stories about the Cougar Creek Monster is a long way from trying to find my killer. If I ran down every crazy urban legend in southern Montana, I'd die of old age before I found anything concrete.

It seems silly, especially given how outlandish some of the accounts are—Indian ghosts, animal orgies—but still . . . there's something about the haunted look in young Elizabeth's eyes. I want to know what she saw.

Impulsively, I dial the number and curse myself for not thinking up what I want to say beforehand.

"Aquaculture Supply. How may I help you?" A woman's voice.

"Elizabeth Lee?"

"It's Collins now."

"Sorry. Yes, of course. This is rather, um, awkward. But I've been doing some research and wanted to ask you a few questions."

"Oh, dear. This about the Cougar Creek thing, isn't it?"

"Uh, yes."

"Listen. That was just a hoax some of my friends pulled. I had a feeling that once these animal attack victims started surfacing I was going to get pulled back into it. I have nothing to add."

"A hoax."

"Yes," she says, rather pat. "If you want to know what that's about, I suggest you go ask that crazy professor who keeps finding bodies."

I hadn't realized how well known that had become. "How do you know about that?"

"My husband is a cop. Everyone knows. Anyway, go talk to the professor."

"I am him."

"Pardon me?"

"Theo Cray. I'm the one that's been finding the bodies."

She takes her time to reply. "You're the one that found those girls?"

"Yes, ma'am."

"And what do you think killed them?" she asks.

"A man."

"A man?"

"Flesh and blood."

"What does that have to do with me?"

"You saw something that night."

"I said it was a hoax."

"I'm looking at a photo of you taken just a few days later. That girl doesn't think it was a hoax."

"That was a long time ago. She didn't know much."

"I'd like to talk to you either way."

"Did I mention my husband is a cop?"

"Yes, ma'am."

"All right." She sighs. "You have our address?"

CHAPTER FIFTY-THREE

SHADOWS

Elizabeth and her husband live in a well-kept two-story home on several acres of property. Three slobbering mutts clamber over one another to greet me when I let myself through the gate. After I dutifully scratch each one behind the ear, paying the entry fee, they run off to chase some invisible foe.

Elizabeth is sitting on the porch with a pitcher of iced tea sitting on a table. She's a bit more robust than the photo taken shortly after high school, but the eyes and hair are the same.

"So you're the man who keeps digging up bodies?" she asks.

"I guess you could say that."

She motions for me to sit down. "Thomas says you lost a friend?"

I assume Thomas is her police officer husband. "A former student."

"I hear they hauled you in as a suspect at first?"

"That was an experience."

"I bet. I bet. But you're here to talk about Cougar Creek. Really, you're wasting your time. Like I said, it was a hoax. That's all there is to say."

She delivers this as a prepared speech. I can tell that this has been weighing heavily on her.

"Two people think there is," I say.

"Pardon?"

"Two people see a possible connection. Me and you. When I called, you said you were expecting someone to reach out to you sooner or later. So far we're the ones with the most intimate knowledge of this, and we've both drawn the same conclusion that they might be related."

"Maybe it's time for you to go. I don't want to have to sic my dogs on you." She says this only half-heartedly.

"Good luck with that. I met your dogs."

She shakes her head. "Worthless animals." She resigns herself to accepting my stubbornness. "Fine. Understand that I didn't have a clear idea what was happening at the time, and after the fact, my friends exaggerated parts of what happened. And then others just went crazy with it. I once even read an account that said we were up there having some kind of demonic animal ghost orgy. I went up that mountain a virgin and came down a virgin, thank you very much."

"So what did happen?"

She takes a moment to collect her thoughts. "Well, as you probably know, we weren't the first ones to encounter the Cougar Creek Monster, or whatever. In fact, it was stories about something lurking up there that made Reese Penny and Alex Danson organize the whole trip. They had some idea it was aliens or Bigfoot. Anyway, it grew into a postgraduation campout. Seventeen of us in all."

"What had you heard before?"

"Hikers said they saw an animal on two legs watching them. They'd come back from fishing and found their campsite had been wrecked. There was even a photo."

"A photo?"

"Yeah. I think Alex's cousin took it a few weeks before. I saw a blurry mimeographed copy of it. It could have been anything."

"What did it look like?"

"At the time, I think Reese said it looked like the Black Panther, from comics. He actually put a comic book cover next to the image. Maybe. But these new girls, these victims, they were attacked by a bear?"

"There are five claw marks, which would indicate a bear. A cat would have four, normally."

"Thomas says the folks from Fish and Wildlife think there might be a polydactyl cat running around, and that's why there's all this confusion. Both big cats and bears are known to bury their prey."

"Mrs. Collins, I've seen these burials. No animal did that."

"Elizabeth. But you think the Cougar Man might've?"

"You still haven't told me what you saw."

"Right. Right. So we hike up the hot spring, and some of the others say they think we're being watched. Lucy Plavin and a couple other girls and I started straggling, picking wildflowers and talking. Pretty soon we were isolated from the rest, but the trail isn't too hard to follow. We're walking along, making lots of noise, giggling, whatever, when Carey Sumter stops and asks, 'What's that?' She points to something on the ridge to the left up in the trees.

"We don't see anything. She says it was something big, and I tell her if it was anything, it was just a bear. Now she's bone white. Scared. She saw something, but we talked her out of it. Ten minutes later she's laughing with us and whatever she saw is out of mind.

"It's not until we get to the spring and start making camp that we find out that three or four other people saw something watching us.

"This is where it started to get a little unsettling. There were three separate sightings at different times. When we compared notes, all of them had the same thing to say: it was on the left ridge, at first it appeared to be a man, but then it slunk off like a cat."

"Did you think someone was playing a trick?"

"Well, yeah. I thought Reese or Alex was doing something with a costume or one of their friends was hiding in the trees. But they were the ones that seemed the most skeptical. Trying to convince Carey and the others it was a bear. Only they insisted this was too skinny to be a bear. They said it looked like Alex's photo."

"Did you see it again?"

She locks eyes with me, as if I'd asked the stupidest question in the world. "Did I see it again? Hell, yes. When it tried to drag me out of my tent."

CHAPTER FIFTY-FOUR

ENCOUNTER

"By the time we'd opened up the third case of beer, our nerves had settled down a bit and the ones that came up there to hook up went off to their tents.

"After most of us started to sleep, there was a commotion outside the tents. Carey, Janet, Vivian, and I had decided to share a tent because we trusted the boys less than whatever we thought might be lurking out there.

"One of them woke up at the sound of the tent zipper being opened. At first she thought it was another girl, or one of the boys playing a prank, but when she grabbed her flashlight, whoever or whatever it was had gone. A little while later, Stacey Kavanaugh heard something and yelled. This got everyone up.

"We were back by the fire comparing notes on what happened. Half the tents had said they heard something prowling around and saw a shadow moving past.

"A consensus was reached that it was a bear or a cat. The girls decided to split the boys up among them for protection. Which would have been the perfect plan for Reese and Alex to concoct, only they seemed just as disturbed by what was going on as any of us.

"I knew Scott Cook wasn't as into the ladies as everyone thought he was, so I ended up sharing a tent with him. He was also captain of the wrestling team, so I felt safe. Poor Scott."

"What do you mean?"

"I thought you knew that part. Well, I'm sleeping on the top of my bag because it's hot. Scott is sound asleep, curled up in the corner of the tent with Depeche Mode playing on his Walkman.

"At first I think it's a dream. There's a sound I can't quite place. Later on, I realize it's the tent zipper being raised very, very slowly. My eyes are shut and I'm still half out of it, but then something touches my leg.

"I think maybe it's just Scott being playful. I decide to ignore it and see how far he goes. Then suddenly, something grabs my ankle and I'm yanked out of the tent."

Elizabeth's face gets animated as she recalls this. Her body twists as the muscle memory floods back.

"I scream and grab at Scott's sleeping bag. As I'm getting pulled outside, I try holding the tent flaps, but this thing is stronger than me and I lose my grip. I roll over on my back and I see this shadow . . . this thing.

"Scott comes running out of the tent and jumps on it. Then . . . then, oh, hell, the thing claws at him. I remember seeing its arm pull back and swipe at Scott.

"That's when Reese fired the pistol he'd brought with him. Nobody knew he had it until then. The thing let go of me and ran off into the woods."

"Was he wounded?"

"I don't know. Scott sure as hell was. Not only did the thing claw at him, but Reese managed to clip his shoulder with his shot. That's why none of the stories were straight. It was against the law to have a gun in Beaverhead Forest, and on top of that, Reese had a couple of previous charges.

"Neither of the wounds was life threatening. The gashes were messy, but we were able to patch him up enough to get him to a clinic in Red Hook. The gun wound wasn't too deep and could have passed for a cut.

"We agreed to leave the part about Reese shooting Scott out of it, but with over a dozen people, soon everyone knew. When the sheriff asked Scott what happened, though, he denied being shot and that was that."

"What about the Cougar Creek Monster?"

Elizabeth shrugs. "What about it? Everyone, even some of us who were there, thinks we were making it up or had a drunken encounter with a mountain lion. It made the paper. Some Bigfoot hunters showed up for a while, but that was the last anyone saw of the Cougar Creek Monster.

"A few months later when those California hikers went missing, nobody even mentioned the Cougar Man."

"Hikers? I hadn't heard about that."

"Before we went up, there were at least two people, out-of-towners who were seen going up but never came back. After, there were three hikers, flower children or something, who hitchhiked their way to Red Hook and then went up the mountain. Nobody saw them again, either. There was never a missing-persons report in the area. I think a ranger did a search. But that was the end of that.

"Although I've heard that others—some of the people who came looking for the Cougar Man, again, out-of-town people—weren't seen again. But who knows. You'd think their cars would be piling up at the trailhead parking lot. Right? Probably just talk."

"What do you think grabbed you?"

"I'd say it was a man, but it didn't smell or act like one. Scott still had the claw marks on his chest. Although he started telling people it was a mountain lion shortly after. He got tired of telling people what really happened. He died in a car wreck a few years later. Drinking. Poor Scott."

We fall quiet for a minute, looking away off opposite ends of the porch. Then Elizabeth faces me.

"What was it? The devil. None of us were the same after. Reese ended up shooting himself with the same gun he shot Scott with. Alex got into drugs and started dealing and was in and out of jail. Carey Sumter started having nightmares and moved away. So did most of the others."

"And you stayed?"

"The devil can get me anywhere he pleases. No point in running. Besides, I married a cop."

There's a distant look in Elizabeth's eyes I recognize. I see the same confused, haunted girl on the couch in that old photo.

The similarities between this Cougar Man and my killer are too strong to ignore. It might be coincidence, but I suspect these early encounters could have been the killer testing himself in his younger years, learning how to hunt.

"Were all of the missing persons in the same area?"

"As far as I know. The valley around the spring. Why?"

"Could you show me on a map?"

"Sure, but there haven't been any missing persons or sightings there in decades. I know, I still pay attention."

"I understand. But I want to go there."

"Why? He's long gone."

"But that might be where he started. I have to see for myself."

CHAPTER FIFTY-FIVE

GEOSPATIAL

Back in Jillian's diner, I hunch over a table full of maps and charts, my half-eaten cherry pie pushed to the side as I try to make sense of the data, as if something will leap out at me and connect everything together.

On the surface, the Cougar Creek Monster sightings have nothing to with Juniper's killer. The man who murdered her, and the others, is invisible, to the point the authorities still doubt that he even exists. Whereas this Cougar Man almost wanted to be seen, popping up to the point of becoming southern Montana's Bigfoot, then abruptly vanishing the night he attacked Elizabeth—assuming that was him.

The more I think about it, the idea that this was the killer in his *Batman Begins* phase makes sense. After nearly—or actually—getting shot, he had to change up his tactics and learn how to hide. Which he did all too well.

This younger killer was clumsy and brazen, attacking in the middle of a crowded campsite. The later killer became much more selective of his prey, probably watching them for considerable amounts of time before striking. The patience that must take—or is that the thrill of the hunt? Does he get as much pleasure from stalking his victims as he does from killing them?

"Planning a hike?" asks Jillian, leaning over my shoulder.

She would have startled me, but I could smell her perfume before she spoke. It reminds me of wisteria.

"Kind of . . ."

She slides into the booth across from me. She's not wearing her apron. Instead she has on a white-collared blouse that suits her figure well.

"You look . . . nice," I say.

"You should see me in hiking shorts."

I give her a weak smile.

She taps the map. "That was a hint, Theo. Every now and then a girl drops one. But don't expect many more."

"Oh." I gather the map and charts together. "It's not that kind of hike."

"You're looking for bodies. I know."

"Actually, not in this case. It's more out of curiosity."

"You've been coming and going for two weeks. Your curiosity has taken you all over. Maybe you could use some company on this one?"

I've thought about her more than I realize. As I've gone into darker and darker places, I've found myself looking forward to coming back to this table, eating pie and enjoying some semblance of normalcy.

Sometimes I watch her across the restaurant, the easy way she smiles and how she deals with a variety of human emotions while not losing her own sense of being. Part of me wants to have that presence with me in those dark places. While another part doesn't want to contaminate her with all that evil.

"I don't know how good of company I would be."

"That's why you need company."

"It may not be safe."

"I'll protect you," she replies.

"Ha. We've seen how effective I've been at doing that for myself."

"Gus says you've been taking well to his training."

"You mean his six a.m. sessions where he swings a laundry bag at my head?"

"Call it what you want, but I can see a difference. Your face is leaning out; you're not as hunched. He'll make you a man yet."

"I don't think there's enough time in the universe."

"All the more reason you need company in the big, bad woods."

"I don't know . . ."

"Will everyone at this table who has actually been trained for combat raise their hand?" Jillian lifts her arm. "Right, thought so."

I forget she was in the army—she's so . . . feminine. I'd protest again that it wasn't safe, but I have no reason to think she's any safer here. And the Cougar Creek Monster hasn't been seen in decades. I doubt he'd revisit a haunt that almost got him killed. Still . . . nothing about this makes sense.

"Fine," she says. "It's settled. You'll pick me up in the morning."

"I didn't agree to anything."

"Too late."

I know arguing with her is pointless. And to be honest, I like the idea of not having to share her attention with a restaurant full of people.

"Some men came by yesterday asking about you," she says.

"Really? Who?"

"Didn't say. Looked like cops. Not ones I recognized. One of them had a watch that was two hours ahead. Maybe from out of town."

"Cops? I'm not hard to get hold of."

"It may have just been a casual thing. I hear they're looking for a mountain lion now?"

I groan. "Yeah. Five claws. Polydactylism in cats usually results in six or more, not five. I haven't heard of this happening in large cats, not that it makes a difference. They'll make up whatever theory they want."

"What are we looking for tomorrow? Not bodies, right? I mean, I'd be up for that. I guess."

"No. We're looking for the Cougar Creek Monster, or the Cougar Man, as he's sometimes called."

Jillian raises one eyebrow, waiting to see if I'm joking. "I'll bring my gun."

"I'm sure he's long gone."

"The gun isn't for him."

"Ah, you trust the mad professor to go off on a hike alone with him, but only if you're packing heat?"

"More or less. Also, like I said, wait until you see me in hiking shorts."

CHAPTER FIFTY-SIX

The Ravine

I let Jillian keep a few paces ahead of me, mostly because this part of the ravine is too narrow for us to walk side by side. Mostly. She wasn't exaggerating about the hiking shorts.

As distracted by her as I am, I still can't keep my mind off the unsettling feeling this trail is giving me. Certainly part of that is the vivid imagery of Elizabeth's story and the dreadful thought of what else happened here, but another aspect is geography.

The trail follows a gradual incline between two steep ridges. At one time there was a stream here, but it has been cut off for years, leaving a dry rock bed that winds its way through the hills.

The trees along the sides are so tall, the only time the ravine isn't in shadow is near noon.

"This place feels off," says Jillian.

I'm relieved to hear her say it, because I didn't want to cause her any unnecessary unease.

"It's because we're vulnerable. Nobody feels comfortable pinned down in a tight crevice."

"That's what he said," she replies with a small laugh.

I get the joke a beat too late and have to settle for grinning when she checks over her shoulder to see how it landed.

"Right . . . Some evolutionary psychologists think that we're hard-wired to feel more comfortable in certain landscapes than others. That's what goes into park design. They're not meant to recreate nature, but to soothe us. A small body of water in a wide-open space with a few clusters of trees to hide in if there's a large predator. This is what we looked for when we left the jungle for the savanna. It's what medieval landscape painters tried to represent and how manors and country estates were designed for hundreds of years. This place? It's the opposite."

"Yeah, but I think I can see why a bunch of teenagers would want to come up here. It feels very far away from authority. Especially after graduation."

I keep my eyes on the shadows, trying to imagine how I'd react if I looked up and saw someone . . . or something . . . watching.

There are a thousand places to hide, and undoubtedly we're being watched. This place got its name, Cougar Creek, from some settlers who lived nearby a hundred years ago. Statistically, the number of mountain lion sightings here is lower than in other areas, probably from excessive hunting due to the name. That said, I'm sure more than one carnivore knows we're here.

Jillian stops to tuck a strand of dirty-blonde hair behind her ear, then takes a sip from her canteen. "How you holding up, city boy?"

"This city boy was trekking through Belize when you were holding pom-poms."

"Pom-poms? Softball and volleyball. I liked to hit things. What were you doing in Belize?"

"Hunting a killer," I reply.

"Really?"

"Culicidae. Mosquitoes. We were tracking down a species that had a higher incidence of transmitting malaria than others. I was an undergraduate following a field researcher, collecting specimens while the government tried eradicating them from danger spots."

"How did that work out?"

"A slightly less infectious species filled the niche. Statistically speaking, we saved eleven lives. Eventually, better eradication methods made a more significant difference."

"Interesting." She keeps walking for a while. "This is the same to you?"

"Pardon?"

"The way you found the other victims and what you're doing out here, it's like hunting a disease."

"I'm not really an epidemiologist, if that's what you mean. It's outside my area. I build mathematical models based on biological systems."

"A generalist."

"I guess you could say so. Even biology felt too constraining, so I had to figure out how to make it more exotic."

"Like how?"

"For my PhD thesis, I created a fifth-dimensional environment, inhabited it with synthetic life, then introduced disease vectors."

"I'm not even going to pretend to know what that means."

"It was a little ambitious. What I was after was trying to find common traits between very different systems. The way a funny cat picture spreads on the Internet isn't all that different from how the flu virus might spread. I wanted to create a very complicated model, really bizarre, and then look for similarities."

"Did you?"

"Lots of them. None of them were built in to the system, but certain things are inevitable. That's how I found where the other victims were. My model picked up patterns that were nonobvious."

"Clever."

"Half-clever. I could discover a lot about what their burial locations and potential interception locations had in common, but it doesn't tell me anything about the killer."

Jillian thinks this over for a moment, then replies, "That's why we're here. If this is your killer in his early days, that will tell you more about him."

"Maybe. It might not even be connected to him, but there could be some data point that helps me better understand that kind of behavior."

We reach level ground and continue hiking under a dense canopy of trees. After a half hour, we reach the small spring where Elizabeth and her friends made camp.

The pool is dark and twists around a bend. At one side there's foamy discharge. Occasionally a bubble gurgles up from below. The sulfur smell isn't overpowering, but it's clearly there.

Rocky outcroppings surround the location, creating a kind of steep caldera. The presence of the steaming spring suggests some latent volcanic activity, implying that this may actually have been a volcano in the past.

I point up. "See the way the jagged edges of the cliffs cut into the blue sky like black teeth? In other places I've been, a geological feature like this would be called a hell mouth."

"Creepy," says Jillian, eyeing them with suspicion.

I take out the satellite printouts of the area I brought with me. It takes me a moment to place where I'm standing with the map, but I find what I'm searching for.

"This way."

Jillian follows me as I cut through brush to get to a rock fall. We climb up it until we're a good sixty feet above the spring. I find a narrow ledge where we can both sit.

From up here, the clearing is a grassy circle with the tiny pond in the middle. In my mind's eye, I can imagine the tents spread out across the glade: small, almost toylike, the people insignificant.

"How do you feel from up here?" I ask.

"Like a god."

"Or a devil."

Jillian nods. "Do you think he watched them from here?"

"I think he watched them all the way up the trail. And the others. This spot below us . . . it's special. It would have been his place."

"His killing ground?"

"Probably more than once."

I take a thermal map from my backpack and orient it with where we're looking.

"What's that?"

"Rangers have been all over this area and never found anything. But there are a dozen places you can't see from the ground."

I line up the cooler section on the map with a precipice about twenty yards away. There's a sheer face about ten feet tall with several cracks in it. Above it is a small ledge.

"Hold my pack?"

"What are you doing?"

"I was looking for a place where a cat or a bear couldn't get to, but a primate might."

"What, a ledge?"

"No, a cave."

CHAPTER FIFTY-SEVEN

LAIR

I have to wedge my foot into a small crack in the rock wall and grasp the upper edge so tightly my fingers turn white in order to pull myself up onto the ledge.

I could imagine a mountain lion making the leap or a bear doing a chin-up if they were really inclined, but I don't think they would do it with any regularity if there were better places to reside.

"Theo?" calls Jillian.

"Just a second." I roll over and catch my breath while ignoring the still-healing wounds all over my body. "Fine," I say after I sit up.

The thermal image suggested there might be a deep passage here. Sure enough, there's a gap in the rocks like a sharp triangle. Just wide enough for a man to slide through.

I take my flashlight from my pocket and shine it into the chasm. The wall veers to the right after about ten feet, indicating that the cave twists to the side.

"If I don't come out in ten minutes . . . um, go get help?"

"Why don't I come with you?" she shouts from the base of the wall.

"Just hang. Let me see what's here."

"Fine. But I'm coming after you in ten, not getting help."

I get an anxious feeling and look out at the clearing. I'm not sure if it's nerves for what's inside or the thought of leaving her alone.

I take my gun out and lower it down for her to take. "Here."

"What are you going to use?"

"Common sense?"

"How has that worked out for you so far?" She waves the gun away. "If I need it to go after you, then it would be better if you had it in the first place."

There's no point arguing with her. I tuck it back into my waistband and step inside the cave.

A scent washes over me. Acrid and moist, I can't quite place it. I've smelled plenty of dead bodies in the past few weeks. This is something different.

I go deeper into the cavern, past the twist in the passage, and the walls begin to widen out. The roof gets lower, but I can still walk with only a slight hunch.

The floor is a layer of dirt covering a flat rock surface. I search for any sign of habitation but only find rocks and a few dry branches a storm probably blew in here.

It's certainly deep enough for someone to live in, or at least spend a few days on a murder vacation.

I keep going farther, looking for something. I really don't know what. It's been over thirty years since Elizabeth had her encounter. And assuming the Cougar Man did hang out up here, I'm not sure what I should be looking for.

Okay, that's not honest. I think I was expecting to see a pile of bones from those missing hikers. All I have is a dirt floor.

After another ten yards, I reach the end of the cave. Just to be certain, I double back and aim the light at all the places where the floor meets the wall, searching for small passages into other chambers.

Nothing.

The strange scent is still present, but I don't smell the decay of bodies.

I have a few other spots on my map to check, but I'm doubtful any of them would be as promising as this place. I turn back and head toward the sunlight bouncing around the corner.

When I reach the bend, I flick my light off. I'm able to make out the front of the cave well enough. But in the half second it takes to turn the switch, I see something that tells me to flip it back on.

It's such a subtle feature. A foot to the left or right and I might never have noticed it. When I move the light around, the details stand out quite clearly.

Four long gouges—the kind you'd get if you scratched the wall with metal claws.

I have to be careful of confirmation bias, but I just can't imagine any other explanation. It looks like the Cougar Creek Monster decided to sharpen his claws before going out on the hunt.

I take some photos, take a flake from the groove, check the other walls, then run out to Jillian. "I found it!" I shout down to her.

"Found what?"

"He was here! Claw marks. Four of them."

"How do you know it wasn't a cat?"

"Cats don't leave bits of metal when they scratch rock."

Amid my excitement I can see an uneasiness in Jillian's eyes. Things have suddenly become very real for her. She came up the mountain with me to investigate a decades-old legend. Now I've tied it in to the present.

"Was there . . . anything else?" she asks.

"No. Just the claw marks. The police might do a better job of searching the floor."

"Do you think they'll come out here for that?"

"I don't know. Elizabeth's husband might take an interest now that there's proof."

"Gouges on the wall?"

I begin to realize what she's thinking. While the significance is important to me, it won't be to anyone else—especially when the police are still convinced they're after an animal.

"Yeah. I see what you mean. But this can be helpful to me."

"I guess it's better," she replies, probably glad the cave isn't filled with victims. "Maybe that means the stories of the other missing hikers are just stories?"

"Possibly."

"And there's no way they could be buried up there?"

"No. It's a solid rock floor." I scan the rest of the caldera. "I don't think there's really anywhere else you could stash a body here without burying it."

"Could you find a buried body?"

"Not the way I found the others. It's been too long."

"Maybe there aren't any."

I watch the steam rise off the spring and waft away in the breeze. "Yeah . . ."

"Theo? Theo?"

I let my attention come back to the present. "Yes?"

"What is it?"

I'm still staring at the hot spring. The anxious feeling begins to fill me again.

"He didn't bury them . . ."

CHAPTER FIFTY-EIGHT

EXTREMOPHILE

Jillian watches me as I circle the pond. The outer edge has a yellow sulfur coloration, while the center is a dark void where an occasional bubble of gas breaks the surface. It's shallow around the first ten feet or so; then the back end drops off dramatically.

I reach a hand down and measure the temperature at a few different spots. The dark end, the deeper side, is much warmer. Not scalding, but like a warm bath.

"What are you thinking?" she asks.

"Did you know that they discovered microbes in the hot springs in Yellowstone that thrived at much higher temperatures than we thought possible? Extremophiles. They're the reason we think there might be life on other planets."

She gives me an uneasy look. "Um, great. So, what, you're thinking we're dealing with aliens now?"

"One second."

I turn toward the brush and start digging through for a large stick. I find something like a misshapen medieval rake and bring it back to the pond.

"You think there might be a body in there, don't you?"

I probe the water with the stick and confirm the drop-off is as steep as I estimated.

"Hundreds of people have been in this pool," I say out loud, rationalizing my thought process.

"They would have found something if it was in there." Jillian tries to say this as a fact.

"Not if . . ." I stop talking as my mind starts to zero in on something.

There's no way to avoid it. The bottom of the pond is what I need to investigate.

I take off my shirt and lay it on a log. Still focused on the pond, I begin to untie my shoes.

"Theo . . . you're not going in there."

I glance over at her. "Sorry if this makes you uncomfortable. I have boxer briefs on."

"You're an idiot."

I remove my pants and take a step into the water. My foot is already warmer than the rest of my body. I go all the way in until I'm chest-deep.

As I move toward the darker section, the water gets much hotter.

"How is it?" she asks.

"Nice, right here. Down there? Good question."

"Promise me you're not going to go diving? It has to be boiling down there."

As she says this, a bubble breaks the surface near my face. "Technically, yes. But it's not the water that scares me."

"Your extremophiles?"

"Go for help if I don't come back in ten."

"I'm going home and forgetting I ever met you," she replies.

I take a deep breath and dive under. As I descend, the water gets dramatically hotter. I feel it on my scalp and the back of my neck. When I shove my arms in front of me, my nerves are burning pinpricks.

I kick my legs, bringing me lower, then hit a wall of even hotter water. My hands begin to burn, so I pull back and head upward.

When I break the surface, the cold air slaps me in the face.

"My god," says Jillian, now sitting on the log. "Your face is beet red."

"It's warm."

"Satisfied?"

I dog-paddle closer to the bank. "I'm satisfied that no sensible person would go down there."

"Great. Will you come out now?"

"No. That just confirms my suspicion. Would you hand me my stick?"

"So you can go bobbing for bodies?" She doesn't move.

"Well, if you don't hand me the stick, then I'll have to use my teeth. Your choice."

"Disgusting." She tosses it into the water, splashing it next to me.

"Thank you."

I grab the end, push it in front of me like a spear, and dive back down. I go as far as I went last time and use the branch to poke around the bottom.

The end collides with rocks and what feel like logs. I'm only able to keep probing for a minute before the heat is too much. I swim back to the surface to catch my breath and cool down. Jillian looks none too pleased.

"This is what you signed up for," I tell her. "I told you that there might be bodies."

"I wasn't expecting one of them to be yours. I didn't come here to watch you boil like a lobster."

"I'll be fine."

"You know about the frog and the pot of boiling water?"

"That's a myth. They hop out. They always hop out." Unless they're single-minded professors who don't know any better.

I dive back down and probe around in another area. This time the stick hits a rock that gives way when I push it, as if it were stacked on top of another rock. I have to go back up before I can investigate further.

"Why do you have to be the one doing this?" Jillian asks as I emerge.

"I couldn't even get the police to show up three miles away from their station for the first body. What do you think they'd say if I told them that this was tied to the Cougar Creek Monster?"

I dive back into the water and return to probing. My stick stabs into something that feels wooden. When I pull the stick back, I can tell that it's wedged into something.

I carefully pull it toward me and reach out to touch whatever it is that I speared. My fingers feel a row of something that's curved and slatlike.

I try not to get ahead of myself. It could be a deer's rib cage. I slide my fingers over the back and check the vertebrae for prominent dorsal spines, like you'd find on a deer or a bear.

They're short and blunt. Just like you'd find on a human.

I stick my head out of the water. Jillian's expression changes the moment she sees me.

"You found something."

"Yeah . . ."

I swim to the bank, dragging my find behind me.

I move it into the shallow end of the pond where the water is clear.

Jillian kneels down to look at the rib cage. "Human?"

I leave it in the water and slide myself onto the grass. "Adult. Probably female."

"Is there more?"

"Probably. The water or the bacteria chewed through the connective tissue. We need to leave this one in here until someone can do a proper removal. Once it gets exposed to the air, it will start to decompose."

I study the surface features of the partial skeleton and notice several prominent claw marks across the ribs.

Jillian notices them, too. "It's him."

"Definitely."

"What's that?"

I look to where she's pointing. Something metallic is glittering against the dark bone. I spot a tiny piece of something wedged into the left side of the ribs. Perhaps a little too impulsively, I pry it loose with my fingers.

When I scrape away the grime and algae I realize it's a sharp metal knifepoint. Maybe even a claw point.

I hold it up for Jillian to see. "This didn't come from a cat or a bear. They have to believe us now. They have to."

CHAPTER FIFTY-NINE

HAUNTED

We walk the first half mile in total quiet, both of us processing our discovery. After getting several photos, I dragged the rib cage back to the center of the pool to wait for police divers.

When I got back out of the pond, Jillian handed me a bottle of water to bathe with, telling me that she wasn't going to have someone who smelled like a fart bomb as a traveling companion.

I appreciated her ability to rebound so quickly from what she just saw, then got the drift that she was never all that fazed by it to begin with. I suspect that she's been around death more than once.

Even so, she's still alert. As we head down the narrow pass, I catch her looking over her shoulder several times and scanning the ridgeline.

The return trip is more unsettling than the hike up. At first I put it down to the fact that we just came face-to-face with death, but then begin to get paranoid.

"That was somebody's child," says Jillian, breaking our silence.

"Yes. Missing for over thirty years, I guess."

"Do you think there are more down there?"

"Yes."

"Why do you think so?"

"I found this one without much difficulty. He'd put a rock on the chest to weigh the body down. The chances of me happening to pry loose the one set of bones down there are just too remote. I'm sure there are others."

"Right there, in this pond all this time. All those people swimming and playing—god forbid, drinking the water—with a graveyard right under their toes. It's wrong."

"It was risky."

She looks back over her shoulder. "What do you mean?"

"Those bodies could have swelled from gases and risen to the surface. It's not a smart way to get rid of them. Better to just bury them out in the woods."

"Then why do it?" she asks.

"I don't know. People baffle me."

"He's not a person."

"Yes, he is. He's just a horrible one. If I were to guess, he liked the idea of having all the bodies in one place. He probably got his rocks off watching people swim in that pool."

"It's disgusting."

"It's encouraging."

"What? How?"

"This was his younger phase and he got smarter, but there was and surely still is some thrill in it for him. Enough to drive him to be careless. He's capable of making mistakes."

Jillian stops. I watch as she tilts her head to the side for a moment, then starts up again.

"What is it?" I ask.

"What's what?"

"You stopped."

"Did I? I guess I heard something."

This tension between the instinctive animal and the reasoning human who discounts anything that doesn't fit into narrow sense categories is fascinating to me. I just watched Jillian detect something and then quickly forget about it because she couldn't classify it.

"Do you feel a tingling on the back of your neck and a tightening in your stomach?" I ask.

"Yes. You?"

"Yep."

"I think we're being watched," she whispers without turning around.

We continue hiking without saying anything. We both make an effort to seem less pronounced in our curiosity about what might be following us, keeping our heads forward but searching the trail with our eyes.

After another half mile, we come to a section where the trees thin out. Jillian whispers, "No place to hide here. But after the next bend it gets thicker. If I were a sniper . . ."

"That's where you would be."

"Yes, sir."

"Keep walking."

I let her get farther ahead of me, then quietly begin to climb to the ridge. I wait for her to get around the curve before I go over the top, wanting the focus of any watcher to be her emerging through the ravine.

The forest forms a peninsula as the trail switchbacks in an oxbow.

If whatever or whoever is stalking us is in the cluster of trees ahead of me, there's only a narrow band of woods for them to go through to leave.

I weigh trying to be stealthy against the direct approach and decide to just run full speed into the trees and pray I'm not about to smack into a mountain lion.

A quarter of the way into the woods, a branch breaks somewhere in the distance. Birds squawk and several thrushes take to the air, flapping wildly.

Ten yards ahead of me, a branch swings upward. I'm not sure if I've just seen a shadow pass by or if it's the sway of a tree.

Suddenly fearful of having left Jillian, I run to the edge of the peninsula and see her making her way around the turn.

She stares up at me and raises her eyebrows, silently questioning me. I shrug.

As I start to turn back, I notice a patch of dry ground just under a low overhang of branches.

There's a clear footprint of a boot. I touch it to measure the moisture. It's recent. Not even an hour old.

I take my phone out to grab a photo. When I place a dollar bill next to it for size comparison, I realize how large the shoe that left it is. It's at least a size fourteen or fifteen. The depression indicates that whoever filled it is quite heavy.

"Well?" asks Jillian after I skid down the hill to join her.

"I saw a big boot print. Probably a hunter."

"Hunter? There's no hunting here."

"Right. Maybe a hiker. I know I sometimes try to avoid people."

"Yeah . . . I've noticed. Sure it wasn't our stalker?"

"This person was tall and heavy. Not exactly ninja material."

She seems satisfied with my answer and continues on.

As I think about it, I realize something: a few minutes ago I was analyzing how quickly she ignored her own instincts, and here I am telling her that there's nothing to worry about because the print I found doesn't match my expectation.

I survey the ridge ahead of us and feel my stomach tighten back up.

CHAPTER SIXTY

SCENERY

The sun is setting against a blood-red sky by the time we make it back to my Explorer. Jillian and I climb inside and exchange glances, expressing our relief at making it down before it got dark.

"So what happens now?" she asks as we pull onto the highway.

"You mean about the body? I send an anonymous e-mail to the police with the photo and the location."

"Do you think that's going to fool anyone?"

"No. I've just had too many frustrating experiences with the law enforcement around here." My side still hurts from the beating Gunther gave me.

"So what are you going to do next?"

"Find more bodies, I guess. There's not a lot I can do. They have a lot of forensic tools they can use. Maybe if they get the FBI involved. At some point they're going to have to give up on their stupid wild animal theory."

"More bodies," she says, looking out the window at the darkening sky. There's only one other car on the road, and it's a quarter mile behind us.

"Actually, I want to see if I can find older victims."

"Like the ones here?"

"Yes. And maybe other places. The problem is he's too clever now. He knows how to avoid the police. His kills are free of his DNA, as far as I can tell. The metal fragment in the rib cage? I doubt he'd let that happen now. He's evolved his methods with modern forensics."

"But his older murders . . ."

"He might not have been so clever. The hot spring probably wiped away any trace of him, so it was smart in that regard, but it didn't hide the fact that there was a killer out there. Now he's invisible. Maybe there are more clues to be found looking into his past."

"So you're going to look up old murders?"

"Missing-persons reports. Odd knife attacks. Anything else that might fit over the last few decades."

I realize I missed my exit and do a U-turn.

"I wonder what he's like? Would we recognize him if we met him?"

"I've been thinking about that. I don't think so. He's intelligent and probably not socially awkward."

Jillian watches the clouds in the fading light. "Where does somebody like that come from?"

"Two percent of the population is sociopathic. They just don't feel the way you or I do about others. If you come in contact with fifty people in a day, one of them is a sociopath."

"But not a murderer."

"No. Yet if they had a magic button they could press that would kill someone and they'd gain from it, risk-free, they wouldn't hesitate."

"Would you know if you're a sociopath?"

"I read a lot about it when I was a teenager."

"Self-diagnosing?"

"Perhaps a little. From what I can tell, if you're intelligent, you'd probably suspect it. If you weren't, you'd just assume that's how everybody else felt."

"And what did young Dr. Cray deduce about himself?"

"Socially inept. Terminally."

There's a flash of light in my rearview mirror. I don't think much of it at first, then realize that we've been on a straight road with no other turnoffs for miles.

Jillian catches me looking in the mirror. "What is it?"

"Nothing."

"Theo," she says with an admonishing tone.

"I think someone just did a U-turn, like we did."

"Are they following us?"

"Good question. Take out your phone."

I stop on the shoulder and turn on the interior light.

"Are we pretending we're lost?"

I look away from the road and stare at her phone. "Yep. When the car passes, let me know how many people are inside."

"What if they stop behind us?"

"They won't. Unless they want to make it obvious that we're being followed."

I see the car approach and pass out of the corner of my eye.

"The windows were tinted. It was a dark-green Yukon."

"Did you catch the plates, by any chance?"

"Montana. Not the number."

"Interesting. Probably nothing."

"Nothing?"

"Yeah."

"Okay." She seems more amused than alarmed.

I turn the dome light off. Jillian is still looking at me, the glow of the dashboard illuminating her face. There's a curl of a smile on her lips.

The lingering gaze, I know what that means.

I think.

For her this is still an adventure. I don't think she gets it.

Or maybe I don't.

Impulsively—maybe it's the adrenaline—I lean into her personal space, and her lips part slightly. I give her a kiss. Intense, but quick.

She's smiling when I pull back. "What?" I ask.

"This is probably the most morbid first date anyone has ever been on."

"You asked for it."

"I did. I did."

She puts her hand on the back of my neck, signaling that we're not done kissing.

"You realize that may have been the killer who just passed us?"

"You realize what a turn-on this kind of rush is?"

There's something about her I can't resist in the moment. I grab her by the back of the head and press her lips against mine again, this time more forcefully. My tongue finds hers, and they play back and forth.

I slide a hand under her shirt and feel the breasts I've been obsessing over all day—actually, since I met her.

At some point her hand touches my thigh and travels upward until she's cupping my bulge.

She whispers into my ear, "Are we going to do something about that?"

I pull away and lean against my door. "I'm sorry. I . . ."

"What? Is it me?"

"No! It's me. These are dark things. Dark places. I shouldn't have taken you there."

"If I hadn't gone, then I wouldn't be here."

"An hour ago we were looking at a dead body."

"That had been dead for thirty years."

"And the killer is still out there."

"Yes, Theo. He is. And the insurgent asshole that killed my husband is still out there, too. I'll never get closure on that."

"I'm sorry. I'm sorry."

"Don't say that. Are you sorry you kissed me?"

"No."

"You have to be able to compartmentalize all that. Your problem is you only have one compartment."

"It's how I focus."

"Have you considered the fact that it might keep you running in circles?"

She's on to something. MAAT didn't tell me about the hot spring. That came from a random comment. I've been doing the same thing over and over again.

I stare at her. She crosses her arms and watches me with her little smug smile on the corner of her lips. "Now what?"

I shut off the professor part of my brain and say the first thing that comes to mind.

"Climb in the back seat and find out."

CHAPTER SIXTY-ONE

INTERNIST

Dr. Debra Mead looks up at me through her very large-framed glasses and makes a sound somewhere between a grunt and a sigh, then says, "So you're the nincompoop who spoiled my samples?"

"Probably."

"This way," she directs me down the hallway of the medical examiner's offices.

I was first aware of the existence of her this morning when I was awakened by a phone call before six. It seems that Montana's single medical examiner keeps very early hours.

"Theo Cray?" she had asked.

"Yes?"

"This is Dr. Mead. Are you the one who keeps sending me bodies?"

There was something so direct about her question that I almost blurted out an affirmative.

"Uh . . . maybe," I replied hesitantly.

"I'm told you're a professor of some kind?"

"Biology."

"Don't tell me you teach, too?"

"Uh, yes. What's the problem?"

"I pity your students. Come to the Missoula medical examiner's office."

"When?"

"Now."

Mead hadn't given me anything else to go on, other than the imperious demand that I get there as quickly as I could.

Four hours later I'm being led down a hall by a petite, gray-haired woman who doesn't bother to contain her disdain for me.

For some reason, I like her. Maybe my spirits have been lifted—because a tryst with a beautiful woman on the side of the road like a horny teenager will do that to you.

"So, uh, what's this about?" I ask.

"It's about me retiring from the university only to find myself 'appointed'"—she makes air quotes as she says this—"by the governor as state medical examiner. Apparently I'm the only one in the state qualified after the last asshole left. Total disarray. They were sending bodies to Seattle. Seattle? Jeez."

"State medical examiner? Wait, there's only one in the whole state?"

"Yes. We have plenty of coroners. Any quack that can pass the test can be a coroner. But to do an official autopsy, one that a court will recognize, that has to be done by someone who knows their ass from their elbow or a bear claw from a knife."

"So you know that they were killed by a man?"

She stops at a door and gives me a dumb look. "Yes, Professor Genius. You're not the only one capable of calling a spade a spade."

"So why hasn't that been announced?"

She waves the question away and motions for me to sit in a chair. "Have a seat and take your shirt off."

"My shirt?"

"I'm taking blood, skin, body hairs, and anything else I damn well feel like."

"I'm not sure I understand."

"You teach?"

"We went over that."

"Right. Well, I've got a room full of bodies in there that I'm going to be examining. If I find any DNA other than the victims', I'd like to know if it's yours. Maybe it's all yours. I'll want semen, too."

"Semen?"

"You teach biology?" She shakes her head. "God help us."

"I'm confused."

"Obviously. Let me explain it to you simply. If I find any DNA, I need to know that's it's not yours. I'd rather not have to wait to find out. I'm not a patient woman."

"Clearly."

She gives me a sharp look. "Listen, smart-ass, I can either have you do this voluntarily or I can get a judge to force you. You don't want to know how we force a semen sample."

"Actually, I do. Is it something you assist with?"

"Yes. I shove an eight-inch needle into your scrotum and drain it like a grape."

I break out into a laugh. "Has anyone ever pointed out that's physically impossible?"

"Do you think the normal dumb asses we see here even know how to spell *scrotum*? So what will it be?"

"Resistance is pointless, isn't it?"

❦

After she gets blood and follicle and skin scrapings, she leaves me to provide the final sample. It's much easier than I would have expected, but I'm not surprised, given the recent memory to think about.

When I open the door, she's standing on the other side of the hallway.

"Forget how to work your zipper?"

"I'm done."

"Goddamn jackrabbit. You must be a real treat for the ladies." She holds out her hand for the specimen cup. "Let me put your excretions on ice, then we'll suit up."

"Suit up?"

"Yes. Your notes weren't exactly as specific as you might have thought they were. I have some questions about how you found the bodies."

"Bodies . . . I only told the police I found Chelsea Buchorn. Oh, and then there was Summer Osbourne." I'm honestly starting to lose track.

Mead watches my confused response, then replies, "Right. That was in the notes. We have a bunch of other bodies sent to us by a Mr. Anonymous. Do you think there are any other aspiring forensic examiners out there digging up dead girls I should know about?"

"Well . . ."

She waves my hesitation away. "If you're worried about the legal implications, talk to a lawyer. In the meantime, let's play a game of tell me how this other guy might have found the bodies and in what conditions, okay? The sooner we clear that up, the sooner we can find out who really did this and the FBI will move on to asking questions about him instead of you."

"The FBI?"

Mead shrugs. "I didn't say anything."

Oh, crap. That might have been who followed Jillian and me last night. Mead's little hint makes it seem that I might be the target of their investigation. Christ.

If that's the case, I'll need whatever help I can get to convince them that I'm on their side. That means doing whatever Mead asks.

I spend the rest of the day explaining to her about each body and how I found them. She asks specific questions about smells, depth of soil, and vegetation.

Although the medical technicians who removed the bodies made detailed notes, Mead is very curious about what my observations were when I discovered them. She was acutely interested in skin coloration.

"Any word on the samples from the hot spring?" I ask after we finish going over the last body.

"Hot spring?"

"I found a rib cage in a hot spring near Red Hook."

"For crying out loud. Really?"

"I sent an e-mail to the police last night."

"Great. Do you ever rest?" she asks.

"Do you?"

"Red Hook, you said?"

"Yeah. Does that ring a bell?"

"Maybe. Odd."

"What?"

"When I first saw these bodies, it reminded me of something I examined years ago. A girl, a prostitute from near there. She had a claw mark across her back. Four, not five gashes."

"Really? How long ago?"

"Going on twenty years."

"And nobody connected her to this?"

"No. She died of an overdose. When I did the autopsy, I noticed the scars. She'd healed from them years prior. I just made a note of it and that was it."

"There may be a connection."

"Maybe. But at the rate the police are moving, I wouldn't count on anything turning up for a while."

CHAPTER SIXTY-TWO

NEXT OF KIN

Between being born and ending up on Dr. Mead's autopsy table years ago, Sarah Eaves had a difficult life. Other than a hospital and date of birth, I can't find out much about her childhood. There are arrest records for shoplifting when she's eighteen and charges of prostitution and drug possession in her early twenties.

The three mug shot photos show a pretty, if sad, young girl aging too fast. There's a five-year gap between her last arrest and when she was found dead in a motel room with a syringe in her arm.

This suggests that Sarah may have cleaned herself up but then had a relapse that killed her.

Dr. Mead was able to pull a few strings and get the address of her last employer, Darcy's Hotcakes & Coffee, on the highway outside Red Hook.

As I sit here, sipping my coffee and using all my willpower not to eat the rest of my blueberry pancakes, I try to place the girl in the photo in a waitress uniform and imagine what could have transpired that would have caused her to regress to her darker past.

A balding man in his early thirties gets out of a faded Honda Civic and enters the restaurant. Although Robert Moorhen doesn't share the same last name as his mother, he has the same eyes.

I wave him over to the booth, and he takes off his well-worn parka and has a seat across from me.

He eyes the folder sitting in front of me. "Is that about my mother?"

I'm hesitant to reply because there are autopsy photos in there. "Some of it. Thank you for meeting with me."

"Yeah. Sure. I had today off. What can I do for you?"

"First, you understand I'm not a cop, right? I'm just a researcher?"

He nods. "I'd tell you anything, anyway. If I knew much. She died when I was five. My grandparents raised me."

"What about your father?"

"He wasn't around much. He was an oil worker who spent most of his time in Alaska and Canada. Mom and him didn't last very long. They split before I was three."

"This isn't easy to say, but you know your mother had a troubled past . . ."

"The prostitution thing and the drug stuff? Yeah, you can say it. My grandparents never mentioned it, but when Dad got drunk, he'd go off on her history. I don't want to believe it, but I guess I accept it. You just have to understand that wasn't the woman I knew. I don't have a lot of memories about her, but she was always there for me. A real good mom." Robert points to a corner booth. "After preschool I used to sit there and color. She'd check on my ABCs between serving customers. Then . . . well."

Robert's memory is a sharp contrast to her mug shots, but I believe him.

"When your mother passed away, the doctors noticed some odd scars. Do you remember these?"

Robert thinks it over. "Maybe? Like dog scratches or something?"

"Yes. Something like that. Did she ever mention how she got them?"

"I was five. You kind of just accept the world as it is at that point. Maybe she said something. Like she got them when she was younger?"

"Younger? How much?"

"I don't know. When you're a kid, you just assume your parents were always grown-up. It's weird—I'm older now than she was when she died. Yet she still feels like my mom." He pauses and stares out the window. "The scars. Maybe she got them playing?"

"Playing?"

"I don't know. She just didn't talk about them. She never talked about her childhood."

"I can't find much about it. What do you know?"

"She left the home when she was sixteen or seventeen. That's about it."

"The home?"

"Yeah. The foster home where she lived. She never talked about that. She'd been in and out of the system since she was a baby."

"Do you know anything about this foster home? Who her foster parents were?"

"No. It wasn't far from here. I know that. She grew up in this area."

Interesting. I need to ask Mead if she can get me any information on that. If that's when Sarah got the scars . . .

"Do you have any suspects?" asks Robert.

"No. As I said, I'm not an investigator. I'm just doing academic research."

"I hope you get the guy who killed her."

"I hope so, too . . ." I stop when I realize what he just said. "Wait . . . your mother died of an overdose."

"Right. But she didn't put that needle in her arm. Somebody else did and gave her a lethal dose."

I slide the police report out of the folder and read through it again. The cause of death is listed as accidental overdose. This might be too much for Robert to cope with, although he said that with so much conviction.

"You don't think your mom had a relapse?"

Robert points to the table where he sat as a child. "Last time I saw her was right there. She finished her shift and went outside to grab a smoke. She never did that around me. And she never came back. Two days later they found her twenty miles away in a motel room." His voice begins to rise. "My mother may have been a lot of things—hooker, junkie, thief—but she was a good mother, damn it. She adored me. If she wanted to run off with some old boyfriend and shoot up, she would have dropped me off at my grandparents', not abandoned me."

His face is filled with rage. Not just at me but at the injustice the world did to him.

"I'm sorry, Robert. I didn't mean to suggest otherwise."

He stares out into the parking lot and calms down. "Sorry. It's something that I think about every day. When you called, I just assumed it was about that. That they'd solved the . . . what do they call it? The cold case. I guess it was too much to hope for."

"No, it's not. Why do you think someone would want to kill your mother?"

"I don't know. As a kid, I thought it might be like a crime movie, where she saw something she shouldn't have. Now? I don't know. I couldn't imagine anyone hating her."

"What did your father say?"

"Nothing. We don't exactly have a close relationship. Maybe he mentioned something once about her going to shoot up with a junkie boyfriend. But ask anyone here that knew her and they'll tell you she wouldn't have just left me here like that. Not unless it was against her will. I mean, who would leave a kid here, all alone?"

"I don't know, Robert. I don't know. But I'll look into that."

It's not an empty promise. But to get to the bottom of it, I need to start at the beginning of Sarah's darker life—and possibly where she first encountered the killer.

CHAPTER SIXTY-THREE

HOMESTEAD

Julie Lane greets me at the door with a warm smile on her worn face. There are a few traces of gray in the dark hair she wears pulled back in a turquoise band, making estimating her age difficult.

From the late 1960s to the early '80s, she and her husband ran a foster home out here on this farm at the edge of Red Hook. Her large house, set against the Montana mountain backdrop, is surrounded by tall fir trees that stand out in the otherwise flat grazing land.

"Mrs. Lane, I'm Theo Cray. We spoke on the phone? I'm doing some research on Montana history."

"Yes. Yes, of course." She opens the door and ushers me in.

A faded-orange couch sits in a living room that seems trapped in time from the 1970s. About the only modern concessions are a flat-screen television and an iPad with a crossword puzzle on it.

I take a seat on the couch next to her easy chair. "As I said on the phone, I'm doing some genealogy research and wanted to talk to you about some of the children that came through here."

"Right. To be honest, I don't know a whole lot about where they came from. We had all kinds of children here. White, brown, Indian, mixed. It didn't matter. We just wanted to give them a good home, and we did the best we could."

I want to jump right in and ask if any of the children were potential homicidal maniacs but have to ease my way in.

"What were their ages?"

"We specialized in teens. Troubled teens, as my husband used to say. But they were good."

"No behavior problems?"

She laughs. "They were teenagers. They all had behavior problems. But it was just acting out."

"I see. Do you remember a girl by the name of Sarah Eaves?"

Lane's expression changes for a moment; then she makes a small shake of her head. "No . . . not really. Maybe? Was she one of ours?"

"She was here in the early '80s. For two years, until she left home. She ended up not too far from here."

"Possibly. Perhaps if I saw a picture?"

I show her a photo Sarah's son gave me. "This would have been her around twenty."

"Yes," she says after a looking at it for a while. "I remember her now."

"Do you remember anything about her?"

"No, I can't say that I do. Like I said, I don't remember all of them. So many faces. You know how it is."

It's quite obvious to me that this woman is holding much more back than she cares to say.

"I just spoke with her son. He was quite interested to know what his mother was like as a child."

"Her son? Sarah had a boy?"

The way her face lights up at the mention of a baby and the way she said "Sarah" tells me she's much more familiar with her than she's let on.

"Yes. Nice guy. He gave me the photo."

"May I look at it again?"

I hand it back to her. She cradles it with both hands. "How old is the boy?"

"Thirty-two."

Lane looks to the side as she does the math. "Oh. That young?" There's something about her tone that indicates she suddenly lost interest. She hands me back the photo.

Why would she have been more interested if the boy was older? Would it be because she might have thought she knew the father?

"Did Sarah have a boyfriend?" I ask.

Lane's eyes narrow. "We didn't allow that kind of thing. Girls lived upstairs, and the boys stayed in the bunkhouse by the barn."

"Right. I didn't mean to imply anything."

"We were very strict here. My husband, Jack, didn't spare the belt, for the boys or the girls."

I'm now getting a creepy vibe. As much as I don't want to cause Mrs. Lane discomfort, I'm afraid I might have to push to get more information.

"Do you know why Sarah ran away?"

"No," she replies harshly. "She was troubled. Always causing problems. Getting the boys stirred up. Jack did his best, but she was too wild."

The way she says Jack's name—with conviction and near reverence—is unsettling.

I'm getting the sneaking suspicion that Jack's punishments might have included statutory rape and Mrs. Lane is well aware of that. If I press too much on that subject, she'll probably kick me out.

I ease off on that line of questioning. "When Sarah was here, who were the boys?"

"Mr. Cray, is this about genealogy or Sarah Eaves?" Her voice is stern. "I think it's time you leave."

"Actually, I just want to know about the scars on her back. She got them when she was here, didn't she?"

"That was an accident when she fell on some farm tools. The child services people know that. I don't know what you've heard. But it's a lie. It's time for you to go." The friendly woman who greeted me at the door has vanished.

I've only got one more card to play before she can have the police arrest me for trespassing.

If our killer was one of the foster children staying here when Sarah was, or close enough in time to know her, he could very well have already been playing around with his metal claws back then. I slide a photo of a bagh naka out of my folder and hold it up to her face. "Have you ever seen something like this before?"

She says nothing, but her eyes widen at the sight of the weapon.

I need to keep her agitated, off balance. "Did your husband, Jack, use this on Sarah?"

Her face goes white. "Jack? God, no! He would never!"

She's protecting someone else. "Who? Who else was your favorite? Was he the one that did that to her? Was he angry with her? Jealous of your husband?"

"That's enough." She stands up and points to the door. "It's time you leave. I'm calling . . . the sheriff if you don't."

"Wait, who were you about to say you were going to call?"

"Nobody. Now go!"

Her voice is so strident I'm afraid she's going to have a heart attack.

So close! I was about to get a name!

I get a sudden idea, drop my papers, and go down to my knees to clean them up.

She storms over to the door and holds it open for me. "Now!"

I push them back together and make my way out. "I'm sorry. I didn't mean to upset you."

She slams the door on me, then watches from the window as I drive off.

I'm going to have to think of a hell of an excuse to come back in a few hours to get the phone I left under her couch with the recorder running.

CHAPTER SIXTY-FOUR
Accomplice

After an hour of sitting in my car a half mile down the road, I turn around and head back to Julie Lane's house. I run through several different lies to tell her but can't settle on one that doesn't sound too forced. I decide to just knock on her door and tell her I may have left some government papers behind—without emphasizing what they were, other than government.

I feel like some kind of con artist trying to fleece the elderly with bullshit encyclopedias or insurance policies that are impossible to collect on. Then I remind myself that she may be shielding the killer. And then there's the possibility she might have been sitting by idly as her husband sexually abused their wards.

I think I'm okay with lying to her now.

"I told you to leave," she says from the other side of the door.

"I may have left some papers behind."

"You didn't. Now go!"

"Please, it's important." Impulsively, I grab the doorknob and turn it.

When I open the door, she jumps back with a terrified look on her face. Technically this is trespassing, but I pretend otherwise.

I give her my broadest smile. "Thanks for letting me in. I'll just be a second."

I move past her and get down on all fours by her couch, dropping my folder near where I left my phone. She steps to the other side of the room, making it easy for me to slip it in my pocket. I pull a sheet out of the folder and hold it up as I stand up. "Got it! Sorry to be a bother."

"You just wait until . . ." She doesn't finish her sentence.

I stop myself at the door. "Wait until what? Were you going to tell someone?"

"The police. I'm calling the sheriff right now!" She takes her phone from her pocket and holds it up in the air like it's some kind of talisman, reinforcing how empty her promise is.

I hurry back to my car and drive back to my earlier waiting spot down the road to play back the recording.

I click "Play."

Lane only waited a minute after I left to make a phone call.

"Damn it," she cried into the phone. "I was hoping you would pick up. There's been a man here asking questions about Sarah and you and Pa. You told me to call if that happened. Well, it did. I told him to go to hell and didn't say anything. I have his number if you want to set him straight."

After she hangs up, there's the sound of footsteps as she paces around the house and mutters to herself. I think she took a seat at the kitchen table across from the living room.

Twenty minutes in there's the sound of a phone ringing.

"Hello? . . . Thank god . . . Yes . . . About fifteen minutes ago . . . His name? Kay . . . Leo Kay, I think . . . What was that name? Theo Cray? . . . Yes, that's it! . . . Unpleasant man . . . You'll talk to him? . . . Oh, thank you . . . Thank you!"

So far there's nothing to tell me who this other person is. Although I'd bet anything it was one of the foster children living with the Lanes at the same time as Sarah. A record search should provide some names.

It's a little disconcerting to hear that he knows my name, but I shouldn't be surprised.

There's a long silence; then Lane says, "Okay . . . okay. What about the cars? You said you'd be sending some men to move them? . . . Okay."

After she hangs up, there's just the sound of footsteps until I show up again. I sound like a goddamn door-to-door con man. But it served its purpose. I know she called someone.

Maybe even him.

Short of stealing her phone, which I consider briefly, I don't know how to directly act on that information, but it's a clue. A really big clue.

Damn it. I may be real close to knowing who this is, assuming the man who scarred Sarah is the same one that killed all those other people.

And the cars? What did she mean by that?

There was just an old station wagon in the driveway. I didn't see anything else. Was there something in the barn, or maybe the woods? What's the connection to him?

My curiosity is driving me crazy. I have to go back again.

I wait until dark to return yet again to her house, parking down the road and walking the rest of the way on foot. I follow a wire fence toward the back of the property, keeping a cautious eye on the house in case a light turns on or someone shows up.

I try to convince myself that he won't come over right away, maybe not at all. Especially if he thinks I'm on to him.

This might be more wishful thinking than rational judgment.

I pass the barn and step through some thick weeds on the far side. I'm tempted to use my light, but I don't want to alert her to my presence.

I can barely see my own shoes in the darkness by the time I reach the woods. It probably would have been better to have done this early in the morning in the gray light of dawn, instead of now. I just didn't have the patience to wait that long.

The woods are a mixture of tall trees and overgrown brush. I have to walk around the edge to find a gap in the brambles to penetrate farther in.

I find a small foot trail and meander through wild berry bushes and shrubs. When I look behind me, the house is no longer visible, so I turn on my flashlight.

Immediately, something reflects in the weeds. I get closer and realize I'm staring at the headlight of a car. It's a rusted blue Chevy Citation.

There's no license plate on the front or the back, but I spot another car, a Datsun, about ten feet farther back. Orange with rust, again with no license plate.

When I spin my light around, I realize that there are at least eight or nine other cars around me. All of them at least thirty years old and covered in rust.

None of them has a license plate. I open the doors to some of them and search the glove boxes for anything to identify where they came from, but there's nothing to be found.

Weird.

Damn weird.

I take photos using my phone and try to find the VIN numbers. The ones on the dashboards have all been pried off. I check the running boards and engine blocks and come up empty.

What's with all the unmarked cars? Was old Jack running a car-theft ring?

No.

That's not why they're here.

My breath grows shallow as I understand where I'm standing.

Damn.

Holy crap.

I need to get out of here fast.

This isn't a junkyard.

This is another one of his graveyards.

CHAPTER SIXTY-FIVE

Junker

I have to get out of here. In a flash, this went from theoretical to very real. Lane's mystery foster child could have been one of many potential suspects, but the cars tell me otherwise.

All the missing hikers back in Cougar Creek, traveling there from across the country—as Elizabeth said, their cars would have to have piled up.

And they did.

He brought them here.

I race through the woods, weaving around the rusted junk heaps, and try to find my way toward the gap out of here. My foot hits a half-buried piece of metal, and I trip.

There's an icy pain as my elbow smashes into the side-view mirror of a Toyota Celica. When I pull my arm free, there are bits of glass in my skin and blood on the door.

Damn it.

I try to wipe the blood away with my sleeve, but all I do is smear it over the panel. I see an upstairs light turn on through the trees. Not good. She has to have heard me.

Screw the car. I bunch my jacket around the gash in my arm and take off running again.

I reach the edge of the woods and race over to the property line to follow the fence back to the road. I'm making a hell of a noise as I stomp through the dry grass. My knees clip the edge of a woodpile, knocking it over.

In the distance there's the sound of a door slamming, and lights come on at the edge of the yard.

"I know you're out there!" yells Julie Lane. Then she says something truly chilling. "Wait until he finds out! Just you wait!"

I make it to the gravel road, shoulders hunched, fearful that I'm going to get a spine full of lead from a shotgun blast.

Lungs heaving, I start to wobble as my vision begins to get dim around the edges. Crap. I've lost more blood than I realize.

I brace myself on a fence post, take a deep breath, and check back over my shoulder. I see Mrs. Lane's silhouette on the porch, watching me.

I stumble farther along, using the wooden rail to keep me from falling. Eventually I walk far enough away that she's out of sight. Not that it makes any difference—but mentally it does.

I keep going, afraid that any moment I'm going to take one mushy step and collapse.

Somehow, I make it to my Explorer. When I open the door and see my arm in the interior light, it's covered in my blood.

I want to drive off and leave this damned place, but I'm fearful that I might pass out behind the wheel and slam into a tree. This needs to be taken care of now.

Using my good arm, I pop the hatch at the back of my Explorer and get out my first-aid kit.

I managed to nick my basilic vein. It takes a tourniquet on my elbow to stop the blood.

I pick away the piece of glass holding it open and squeeze the rupture. Thankfully, the vein isn't severed, just slit like a botched blood draw. As I sit on my bumper waiting for blood platelets to coagulate and seal it from within, I keep a watchful eye on the road.

I slide Gus's gun from my waistband to the floor, in case I have to get to it in a hurry. The only problem is that I'm a righty and that hand is out of commission for the moment.

Patience, Theo. Patience.

My heart stops beating so fast and the blood isn't running down my fingertips anymore. When I release the vein, there's still a trickle, but something I can manage with a tight dressing.

Just to be sure, I need to have a two-handed physician examine the cut, in order to make sure I don't have to stitch it up.

❦

Forty minutes later I'm sitting in the emergency room of Fairfax Hospital waiting for them to call my name. The fluorescent lights and antiseptic smell are strangely soothing to me. It's the only relaxing thing in my world right now.

My bandage is bright red, and the blood has started to flow back down my arm. I want to say something to the receptionist, but I'm sure I have another few pints to go before I'm really critical.

The numb arm isn't what disturbs me the most. It's the confirmation of what I suspected.

As I sit here, bleeding out, I use my left hand to operate my phone and search through all the records I could find about missing persons around Cougar Creek.

Six of the cars I found in the woods are the same make, model, and color of cars belonging to missing persons.

It's him.

It's really him.

I compose a text message to the police in Red Hook and cc Dr. Mead. I provide the Lanes' address, a list of the cars, and their connection to Sarah and the murders.

With this information, they can get the names of who was living there and get *his* name.

I hit "Send" and feel a wave of relief that could also be the disembodied euphoria of passing out.

CHAPTER SIXTY-SIX

ALIBI

The Poitier County sheriff substation in Red Hook is a small building attached to the post office. The walls are filled with brochures and notices. Two desks sit in back of a small counter, and the rest of the station is behind a secure metal door where I assume they have a holding cell or a safe.

Sergeant Graham, a female officer who wears a serious expression over an otherwise friendly face, is making notes as I tell her how I came to the Lane house and discovered the cars.

I've had to change the story a little, or rather redact some of the details, because I was clearly trespassing.

"When I knocked on the door, there was no answer. So I went around back to see if she was there."

"Did you have permission to do this?"

"I'd spoken with her on the phone. She told me I could stop by." This part is true, until she told me to go to hell.

Graham writes this down in tiny, very concise script. "And that's when you discovered the cars?"

"I saw the woods and decided to take a closer look."

"Why?"

"I'm a biologist. You don't see as many fir trees at this altitude around here."

She taps her pen on the edge of her chin. "Huh. I never thought about that."

I get the impression that she thinks deeply about a lot of things and make a mental note to try not to be too clever.

"I think it has to do with the soil. This is all glacial flood plain. The top layer is good for farming, but more than a few feet it's too rocky."

"And that's when you saw the cars?"

"Yes. Lots of them. It seemed odd. I wrote down the model numbers and makes and compared them to a list of cars belonging to missing persons in the 1980s."

"And you think this is connected to the bodies that have been turning up?"

"Yes. They've all had similar claw marks. I was told that a foster child under care of the Lanes had suffered something similar, so I went to investigate."

She leans back in her chair and assesses me. "That's quite a leap."

"One of the victims at Cougar Creek had a similar wound. It seemed worth looking into."

"On your own . . ."

There's something about the way that she says this that's slightly condescending.

"Let's just say that the other authorities I've spoken to haven't been very proactive."

"Probably true. Can't say that I'm much better. I've got a stack of reports and incidents that keeps growing."

"I understand. But we're talking about murder."

"And I take this very seriously." She picks up her radio shoulder mic. "This is 163. Do we have anyone near Highway 30 and Harris Road? Over."

"Hey, Graham," a man replies. "Finley is about ten minutes away from there."

"Could you connect me to him?"

Seconds later an older voice announces himself. "Finley here. Over."

"Hey, Fin. This is Graham. I've got a witness here with an interesting lead. Could you go over to 848 Harris and check on some possible stolen cars in the back of the property? Just ask the owner if they'll let you do a search. If not, we'll ask the sheriff what to do next."

"Sure thing. That's the Lane place, right?"

"Affirmative."

"She doesn't seem the type."

"Maybe one of her foster kids."

"Foster kids? I thought she lived alone."

"This is going way back."

"Roger."

She turns her attention back to me. "We'll see what he finds. If the owner won't let us search, then we'll see about a warrant. I'll need you to speak to the sheriff at that point."

"Whatever I can do."

"So you think one of the foster kids is the fella that was killing all those girls?"

"I'd say there's a definite connection there. The cars are what convinced me." Since she seems at least into the theory and hasn't locked me up or kicked me out, I decide to go a little further. "Can you pull up a list of names for the foster children who stayed there?"

"I'd have to call family services." She checks her watch. "But . . . it might not be a bad idea to be a little proactive."

She picks up her desk phone and dials. "Hey, Bonnie, this is Graham calling from the Poitier County sheriff's office. I wanted to find out about getting the records for some foster parents going back to the late 1970s and early 1980s . . . uh-huh . . . Helena? . . . Can't you do it electronically? No? . . . Well, if it's not too much trouble, could you go ahead and have them pull them and set them aside? The department has a liaison there."

When she hangs up, she shrugs. "That's half my day, asking for things that I should be able to find in a second. My friend is calling over to Helena to have them pull the records. If your story pans out, then we'll be able to dig in a little farther."

I have no doubt that it will pan out. There's no way the killer could remove that many cars overnight without leaving evidence.

Her radio bursts to life with an urgent announcement from the dispatcher. "All available units to respond to a fire at 848 Harris Road!"

Graham and I both look up in shock. Hers is more subdued than my own.

Her radio crackles. "Graham, this is Fin. Is that witness with you right now?"

"Right in front of me."

"What time did he say he left the Lane residence?"

"Dr. Cray?" she asks.

"Last night. I went to the hospital after. You can talk to them," I reply.

Graham relays this into her radio. "He says he was there last night. The department also got an e-mail from him last night as well."

"Okay. Well. Damn it. The woods are on fire. Looks like it may have started a little while ago. I think we need you out here."

Graham bolts upright. "Dr. Cray, I have to lock up the substation, but if you can stick around in this area, that would be helpful."

"Of course. Anything."

Jesus. He set the whole woods on fire to keep them from getting to the cars. But how much will that really help?

Dumbfounded, I follow Graham out the door and watch as she locks it.

As she heads to her car, there's another call on the radio I can hear clearly. "Dispatch, this is Finley. I'm at 848 Harris and have a 10-54."

Graham turns around and stares at me for a moment from the side of her police car, her hand hesitating on the door handle.

I force myself to give her a nod. "I'll be at Darcy's Hotcakes & Coffee if you need me," I say.

"All right. Stay close," she says, then climbs into her cruiser and drives off.

I wait until she's around the corner to fall to my heels and take a deep breath. I'm amazed I lasted this long. The last radio call sent me into a panic it took all I had to suppress.

A 10-54 is police code for a possible dead body.

The killer not only tried to make the cars difficult to investigate, he murdered Mrs. Lane, the woman who raised him and the one person who might be able to connect him to his past.

CHAPTER SIXTY-SEVEN

FOUNDLING

I walk to my Explorer expecting Graham to come tearing back down the street, siren blazing, ready to jump out of the cruiser with her gun drawn and tell me to go face-first into the pavement.

It's not until I'm on the highway, heading in the opposite direction, that I feel a modicum of relief.

I try to process what happened after I left Lane's house. The killer must have been concerned that I would go to the authorities, so he attempted to cover up a long-forgotten connection.

He probably assumed that the cars were safer back in the woods than trying to move them. And they probably were. Even if someone else had stumbled on them, abandoned cars aren't exactly out of the norm around here. When I do searches on Google Maps, I spot old cars all the time, sitting in yards on blocks or just half-buried in the weeds with rotten tires.

The cars at the Lane property would be no big thing—unless you knew whom they previously belonged to. That's what spooked the killer.

Torching the woods would only delay identifying them, even if he put some thermite on the engine blocks.

His real motive was to kill Julie Lane. Doing that would not only silence her but attract attention to me and misdirect the authorities. The killer wasn't just getting rid of a loose end, he might be trying to frame me.

I'm the last person to see Lane. I'm also the one with a bizarre story involving the Cougar Creek Monster and the recent murders . . . and I left a trail of blood from the woods to the road.

If the killer strangled her and dipped one of her kitchen knives in my blood to make it look like she was trying to defend herself, I'll have a hell of a time proving my innocence.

I take the exit leading to Helena instead of going back to Gus's place. I have to get to those foster parent records and find out who I'm dealing with. Then I need to get a lawyer.

I also need to warn Gus and Jillian. I call her first.

"Hey! What's up? How did the research go?" she says as soon as she picks up.

My words come out in a rush. "Jillian, I think I found out who he is, or least where he's from. I think he just killed his foster parent to cover his tracks."

"In Red Hook?"

"Yes. I was there yesterday talking to her. I found the cars in the woods that belonged to the missing hikers. There were ten of them."

"Oh, my god!"

"That's not all. He knows about me. He knows my name. That means he might know about you and Gus."

"What are you saying?"

"I don't know. I'm so sorry. I didn't mean to bring you into this."

"You didn't. Stop blaming yourself."

"He might come for you."

"Why?"

"Why does he do anything?"

"Where are you? Come here so we can talk about this."

"I have to do something first. I need to get his name."

"Then you'll come straight here?"

"Yes. But call Gus and warn him. Also, call Hudson Creek PD. Tell them whatever you have to. Hell, tell them you're afraid of me."

"I can't do that."

"You need to do something."

I hope I'm overreacting. I don't know what I'd do if anything happened to Jillian.

❧

I spend the rest of the drive to Helena worrying about two things. What if he's using the fire and the murder as a distraction to get away? He could be long gone by the time the authorities realize they should be pursuing him.

The other concern is what if he's not using this as a cover to run away? What if he's staying put and killing anyone that could connect him?

Sarah Eaves's son was convinced his mom was murdered. What if that was the killer eliminating one more witness?

When I get to the Child & Family Services office, my stomach is a knot of agitation. I don't know which way is up. Making my anxiety worse, I have to go inside the building and lie.

I pull in to a parking spot in front of the blocky building and spend a moment calming myself down. His name is inside there. All of this could be over very quickly. I just have to go in there and get the paperwork Graham requested.

Yeah, that's probably a felony. But that's the least of my worries right now.

I step out of my Explorer, make sure I'm wearing a clean shirt without any bloodstains, and enter the lobby.

A security guard sitting at the front desk looks up from his phone. "Can I help you?"

"I'm here to pick up some records for Poitier County."

I'm ready to try to bluff him with my National Parks research permit and university ID, in the hopes that those official-looking documents would give me some credibility.

"Third floor. Room number four."

"Thank you."

❧

Two minutes later I'm standing at the front desk. My leg is shaking so hard I have to press it against the counter to stop.

"May I help you?" a woman asks as she takes a seat behind the desk.

"Hello. I'm here to pick up some foster records requested by Poitier County?"

"When did you put the request in?"

"This morning."

"Sorry. That takes about ten days. I'm surprised they didn't tell you."

Damn. Damn, damn.

I'll be in jail or dead by then.

A voice calls out from an office. "Is that the Poitier County Sheriff's Department?"

"Yes," the woman in front of me replies. "I told him that it'd take at least ten days."

"I have them on my desk," says the person in the other room. "We had another call come in an hour ago, an urgent one. Apparently there's a murder investigation."

A woman dressed in a sharp pantsuit steps out of her office holding a thick binder. "I just finished putting these together. Here you go."

I try to keep my hands from trembling as I take the binder from her. I casually flip it open. It's filled with forms and photographs of children. There are at least thirty of them here.

"Thank you."

I almost walk into the door as I scan through the faces, trying to find the one that belongs to the killer.

CHAPTER SIXTY-EIGHT

COUNTERMEASURE

"Are you going to get that?" asks the guard as I walk past the front desk.

"Excuse me?" I look up from the binder.

"Your phone." He points to my pocket.

I just now realize that it's been ringing. "Oh, yeah." I tuck the folder under my arm and take out my phone.

It's a long-distance number from some area code I don't recognize. I'm tempted to not answer but decide to take the call as I sit on a bench outside the building.

"Hello?" I say, only half paying attention. I'm trying to sort through the dozens of faces and find the ones that match up with when Sarah Eaves was at the Lane home.

"Theo?" asks a deep, basso voice.

"Yeah . . ." I flip toward the back when I realize that's where the late '70s and early '80s are grouped. I stop on Sarah's face. It's a younger one than I've seen.

"Do I have your attention? Because you certainly have mine."

The tone of the voice makes me look up from the folder. "Who is this?"

"Who do you think it is?"

I feel a cold finger touch my heart. "I'm not sure . . ."

"Let's get right to the point and what you're going to do."

"About what?"

"First, you're going to destroy all your notes and anything you haven't turned over to the police."

Fuck, no . . . it can't be . . .

"Wait a second . . ."

"Theo, I'm not finished." His voice is firm, like a K9 instructor telling a German shepherd to sit. "After you destroy your notes, you're going to go to make a videotaped confession to the murder of Julie Lane."

"But I didn't kill her . . ."

"Of course you didn't. I did. She was like a mother to me. And look what you made me do."

My breathing is shallow. "Why?"

"Why do you think? If you hadn't knocked on her door, she'd still be alive. You did that."

"No, you did . . . ," I say feebly.

"I may have been the instrument, but you were the cause. You know this. It's just one more mess you've created that we have to clean up."

"All of those people . . ."

"We're all going to die. What difference does it make?"

"How . . . could you?"

"It's what I am. Now let's talk about what you are and what you're going to do. After you destroy those notes and confess to killing Julie Lane, they'll want to know about the other bodies. That's why you're going to say in your confession you manipulated them to hide the fact that you killed Juniper Parsons."

"That's insane. That's not even possible."

Everything feels like a dream. I have to stare out at the passing cars and smell the breeze to convince myself that this is really happening.

"Trust me. They'll believe you. They already suspect you. Use your brain to think of methods and explanations. You're a clever man. Too clever."

"They won't believe me."

"They will, some of it. It's up to you to convince them of the rest. Trust me, they want a simple explanation. They always do."

For some reason I don't protest. I just ask questions, as if this was inevitable.

"And if they don't?"

"If you don't convince them? What do you think, Theo?"

I hesitate. "I don't know . . ."

"I'm sending you a photo."

My phone chirps as a text message arrives. A black-and-white image pops up. I have to squint to see the details at first. When I recognize what I'm looking at, the world stops.

It's an image of Jillian, taken with a night-vision camera.

She's sleeping in her bed.

"I was there last night, Theo. I stood over her for an hour, watching. I'm very quiet. But I don't have to go to her house again. I could sit at a table in her restaurant and slip a knife into her ribs as she refills my coffee. I could grab her as she goes to her car at night. I could shoot her from a hundred yards away. I have a lot of ways. And your friend, the old man, how hard do you think that would be? I could kill them both in twenty minutes and then be on my way to Florida to visit your mother. Or I could go to Texas and start killing random students at your college."

I snap out of my dreamlike state and feel my blood boiling. "You fucker . . ."

"You started this. Now you have to end it. Right now you're weighing the odds. Do you tell the police everything I told you? Or do you do exactly as I asked? Do you think they could protect everyone? They don't even think I exist."

"I know your name. I'll tell them." I don't yet, but I know it's in the binder.

"No, you don't. You know an old name I haven't used in thirty years. That boy, the one that . . . He doesn't exist anymore."

"Is that what it is? Some hick molests you and you become a serial killer?"

"It's not that simple, Theo. Deep down we're all animals. But that's not important. You know what you need to do."

"How do I know you won't harm them anyway?"

"You don't. But you're a logical man. It's not in my interest to do that. I just want to hear on the news tomorrow that you confessed."

"What if I do everything you ask me and they don't believe me?"

"That's why you need to do one more thing to convince them. I can't trust you not to eventually tell them. That's why you're going to use that gun of yours to put a bullet in your head after you make your confession."

"I . . . I'm supposed to kill myself?"

"Yes, Theo. Videotape a confession. It had better be the performance of your life. Then shoot yourself. It'll be quick. You won't feel a thing. Jillian will be safe. And if you don't, someone you care about will be dead by tomorrow night. Maybe her. Maybe Gus. Maybe someone I haven't mentioned."

I don't know how long after he hangs up that I sit here, staring at a swaying tree branch, hypnotized.

My ringing phone wakes me out of my stupor.

"Hello?"

"Hey Dr. Cray, it's Sergeant Graham." Her voice is friendlier than the professional tone she struck with me this morning. "We didn't get to finish up. I have a couple more questions for you. Are you still at the pancake place?"

"I . . . had to run an errand."

"Okay. Well, if you could pop by the substation, we can wrap up. Can you be here in an hour?"

"Sure," I lie.

"Great. See you then."

I'm not the only liar. She was too friendly, too cordial. I'm sure she went by the pancake place and realized I wasn't there.

They want to talk to me about Mrs. Lane.

Right now they're wondering why I would kill her, torch the woods, then go to them with a story about the Cougar Creek Monster. It doesn't make any sense. It's insane. But it all leads back to me.

Damn.

If I want to keep Jillian and Gus safe, I better think of something.

CHAPTER SIXTY-NINE

ADMISSION

Joshua Lee Clark, that's his name. At least that's what it used to be. When I turn to his page in the binder, the eyes give it away. Dark green, sitting under a mop of reddish hair. The eyes are intelligent but unsure. It's not a photo of a scared eleven-year-old. It's a wary animal caught in the flashbulb's glare.

He was placed in foster care after his mother was found stabbed to death in the kitchen. Joshua told the police it had been a domestic dispute between her and his estranged father. Nobody else saw his father come or go, but there had been a history of violence and the police found Joshua's story credible.

I'm not sure I do, knowing what I know now. The calculating voice on the other end of the phone was capable of anything. He admitted to killing Julie Lane, his foster mother, in an attempt to silence her and frame me.

Killing for him is effortless, whether it's for pleasure or expedience. And now he's threatened to kill people I care about if I don't do what he says.

I have to lie and invent explanations that will be paper thin. I have to do everything I can to convince the people I was trying to get to believe there was a killer out there to now think it was all some scheme I concocted.

It's absurd and won't stand up to scrutiny. But Clark is right: if I punctuate the lie with my own death, they'll make it fit.

If I admit to killing Juniper, they'll believe me. I can convince them I arranged Chelsea's death if I say it happened on a trip I made up here the year before.

Same for the other bodies. If the time frame doesn't match up, if I was out of the country when they were killed, I'll concoct some story about putting their bodies in a freezer to hold them longer or something like that so I would have an alibi.

I'll say the Cougar Creek bodies were ones I found elsewhere and planted years ago at the hot spring.

How hard will they try to debunk the testimony of a dead man? If I give them everything they need, they'll be happy.

Whatever it takes to keep Jillian safe.

They'll want a motive, too. I can't just explain how I managed all of the killings—they'll want to know why a sick mind would conceive of such a deranged plot.

I'll tell them I've always been off. Obsessed with violent thoughts toward women, the desire to pull off the perfect murder. I'll tell them I killed Juniper because it wasn't enough to watch strangers die; I wanted to murder someone who knew me.

Why would I kill myself?

If I'm a sociopath, it can't be due to guilt. Is it because I want to gloat openly? Or is it that I fear they're closing in on me?

When they arrested Ted Bundy, he told the police officer who caught him it would have been better to have just shot him. He felt no remorse but wasn't immune to anxiety.

I'll need to make a detailed timeline to explain when I did my crimes. I should also be prepared with some explanations of how I fooled the methods for dating bodies, like the refrigerator. I could name some preservatives as well as some enzymatic accelerants.

To make it more convincing, I should see to it that when they search my car they find the necessary tools and chemicals. There's probably one or more chemical supply companies nearby that can provide me with what I need.

Yes, I think I can do this. Hell, I'll post my video confession online for everyone to see. That would be too much for the news to resist.

That should convince him of my sincerity.

There's a clarity that arrives when life forces you into a binary situation.

If I had more time, there might be other choices. Regardless of the name change, I'm sure I could have found him. But I was too late and too clumsy. Any attempt to bid for more time would be transparent to him. He has the upper hand.

I devote my mental energy to the chemicals and materials I'll need to convince the police I was able to muck around with the bodies, screwing up their estimated time of death.

There's an enzymatic solution used as an industrial cleanser that would cause advanced necrosis before breaking down. A few gallons of that would be convincing. A mild acid wash in a bathtub would cause skin discoloration and aging.

I could say I used a CO_2 tank to cause the internal organs to rupture from decomposition.

If I wanted to really screw with forensics, I could say I drew blood from one body and placed it in another to mess with their DNA analysis.

Hell, I could even convincingly turn a corpse into a dead clone of a living person if I transferred enough blood, used a clotting agent to have it solidify in the veins they'd tap, then destroyed the dental records by using hydrofluoric acid to wear down the teeth—as if they were attacked by aggressive bacteria.

Okay, I know what I'll say. I know what I need to do.

I'll write up a summary of my methods, make a video confession, and then let the police know where to find my body.

It's the only way to keep Jillian safe.

CHAPTER SEVENTY

SURROGATE

> In my solitude I have pondered much on the incomprehensible subjects of space, eternity, life and death.
>
> —*Alfred Russel Wallace*

Faking my own death is easier said than done—especially with such short notice. While there was no way in hell I could convince someone conducting a thorough forensic examination that somebody else's body was my own, I could buy myself some time. I have three or four days at most until Mead and her staff take a look at the corpse and realize that the whole thing is a sham.

I have to find Joshua Lee Clark before then. Once he realizes what I've done, he's going to go ballistic and Jillian and Gus won't be safe.

If I thought Clark would leave them alone, I might have put the bullet in my head. But I don't trust him. Once I'm dead, he'll probably eventually kill Jillian just for kicks. It's what he does. While he presented himself as a coldly rational person on the phone, he's a murderer who enjoys killing. It's in his DNA.

To buy time I have to let him think I'm dead. To do that, I need a body. On average, twenty-four people die a day in Montana. The number of males around my age averages about two to three per day.

According to the *Montana Gazette*, Christopher Dunleavy, age thirty, was found unresponsive two days ago and taken to Missoula Memorial Hospital, where he was declared dead on arrival from a prescription-drug overdose. Authorities say they're trying to contact family members. Translation: his body is sitting in the hospital morgue waiting for someone to make burial arrangements.

The social media profile I found for him shows someone that doesn't resemble me facially but has a similar body type—close enough for what I have planned.

❧

I dial the hospital and have the switchboard connect me to the morgue.

"Cold storage," says a friendly woman.

"Hello, I'm calling from Hudson Creek sheriff's office. Do you still have Christopher Dunleavy's remains?"

"Yes. Still waiting on next of kin. What's up?"

"There's been a wrinkle. I think the state crime lab wants to have a look."

"Says who?"

"Mead, I believe." Better to throw her name around.

"She doesn't trust our forensic examiner?"

"No. No. There might be a criminal element. Trying to identify the source of the pills."

"Oh, got it."

"Yeah. Anyway, DEA has asked for an examination."

"Just have someone come sign for it and they can do as they please."

❧

After laying the groundwork for taking the body, I have to actually pull it off. Sadly, I can't just drive up to the hospital in my SUV and have them load the body in the back.

Fortunately, in Helena I find a truck rental company with a new high-top black van—exactly the kind of thing you'd expect a government agency to use.

I put the vehicle on my credit card, assuming that by the time police check those records I'll be dead or Clark captured.

When I arrive at the hospital, my hands are clammy and I'm not quite sure if I'm up to pulling it off. I've hastily bought a dark-blue windbreaker so I look like some kind of officious person. My cover story is going to be that I am a federal examiner brought in by the DEA—if they even ask.

I park in back near the loading zone. As I walk toward the rear entrance, I spot a young cop on break leaning against his car, smoking a cigarette. Immediately I become apprehensive, but then I get an inspiration.

"Excuse me," I call out.

"Yes, sir?"

Perfect, a cop with good manners. "Do you know where the morgue is? I'm picking up a body for the state crime lab."

He points to a set of doors. "I think it's through the entrance and to the right. I don't work this place often. I'm just waiting for my partner to check on a witness."

"Well, if you have a second, could you help me out? I got to load the thing. I could use someone to hold open the doors. My partner's wife went into labor in Bozeman, and he had to head there."

"Sure thing," he says, dropping the cigarette. "As long as I don't have to touch anything."

"Thanks, Officer . . . Patel," I reply, after seeing his name tag. "I'm Bill Doff." I give him the name of my high school algebra teacher.

"Nick," he says, shaking my hand.

As we walk inside, I make sure the small talk isn't professional and call attention to an attractive nurse who passes us in the hallway.

"It's why I like hanging out here," says Nick.

When we get to the front desk, we're greeted by the same friendly voice I spoke to on the phone.

"Hello, we're here to pick up Christopher Dunleavy. I believe somebody called?"

"Oh, you're from the state lab?" She gives Nick a smile, implying that he might be a more frequent visitor than he let on.

"Yes."

She slides over a form on a clipboard. "Just fill this out."

I bluff my way through the boxes and put Mead's name in the field for requesting official.

She looks it over and nods. "I'll just need a transfer form."

A what? I was afraid there would be some kind of paperwork I didn't know about.

"Right." I hesitate. "Mead didn't send me over with one."

I'm about to ask to see what one looks like so I can try to forge it at a FedEx office, but the clerk relents. Probably because I have a police officer standing next to me—which clearly means I'm an official person doing official things.

"That's okay, just fax it over ASAP. I'll have an orderly load the body on a gurney and bring it out back in ten minutes."

"Wonderful."

Fifteen minutes later I'm driving away with a stolen corpse. I make one more stop at a medical supplier to get whatever I can legally obtain, then steal the rest from a parked ambulance using my secret door-opening trick.

CHAPTER SEVENTY-ONE

FATALITY

Christopher Dunleavy's dead eyes stare out at me from behind the wheel of my Explorer. There's a little more color in his skin. There should be—I pumped two pints of my blood into his body. I was already running low from my previous accident and not sure if I should have spared even that much.

But to make the thing work, it's absolutely critical that the medical examiner who shows up on the scene to pronounce the body dead doesn't see immediate signs of lividity. To minimize those, I put heparin, a blood thinner, in my donor blood and used a syringe to inject the liquid into his body, then massaged the surrounding area.

As I did this, I kept the heater running at full blast and put pocket warmers around his neck and under his armpits, so when they check for a temperature he'll seem recently dead, instead of freshly sprung from a hospital freezer.

It's a sloppy job, and I know it. If I can confuse the initial examination, I'll be fine until Mead or whoever cuts open poor Christopher and sees all my shoddy craftsmanship.

To fit him into the driver's seat, I had to loosen up his limbs, which had already stiffened from rigor mortis. A syringe filled with muriatic acid injected into the major muscle groups decalcified the filaments enough to make him fairly pliable.

The final result is a semi-stiff corpse sitting in my Explorer with his hands poised around Gus's shotgun, ready to pull the trigger and blow off his face—which also proves easier said than done.

Besides the emotional difficulty of literally defacing another human being, I become aware of the practical problem. How could I pull the trigger and make it look like he did it? If the door was open and I stood there, it would leave a rather odd blood splatter with a missing section. The same if I sat in the passenger side.

I consider trying to wire up something through the brake pedal but settle on reaching a garbage bag–wrapped arm through the window and manually pulling the trigger.

I'm sure a competent forensic technician would notice something amiss, but again, I just need a few days, not an unsolved mystery that lasts for years.

I toyed with the idea of setting Christopher on fire as well. While that would certainly complicate a forensic examination, it might make Clark too suspicious. If news reports said the body was burned beyond recognition, I'm sure he'd suspect something is up.

I have to give him exactly what he asked for.

I toiled late last night trying to make Christopher look fresh and planting all the identifying pieces of evidence so it would seem pretty clear-cut who was in the car. I dressed him in my clothes and put my wallet in his pocket.

As I tied my shoes on his feet, I became aware of all the subtle things I was probably getting wrong—like doing the knot upside down. I did my best to fix all those details and spent an hour obsessing over everything, trying to make certain that it wouldn't be immediately obvious.

In the end, I had to just settle and tell myself that it would be enough to convince first responders and make the news with enough information for Clark to draw the conclusion I want.

Beyond all the forensic details, the most important element will be my confession. Working on Christopher, I laid out what I was going to say in my head. It took my mind off the horrible things I was doing to this man's body.

I'd worked with plenty of dead bodies before I came to Montana, but this was crossing a line. How far apart was I from Clark? Yes, Christopher was already dead, but I was violating him in some way. The last thing he could have wanted when he took that fatal overdose was some asshole to desecrate his corpse. And what about his family? What happens when they finally come to collect him for burial and see what I've done?

This is getting to me to the point I have to sit down and take a break.

I drop down on the hard dirt where I parked the Explorer and stare at Christopher's face. The moonlight reflecting off his red and white cheeks makes him look like a creature half in this world, half not.

"What the hell are you doing, Theo?" I ask myself.

"Surviving," I reply. "Surviving."

Even if I see my way through this mess, I'm positive nobody would ever understand why I did what I did. "Why didn't you tell the police? Why didn't you warn everyone?"

Those are questions that will haunt me for the rest of my life if things don't work out the way I need them to.

All of this preparation and planning was a distraction from the real problem. Assuming things do work out and I create a convincing suicide, that still leaves one very large problem: I still have no idea who or where Clark is.

He told me to kill myself because he feared I was close. But the truth is, I don't know any more than what he suspected I'd already told the police.

I'm at just as much of a dead end as they are.

My only hope is that Clark feared me, not because of what he thought I knew, but what he thought I was close to knowing.

CHAPTER SEVENTY-TWO

BREAKING

At 7:22 a.m. a body was found in a car parked in an unfinished housing development northwest of the city. Unconfirmed reports say the victim, a man in his midthirties, may have died from a self-inflicted shotgun blast to the head. While no motive is immediately known, we can confirm that earlier this morning our news bureau received a link to an alleged confession on YouTube from a person involved with the string of alleged murder victims that police agencies across the state had previously identified as animal attacks. This video confession was made in a vehicle in what appears to be the same area where the body was found. Developing.

CHAPTER SEVENTY-THREE
DEAD MAN

I sip my stale coffee and watch the parking lot of the motel from my second-floor room. I'm not paranoid yet. I'm just tired of looking at a computer screen for hours on end.

A big rig pulls up to the diesel pumps, and a stocky man in a tan leather overcoat gets out and walks into the service station. He's about the eighth guy I've seen do the same thing. It's like there's a casting office down the road they're sending them from.

The news announced my name and death eighteen hours ago, along with the video confession I sent to the stations. I've spent the last twelve holed up in this motel two hundred miles from Helena, trying to crack Clark's pattern. As each hour goes by, I nervously check the Internet to see if they've caught on to me yet.

I keep the TV on in the background with the volume low, anxiously awaiting another "breaking" report. I've seen parts of my confession air three times on the evening news as well as footage of the scene of my fake death, shot from a distance. There hasn't been a press conference yet, just a graphic of police letterhead saying that the investigation is ongoing.

Ongoing . . . It certainly is.

I try not to think of what the news has done to Jillian or Gus, let alone my parents. I've had to stop myself several times from picking up the phone and telling them I'm okay.

I can't just yet.

I have to find him.

I know he won't make a move on Jillian or Gus so soon after my death. It would attract attention and let the authorities know there's another killer out there. He's smart and patient. He'll wait it out—then go after them and close that book.

Constantly checking the news was getting distracting, so I created a little script that searches the web for my name and sends me a text update any time it appears in the Montana newspapers.

I also have a police scanner that lets me know what the cops are up to around here—the ones that aren't using an encrypted channel. If they've seen through my ruse and are closing in on me, I think it might give me some heads-up.

The van is parked out back, near the fire escape. I can get to it from the front door, or through the back window that I already have open, with a coil of rope tied to the toilet. Probably overcautious, but the cops aren't the only ones I'm afraid of finding me.

Clark is a skilled hunter. While I don't doubt his threats toward Jillian and Gus, I'm sure he'll come for me if he thinks I'm on the loose.

That's why finding him first, while I'm dead, is so critical.

Unfortunately, my hunt has been a bust.

Joshua Lee Clark vanished in the 1980s, not long after the Cougar Creek Monster sightings stopped. The next time I know he reared his head was when the oldest victim I found outside of Red Hook was killed six years ago.

I suspect he was active before then in the state, but it wouldn't surprise me if he went somewhere else for a decade or two.

Using some anthropology software designed to reconstruct facial features from bone structure, I created an adult version of his face and then used that as a comparison to scan through online mug shots. Then I sorted through thousands of possibilities and discounted ones that had traceable family connections.

This narrowed the field to just under two hundred people. To sort through these, I looked at their arrest records and the crimes they committed, and went on instinct.

This yielded a dozen maybes, although none of them felt right. I knew that wasn't exactly a scientific thing to go on, but I suspected that Clark might be too clever and focused to get busted for the simple things, like robbing a convenience store or selling meth out of his car. However, given his violent tendencies, I considered it highly possible that he might have been arrested at some point when his temper got out of control, so I kept checking.

When this line of attack began to seem less likely to find him, I started trying to think out of the box. For the last two hours I've been hypnotized by his purple band of activity that MAAT singled out for me.

Watching all the big rigs pull up, I have an inspiration and try to find a trucking route that lines up with the killings. Nothing matches.

There's also the problem that MAAT insists overwhelmingly that Clark's hunting ground is based on victim availability. This suggests that he adjusts his route to the victims, which would be hard if he had to drive a proscribed route. I'd see clusters around specific dates, but I don't.

My sense of dread is growing with every dead end. I'm running into the walls of the public data sets I have access to. I've paid for dozens of background checks, but that's just not enough. If I had FBI-level resources and an unrestricted warrant, maybe I would have better luck.

Or maybe not. I might still be looking at this the wrong way.

I've had a few exciting leads that have given me hope, but they quickly faded.

When I was in the gas station bathroom, I realized for the first time that there were vending machines selling condoms and breath mints. I'd seen these all over the state.

I ran back to my room to see if I could find a connection, thinking that maybe the person who refills them is Clark, but came up empty-handed. MAAT gave that as much probability as Clark just being a random person driving long distances from his home to kill.

It's obvious. I'm sure of it. I just don't know what that connection is. I'm going to make some assumptions and see if MAAT comes up with something that jumps out at me.

Clark is familiar with his victims in some way. He sees them, he knows their routines. He has opportunity to watch them and wait until they're vulnerable.

I type these factors into MAAT, converting them to code. Familiarity with the victim would imply that he has a chance to see most of them more than once. Knowing their routine means he has some idea of their circuit—their own work and social patterns. Vulnerability is coded for by looking for when he could be alone with them in a professional situation—like being a taxi driver or a mailman.

It takes MAAT a fraction of a second to come back with a high-probability suggestion that chills me. Under those criteria, the likeliest occupation for Clark is highway patrolman.

CHAPTER SEVENTY-FOUR

Reality Check

It's a wonderful theory and would explain so much. Yet it only works in the limited reality that I programmed into MAAT. Clark would have to be close to sixty now. There aren't any Montana State troopers out on the road that old.

He might be senior law enforcement, but that seems doubtful. I'm not sure if he would want to risk the background checks that go with that. I'm not ruling it out entirely, but putting that under the maybe category.

I'm getting stir-crazy and decide to go for a drive. It's risky going out on the road. But so is hunting a serial killer.

In the back of my mind, something tells me I need to start where this began. I do a U-turn and head toward Filmount County, where Juniper was murdered.

That was the last location I can place Clark. He was there the night Juniper got murdered.

Something brought the two together. Had he been watching her for days? Was it an impulse?

As I drive into the night, I assess the other patterns MAAT created when I inputted known serial killers. A strikingly obvious fact came to the surface, something I should have considered earlier.

MAAT saw three distinct killing patterns. There was the wide-ranging type like Ted Bundy, who had a cross-country murder spree. He was a drifter and moved often from place to place. Even still, he sometimes stayed too long and attracted attention—to the point of getting arrested, only to escape and keep killing.

Drifters like Bundy aren't very cautious. They rely on law enforcement not catching up with them before they move on.

Clark isn't a drifter. He frequents the same areas over many years. Killers who stay in one place are able to do this if they're invisible, somebody in the community you wouldn't suspect, and if the bulk of their victims are socially ignored: hookers, drug addicts, the homeless.

Really prolific killers who stay in one place either prey upon one group exclusively, such as prostitutes, or have elaborate means of concealing their crimes.

Jeffrey Dahmer lived in a poor neighborhood, and his victims were largely young male homosexuals who were separated from their families.

For over two decades, the Grim Sleeper, a Los Angeles serial killer named Lonnie David Franklin Jr., murdered mostly African American prostitutes with drug problems.

John Wayne Gacy broke this mold, preying on victims from a variety of socioeconomic backgrounds. Some were young men that worked for his construction company; others were gay men he picked up cruising and took back to his house to kill.

Both the Grim Sleeper and John Wayne Gacy were well known in their communities, which had the paradoxical effect of contributing to their invisibility. Even as people were disappearing or being abducted, sometimes literally in front of their houses, they remained above suspicion.

One recurring theme in these cases is that the culprits were people the police spoke to early on. Bundy was stopped multiple times. Police returned a teenage Laotian victim to Jeffrey Dahmer's apartment, afraid to interfere in what they thought was a lovers' quarrel. The parents of one of Gacy's victims called the police more than a hundred times, imploring them to investigate him further after their son disappeared in connection with Gacy. They didn't. Three years later, the boy was one of twenty-seven victims found buried under Gacy's home.

It's extremely likely that Clark has already spoken to the authorities in some capacity, either as a witness or someone ruled out as a suspect.

Given the fact that nobody even acknowledges that there is a serial killer operating in Montana, it's possible that the parents of some missing girl have pointed to Clark but have been ignored.

I'm missing something . . .

Something important.

I need to go back to basics.

When they thought Juniper was murdered by a human, before the bear nonsense, they had two suspects: me and the mechanic, Bryson.

They discounted both of us readily. I know why they did in my case, but what about Bryson?

Did he have some airtight alibi? Or did they not do their due diligence?

Bryson seemed pretty fit. I remember him to be in his late fifties, close to Clark's age.

This is too much. I take the next exit and pull into the parking lot of a defunct gas station ten miles away from Filmount County.

I look up the property records for Bryson's repair shop and get his full name. Philip Joseph Bryson. A background check reveals that he's had the shop for twenty years. He's married to his second wife, and he has a mother still living in Missoula. He also has two sisters.

Damn. If only.

He can't be Clark.

It doesn't mean he couldn't be the killer, but it would throw out the window everything that led me to Lane and the cars.

The cars.

The goddamn cars . . .

Juniper's car was at Bryson's service station getting repaired. That's why she was taking walks through the woods.

Jesus Christ.

Juniper's killer wasn't someone who saw her in town or just walking along the road.

He saw her car at Bryson's.

He knew she was stranded.

She talked to him. Bryson might even know him.

The cars at the Lane farm . . . why are they important still?

Fuck.

I understand the pattern now!

I know what Clark is. He's everywhere. He's invisible. He can do what he does in plain sight and nobody would ever give it a second thought.

Christ, I have to warn Jillian and Gus.

CHAPTER SEVENTY-FIVE

STALKER

All the lights are on in Jillian's house, but she's not answering her phone. I tried calling Gus as well but only got his voice mail. I try to tell myself that it's because they don't recognize my burner phone number. I pray that's why.

I almost called into 911 to warn them but decided against it when I realized that, at most, they'd send a patrol car by. And if Clark is watching the house, this might make him suspicious.

At best, the police might stick around for a few hours and watch her place, but if he wants to get to her, he will. There's no way Hudson Creek will put in the kind of manpower necessary without more credible evidence. Even then, I don't know how much faith I have in Whitmyer.

My fear is that they know Joshua Lee Clark personally and will laugh off my suggestion of what he truly is without more evidence. To make sure they don't ignore him, I have to yell his name far and wide, as loudly as I can. But first, I have to make sure Jillian and Gus are safe. It's a dangerous gamble.

I park down the block from her house, a two-bedroom home across the street from some wood-covered property. This is what scares me. A man like Clark could hide in there like a sniper and never be found.

The street is quiet. Jillian's car is in her driveway. Nobody else has their car on the street.

The woods make me nervous. I'm afraid he might be in there watching. So I decide to take the long way around and approach her house from the back, cutting through the neighbor's property and her backyard.

This part of the street is quiet, too. Somewhere in the distance a dog barks, but there isn't anyone stirring.

The whole house is brightly lit. I crouch behind a bush next to a woodpile and watch for a moment, waiting to see if she's up and about. Her porch light is on; so are the kitchen and dining room lights.

After five minutes of no movement, I decide to give her phone a call again.

It rings five times, then goes to voice mail.

Damn.

I go to dial again but stop when I see a notification from one of my computer scripts.

BREAKING: SUSPICIONS MOUNT IN ALLEGED SUICIDE.

No. Not this soon! I click through the article. An unnamed person in the Helena police department says that they're hesitant to confirm my identity because of "forensic discrepancies."

Fuck.

He knows.

I call Jillian again. This time I put my phone on silent and listen.

Across the yard I can hear her phone ringing from inside the house.

Why isn't she picking up?

I can't wait any longer.

I rush to her back porch, setting off a motion-sensing light.

When I get to the sliding door, I press my face against the glass and peer inside. I can't see into the bedrooms, but this part of the house is empty.

I try the door, but it's locked. I want to knock, but I'm worried that the sound might tip off Clark that I'm here.

I climb over the porch railing and go to the side of her house. The shades are drawn, but I can see light from behind them.

I creep toward her bedroom window and put my ear to the cold glass.

I think I hear her voice.

I raise my hand to tap gently but freeze when something snaps in the woods directly to my right.

Somebody is out there.

I press my body flat against the wall and search the shadows for the source of the sound. All I see is darkness.

If I go out there, he'll see me. If he has a rifle trained on the house, he'll drop me before I know what hit me.

I take my phone out of my pocket and crouch down, using my jacket to shield the glow, which kills my night vision.

I try calling Jillian again.

Her phone rings from just a few feet away.

On the third ring she picks up.

"Hello?"

"Jillian! It's me!"

"Theo!"

I can hear her voice through the window.

"Listen carefully. You're in danger."

Something moves behind me. Still blinded by the glow of my phone, all I see is a distant yard light.

"Don't move," says a voice in the shadows.

I slide my arm behind me to grab my gun, but a man in a mask runs toward me and fires something.

My chest explodes in pain, and I collapse.

CHAPTER SEVENTY-SIX

PROTECTION

There's a bright light in my eyes, and somebody is talking to me.

"Are you okay, Theo?"

I begin to focus and see a male paramedic peeling back my eyelid and looking at my pupil for dilation.

When I try to move my arms, I can't. For a moment I think they're paralyzed, then realize they're handcuffed behind my back.

"What happened?"

"What do you remember?" the paramedic asks.

"I . . . was checking on Jillian. Jillian! Where is she?"

"She's in the house."

"I need to talk to her."

The paramedic steps back and takes off his gloves. "That's going to be up to these men."

Detectives Glenn and Whitmyer are standing off to the side. There's a third man I don't recognize.

I remember why I came here. The flashing red lights of the ambulance reflect off the trees in the woods behind it, and I get a knot in my stomach, feeling suddenly exposed. I want to shout out, to warn them, but I'm afraid it'll only make me look crazier.

My shirt is ripped down to my chest, and there's a Band-Aid right where I felt the exploding pain. Someone—probably one of the cops standing in the street wearing camouflage—shot me with a stun gun. I guess I should be happy it wasn't a real gun, but I still feel sore all over.

They must have been waiting for me. And that means they probably never bought my faked death, or didn't take long to see through it.

A man I don't know takes a seat on the porch deck next to me. He's wearing a black windbreaker and has a real clean-cut face. If I had to guess, he's some kind of federal agent.

"Dr. Cray, do you feel like talking?"

"Is Jillian safe?"

"Yes. She's inside."

"What about Gus?"

"He's inside, too. Care to tell us what you're doing here? Or, for that matter, why you're alive?"

My eyes are still on the woods. "The killer. He said he'd hurt them if I talked to you."

"Did he? When did he tell you this?"

"Two days ago."

"Was this in person? Did he write you a letter?"

I turn to the man. "Why are you patronizing me?"

"Am I? I'm just trying to figure some things out. Let's talk about your confession."

"Who are you?"

"I'm Special Agent Seward with the FBI. You came to my attention after you started finding all those bodies. Ones you now say you planted."

"That was a lie."

"Really? It was a convincing lie."

My mind finally focuses. "Seward, listen to me very carefully." I speak up so Whitmyer and Glenn can hear me. "The man who killed those women. The man who killed Juniper Parsons. I know who he is."

"Joshua Lee Clark," says Seward.

"Yes, but that's not his name now. He left Montana and came back with a new identity."

"Okay, what is his name now?"

"I don't know."

Seward makes a smug little grin and turns to the others. "Well, that's not very helpful."

"They know who he is," I say. "They've probably talked to him dozens of times."

"Gentlemen?" Seward says sarcastically. "Have anything you need to tell me?"

Whitmyer rolls his eyes and shakes his head, but Glenn is listening intently. "Who is he?" he asks me.

I ignore Seward and speak directly to Glenn. "He knew Juniper was stranded. He drove past Chelsea and the others. He knew when someone was from out of town and didn't have any connections."

"And how is this?" asks Seward, trying to take control of the conversation.

I stare at him, unflinching. "Because he's the fucking tow-truck driver. He's the first person you call when you're stuck in the middle of nowhere with a flat tire or your car runs out of gas. He's the one you tell your whole story to when you sit in the cab." I look up to Whitmyer. "Did you ever find Chelsea's car?"

"No . . ."

"No. But we found her body. Somebody hauled her car away."

Seward stands up and walks over to Whitmyer and Glenn to talk. I can tell this has hit him by surprise. From his dismissive attitude, I got the sense that he believed my confession but not my death. He wasn't really expecting me to name someone.

Glenn is nodding his head. Whitmyer is shaking his. They have a name in mind. They know who I'm talking about. They just don't want to accept it.

"Who is he? What's his name?" I shout.

Seward turns and glares at me. "Just wait."

"Wait? My family isn't safe. Nobody is safe!" I'm frantic. "Let me talk to Jillian. Jillian!"

There are footsteps behind me. I turn and see her standing at the door.

"Theo!" She puts a hand to her mouth when she sees the handcuffs.

"Go back inside!" shouts Seward.

"What's going on?" she asks.

"He's coming for you and me and Gus and anyone else," I yell.

"Who?"

"The tow truck guy. Whoever has this area and Filmount."

"Joe Vik?" she says, then looks at the gathered cops. "Is this true?"

"We don't know anything about that," says Whitmyer. "We're going to send someone to go talk to Joe."

"You're on a first-name basis with him?" I ask incredulously.

"Shut up, Dr. Cray," snaps Whitmyer, "or we'll have you tased again."

"You don't understand."

Whitmyer pushes past Seward and crouches down in front of me. He shoves a finger in my face. "I'm sick and tired of your bullshit. Keep your mouth shut!"

"You don't know what you're messing with," I say under my breath.

"Oh, really? What are you going to do?"

"Not me, dumb ass. Him! This Joe Vik. He's a killer!"

"I've known him for twenty years. You've been here what, two weeks? I have a pretty good idea what I'm dealing with here."

Glenn steps over and tries to calm things down. "Dr. Cray, we'll take him in for questioning. We'll see if his story matches up. This is under control."

I shake my head. "You don't get it. You don't know what you're dealing with. I've looked at his patterns. He's not a man. He's a monster that's excellent at pretending he's one of us, but all he really wants to do is kill. The bodies I found, they're only part of it. This is only the beginning."

A police radio crackles in the cool air, and we all freeze as a dispatcher calls out, "Officer down! Backup requested at 239 Valley Pine. I repeat, officer down."

Whitmyer looks to the nearest Hudson Creek police officer and says, shocked, "That's Joe's place." He runs to his police cruiser and motions for his other cops to follow. "Let's go!"

"You want backup?" asks Seward.

Whitmyer gestures to a cop and points to me. "Keep track of that asshole!"

"Goddamn fool," I reply. "He doesn't understand. None of you do. Joe Vik has been waiting for this day. All these years, killing in secret. Hiding. Now he doesn't have to. He gets to show you what he really is."

"What do you mean?" asks Glenn.

"All he wants to do is kill."

"I think our cops can manage this," says Seward.

"How long has it been? Ten minutes? You've already got one, probably two officers down. Vik was waiting for them. He's going to kill Whitmyer and the others. Then he's going to come here."

CHAPTER SEVENTY-SEVEN

PERIMETER DEFENSE

Seward is pacing around the yard, his hands clenched in fists pressed to his hips as he listens to the radio from the remaining Hudson Creek police officer at Jillian's home.

The reports have been sporadic. A second police unit approached Joe Vik's home and found one officer sprawled out in the driveway and the other crouched behind his cruiser, bleeding from the neck.

All we've heard from Whitmyer is that they are approaching the house and taking positions around the property to try to contain him.

Glenn has been on his phone talking to Filmount County, prepping them on what's happened so far. I've overheard him say "Joe Vik" at least three times. I don't think he knows him as well as Whitmyer, but he seems to be aware of the man.

The door opens, and Jillian steps out onto the porch and takes a seat next to me.

"Ma'am, we need you to step back inside the house," says Seward.

"Technically, I think I can ask you to leave my property."

"Interfering with an arrest is a crime," he replies.

Jillian nods to my handcuffs. "It looks like you arrested him. What is there left to interfere with?"

Seward turns away to check the radio.

"We've formed a perimeter. I'm going to get on the PA and ask Joe to come out," says Whitmyer over the radio.

"Tell him to hold back and call in a SWAT unit," I shout.

"Maybe we let Whitmyer do his thing?" says Seward.

Glenn stops talking to listen to the radio. "Maybe Whitmyer should hold off?"

"He and Joe go back. Probably better he deescalates it this way," says a Hudson Creek deputy.

"What's going on?" Jillian whispers to me.

"Joe Vik is going ballistic on the police. At least two cops are down."

"Joe Vik . . . huh."

"Who is he?"

"Joe runs the tow service, owns a parts yard and some other businesses. Sponsors Little League."

"Yeah, but who is he?"

"Everybody knows him, but I don't know if anybody knows him that well. He has a wife and two daughters. I think from her first marriage."

Damn. I yell to the deputy, "Get someone who knows the wife and kids to call them!"

He waves me off. Seward glares at me.

"You don't think he'll hurt them?" asks Jillian.

"They're probably already dead. They were a disguise. Now that they're not needed anymore . . ."

People are beyond my understanding, but animals I can grasp.

"Going—" Whitmyer's voice is stopped by the sound of rapid-fire shooting.

"Was that a TAR-21?" asks the deputy, his face wide with shock. "I need to go to this."

He runs over to his squad car, turns the lights on, and races off.

"Can you get their channel?" Seward yells to the paramedic, still standing by.

"I'll check," he says, then starts flipping through frequencies on his radio.

Seward turns to Glenn. "Jesus Christ. How far out are your people?"

"Twenty minutes." He points toward me. "Let's all go inside and find out what we're dealing with." Glenn grabs me by my arm, helps me to my feet, and steers me through the door.

"Can't you take the handcuffs off?" asks Jillian, following us in.

"This man is a suspected felon," replies Seward. He shuts the door after us. "They stay on."

"Let's at least put them in front of him," says Glenn. He takes out his keys and unlocks one cuff so I can bring them to the front of my body. "Sit down."

I drop onto Jillian's couch and realize how sore my arms are. She takes a seat next to me. Seward gives her a look, but she ignores him.

"What does Joe Vik look like?" I ask.

"Big guy," says Glenn. "Maybe six and a half foot. Built like a linebacker. Red hair and beard. Quiet. Hard to imagine him as some stealthy killer."

"Well, when he was leaner they used to mistake him for a cougar. Now he pretends he's a bear."

"Pretend to be a bear?" Seward is shaking his head. "I'm still not sure I buy your theory."

"So, do you think an actual grizzly with a machine gun just killed those police officers?"

Glenn cuts me off. "Why do you think he's coming for you? Revenge?"

"No. I don't think he feels that the way we do. He said he'd kill Jillian and Gus if I didn't do as he said. I think he puts a high value on following through on those kinds of threats. But that could be today or ten years from now. As far as I'm concerned, he wants me dead for a very practical reason—once he escapes, he wants to make sure that he can't be found again."

"And you're the only guy that can do that?" Seward says derisively.

I glare at the asshole. "I'm the only guy that knew he existed. Where was the FBI during all this? Where were any of you? I had to literally drag up bodies to drop on your doorstep to prove my point. Even then—"

"Bodies you said you tampered with," Seward cuts in.

"Jesus Christ. Are you still on that? Look around you! I made that whole thing up so he wouldn't go after Jillian. I didn't have a choice."

"You could have contacted us."

I groan. "To do what? You think Whitmyer is just playing radio hide-and-seek? The man is dead. I tried to warn him. But no!"

"All right," says Glenn. "What do we need to know now?"

"Once he gets past the cops, he'll probably be coming here."

"Assuming he gets past the backup units," replies Seward.

"He's probably already left his house. He shot Whitmyer to draw everyone there." I motion to the street. "The Hudson Creek cops already took off."

"And you think he's coming here?" asks Glenn.

"He's coming to where he thinks I am. Here or the Hudson Creek police station."

Seward shakes his head. "He's not going to attack a police station."

"How many cops do you think are there right now? One? Two?"

The paramedic steps inside and has a stricken expression on his face. "I just heard on the radio. Five down, possibly dead, including Whitmyer. They went into the house and found Vik's wife and kids dead, too. Bullets to the head, killed in their bedrooms."

"He did that before the cops even showed up," I say, feeling a heaviness at the back of my throat. Guilt. "Vik probably did that the moment he heard my death may have been faked."

"What about Vik?" Seward asks the paramedic.

"Gone. They're not sure how. But they say he's gone."

"All right, we're taking my car, the ambulance, and your car to my office," Glenn says.

"That's five times as far away as Hudson Creek PD," says Seward.

"You're welcome to hang around there when Vik shows up. I'd rather take my chance somewhere we can defend."

Seward makes a disgusted sound. "He's just one man."

CHAPTER SEVENTY-EIGHT

SAFE HOUSE

The ambulance wails ahead of us as we race down the highway toward Filmount County. Glenn drives, Seward is shotgun, and Jillian sits in the back next to me, her hands cupped around my handcuffed fists.

She's still trying to make sense of things. "So he's really coming for you?" she asks.

"If he thinks he can get to me, then yes. He would have killed me before, but he thought he had a perfect way to tidy things up and buy time."

"By asking you to kill yourself?"

"Yes. I think he was expecting me to run to you if I didn't go to the cops or do as he asked. He may have been near your place waiting."

"Why doesn't he just run?" asks Seward. "It's what I would do."

"As I said, he's afraid that I'll help you catch him. But he overestimates me."

"So he comes straight at us? I don't see it."

"It won't be straight. We won't see it coming."

"I'll have more manpower in the next two hours than he knows how to deal with. He won't see it coming."

"I hope you're right, but I don't think he'll go down easily. He took out the Hudson Creek cops because they underestimated him. When he comes for me, it'll be indirect."

"You think you know this guy?" asks Glenn.

"All I know are a bunch of numbers and equations that relate to him. Those bodies I found in the woods aren't his only kills or type of victim. You said he ran several different businesses? Do you know who has been moving meth around your counties? How many warrants do you have out for dealers that you can't locate?"

"You're saying he's a drug dealer, too?" says Seward.

"Anybody seen the two junkies that helped me find Chelsea Buchorn's body? You think they could go this long without getting stopped for some minor infraction?"

"He got them?" asks Glenn.

"That'd be my bet. I think killing is both a hobby and a profession for him."

"Maybe so," says Seward, "but serial killers run—they don't try to pull a Terminator."

"What do you know about a man like Vik? How many serial killers have we ever encountered that were this prolific?"

"How prolific?" asks Glenn.

"We won't know until we start retracing his steps. But a conservative estimate? Three hundred."

"Three hundred people?" Seward sneers. "Somebody has an inflation problem here."

"Yeah? Ten or more a year over thirty years. Do the math yourself. Then take a look at Montana missing-persons numbers and ask yourself why they're higher than Florida or California. It's not just reporting anomalies. It indicates the presence of a highly active serial killer."

"Yeah, but three hundred?" says Glenn.

"Gary Ridgway, the Green River killer, murdered forty-two women in just a two-year period. He wasn't caught for another two decades. He had an IQ of eighty-two. How intelligent does Joe Vik strike you?"

"Very."

"So if a low-IQ necrophiliac who liked to return to the woods to have sex with his victims can kill that many women in such a short span of time and get away with it for twenty years, how much damage do you think someone like Vik could do?"

"Three hundred people?" says Seward, still rolling the number around.

"Conservatively."

"We've never seen anything like that."

"That you know about. Ridgway left lots of DNA evidence. Gacy left bodies under his house. Robert Hansen, the guy that abducted hookers and hunted them down in the Alaskan woods, did this over thirty times and was only discovered when one of his victims managed to escape.

"I ran the numbers. Here's a cold fact for you: statistically speaking, you don't catch the majority of highly organized serial killers. And the really expert ones, the killers that don't leave DNA, don't kill within five miles of where they live, and carefully choose their victims and method of burial, you don't even know they exist. You don't have profiles for them at Quantico because you've never knowingly encountered one."

"But you have all the answers," says Seward.

What an asshole.

"Just the numbers. They tell a terrifying story. There are at least thirty or more Joe Viks operating out there."

"Let's get this one, then worry about the others," Glenn says.

"It'll give you something to do from jail," adds Seward.

"You're still going to go through with this arrest?" asks Jillian. "After all he's done?"

"Tell that to Christopher Dunleavy's family after they see what your boyfriend did to their son's corpse," says Seward.

"The operative word is *corpse*," I fire back, but I can't pretend he doesn't have a point. I give Jillian a sorrowful look. "I didn't think I had any other options."

She squeezes my hands. "I believe you."

"It was kind of stupid in retrospect. I should have tried to draw him toward me."

"We'll be okay—"

She doesn't finish her sentence.

"Shit!" yells Glenn as he swerves to the side of the road.

I look out the windshield in time to see the ambulance tumbling over on its side and skidding toward us.

The roof of the ambulance clips our front end, and we go into a violent spin, smashing a guardrail and careening into a ditch.

As we skid off the highway, I see a massive black tow truck fly past, flash its brake lights, then do a screeching U-turn.

CHAPTER SEVENTY-NINE

CRASH

Our SUV slides backward down the grassy slope and rams into a line of trees. The back of my skull rockets off the head rest, sending my face slamming into my handcuffed wrists, cracking my nose. I see stars for a moment and smell the tangy scent of blood.

"Are you okay?" Jillian asks, unfastening her seat belt and sliding over to me.

"Yeah . . . I'm okay."

She reaches up and grabs Seward by the shoulder. "Can you get these damn handcuffs off him?"

He doesn't move.

His head is slumped over to the side. His window is shattered.

I grab his neck with both hands and feel for a pulse. "He's alive."

Glenn rubs his temples. "Holy crap! Everybody okay?"

Jillian thrusts her hand in front of his face. "Handcuff keys. Now!"

"Just a second . . ." He's still shaken from the impact. "Let me call for help."

He takes his phone out and starts dialing. Frustrated, Jillian leans into the front section and starts to riffle through Seward's pockets.

"Careful. He might be hurt," says Glenn.

"You think?" she says.

Something moves through the bright beams of light shooting out over the edge of the road near the gap where we tore through the guardrail.

Reflexively, I grab Jillian by the collar of her jacket and yank her into the back. "Duck!"

"What is it?" asks Glenn.

A split second later, the windshield is punctured by a barrage of gunfire, blasting bits of glass at our heads.

I press Jillian to the floorboard and throw my body on top of her.

There's a second burst, and the truck makes popping sounds as bullets penetrate the hood and grill.

"Anyone hit?" Glenn shouts from the front—presumably crouched down like we are.

"I'm good," whispers Jillian.

"I'm okay."

The light beam flickers again.

"He's moving."

"Stay down," says Glenn. I hear him slipping his magazine out of his gun, then pushing it back. "I'm going to count to three, then fire back."

"He won't be there," I say.

"What?"

"He's going to try to make a feint. Probably on your side."

"What makes you say that?"

"Because he knows you're armed and needs to take you out first."

"Are you—"

BANG! BANG! BANG! BANG! BANG! BANG!

Bullets fly above our heads and send more glass fragments raining down on us like angry hail.

"FUCK!" Glenn screams.

"Are you hit?"

"Grazed. Went through the door. I'm going to return fire. You two get out on the other side and stay behind the vehicle!"

"Hold on," says Jillian. I realize she's got Seward's keys. Her nervous fingers find the handcuff key, and she unlocks me. "Okay."

Glenn begins to fire his gun, filling the cab with a deafening noise.

I fumble with the door handle and climb out, keeping low. Jillian slides out after me.

"Are you out?" yells Glenn.

"Clear."

"He's lying down in the grass. I think I may have got him."

"Or he's just taking up a sniper's position," Jillian replies.

"Maybe. I'm going to fire again. When I do, head deep into the woods."

I have a bad feeling about that. The forest is his home turf, but I don't have a better idea.

"Go!" Glenn shouts, then starts shooting.

Jillian and I start through the woods, but I freeze the moment Glenn's shooting stops.

"What is it?" asks Jillian.

We're about ten feet away from the truck. I can see patches of grass beyond the tree trunks. Joe is nowhere to be seen.

"Other way!" I yank her by the arm. "He's already in here!"

We race around the truck, putting it between us and the forest, and climb up the hill toward the highway.

I look back and see the tip of Glenn's pistol above the dashboard.

I yell, "He's in the trees, coming up behind you!"

Glenn pops his head up and spots us running toward the road. Without hesitating, he crawls through the open windshield, rolls across the hood, and chases after us.

I see him stop and look back at Seward, afraid to leave him.

Bang! Bang! Bang! Bang! Bang! Bang!

Rifle fire emerges from the woods, and bullets ricochet off the truck.

"Run!" I scream.

Jillian is pulling at my arm, trying to get me to move as well.

We hop over the guardrail as bullets puncture it, making a loud metal twang. Glenn hits the side of the hill, twists around, and returns fires back in the same direction the shots originated.

The rifle fire comes to a halt, and he picks himself up and races over the top of the rise, catching up to Jillian and me.

We run to the ambulance lying on its passenger side. The lights are still flashing and the back wheels are spinning, having crashed only moments ago.

The paramedic is bent over the passenger side door, getting to his knees.

We pull him to the far side of the vehicle, away from the forest.

"Are you okay?"

"Yeah. I think."

I point down the road. "Then take her and run."

"No," Jillian says flatly. She turns to the paramedic. "Go!"

Already spooked by the gunfire, he breaks off into a sprint.

Behind us, red and blue lights flash as a Hudson Creek police cruiser comes to a skidding halt. An older cop jumps out of the driver's seat. "What's going on?"

"Shooter in the woods!" says Glenn.

The cop starts to stride toward us, exposed to the trees.

"Stay back!" yells Glenn.

Bang! Bang! Bang!

The officer's shoulder is ripped open, and he drops to the ground, screaming.

"Help me get him!" I say to Glenn, then hunch over and hurry toward the fallen man.

"Let's take him to the car and use it to get out of here," replies Jillian.

Bang! Bang! Bang! Bang! Bang! Bang!

A burst of automatic fire sprays into the cruiser, puncturing the radiator and sending up a cloud of steam.

"Shit! He has us pinned!" says Glenn. "I'm going to fire. You grab him and bring him to the ambulance."

Glenn fires his gun twice, then ducks behind the cruiser, using it as a shield.

Jillian helps me drag the downed cop to the inside of the ambulance. He valiantly tries to stifle his screams as we lift him across the sideways door.

I start searching through the medical supplies all over the floor—which was once a wall—for some bandages, find them, and start wrapping the man's shoulder wound. It's a mess.

Through the back window, I spot Glenn climbing into the police cruiser and taking out the shotgun.

He moves toward the hood and puts a finger to his lips when he sees us watching. He points to his eyes then toward the back of us.

Joe has changed positions again and is sneaking up behind where we're hiding.

CHAPTER EIGHTY
VALIANT

My impression of Glenn has crystallized in these moments. When I first met him, I thought he was a hard-ass, and I resented the way he manipulated me into spilling my guts, embarrassing me with my own naïveté. He knew my intelligence but used it against me in some kind of judo move. For all my theoretical smarts, his knowledge came from talking to real people all day long, spotting the liars and thieves among them.

He's been my antagonist, but in the last few minutes he's put his own life on the line several times to protect Jillian and me.

Glenn is checking the shotgun he borrowed from the police cruiser and getting ready for an assault from Joe.

Right now Glenn has the ambulance and the car to block a retreat and could make a run for it and abandon us. He won't. He's not even trying to get to our hiding space, where we have more protection from the assault rifle.

He might be able to make a better last stand from here, but his position is better suited for firing at Joe if he comes at us.

It's a selfless thing Glenn is doing. He'll get the better shot from there, but it will probably be his only one.

He catches me staring at him. He gives Jillian a small nod, then locks eyes with me.

Protect her.

It's primal. It's chauvinistic. It's what we're biologically programmed to do—well, the best of us.

I turn my attention to our patient. He's leaning against the wall, grasping his arm below the wound.

I notice for the first time this ambulance is actually a mobile medical center, with refrigerated storage and a mini pharmacy.

"How are you doing, Sergeant Bryant?"

"Wonderful," he groans. "I had the night off."

I slide open a panel and find the hard stuff. "Want something for the pain?"

"God, yes."

I give him a shot of morphine, and his face slackens.

"Is that a good idea?" Jillian whispers to me.

"He was still in shock. He was a minute or two away from screaming his lungs out. He lost a lot of his shoulder."

I'm afraid to try to redress the wound without a proper surgical environment. If I move the bandage, I risk uncorking whatever is keeping him from bleeding out. Instead, I put another layer over his shoulder, making sure there's plenty of pressure.

The first bandages I used had a built-in clotting agent and seem to be working pretty well.

To be on the safe side, I get a syringe of clotting medication ready, as well as a bag of synthetic blood in case Bryant loses too much of his own. Synthetic isn't meant to replace your blood—it just dilutes it better than straight saline, helping you maintain blood pressure.

"What are we going to do?" asks Jillian.

"Glenn called for backup. I'm sure help is coming."

We're both well aware that Joe is close by and will be here before any help.

Glenn is creeping toward the front of the cruiser. He has the shotgun trained on a point off to our right.

Boom! He fires at something.

Glenn moves to the other side of the hood, then shoots again. *Boom!*

Bang! Bang! Bang! Bang! Bang! Bang!

Bullets fire into the police car, making ice-pick clangs as they hit.

Glenn lurches forward and groans loudly. A bullet hit him in his side.

I rush toward the back of the ambulance to help.

"Stay back!" he snarls through gritted teeth, then pumps the shotgun.

He bounces up and fires another volley. *Boom! Boom! Boom!*

Bang! Bang! Bang! His chest is covered in red blossoms, and he falls to the ground.

I leap out of the ambulance and pick up his shotgun. When I try to run back to the door, my leg collapses under me, and even before I hit the road I know I've been shot.

My chin hits first, splitting open on the rough asphalt.

When I look up through hazy eyes, I get my first view of him twenty yards away.

My initial reaction isn't terror or shock.

It's awe.

Joe is enormous. He's clad in body armor from head to toe, and his face mask is a metal shield with narrow slits and war paint. Across his Kevlar chest is a necklace of bear claws.

At his waist I see the stainless steel metal claws, waiting to be unleashed.

He walks slowly toward me with his rifle aimed at my chest. He could have fired already, but he's enjoying this. He's enjoying watching me as I see him for the first time.

I raise myself up on my good knee and limp back toward the ambulance. As soon as I get near, Jillian grabs me under the arms and pulls me into the back.

I see her eyes widen as she catches a momentary glance of Joe.

"Did you see him?" I ask.

"Yes." She rips open my pant leg to examine my wound. "Help me with this—what do I do?"

"He's . . ." Words fail me.

"Theo! Help me with this!" she yells.

I'm staring out the window at the shadow of Joe as he gets closer. What's it like to have caused so much death? Do you think you're no longer human? Do you imagine yourself a god trapped in flesh? Do you even feel anymore? Or are you just a creature of pure reaction—like lines of code?

So many questions.

CHAPTER EIGHTY-ONE

HUNTED

Joe raises the rifle and fires at the back window. I throw myself over Jillian and Bryant, turning my back to the barrage.

The inside of the ambulance is chaos as bullets shatter glass, burst through metal walls, and riddle the doors with holes.

I feel a searing pain in my thigh and another in the side of my body.

The staccato beat of the rifle comes to a halt, and the only sound is our breathing. I can feel Jillian under my chest, her head tucked beneath my chin.

Her body is shielding the wounded cop—one more layer of humanity trying to protect him.

There's a deep, whinnying sound as someone labors to breathe.

Jillian turns to look at me, wipes away strands of dirty-blonde hair, and mouths, "Are you okay?"

"I think so," I try to say but only sputter blood.

Her face, inches away from my own, is a wide-screen vision of terror as red-tinged saliva trickles out of my mouth.

I realize the wheezing sound is me. One of Joe's bullets grazed a rib, fracturing it.

"Hold on," says Jillian. She crawls out from underneath me and goes toward the door.

I try to say, "Don't go out there," but start to cough.

She grabs the handle of the open lower door and pulls it shut, sealing us in.

The upper window is filled with holes, but it's largely intact. Although I don't know what difference it will make. One more spray of bullets from Joe and the glass is likely to give way.

Seconds later, the handle begins to rattle as Joe tries to open the door.

Jillian and I watch anxiously; then the noise comes to a halt.

"I think he's gone," says Jillian.

"No, he's not," I gurgle.

"Theo, tell me what to do!" She runs her hands across my body and finds the wound on my rib cage.

"How's he?" I ask through gasps.

She touches the cop's neck and measures his pulse. "Alive. Now help me patch you up." She assists me into a sitting position.

"No time . . ."

"Bullshit. Tell me what to do!"

"Gloves," I say through labored breathing.

She digs through a pile of supplies and finds a box of blue gloves and slips them on. "Now what?"

"Is the wound deep?" I ask.

She probes the injury, trying to gently see if there's a bullet hole, implying there could be a bullet inside me.

"Fuck!" I scream when my body is attacked by white-hot, searing pain.

She pulls back. "I'm sorry!"

"It's okay . . . It's a good sign."

"I can feel your rib. I think it's fractured."

"No hole. Get . . . the clotting . . . bandage," I gasp.

The internal bleeding is just a temporary symptom, I hope. If there had been a bullet hole through my chest and lungs, I could be dead in minutes.

Jillian rips open a pack of the same bandages I used on Bryant and sticks them to my skin. The clotting agents mix with the blood and start to form a seal, stopping the flow of blood from the wound.

Still, I feel woozy.

"Theo?" Jillian raises her hand from the floor. It's covered in blood. "I think you got hit on the leg in two places."

She searches my body and presses on my thigh. I feel like I just got stabbed.

"I'm so sorry! I think it went through, at least."

She finds a pair of scissors and cuts away at my jeans.

"Should I wrap it, too?"

"Plug . . . ," I say through gritted teeth. "Like a tampon . . ."

Sometimes the best field dressing is a round plug that fills the wound. It can be a lifesaver or make things worse, depending on the type of wound. For a hole straight through my thigh muscle, it's the most expedient solution.

"Like this?" she asks, holding up a syringelike applicator.

"Yes . . ."

Without warning—which is probably for the best—she shoves it into the wound. The pain is so intense I pass out for a moment.

I come to with Jillian slapping me and calling my name.

I feel cold and weak. "Yeah."

"You've lost a lot of blood."

"Because I'm bleeding," I reply nonsensically.

"Should I give you artificial blood?" She holds up a packet.

"Can you . . . can you . . . tap a vein?"

"Yes. Probably."

I'm so tired I don't even feel like answering.

"Theo! Stay with me!" She slaps my face again.

"So . . . violent."

Things begin to darken around the edges of my vision. I feel a sharp pain in my arm, then gradually focus.

Jillian has a bag of artificial blood suspended from a door handle above our heads. The end is poked into my arm.

"Like this?" she asks.

"Yes. Am I still leaking?"

"I don't think so."

She wraps a bandage around the needle in my arm, fixing it in place.

"Joe?" I ask.

"He's been gone for a few minutes. I think help is on the way."

I wish I could believe that was true. I have a feeling we're a long way from anybody coming to our rescue. It makes no sense that he would just walk away from us.

I try to scoot myself upright but can barely move. I fall back on the side wall and try to catch my breath.

Jillian hovers over me, checking my bandages, then making sure the wounded cop is still okay.

She freezes and looks up as she leans over me.

I'm about to ask her, "What is it?" but then I hear the sound of heavy footsteps walking toward the back of the ambulance.

Through the shattered glass we can see the passing of a shadow.

A horrible screeching sound fills the air as Joe starts up some kind of mechanical device. The ambulance is filled with noise as he uses a metal saw to cut away at the doors.

Jillian spins around and sprawls out over my body to shield me.

"Check the cop for a gun," I whisper through pained breaths.

She reaches around me and starts to feel for his holster.

"I can't find . . ."

The words freeze in her mouth as the upper back door falls to the ground.

Past her shoulder, I see the mountain of man that's Joe.

A huge hand reaches inside and grabs Jillian by the ankle.

"Theo!" she says as she's yanked away.

I try to take her hands and hold on to her, but she's out of my reach before I can even move.

She clings to the door frame, trying not to be taken. Joe is too strong. He pulls her free, then drags her away out of sight.

He took her.

He took her first.

He knows I'm in here, barely alive, unable to do anything.

This is how he makes me suffer.

CHAPTER EIGHTY-TWO

VIGILANT

She's gone.

I try to get up. The world begins to move around me, my legs give way, and I fall back down, landing on Bryant.

He makes a groaning sound.

He needs help. Hell, I need help.

I attempt to get on my hands and knees to crawl but find my arms aren't strong enough to support me.

He took Jillian. And the worst part about it is she didn't even scream. She knew I was too injured to do anything.

I've lost so much blood. I'm still leaking out.

I'm allowed to give up.

It's okay to throw up my hands and say I did the best I could.

I can't save her.

I couldn't save Juniper.

I deserve to die.

When Joe comes for me, I won't protest.

I can't go on knowing I lay helpless as he carried Jillian away.

Can't go on . . .

I realize that I truly have nothing to live for if I let him kill her.

My hand falls on a pile of vials.

Dextroamphetamine sulfate.

Speed.

I dealt with more than one speed freak as a paramedic. It took several cops to hold them down. Even then that wasn't enough. Their brains didn't know they weren't supposed to keep going.

Weren't supposed to keep going . . .

Ultimately, their bodies paid a price. Cardiac arrest or worse.

But what could be worse than this?

The blood bag hovering over my head gives me an idea. More accurately, it's a suicide plan. But it might give me a few more minutes . . .

I find a syringe and inject the bag with the amphetamine.

I dig through the cabinets and find epinephrine, adrenaline, and add that, too.

I use way too much.

You wouldn't use this much on a racehorse, not unless you hated the animal and wanted his heart to explode on the last lap.

But that's exactly what I want.

My body is already forfeit.

I'm going to die one way or another tonight. It might as well be fighting.

I use a bandage wrap to strap the blood supply to my chest and move the needle to an artery on my thigh, inches from where I was shot.

I try to push into my skin, but I'm too weak. I feel like I'm slipping back into a dream.

"THEO!"

I don't know if that was Jillian screaming or some voice in the back of my mind. Either way, it makes all the difference in the world. I find the artery, and the needle goes in . . .

I'm already beginning to feel tingly. Waves of electric ants start marching across my skin.

My breathing picks up. My heart starts beating faster.

HOLY SHIT.

I'M ON FIRE.

My head feels like one of those novelty-store plasma balls.

In a moment of clarity, I grab some syringes from the floor, fill them with different concoctions, then shove them into jacket pockets.

There's a lot of my blood on the floor. I strap two more pints to my chest and tape a small pump to my side. They won't kick in until my blood pressure drops even farther. For good measure I inject them both with adrenaline.

This is some next-level Lance Armstrong bionic shit going on.

I'm stronger now—I don't just stand up, I bounce to my feet.

I step out of the ambulance feeling like I'm made of pure energy. I run toward where I last saw Jillian.

I'm moving fast. Subconsciously I'm aware of the fact that my left leg is dragging because of the puncture wound, but the stimulants keep the nerves firing, and the muscle fibers do what I ask them, all their overrides having been shut down.

The Nazis used to pump their soldiers full of shit like this to turn them into super soldiers. They paid a heavy price for it physically, but it's not like Nazi physicians had the best intentions to begin with.

A moment ago I was despondent, ready to let Joe end me. Now . . . fuck that. I'm a GODDAMN LOCOMOTIVE READY TO TEAR THROUGH HIM.

Some part of me is saying that this is the drugs talking.

FUCK THAT NOISE.

I'M GOING TO RIP HIM TO PIECES.

Way to go, hotshot. Now think for a moment. Maybe you should pick up that shotgun by Glenn's body? He might have one or two rounds left.

I grab it and jog into the woods. There's a break in the trees he probably took her through.

I check the chamber. One shell left.

MAKE IT COUNT.

I run down the hill and jump the last few yards.

My leg buckles, but I keep going.

He wants me to chase after him. He saw me wounded in the ambulance and wanted to see what I was made of. Would I let him drag my girl off? Or would I find the strength to be a fucking man?

I stomp through the bushes, using the shotgun barrel to swat away branches.

I reach a small clearing.

A large shape is standing at the other end. Jillian is kneeling on the ground, blood trickling from her lip and a bruise around her left eye. Joe has one hand around her throat and another with his claws ready to puncture her jugular.

He looks my way. Silent, yet full of rage.

I contemplate trying to take a shot but notice how the barrel is shaking in my hands.

I'm too high to aim straight.

I'd be just as likely to shoot her as him—and he has body armor.

I toss the shotgun to the ground.

Fast, really fucking fast, Joe shoves Jillian to the side and sprints toward me.

He wants to show how fast he is. He wants me to see that he's really some animal spirit in possession of a man's body.

He wants me to die knowing that he's not just a depraved whack job.

He wants me to believe he is a demigod.

For a fraction of a second, I believe him. I think no man his size should be able to move that fast. I think that no human could react that quickly.

Then I remember that I'm a scientist.

And I just injected my body with a lot of powerful shit that's going to kill me.

But for one brief moment . . . I'm a demon-powered soldier of vengeance.

And I have a fistful of syringes he doesn't know about.

CHAPTER EIGHTY-THREE

ADAPTATION

I had a friend who was a marine biologist who tagged great white sharks. I asked her how the hell she did that.

First, she explained, you get a long pole and stick your tranquilizer on the end. Then you chum the water and get the shark really close to the boat. When the shark is chomping down on the chunks of fish, you stab it. After it goes limp, you keep it stationary in the water using a special hammock. Someone counts out the minutes left on the dosage and you go about your work.

The real problem, she said, wasn't the great white sharks.

It's what happened after the thing was immobilized and lying helpless in the water harness.

You had to protect the shark from dolphins.

The clever little bastards didn't waste any opportunity to strike at the sharks. They'd come flying out of nowhere and ram their noses into the great white's gill slits, trying to fuck it up.

I can't blame them.

The researchers had to watch their backs and make sure there wasn't an eight-hundred-pound torpedo aimed at their patient.

Sharks have been swimming around in the ocean for more than four hundred million years—dolphins less than a tenth of that time. Yet, in that short period, dolphins adapted to become their fiercest enemy.

While dolphins have blunt baby teeth compared to a great white, they have one advantage a shark doesn't—their brains. Dolphins are incredible improvisers.

Sharks have millions of years of preprogrammed strategies. Dolphins have cheat codes.

I'm not a fighter, despite Gus's best efforts. But neither is Joe. He's a killer. He's a great white shark on two feet, and like a shark, he uses the same strategy over and over again. He preys on the frightened and the weak and the vulnerable. I have to think like a dolphin.

Joe bears down on me, and I drop to my knees. His arms swing out over my head, slicing the air with his claws. Moving too fast to stop himself, his right leg kicks into my shoulder, and he stumbles.

I roll to the side.

Before I can gather myself, Joe has already spun around.

Goddamn, he's fast.

Four scimitars come at me. I duck my head and feel them slice into my back. I'm high, so it's not painful so much as a curious sensation of being carved open.

I shoot my arm out with a syringe and aim for his calf. I loaded enough sedative in the syringe to stop the heart of a grizzly.

The needle goes into the leather. I start to squeeze the injector, but Joe jerks his leg and the tip snaps in half.

FUCK!

This is the last time he'll let me get this close.

I use the distraction to jump back and out of his reach for a second.

I hold another syringe in front of me with my left hand.

He pauses for a moment and watches me. I can't see anything behind his mask, but I can tell he's assessing me.

I have to try a new tactic.

I need to do something his victims have never done.

"Bad night, Joe?"

I know his only response is to attack, so I leap to the side as soon as I finish the sentence.

Joe lunges at where I was standing, swiping the air and exposing his left deltoid. I launch myself at him and cling to his arm like a monkey on a tree trunk.

Before the needle goes in, Joe's claws go into my shoulder, and he stabs me.

A geyser of blood shoots into his mask.

Fuck. He hit my artery.

The blood keeps gushing.

I fall off him and land hard on my back.

Joe stands over me. Triumphant. He swatted me away like King Kong.

My blood is still spurting out, spitting into the air and pooling around my head.

He just watches.

This is his thing, wounding someone and waiting for them to bleed out.

This is how he gets his jollies.

I'm so full of shit my brain is too wired to know that it's not getting any more blood.

The fountain turns into a trickle, then stops.

My heart should go next.

My last image will be the man who murdered me.

The man about to kill Jillian.

CHAPTER EIGHTY-FOUR

Thrombosis

Joe looms over me, taking quiet satisfaction in my death, letting me ooze out like a stuck pig.

I lie here helpless, staring up at the sequoia of a man, waiting for my vision to fade and the ferryman to take me across the river Styx.

Still waiting . . .

And waiting . . .

Shit, dying takes a while.

Has time slowed down?

I'm experiencing my death remotely, like my Marvel Comics Watcher, who is there for the end of things.

Is death like the event horizon of a black hole, where you fall forever?

I know it's subjective and all, but shit, I should really be dead now.

It doesn't matter how many drugs are in my system—once you bleed out like that from an arterial wound, it's a matter of physics. You should be dead.

But I'm still alive. Or at least aware.

Joe starts to kneel down. I can hear him inhaling under his mask. He senses something.

"Theo . . . ," moans Jillian.

She's a crumpled rag at the edge of the clearing.

Joe's head turns to face the sound she made.

Then it hits me.

Joe didn't strike an artery.

He sliced into a blood bag.

I'm sure I got punctured, too, but that geyser wasn't my blood.

My pressure is dropping, to be sure . . . which also means that any moment now—

Buzzzzzzzzzzzz.

My little blood pump kicks to life. Joe whips his neck around to look at me.

I continue to play dead.

The pump sounds a lot like a pager.

He leans over me, trying to identify the source of the vibration.

I.

Don't.

Fucking.

Breathe.

Joe slides his right glove off and holds it in his left. His massive hand pats me down on the side.

I spot his thick, pink neck under his mask. It's his soft spot. His gill slits.

Like an opportunistic dolphin, I slam the syringe I'm clenching into his neck.

"Motherfucker!" he bellows.

"Made you break character, asshole."

His fist pounds into my face, pulverizing my nose.

Joe starts to put the claws back on, then leans backward on his heels. He stands upright and wobbles.

I roll away and pull myself to my knees. Now I feel wobbly.

Joe stumbles to the side, then stops himself. He gets the glove all the way on, then lumbers toward me.

Weak, but slightly more coordinated than him, I shift to my side. He passes, then collapses like a drunk.

My bad leg gives way, and I fall to my knees, then hit the dirt face-first.

Blood runs down my neck and into my mouth. I can't see Joe.

I can't see shit.

I think I'm crashing.

A hand grabs me by my upper arm and pulls me upright.

I try to swing a fist at my attacker but can't tell where they are.

"Theo!" Jillian yells.

Shit. I almost hit her.

I stop resisting and let her drag me over to a log and sit me upright.

"Are you okay?" she asks, squatting in front of me.

There's blood running down her face from where Joe knocked her out. "Are you?" I ask.

"Better than you. Hold on." She limps over to where I dropped the shotgun and picks it up. "Stay with me."

She sits down and cradles my head in her lap with one hand and keeps the other on the shotgun facing Joe's unconscious body.

I start to drift off.

"Theo!" She slaps me awake. "Ambulance is on the way. Stay with me."

I look over and see Joe's body is still there. I try to do the math and warn her that if he's not dead, he'll be up any minute now. We need to think like dolphins.

I fall into a daze before I can say anything.

I think I'm dreaming.

Boom!

I bolt awake and look for Joe's body—it's gone.

"Jillian!"

"It's okay," she says.

"He's gone!"

"To hell, Theo. He's gone to hell."

Then I see it—Joe's corpse sprawled against a tree. His mask is ripped away, and there's a bloody pulp where his face should be.

I don't know if he was coming or going, but she dropped the son of a bitch.

I like this woman.

❧

They're carrying me away.

Red and blue lights wash over the trees.

EMTs pull at my clothes, detaching the tubes.

I expect the face of the paramedic to be my own.

But it's not.

I don't even think I'm here.

I decide I'm not.

I'm back at that campus pizza parlor with my students. Juniper is looking at me. She leans in, our fingers almost touching on the bench between us.

She has Jillian's face.

This time I don't pull away. I move closer and cover her delicate hand with mine.

She smiles.

Acknowledgments

Thank you to Erica Silverman-Spellman for making sure that Theo didn't get lost in the woods. Special thanks to Jacquelyn BenZekry for helping Theo find a home and Liz Pearsons for making him feel welcome. I'd also like to thank my parents, Jamie & Zory Harter, Justin Robert Young, Kenneth Montgomery, Hannah Wood, Mary Jaras, Peter J. Wacks, Steven L. Sears, the Winner family, Chris Brennan, Brian Brushwood, Paul Zak, Jack Horner, David Sands, Richard Friedman, James Randi, and everyone else with whom I've had the pleasure of talking about our mutual love of science.

About the Author

Andrew Mayne, star of A&E's *Don't Trust Andrew Mayne*, is a magician and novelist ranked as the fifth bestselling independent author of the year by Amazon UK. He started his first world tour as an illusionist when he was a teenager and went on to work behind the scenes for Penn & Teller, David Blaine, and David Copperfield. Andrew's novel *Angel Killer* is currently in development for television. He's also the host of the *Weird Things* podcast.